P9-DOE-343

MACHINE

Other books by Denis Hamill:

STOMPING GROUND

MACHINE

Denis Hamill

DELACORTE PRESS NEW YORK

Published by
Delacorte Press
1 Dag Hammarskjold Plaza
New York, N.Y. 10017

Manufactured in the United States of America

First printing

Designed by Judith Neuman

Library of Congress Cataloging in Publication Data

Hamill, Denis [date of birth].
Machine.

I. Title.
PS3558.A4217M3 1984 813'.54
ISBN 0-385-29271-6
Library of Congress Catalog Card Number:
83-15309

DEDICATION

This book is for my brother Pete, the most generous man I know, and for Don Forst, a great editor, teacher, loan officer, and friend.

ACKNOWLEDGMENTS

I would like to thank my friend Morgan Entrekin who was more than just my editor on this book. His advice, ideas, guidance, patience, time, assurances, and lunches are all in here somewhere.

MACHINE

1

Be Be Gonzago hated his eyes.

In the end, more than any of his personal or political enemies; more than the investigative reporters or the legislative investigating committees; more than reformers and campaign-spending laws; more than Republicans, right-wing fanatics, pain-in-the-ass liberals, attorney generals, DAs, grand juries, IRS agents, watchdog committees, consumer-fraud assholes, and hot-dog lobbyists—more than any of the other ball busters, Be Be Gonzago had been defeated by his own eyes.

It was ironic, for Be Be Gonzago had gotten to where he was in life because of his uncanny ability to see through people. He didn't make the tough, long climb to chairman of the Kings County Democratic party by going to law school and then working as a flunky for two-bit councilmen who would toss him a crumb, pat him on the back, and give him a promotion every couple of years until he was indoctrinated enough to assume the mantle of Brooklyn party boss.

No, Be Be Gonzago did it his way. He took power without ever bothering with a formal education, without begging at the feet of the established bosses. Be Be Gonzago understood the most crucial element of power from a very young age—you did not barter, bargain, or bid for power. You took it.

So he sat there now in the total darkness for a long time, staring inward instead of out. Darkness had become a constant companion in the last few years, ever since the hard little beetle shells called cataracts had grown over his eyes. Be Be Gonzago had tried to fight it. He had the best surgeons flash their blades. But the darkness had won and Be Be Gonzago accepted it as part of the final condition of his life.

The brown suede couch in his dimmed living room held his short, stocky body like a huge gloved palm. On the table next to him was a box of De Nobile cigars, a bottle of Rémy Martin V.S.O.P., a large pot of freshly brewed espresso, a polished glass, a demitasse cup, and an ashtray. On another table was the Bell and Howell movie projector, sitting mute and blind in the large silent room.

Be Be was not yet totally blind. Without the thick glasses the doctors had given him, he could see only ghostly shapes and figures, making the whole world look like a steam bath with silhouettes moving in and out of focus. With the glasses he could see much better; the details came together like the moving parts in a kaleidoscope. But he would never wear the glasses in public. He was too vain to admit he was weakening.

Be Be Gonzago reached into the pocket of the silk robe and took out the thick glasses, slowly unfolded the flimsy arms, and placed the eyeglasses on the bridge of his nose. The frames were thin and light but the weight of the half-inch-thick glass lenses annoyed him. It made him all too aware of his handicap. He reached for his cigars, produced the gold lighter from his robe pocket, and felt the small ache behind his eyes as the flame pierced the gloom. He puffed heavily on the cigar until the ember was a bright hot orange and let the strong taste and smell of the tobacco relax him. He splashed himself a hefty snifter of cognac and poured some of the scalding espresso into the small ceramic cup and stirred in two sugars. It was this combination of alcohol and coffee that made smoking an irresistible temptation regardless of what the doctors told Be Be. A strong cigar mixed with the tastes of cognac and espresso was almost worth dying for because it made what was left in life just a little more pleasurable. The doctors had said death wasn't far off, although they couldn't pinpoint it. When it came it would take him by the throat and strangle him from the inside.

Nobody, not even old faithful Johnny Quinn, knew about the throat cancer. The cigars and the brandy and the coffee would probably speed up the process, Be Be thought. But what's the difference? When the bandit finally comes it might just as well come from inside as from outside. Better to abdicate than be dethroned. It would be a last laugh on all the vultures. Let them come and pick the bones of the dead rather than try to eat me alive.

The only real regret was his son, Joseph, whom he had not seen in over ten years. Joseph had been the most important thing in Be Be's life, and when Joseph had left, Be Be had stopped caring about a lot of things. Perhaps if he had agreed to see the doctors when his eyes and his throat started to die there would have been some hope. Perhaps they could even have saved him.

Be Be loved that boy—maybe too much, some people, including Joseph, thought. Was there ever a baseball or football game that Joseph had played that Be Be had failed to attend? Be Be had even skipped the Johnson inauguration to see Joseph play a championship football game for Madison High School in his sophomore year. And Be Be's presence always made Joseph nervous because Be Be expected nothing short of perfection from his son. Be Be had wanted to groom Joseph Gonzago to be the first Italian-American president of the United States. Just as Joe Kennedy had groomed his son Joseph, and then later John, to be the first Catholic Irish-American president.

Be Be had even named his own son after Joe Kennedy. Be Be admired that man. And, as Be Be sat there now in the dark room where he had once bounced young Joseph on his knee, he thought about how he could have succeeded in doing the same thing for his own son that Joe Kennedy had done for his. If it hadn't been for that fucking war, he thought. If there had been no war in Vietnam, Joseph might now be in the Congress, or even the Senate—young, good-looking, with all the right connections to launch him into the White House.

But Be Be knew it was more than just the war that had torn father and son apart. The war was part of it, but there was more. Be Be knew that in his mad desire to have a son become president he had overlooked that maybe the kid should have his own say in the matter.

There was also Angela. Joseph's mother had taken her own life because she could not live with the idea that another woman had taken Be Be's heart. Joseph would never be able to forgive his father for that. Be Be knew. Ten years of silence from a son he adored assured him. How does a son forgive a father he holds responsible for his mother's suicide?

Be Be remembered the day Joseph was born, the first glimpse he got of him. The hair was so thick and dark for a newborn infant that even the nurses gathered around in awe. When the baby began to cry Be Be had smiled wide. He knew beforehand it would be a boy and that his name would be Joseph, and he knew one day that little blanket-wrapped infant would run the United States of America. It was Be Be Gonzago's great dream. He would get him into the New York assembly first, then into Congress, then the Senate, and then into the Oval Office. Even then, this did not seem such a monumental task to Be Be Gonzago, because he had seen how it could be done.

Presidents are made not born. But they have to be born to king makers and Be Be knew he was a king maker. In Be Be's political career he had taken the biggest has-beens in the State of New York and made them into senators and governors and mayors. When Be Be Gonzago had an infant, his own son, he knew he could raise him into perfection, tailor him for the highest office in the land.

And then it had all fallen apart. That little baby grew into his own man, with his own dreams and desires. Be Be had never considered this. He had tried to raise a candidate instead of a son, and this would be the greatest failure of his life. He knew that now. Funny how you always learn the most important things in life when you are learning how to die.

After Angela was buried Joseph had packed a single bag and taken an airplane out to the West Coast. Be Be had not heard from him since. He saw young Joseph on the television from time to time, running around with the other campus radicals, like that Tom Hayden and Tim Harris and Abbie Hoffman, talking about overthrowing the government. Be Be could not understand Joseph in those insane days of the late sixties and early seventies. If the kid had been patient he could have taken the country legitimately. Instead he thought he could take it with a bull horn and a protest march.

The times when it hurt most were when Joseph would publicly denounce Be Be, his own father. Like the time he gave that interview to that investigative reporter for *The Village Voice,* Jason Gotbaum, about how his own father, Be Be Gonzago, was guilty of murder for backing Lyndon Johnson's war policy. Or when he would go on national network news shows and bad-mouth the old man.

All of Be Be's friends would ask him how he could let his own son do that to him. But Be Be couldn't explain it all. It wasn't just the war. Be Be knew it was also Angela, Joseph's mother, his son was talking about and there was no way Be Be could respond to that.

Be Be poured himself some more coffee and brandy and then reached over and switched on the movie projector. The blinding glare of the high-intensity bulb made Be Be shield his eyes until the pupils in his fading eyes adjusted to the light. Now the faint scratching of the old film was audible over the chattering of the sprockets biting through the celluloid. Johnny Quinn had gotten some film lab to assemble this ninety-minute montage of Be Be's life. It included news clips of some of Be Be's public appearances with the high and mighty over the years, spliced together with more intimate fragments of his personal life, including his wedding, Joseph playing football, anniversaries, birthdays, Christmases. It was a biographical montage of the life of Be Be Gonzago.

Be Be cherished the film and had it set up on the projector at all times for nights like this one when he was feeling particularly empty. It filled him up with nostalgia and gave him back a few of the old laughs and always made him cry. Especially those clips that included Angela and Joseph.

Be Be had gotten his hands on a home-movie camera when they had first came on the market and had learned how to use it so that he could preserve for posterity all the special moments of Joseph's life on the way to the presidency. It seems a little silly now, he thought. But he had wanted to show the world the footage of President Joseph Gonzago taking his first step in life, the first time he rode a two wheeler, his first Holy Communion and his first day at school and his Holy Confirmation, and graduation from elementary school and quarterbacking the high school team to a championship.

These fragments of time were all preserved, but they would never be for general viewing now. They were for the half-dead eyes of a father the son hated. Be Be knew this but treasured them anyway in the hope that someday Joseph would understand and forgive him. But that someday now looked as if it would never come because there weren't too many somedays left in Be Be Gonzago's life.

There was no soundtrack on the film, but Be Be Gonzago could remember the crack of the Louisville Slugger as Joseph smashed the home run up there on the screen. Be Be recalled that particular game vividly. Angela had accompanied him and she had stood quiet and confused on the sidelines out on Shore Road, Brooklyn. She had never understood this game called baseball, and she wondered why sometimes people cheered when Joseph made a strike and other times they cheered when he hit the ball. Be Be had spent that entire afternoon trying to explain that they cheered his strikes when he threw them from the mound and cheered his hits when he was at the plate. She insisted this made no sense. The object of the game had to be either making strikes or making hits—not both.

Be Be had thrown up his hands and laughed. It was not important for a woman from Naples to understand baseball, he told her. The only thing that was important was that Joseph played it well because being a high school baseball star would look good in any biographical stories about Joseph Gonzago, candidate.

This had confused Angela even more. She did not understand

what baseball had to do with politics. Be Be assured her they were both only games.

Be Be watched Joseph run around the bases up there on the small screen as the sixteen-millimeter film chewed on. Now Be Be was a black-and-white image, looking younger and dapper, dressed in one of the tailor-made suits that the Old Ginzo had sewn to order for him. Be Be was standing on the steps of City Hall shaking hands with Mayor Wagner. Wagner was presenting Be Be with some bullshit plaque, the nature of which Be Be could not remember.

Now there was footage of Joseph's fifth birthday party. Be Be smiled there in the dark as he looked at young Joseph without any front teeth, shoving cake and ice cream into his face. Joseph's boyhood friends, Gulatta and Rosario, mouthed the words to "Happy Birthday." Those two had grown up to become low lives but they had been good friends to Joseph when he was a kid. And there was Frank Donato, the poor bastard, starting the cake fight. Always in trouble, that Frank Donato. Like now, facing big time for waterfront racketeering. I'll have to get him out of this jam. Horse trade . . . Be Be thought it funny, how they had all gone such different ways. How simple it was when they were just kids and how complicated adulthood had made their lives.

Soon the screen went bright hot white as the film ended. Be Be turned the rewind button on the projector so that the film would be ready to roll again whenever he needed the fix it gave him. As the film rewound, Be Be took a large gulp of the brandy and washed it down with a half cup of cool espresso. It was time for the sack. Almost eleven P.M. Johnny Quinn would be picking him up at seven in the morning to bring him down to the Court Street office where he would meet with that horse's ass of a governor Wolfington. Little did Wolfington and his clique of flunkies know that Be Be was not going to endorse him for his re-election. He was going to go for this Kelly kid, the reformer, in the Democratic primary. That was going to shock the shit out of them. Be Be the Boss Gonzago, machine hack, touting the liberal knight on the white steed.

But there was something about this kid Kelly that Be Be truly liked. He reminded him of Joseph. He was the kind of candidate who could parlay a New York governorship into a horse race for the White House if he didn't trip himself up along the way.

Kelly believed in a lot of the same things as Joseph. Kelly came from that campus activist background but had clawed his way into establishment politics as a maverick assemblyman. He even rounded up a bunch of the old college radicals to run his campaign —Tim Harris was virtually running the show in that campaign and he came out of the Columbia University SDS crowd. Kelly was running hard against the death penalty and nuclear energy and was proabortion. None of these issues were popular, but Be Be admired guys who ran against the grain.

Maybe Joseph would have liked the idea of his old man backing a young progressive candidate in what was surely Be Be's last campaign. But that's just more bullshit, wishful thinking, Be Be thought. Joseph wouldn't give a damn what Be Be Gonzago did in his public or private life.

The film was completely rewound now and Be Be snapped off the machine. He removed his glasses, folded them, and placed them into the pocket of the silk robe. He slowly pushed himself to his feet, feeling now, finally, all of his sixty-eight years. He also felt his own size now, which was just five foot six. There had been so many years, the good ones, when Be Be felt like a man of more than six feet.

It was a demeanor he had practiced, a way of cocking the blocky head on the bull neck in such a fashion that his eyes appeared to look down when they were looking up. It intimidated a lot of people, made it seem Be Be was actually taller than he was. In those days, when Be Be's eyes met someone else's, they locked like dead bolts and only Be Be could break the stare.

Now those days were gone and Be Be felt like the smaller man he was, his body dying and shrinking and revolting against all the years of overuse. His walk was lighter, his heels no longer assaulting the floor beneath him but rather groping upon it for security. He cautiously made his way across the thick Persian carpet, swung open the knotted-glass doors, and slowly climbed the wooden stairs to the bedroom, using the banister to deliver him to the top step.

Be Be removed his robe and slid beneath the blankets of the large bed and rested his head upon the pillow and slid his right hand instinctively underneath it and grasped the cold steel of a Smith and Wesson .38 revolver.

You're not such a fucking big shot anymore, he thought. You're an old man. You're dying. You have no wife and your son prefers not to have a father. The vultures are circling overhead but you cannot even see them, because your eyes have betrayed you. All you are left with is their hideous screeching laughter as they wait for you to fall. Silly fools, they don't know you already have . . .

2

The guy with the bull neck named Hanrahan in the back of the classroom did not bother to raise his hand. He just started shouting and Joseph Gonzago paused in the middle of his lecture to listen.

"You know what I think," Hanrahan said. "I think you're full of crap, Mr. Gonzago. You might be able to bullshit a lot of those younger kids, too young to remember you. But I remember you. Me and you are the same age. Maybe I wasn't in college back then in the sixties and early seventies. That's because I was in the police academy. And now I'm getting my degree nights. But I remember you and all them other clowns, Jerry Rubin, Abbie Hoffman, Tim Harris, the Black Panther guys. You thought you were big deals."

Joseph Gonzago smiled patronizingly as he leaned against his desk in the front of the classroom.

"Why don't you shut up and let Mr. Gonzago teach the class, Hanrahan," a younger student snapped.

"No, it's all right," Joseph Gonzago said with an entertained grin. "Let's hear Hanrahan out. Let's hear how the other half thinks. Or doesn't think."

"Thank you, Mr. Gonzago," Hanrahan said, and cleared his throat. "As I was saying, I think you're full of shit—"

Hanrahan was interrupted by a barrage of laughter from the other students. He waited until the giggles died down and then looked around the room, his face flushed with anger.

"See what I mean," Hanrahan said. "Whenever anyone disagrees with the liberal way of thinking people laugh at him. But you can't ignore the fact that there are a lot of us out there."

"A lot of *what* of you out there, Hanrahan?" Joseph Gonzago asked as he gingerly slid a Vantage Blue cigarette from his pack and tapped the filter on the face of his gold watch.

"You know, people who aren't liberals," Hanrahan said. "You know, regular people, like."

"Regular people like?" Joseph said as he snapped open a slim butane lighter and put the flame to the tip of his cigarette. "What exactly are 'regular people like,' *like,* Hanrahan?"

"Someone who works for a living and doesn't think the world owes him a living, and he doesn't want to overthrow the government so a bunch of Marxists can come in and tell you what job you have to do."

Joseph winked at a pretty redhead named Cynthia sitting across from Hanrahan and she smiled back. Joseph Gonzago was dressed in a pair of faded, tight designer jeans, Gucci loafers, and a V-neck cotton pullover that exposed the hair on his chest. His hair was jet black and styled neatly over his ears, and the bushy dark canopies of his brows made his bittersweet chocolate eyes appear darker and mysterious. Joseph was six foot one and was thirty-two years of age with a slim but athletic build. He was a long way from being Mr. Chips, but he was one of the more popular professors on the UCLA campus—especially among the women.

"Hanrahan, how did we get off the topic?" Joseph asked. "We were discussing big-city politics and the influence of party machines in big cities. What does any of this have to do with overthrowing the government and Karl Marx? Or were you referring to Groucho? Harpo?"

The class laughed and Hanrahan flushed red. "See, you always try to put a guy who doesn't agree with you down. But look at you. In the sixties you ran around with all of them clowns. Now Jerry Rubin is on Wall Street. Abbie Hoffman writes rotten books that he makes a lot of money on. Tom Hayden is married to Hanoi Jane and isn't missing any meals. Bob Dylan found Jesus. And you, who wanted to burn the campus down, you teach political science at UCLA and you're up for tenure. How come all you guys went for the capitalism in the end? Because you know that the Marxism don't work."

"Hanrahan, Hanrahan, Hanrahan. Please get a grip on yourself. You are a Los Angeles city policeman, right?"

"What of it?"

"Ten years ago you thought all college kids were bums, pinkos, and radicals."

"Most of them were."

"But today you are able to sit in a college classroom and tell your teacher that he is full of shit. And maybe I am. But if it wasn't for the students in the late sixties and early seventies who demanded an equal say in university matters, the administration here would still have you wearing jackets and ties to class and they'd make you so intimidated that you'd be afraid to contradict the almighty teacher. Am I right, Hanrahan?"

Hanrahan shifted his head to the side and thought it over.

"But you gotta burn down ROTC to get that?" Hanrahan asked.

"No," Joseph said. "But it helped."

The students broke up laughing again and Hanrahan retreated into a cocoon of silence.

Joseph winked at Cynthia again and then checked his watch. He took a long drag on the Vantage Blue and exhaled dramatically.

"Okay, look, almost time to go. Tomorrow we'll discuss machine politics in more specific terms. We'll be discussing a man I once knew quite well in fact. Be Be Gonzago, my father, the boss of the Brooklyn Democratic machine. Okay, good night."

The students began collecting their books and making for the door. Hanrahan was still silent, perhaps a little embarrassed.

"Hanrahan," Joseph shouted, "can you stay for just a minute?"

All the other students left the classroom except for Hanrahan and Cynthia. She remained seated and Hanrahan approached Joseph.

"Hanrahan, I'm going to level with you, pal," Joseph said. "So far, your test scores have been rotten and your papers are awful. But your class participation has been excellent. I know we don't see eye to eye, never will, thank God, but I think you give this class the inoculation it needs. Because of that I'm giving you a C instead of a D on your midterm. I think if you study just a little more and stop writing papers like they were letters to the editor of the *Birch Log* you could boost your grade to a B by the end of the term. I admire you for speaking up and I hope you will keep doing it. A deal?"

Joseph put his hand out and Hanrahan looked at it and smiled at Joseph.

"Never thought I'd shake hands with a fuckin' commie," Hanrahan joked, and accepted Joseph's hand. "Thanks, Mr. Gonzago."

Joseph looked at the redhead in the back and pointed to Hanrahan and said, "Handsome bastard for a cop, isn't he, Cynthia?"

The young woman broke up laughing. Hanrahan laughed too and left the classroom. When Hanrahan was gone Joseph shook his head.

"You couldn't invent a guy like that," Joseph said. Cynthia swaggered up to Joseph and leaned over to kiss him. Joseph pulled away.

"Not here," Joseph said.

Later, when they were through, Joseph propped himself up on the silk pillows and lit a cigarette with the thin silver lighter and blew the smoke up toward the ceiling. Cynthia lay next to him, the sinewy body glistening with perspiration was accentuated in the soft pink lighting. The room was decorated in a gentle feminine motif of lace and satin and silk. The sound of the surf beating like a massive pacemaker on the shore of Venice Beach was the only sound audible over Cynthia's breathing. Joseph took a long drag on the cigarette, and without looking at Cynthia he gave her the news.

"I'm giving you a C in the course," Joseph said as he watched the smoke curl toward the stucco ceiling. Cynthia was re-emerging from the dreamy-eyed world of eros. She smiled and snuggled her face into Joseph's deep pile chest, her arm going around his waist.

"I was hoping for a B."

"You only did C work, Cynthia."

She propped her head up and looked into his eyes, smiling lustfully.

"You call what I just did a C performance?" she said, pursing her lips.

Joseph stared at her in silence for a long moment, then crushed out the cigarette in the ashtray, annoyance building in him. He was perturbed that the young lady was trying to exploit sexually a university grade from him. He had been seeing Cynthia for a few weeks in what he had thought was nothing more than a recreational interlude between two adults who found each other attractive. It didn't occur to him until now that ulterior motives might be involved.

Joseph was finishing dressing less than five minutes later as Cynthia, equally angry, lay beneath the sheets of her bed, her arms folded, silent. Her eyes followed Joseph Gonzago as he moved about the room, combing his hair, strapping on his gold watch, buttoning up his shirt. When he was ready to leave he walked to the bedside and leaned over and kissed Cynthia's cheek, a polite expression of sexual farewell.

"If you put in more classroom participation you might boost the grade to a B by the time finals come. But right now you're only doing C work. I'm sorry."

Cynthia said nothing, just lay there fuming as Joseph walked to the door. He was unbolting the lock when Cynthia's voice stopped his movements.

"That's okay, teacher," Cynthia said. "In school you might be teacher and I might be student. But we both know that in this room it's the other way around, don't we?"

Joseph stood tree-still with his back to the woman. The sharp words stung.

"I'll see you in class," Joseph said softly.

"Yeah," Cynthia said. "Well, you've just been dropped from this one, fella. I'm giving you an F as in fuck off."

The red Ford Mustang whispered along Pacific Coast Highway as a sports talk station played on the radio. Joseph wasn't really listening to the chatter about the Dodgers, Angels, Rams, Raiders, or Kings. His mind was a continent away, back in New York, where a heated gubernatorial race was going on between Wolfington and Kelly. He'd read a story about it that morning in *The Village Voice,* which came out about a week late in L.A. Jason Gotbaum had written the story and it was his impression that Kelly was making large gains against the organization-backed Wolfington. Kelly's support was coming from the blacks, Puerto Ricans, and other minorities because of his liberal stance on jobs programs and social-aid legislation. The white liberals liked his anti-death penalty position, but a great deal of his support was beginning to emerge from the nuclear freeze movement, which threw its support behind Kelly because of his opposition to nuclear power plants in New York State.

The news of the New York election was often sketchy out here in the land of sunshine, blondes, and the combustible turbine engine. But Joseph scrounged for as much news of it as he could because an old SDS friend named Tim Harris was working on the Kelly campaign. Joseph was hoping Kelly would trounce Wolfington, not just because of his friendship with Harris, but because Be Be Gonzago, his father, would certainly be backing Wolfington. Joseph would have liked nothing better than to watch Be Be Gonzago's infamous Brooklyn Democratic machine take a nose dive.

As he drove, a three-quarter moon hung to his left over the Pacific. In the distance the Pacific Palisades rose in the night, the tenacious sea snarling at the sheer walls of rock. Lights shone in the homes precariously balanced on the edges of the cliffs. Cars sped past Joseph in the opposite lane, heading south into the city of Los Angeles or farther into Orange County, which Joseph thought should have been renamed Caucasian County.

He exited up the California Incline and took California Avenue down to 19th Street in Santa Monica. He parked the red Mustang in his appointed carport and took the back steps up from the alley to apartment number five, a furnished studio of the type so abundant near the beach. He flicked on the lights and walked across the burned-orange shag carpet to a small service kitchen, jammed a glass with ice, and poured the J&B on top of it. He took a long swallow and went in and dropped himself on the folded-out Castro bed. He never bothered to fold the Castro back into a sofa since the only visitors he ever had here usually shared the bed with him one night at a time.

Outside his window a typing pool of crickets sent dispatches into the night. It had taken him a long time to adjust to the sound of crickets after hearing Brando say how they made him nervous in *On the Waterfront.* To city people crickets were like spies sent down by the farmers to make sure there were no conspiracies being hatched against pork-belly futures.

Joseph searched the channels of the television to see if any late-night news programs might give him some information about the New York campaign. *The Village Voice* story had said that Kelly had closed the point spread to ten. Not bad. Joseph wanted more recent news, but there was nothing on the tube but cut movies and series reruns.

He took another good gulp of the whiskey and felt his insides buck as it hit the walls of his stomach. He leaned against the back rest of the sofa bed and closed his eyes. He imagined for a moment what his father's face would look like if this Kelly beat Wolfington. But the image would not come. He had never witnessed his father in a moment of true defeat. He was a man who almost always had gotten his own way. When the only image that would come was that of Be Be Gonzago smiling in victory, Joseph opened his eyes to escape the ghost.

He thought about the tawdry scene with Cynthia and wished it had not gotten so petty and ugly. But he felt little guilt over the incident. After all, she had tried to use him to her own advantage.

What did disturb him was his inability to be truly close to a woman for so many years. There hadn't been a single woman with whom he had felt an emotional connection for ten years. Since *Her.* He refused even to let her name form in his mind. Joseph Gonzago had decided a long time ago that the only way ever to escape her, that woman of yesterday, was to bury her name, disfigure her face in his memory, strip her of identity, reduce her to a symbol, and so the woman who had once been the center of his life, became simply *Her.*

Joseph got up from the bed and walked to the window and looked out over the city of Santa Monica, a series of low multiple dwellings, parades of palm trees, ersatz British pubs, plastic-roofed fast-food depots, gasoline stations, and automobile dealers. It certainly wasn't Brooklyn, but Brooklyn, like *Her* and Be Be Gonzago, were part of another world, a different dimension called the past. Be Be Gonzago had helped send Joseph's mother to the grave, and Joseph's heart had been cut out and halved by *Her.* You do not go back to such people and ask for an encore.

You live with yourself, Joseph thought. Sometimes you cannot even trust who that person is. He had an early morning class and it was getting late, almost midnight California time. He undressed, carefully hanging his clothes on a wooden valet next to the sofa bed, and slid under the sheets. Both pillows were on one side of the bed. His last conscious thought was that back in Brooklyn *She* was three hours ahead of him and probably always would be.

3

At midnight the Plumber stepped off the elevator on the fourteenth floor of the office building on Court Street in downtown Brooklyn. The building was empty and the hallways were silent, and the eight short steps the Plumber took across the marble floor to the men's room facing the elevator sent small thunderclaps resounding off the high ceilings. The Plumber held a toolbox in his left hand, and with his right he opened the men's room door with a small brass key.

He walked to one of the old-fashioned tall urinals and emptied himself of a minor case of the shakes. After zipping up, he walked across the cracked tiles to the window. The window would not open; it had been sealed by twenty-five years of gray enamel paint. He hoisted the toolbox up onto the dusty sill and opened it. The top portion of the toolbox was designed to be lifted out. He took an eight-inch Stanley screwdriver from the top tier and then lifted this level out. From the bottom half of the toolbox he took out a three-pound lump hammer and placed it alongside the screwdriver on the windowsill.

Now he removed the most important tool of all for this job—a .38 Smith and Wesson revolver with screw-on silencer. He placed this on the windowsill alongside the other tools. Then he went to work on the window, hammering the paint and wood of the window where it stuck to the frame. The job took fifteen minutes. And finally, using all the weight in his five-foot-eight, hundred-and-fifty-pound frame, the Plumber shoved the window open wide. The window led out to a fire escape that probably had not been used for fifteen years—when the new fire stairs had been added to the interior of the building and a sprinkler system put in to meet the more modern fire code.

A wet April breeze came through the window and the Plumber shivered, but he left the window open. It was going on twenty past twelve. The Plumber now took three three-quarter-inch slide-bolt latches from the toolbox and walked to the heavy wooden door, and with four-inch wood screws he fastened the latches every two feet on the eight-foot door. The exertion of driving the wood screws into the mahogany brought a film of sweat over his body. When he had finished he bolted each of the latches and yanked as hard as he could on the door. The door would not give even a fraction of an inch. The Plumber calculated that it would take several men with a crowbar at least fifteen minutes to open the door. That would provide ample time.

Now the Plumber took out his stopwatch and walked to the door again and opened the latches. He took the pistol in his hand, activated the watch, opened the door, pointed the pistol at the elevator door, slammed the men's room door quickly, and bolted the latches as fast as possible. Now he made for the window, climbed out, and began his sprint down the rusted old stairs. The stopwatch ticked away in his hand. He made the parking lot in one minute thirty-three seconds, jumped into his Oldsmobile, and raced out of the lot. He was two blocks away when the stopwatch showed three minutes had elapsed since he had pointed the pistol at the elevator door. That gave him an estimated twelve minutes to play with. You could read the whole sports section of the *News* in that long. There would be no problem.

Now the Plumber drove back to the parking lot, killed the lights, and shut off the engine. He hid the keys under the dash and stepped out of the blue sedan and across the tarmac of the lot to the ladder leading to the fire escape and started the long climb back up to the fourteenth floor.

The Plumber was panting heavily when he climbed back into the men's room. Your wind starts to desert you when you reach your fiftieth year. His hair and clothing were damp with sweat and the light spring mist. The only sounds in the building were the anonymous commotions of the plumbing and air ducts that brought water and heat from the basement to the top floor.

The Plumber now made himself as comfortable as possible on the floor of the men's room. He took a Thermos of hot coffee from the toolbox and unwrapped a peanut butter and jelly sandwich on cracked whole wheat. It was nearly one o'clock in the morning and the Plumber had now regained his breath and had shaken the nervous chills from his body with the strong warm coffee.

The governor of New York State would be stepping off that elevator in seven hours. He would be coming to Brooklyn for a meeting that would weigh greatly in his political future. His re-election after a stormy two terms might depend on the support of Be Be Gonzago, Brooklyn Democratic machine boss. The money and manpower of the Brooklyn machine could well be the deciding factor in the Democratic primary. The governor had a strong challenger in the reform candidate Brendan Kelly.

Ever since the nuclear accident that claimed six lives at Indian Point even the more conservative upstate farmers were starting to get terrified by the possibility of a nuclear catastrophe. Wolfington had fought hard for the federal dollars to build nuclear power stations because he needed to alleviate the local unemployment. So now he could not very well take the popular and expedient stand against nuclear energy. He had to stick to his guns even if it might spell political disaster. The alternative was making himself vulnerable to accusations of hypocrisy and political opportunism. His antiabortion stance would help secure the Catholic and scattered fundamentalist blocs. His pro-death-penalty stance would lose him the urban liberals but get him the blue collars.

Still, Wolfington was no fool. Kings County, as Brooklyn was also called, had the highest concentration of registered Democrats in the State of New York, which also made it one of the largest Democratic strongholds in the nation. There were over three million people in the borough of churches, and 491,000 of them were registered Democrats who would be voting in the upcoming primary.

Henry Wolfington had been made by the media. Once a somewhat obscure upstate congressman, he had capitalized on that obscurity by offering himself as a fresh face with new ideas. He did this with the help of Daniel Gunther, considered to be the best, if most ruthless, media manipulator in the state. Gunther had also worked in a few national elections with a certain degree of success. But he knew the New York arena best, and how to sell a candidate on television to both city slickers and country bumpkins.

It had worked magnificently the first time because Wolfington was such an unknown quantity that voters were willing to take a chance on a new product. Four years later it was a little harder and the percentages had narrowed at the polls. Now after eight years of Wolfington it would be hard to sell him as a new and improved version of an established product. Gunther did not like backing nags ready for the glue factory. The pundits saw Gunther's jumping to the Kelly camp as an investment in youth and the future even if Wolfington did have Pennsylvania Avenue on his mind.

Now Brendan Kelly had the same fresh-face advantage Wolfington had had eight years ago. Gunther could sell that.

For weeks the political gossips and pundits had been speculating that Governor Wolfington was beginning to realize he needed more than just "good packaging" to get a third nod from the New York voters. The press was reporting that sources inside the Wolfington camp were trying to urge their candidate to meet with more of the political bosses, the behind-the-scene power brokers such as Be Be Gonzago whose machine could go out and canvass and pull the street-level vote.

But Wolfington was reluctant. He and Gonzago had had their differences over the years. Some of them public. Others behind oak doors. The press was saying the Wolfington strategists were assuring their candidate that these skirmishes could easily be rectified if the governor were willing to come across with a few hundred state patronage jobs for Brooklyn party loyalists and a public endorsement here and there for a tolerable machine candidate.

The scuttlebutt was that Gonzago resented Wolfington's "outsider" status and his "hayseed priorities," which often led to neglect of big cities, especially New York City. They pointed out that Gonzago's power had been slipping slightly in the past few elections, but the pundits were quick to say that he still mattered. In his home territory of Brooklyn he still carried plenty of clout; most of the judges were still Be Be Gonzago hand-picked and boxed. William Marcy Tweed had once said, "It is better to know the judge than the law." Be Be Gonzago was fond of saying, "It is better to know the people who make the laws." Which Be Be Gonzago certainly did. Most of the councilmen and state legislators from Brooklyn owed at least one favor to Be Be Gonzago, the Brooklyn party boss. So for Wolfington to get the endorsements of these men in their constituencies, it was crucial that he approach Be Be Gonzago. The press had been saying for weeks that such a meeting was imminent. It was no different than a candidate sitting down with the editorial boards of *The New York Times*, the *Daily News*, or the various TV and radio stations looking for endorsements.

Be Be Gonzago started in politics before television controlled so much of it, and today many people thought his style of politics anachronistic and downright immoral. There were others who found a certain charm in men of power such as Be Be Gonzago who dressed like Frank Costello and expected the same respect just short of the kissing of the ring. For still others machine politics brought out a melancholy nostalgia, a longing for the good old days of Christmas turkeys and free beers on election days. The new power brokers had initials like ABC, CBS, NBC. These were monolithic, impersonal institutions that commanded respect and influence.

But those who made their living peeking up petticoats in the ballrooms of New York politics knew that before the orchestra played the last waltz Governor Henry Wolfington would walk up to Be Be Gonzago and ask him to dance.

The Plumber turned the pages of *Playboy* magazine. He studied the beautiful girl in the centerfold and smiled to himself. By tomorrow night he would have enough money to buy a woman like that. He had heard that you could purchase women with bodies like playmates in Los Angeles. And tomorrow he would leave Brooklyn, just as the Dodgers had over twenty years ago, looking for sunshine and with the money to buy it. The Plumber turned the pages slowly, stopping to buy each woman that glorified the glossy pages without waiting for change.

4

The garbagemen awakened Johnny Quinn every weekday morning at 6:30 A.M. There was no longer any need for an alarm clock. He had grown accustomed to the banging of cans, the whine of the sanitation trucks, and the crunch of the heavy machinery eating part of the fifteen thousand tons of garbage collected from the streets of New York each day by the sanitation department. The sanitation commissioner was a Be Be Gonzago protégé, and Be Be saw to it that the streets where his friends lived got prompt and frequent pickups.

Johnny Quinn was a tall gaunt man whose hair was snowy white. His eyebrows were bushy and still jet black. His soft, startling blue, fluttery eyes never focused on any one thing for very long, but rather scanned a broad field in a nervous, cautious manner. His body was going soft from underuse and a small potbelly had formed on an otherwise thin frame. He stepped out of the single bed onto the linoleum floor of his box-shaped living room and moved toward the large kitchen furnished with a small Formica table and a single chair.

He removed the prune juice from the small refrigerator and poured himself his usual five ounces, which he finished in two small gulps. He stared out the kitchen window and could see the early sun gilding the harbor ten blocks away. Barges moved past the Statue of Liberty, and the skyline was coming to life. The view of the harbor and the skyline from Sunset Park, Brooklyn, was one of the best in the city.

Sunset Park was one of those overlooked sections of the city where successful integration had taken place without mandates from judges or urban planners. The neighborhood was sandwiched between better-known Bay Ridge and Park Slope and was treated by the people of those areas as a sort of stepson who had never really made the grade.

Like everywhere else in New York City, Sunset Park had its share of violence and assorted crime. People stuck up delis and late-night bartenders. Drugs were popular among the teen-agers; rival gangs would clash in Sunset Park at night. That was the stuff that made filler copy for the city-wide daily newspapers and provided headlines for the small local weeklies. But the neglected story in neighborhoods like Sunset Park was the Puerto Rican bus driver who awakened early each morning, had breakfast with his wife and kids, grabbed the brown paper bag with the ham sandwich and an apple, kissed the wife good-bye, and got a ride to work with his Italian-American next-door neighbor.

It was a neighborhood where people still hung wash above back yards, where locals shopped in corner markets, where you went to watch the Mets at Frank's Tavern on the corner, and where women congregated at bingo halls and Laundromats.

Johnny Quinn loved Brooklyn, so he stayed and intended to stay until he made the final move ten blocks north to Greenwood Cemetery, which was the northern border of Sunset Park. One of the reasons Johnny Quinn loved this neighborhood was that the Manhattan professional types who had moved into neighborhoods like Brooklyn Heights and Park Slope had not yet discovered Sunset Park.

Johnny Quinn finished his shower, dried himself briskly with a thinning towel, and began dressing in a dark blue suit, white shirt, and red and navy striped tie.

As he left the building he noticed that the morning was turning bruisy—dark swollen rain clouds moving in to smother the promising sun. Johnny Quinn thought about going back up for a trench coat and umbrella but decided against it after he checked his watch and saw it was nearing seven thirty. Be Be would be waiting and the appointment with the governor was on top of the list.

He climbed into Be Be's green Plymouth, which had been purchased almost at cost through the police department because these were the cars New York City detectives used. He took Fifth Avenue because he enjoyed the way the commercial strip exploded with life at this hour of the morning—the clothes stores and supermarkets, butcher shops and candy stores, were all removing the modern urban armor of accordion gates. Factory workers waited at bus stops or hurried for subway stations. Truck drivers were unloading their cargoes of milk and bread and cheap cakes, and cops sat in 89¢-two-eggs-any-style-coffee-toast diners and read about last night's rage of crime in the first five pages of the *Daily News*.

Johnny Quinn passed the Transit Authority bus terminal at Thirty-sixth Street and Fifth Avenue and saw that the drivers and the buses were about as active as the people who occupied Greenwood Cemetery across the street. That's because the MTA is a state agency, Johnny Quinn thought to himself. But this guy Wolfington didn't care much about the City of New York, especially the transit system, which he had been overlooking for the past eight years. Be Be had told him on a hundred occasions that the city should be eligible for some of those federal highway improvement dollars that were mostly spent in towns upstate. Be Be had told Wolfington that the subways were New York's highways—that over three million people used those "highways" every single day as the only way to get to the jobs that provided Wolfington with his state income taxes. Wolfington had balked at the idea that highway money be spent on the improvement of New York City subways.

Wolfington now had the gall to come and ask Be Be Gonzago for his support. He would be in for a very unpleasant surprise. Be Be, if he did support Wolfington, would stick him up for a whole bunch of promises. Be Be had a way of making you keep your promises—he did this by secretly tape recording them when they were made. Long before Nixon and his gang first heard of the word Sony, Be Be had been preserving for posterity, and maybe eventual insurance, the secrets and schemes of almost every public official in the city and state government of New York. Only two people knew these records were kept—Be Be and Johnny Quinn.

He made a right at Twentieth Street and thought how things might have been different if it had not been for Be Be's son, Joseph, leaving when he did. It had stolen some permanent source of fuel from Be Be Gonzago's life. No political rival had ever been able to affect Be Be that way, Johnny Quinn thought. He had been with him from the beginning, watched him go from clubhouse worker to the top of the Brooklyn Democratic party. Sometimes he had been ruthless, perhaps too much so, but he had mellowed in his later years, even passing up the opportunity to destroy a man like Sydney Weingarten, speaker of the state assembly. This would be Be Be Gonzago's final campaign. The fun had gone out of it all for Be Be. Politics had been reduced to a series of grueling headaches: people investigating each other all the time, grand juries sniffing around your door, watchdogs sitting at the next restaurant table.

Be Be Gonzago had never been indicted in his life. He had been investigated all right. But never once was he formally charged. It looked now as if it was only a matter of time before some cockamamy indictment would fall. You could do time now for squashing a littering ticket, Johnny Quinn thought. Be Be was probably right in wanting to hang up the guns and go lie in the sun somewhere.

Johnny Quinn drove through Bartel-Pritchard Square, past the monument to the war dead and the now-shuttered Sanders movie theater. He took Prospect Park Southwest up toward Park Circle.

Just as he entered the service road of Prospect Park the rain fell as if a hole had been cored in the sky. The wipers peeled the sheets of water off the windshield. Needles of rain stitched the soft green earth at the side of the road, causing streams of muddy water to chuckle along the curb. He stopped for a red light on the park road just outside the small, crumbling zoo. The only animal visible was an aging gray elephant who walked as if he needed orthopedic shoes. The rain didn't seem to faze the mammoth animal. Johnny Quinn laughed to himself and said aloud, "Typical dumb Republican." The light changed and he drove on, the tires whispering through the rainwater.

Johnny Quinn took the Coney Island Avenue exit from the park and made for Albemarle Road. Flatbush Heights was the last thriving section of Flatbush—the area cut off from the deteriorating section by the subway tracks of the D train where it emerged from the tunnel on its way to Coney Island. The neighborhood was first settled by rich Protestants from Manhattan in the late nineteenth century who built great mansions in the bucolic Dutch settlement called Flatbush, taken from the Dutch "Vlackebos."

These were summer houses ideally located between the sandy shores of the Atlantic Ocean and the low hilly region now called Prospect Park. The rich were attracted by the hunting and swimming available on the other side of the river from Manhattan, and the street names now reflected those of the people who settled there—Marlborough, Albemarle, Beverley, Cortelyou. These twenty- and thirty-room structures had survived the test of time and vandalism. Most of the homes were owned by doctors and lawyers and white-collar professionals now, who kept a minimum of two foreign cars in each large driveway. The huge overhanging trees transformed the streets into virtual tunnels when in leaf. The community had its own private security patrol, supported through block associations.

Johnny Quinn slipped the car into the driveway and hurried up the four steps of the stoop. Be Be Gonzago opened the door after the first ring. He was dressed in a beautiful gray pin-striped suit that fit his stocky body perfectly. It accentuated the shoulders, which helped to broaden his dimensions while at the same time giving the illusion that his legs were longer than they really were. His tie was a little askew and Johnny Quinn instinctively straightened it and brushed the shoulders of Be Be's suit.

"Morning, Johnny," Be Be Gonzago said.

"Good morning, Boss."

"I like the smell of the rain this time of year," Be Be said as he gulped the sweet, rain-laundered air. "Spring rain. Nice."

"Yeah," Johnny Quinn said.

"I look all right, Johnny?"

"Perfect."

"What about the shave?" Be Be asked. "I can never be sure if I get the shave right. Even with the glasses. Terrible thing, not being able to get the shave right. How's it look, Johnny?"

"It looks just fine, Be Be, just fine."

"I don't want to give this Wolfington anything to talk about, you know. One of those Protestant types, likes to talk about ethnics."

"Just remember who's coming to see who, Boss."

"Yeah," Be Be said, as he handed Johnny Quinn an umbrella, which Johnny Quinn held over his boss's head. Be Be climbed into the front seat of the car and Johnny Quinn clunked the door closed behind him.

Johnny Quinn turned on 1010 WINS news and Be Be listened distractedly as they drove out of the driveway and down toward Flatbush Avenue. The news reader delivered his litany of violence and fires and threw in a humorous spot here and there to keep people from snapping off their sets. Now he announced that a new *New York Times* poll showed that Brendan Kelly had closed the gap between himself and incumbent governor Henry Wolfington to just ten points.

Johnny Quinn made the left onto Flatbush Avenue, which was bustling with morning shoppers and students from Erasmus Hall High School.

"Kelly's gonna win this thing, Johnny," Be Be said.

Johnny Quinn turned to Be Be, a little surprised.

"Really think so, Boss?"

"I'm gonna support him, Johnny. I made up my mind. I support him and I'll help deliver this borough and I think it can make a difference."

Johnny Quinn smiled broadly and slammed the heel of his hand off the steering wheel in delight. He did it again.

"Keep your eyes on the road, Johnny. Christ sakes, I don't wanna go into the tankeroo before I get the chance to back the guy."

"Can't believe it, Be Be," Johnny Quinn said, and sped up the car and laughed. "I mean I can't believe it. Son of a gun, I just can't believe it. I can't wait to see the look on Wolfington's face when you tell him."

"It might make things dangerous," Be Be said. "A lot of people are counting on Wolfington winning. It means a lot to them. If he wins again he could take a stab at the presidential primary in two years. And you know as well as me there's no competition for that and he could make a good run. But not if he loses his own state this time around. I just don't think the country could afford to have this dumbbell in the White House. He's gotta be stopped."

"There are an awful lot of people counting on him winning," Johnny Quinn said more soberly. "Weingarten wants that state supreme court seat so bad he can taste it. If Wolfington goes down the drain so will Donnelly's campaign for attorney general. Not to mention all the other hangers-on who could get soft jobs."

"That's why I'm telling you to keep your eyes on the road," Be Be said as the car slipped by the entrance to the Brooklyn Botanic Garden. "I don't wanna die before I get to screw 'em all."

Johnny Quinn laughed. Be Be Gonzago opened his window to take in the smell of the Botanic Garden. Since his eyes had begun to fail smells had become very important to Be Be Gonzago. The scent on the wet, flowery spring air reminded Be Be of the perfume Angela used to wear. Joseph also came to mind, but Be Be did not want the weakness that accompanied such thoughts to dull the duties that lay before him that morning. He began to slam his fist into his broad palm.

"We'll mop the goddamn floors with them, Johnny," Be Be Gonzago said. The scent still came to him from the Botanic Garden. He rolled up the window and lit a cigar to kill the sweet scent and the memories that escorted it. He bit deeply into the end of the cigar, took a heavy inhale.

"Slaughter the sons of bitches," Be Be said. "Maybe this is the last one, but it'll be a honey for the money. I'm gonna make Brendan Kelly the governor of New York and Henry Wolfington the unemployed actor he deserves to be."

Johnny Quinn banged the steering wheel again as he sped down Flatbush Avenue. Both men started to laugh.

5

Johnny Quinn pressed floor number fourteen and the elevator door snapped shut, and Be Be stood silently as the lift rose in the shaft, instinctively raising his eyes to the floor number indicator. Finally he spoke.

"Can you tell when you look at me, Johnny?"

"You ask all the time, Be Be, and I tell you the answer is no. Ever since I've known you, which is over thirty-five years now, Boss, you always squinted. They don't know if you're looking at them, through them, over them, or falling asleep with boredom. Your eyes make them all nervous because they don't tell them anything."

"Yeah? Well you make sure you get a good look at their faces when I drop the bomb on them about Kelly. I wanna know what Wolfington's face looks like. And Weingarten and that Donnelly. The rest of the mutts too."

"Don't worry, Boss, I'll be looking. I only wish I could photograph it."

The doors opened at the fourteenth floor and Be Be stepped off first. He was in public now and so he would not allow Johnny Quinn to help him down the corridor to the office. He knew the steps by heart from the more than twenty years of walking to the throne of political power in Brooklyn, the fourth largest city in America. The corridors were still empty and would remain so until after nine A.M. when the bureaucrats would arrive.

Johnny Quinn unlocked the office door and stepped inside and held the door open for Be Be. A huge map of the borough of Brooklyn covered the wall to the right of the front door. An American flag stood on one side of a massive oak desk and the flag of Brooklyn stood on the other side. A portrait of Be Be, painted when he was much younger, hung on the wall behind the desk. A small plaque sat on his desk: I SAID MAYBE AND THAT'S FINAL. Another one said: THE BUCK STOPS HERE—A LOT OF THEM.

Be Be sat in a swivel chair and relit his cigar and rested for a few moments. Johnny Quinn filled the Mister Coffee pot in the small bathroom off to the left and soon the rich aroma of brewing coffee filled the room. Be Be rose from his chair and walked to the bay window and stared out over his domain. It all looked watery to him now—a vast sea of steel and concrete and citizens. He did not have to be able to see it anymore to know what was there. It spread before him like the result of a few million rash and contradicting decisions.

Over there to the southeast was Red Hook and the famous Gowanus Canal which a man named William Adriaense Bennett purchased from a Mohawk chief named Gouwane in 1636. Bennett named part of his 930 acres "Gowanus" after the poor old redskin. The Dutch called the other part of it Roode Hoeck, later anglicized to Red Hook. It got its name from the color of the red clay earth in the area and the wild cranberries that flourished there. Today modern technology had transformed this section into a meandering series of empty lots, burned-out warehouses, crime-ridden housing projects, and the famous Gowanus Canal where mob snitches received the equivalent of full Naval burials at sea.

Brooklyn itself was named after a Dutch city called Breuckelen, meaning Broken Land, because the topography of the borough resembled the city of that name in Holland. Maybe it resembled it then, Be Be Gonzago thought. But not today. Today Brooklyn was a Broken Land all right, busted up with the help of guys like former power broker Robert Moses, who shoved highways and public works monstrosities into every orifice in the borough, breaking it up into isolated hamlets with steel and concrete borders, sometimes impossible to cross, and in this way pockets of poverty festered so that once a neighborhood imploded from squalor and neglect, the inhabitants moved to another walled hamlet where the same process repeated itself.

To Be Be Gonzago's left was the greatest monument to Brooklyn —the Brooklyn Bridge, the dream of an engineering genius named John Augustus Roebling. The bridge took thirteen years, five months, the lives of twenty workmen, and the lives of Roebling and his son to complete. But on May 24, 1883, when the bridge opened there were few who could deny it had been worth the effort. Even today no other bridge in the world equaled the beauty and majesty of the Brooklyn Bridge. Be Be Gonzago took a special pride in knowing that when the bridge was built Brooklyn was still an independent city and that two thirds of the bridge belonged to the City of Brooklyn, while one third could be claimed by the City of New York.

"Here's your coffee, Be Be," Johnny Quinn said as he placed a steaming mug in Be Be's hands.

"It's still beautiful, isn't it, Johnny?" Be Be asked as he looked out over the borough.

"The best, Boss," Johnny Quinn said.

Below the traffic moved in bizarre directions, as if it all intended to converge at the same intersection; people scurried haphazardly, obeying no traffic laws; pigeons flew in flocks from a thousand rooftops; buildings were being erected and torn down; a helicopter moved overhead; across the street the courthouse was coming to life as men and women with briefcases moved in and out of the revolving doors; citizens surfaced from the subways carrying umbrellas and newspapers and pocketbooks; Prospect Park, the emerald of the great landscapers Frederick Law Olmsted and Calvert Vaux, slurped up the April rain to help feed the coming summer; steam rose from sewers; bicyclists defied the daredevil stunts of the yellow taxis; buses honked, trucks snorted, cops blew whistles, winos drank, junkies schemed, mothers wept.

Brooklyn, the Broken Land, was out of bed.

"He'll be here in twenty minutes, Boss," Johnny Quinn said. "Weingarten and all the others will be here too, so maybe we should use the conference room."

"Sure, Johnny," Be Be said. "Yeah, use the conference room. It won't take long anyway."

Be Be sipped some of the hot coffee and felt it scorch the dying flesh in his throat. He puffed at the cigar and stared through the rain-splashed window one last time.

"So fucking beautiful," he mumbled to himself. "And so fucked up."

"Whadja say?" Johnny Quinn asked.

"Oh, nothing, Johnny," Be Be said. "Just that they need somebody younger to do this. I'm too old, I can't see, it's all over. I think we can have fun with this last number, but that's it.

"I have a few guys in mind, younger guys, but none of them are hungry enough, Johnny. You need a young, hungry guy for this job. I'm full up, Johnny. But so are all these young turks. They come into the business with their bellies filled with law school and political science degrees and they think they understand what people think. They don't know hungry, Johnny."

"You think Kelly is hungry, Be Be?" Johnny Quinn asked.

Be Be thought for a moment. "I'm not sure but I think he could eat," Be Be said.

With fifteen minutes to kill before his eight A.M. class Joseph Gonzago strolled leisurely to the main building from his Ford Mustang, which he parked in the faculty lot of UCLA. Even at this early hour the temperature was nearing eighty degrees. A warm breeze was blow-drying the dewy green of the campus grounds. Joseph noticed the distant brown collar of smog strangling the neck of the San Fernando Valley. But here in Westwood the skies were bright blue.

Joseph was trying to put back together a dream he had had the night before. The pieces lay scattered around his consciousness. His sleep the night before had been sweaty and twisted. When he awakened the sheets were damp with perspiration and twined like taffy and most of his body lay exposed.

As he walked across the campus toward the main building, he sorted and collated the pieces of the dream.

There was a young boy. The boy had very dark hair. He was well-built even for his age. Maybe he was seven, eight, nine. Not sure. That boy must have been me even though I couldn't see his face through the smoke. The smoke. It was dense, bluish gray, clouds of it. Can you smell what you see in a dream? Was it cigar smoke? Must have been. It was coming from the mouth of a huge face that floated above the boy. Boy was me. And the big lips of the big mouth were talking into the small ear of the small boy. There was another man in his thirties. He was also me, I think. Do you see your own face in a dream? Don't know but it must have been me. I was that man in his thirties because it was me that was yelling at the young boy. I told him to run, run back. But where the hell were we? A house with no rooms and no furniture and no windows or doors. A church? No. A mausoleum. I was yelling for him to run. But the small boy could not hear above the roar of the huge face that shouted instructions to the young boy. What were the instructions? "Go up! To the top! You must go to the top!" Top of what? The house? No. The face—the face was massive and frightening. It was telling the boy, "Go to the top of the world." The face was made of colored smoke, and as it started to fade the boy chased it, his hands outstretched. Ran from me. Ran when I told it to go back and listen to someone else besides that face . . .

"The face," Joseph said aloud, as he instinctively reached for the door of the school, "was Be Be Gonzago's face . . . ."

"Excuse me, Mr. Gonzago?" said a young man who was leaving through the other door. The young man stopped and stared at Joseph Gonzago oddly. Joseph did not answer; he just walked through the door on his way to his morning class.

As Joseph neared his classroom his casual gait became a deliberate strut. His hard leather heels clacked off the floor like a blind man's cane. He threw his shoulders back, tensed the knotty muscles of his stomach, tilted his head a little higher, and narrowed his eyes. Now he stopped just outside the classroom, smoothed his hair, took several breaths. He was now ready to "go on." When he had taken dramatic arts classes in college he had learned to prepare himself for going on stage a different way before each performance. Teaching was similar to acting. Sometimes the words and nature of the drama would be the same, but each audience and performance was approached differently.

Joseph could hear the loud din coming from inside the classroom —laughter, chairs scraping on the tile floors, people yawning and coughing, matches being lit, books slamming, windows being opened and shut.

Then in one single flourish Joseph Gonzago strode through the door, a long sweeping entrance across the front of the room. The gesture took the room by surprise and people tried to settle themselves. As they did, before they were even at full attention, Joseph Gonzago began his lecture in a deep, authoritative voice.

"Today we are going to discuss organizational party politics, better known as machine politics, and we will cover such subjects as legal graft, bossism, ward heeling, kickbacks, and a man named Be Be Gonzago. There are many people in this country like Be Be Gonzago, but I choose him as an example of this lesson because I think my personal knowledge of this man will help you to understand better exactly how machine politics really work. You can agree, disagree, or be uncertain. But I want and expect full participation. If the name Be Be Gonzago sounds familiar to you, it is because the man, in the conventional sense of the word, is my father."

Now Joseph had their full attention. Whenever Joseph spoke of his father to classes he commanded attention. It was his very best performance.

The Plumber paced back and forth in the men's room, checking his watch almost every two minutes. It was almost time now. Several people had tried the men's room door since Be Be Gonzago and Johnny Quinn stepped off the elevator earlier in the morning. None of them had lingered very long at the door, but all of them had made the Plumber nervous. The Plumber was awaiting the coded knock on the door that would tell him when the governor of the State of New York would be stepping off that elevator.

The handle of the .38 was damp in his sweaty palm. A few times he had tried to urinate but to no avail. He tried again but his bladder was filled only with fear. He zipped up and continued to pace.

Nothing can go wrong, he assured himself. The details have been seen to. A single shot and it will be over. Keep calm, no panic. The contractors had told him that only panic could ruin the plan. Stay cool and all will go smooth.

The Plumber repeated this over and over and over in his mind. It helped soothe him. He sat on the windowsill and listened to the soft melancholy chatter of the rain. The pistol in his hand felt like a ticket to the future.

6

The Cadillac limousine moved across the Brooklyn Bridge at an even forty miles per hour. The hum of the tires licking the wet iron gratings of the bridge irritated Governor Henry Wolfington. The vibrations made his nose itch and he rubbed it repeatedly. Two state troopers sat in the front seat next to the driver. Matthew Brideson, the governor's top aide, sat next to Wolfington with a pile of papers on his lap.

"I hate driving over this damn bridge," Wolfington said as he continued to scratch. "It's like holding on to a pneumatic drill. Makes your whole body itch."

"For God's sake," Brideson said with a smile. "Don't knock the Brooklyn Bridge in front of Be Be Gonzago. That would be like telling the Arabs the pyramids are an eyesore. Besides, Gonzago thinks he owns the damned bridge."

"His father probably bought it when he got off the boat," Wolfington said.

The two men chuckled.

"Seriously now, Hank," Brideson said. "We really need him. He could make the difference this time. Brooklyn is the largest Democratic district in the state."

"I'm aware of that, Matt," Wolfington said. "I should know, I carried it twice already."

"You mean Gonzago delivered it twice for you," Brideson said. "There is a difference, Hank."

"Quit calling me Hank," Wolfington said. "Especially when we're in public. And I'm well aware of Gonzago's strength in Brooklyn. But don't tell me he did it all. The people there are my kind of people. Working people. Just be sure you call me Mr. Governor in front of Gonzago."

"All right, all right," Brideson said, testily. "But I'll be calling you Mr. Ex-Governor if we don't have Gonzago on our team. So try to hold on to your temper with him. Don't be argumentative."

"Matt, do me a favor, will you. Stop lecturing me."

"It's called briefing," Brideson said. "I'm not lecturing. I just want to make sure we don't lose this guy because you're in one of your fighting moods, Hank. That's all."

"All right, all right, I'll handle it."

Brideson looked over the papers on his lap, sifted through them quickly as his brow wrinkled like a hand bellows.

"By our best estimation, rural upstate could split," Brideson said. "Not that the farmers are big Kelly fans, but because of this damned nuclear-energy issue. Even farmers are afraid of radioactivity. Especially since the big accident . . ."

"Enough Matt," Wolfington said with a wave of his hand. "I know the figures. I know we need Brooklyn. I know the breakdowns. Just let me think for a few minutes. I want to prepare for this meeting. Please . . ."

"Sure, Hank."

Wolfington looked out over the river, ferries moving toward Governor's Island, Liberty Island, Staten Island. Fog horns told sad stories and freighters and tugs carved up the rain-dimpled bay. The two policemen in the front seat stared straight ahead as the car passed the large yellow buildings that were the worldwide headquarters of the Jehovah's Witness organization. READ GOD'S WORD DAILY, the legend on the main building read. I do, Wolfington thought. In the polls.

Finally the car skimmed off the metal gratings onto the smoother asphalt of Brooklyn. The limo hit a pothole deep enough to drown in, and Wolfington took the bounce with heavy effort. It reminded him that Gonzago would be giving him a hard time about highway money. He'd have to prepare for that. There were answers. Austerity usually worked. But not with machine bosses. Blame the feds. Dwell on crime and new dollars for more cops. Talk about dollars that are forthcoming, not those already spent upstate. Keep in mind you are the governor of New York State. Gonzago is just a hack boss, part of the old guard, hanging on to the last vestiges of power.

Wolfington smoothed his dark blue Pierre Cardin suit as the limo moved along Adams Street past the General Post Office and the New York State Supreme Court building toward Court Street.

"You look fine, Hank," Matthew Brideson said. "You look like a governor."

"I should. I am."

There were no reporters outside the office building when the governor's limo pulled to the vacant spot at the curb near a fire hydrant. The press had not been informed of this visit. The two state troopers climbed out first and reconnoitered the area. One trooper went into the large marble lobby. It was empty except for the uniformed security guard who stood near the large directory smoking a cigarette. The trooper summoned an elevator as his partner escorted the governor and Brideson into the lobby, shielding them with a large umbrella.

The security guard recognized the governor immediately and said, "Hello, Mr. Governor." Wolfington detected a Brooklyn accent and, realizing every vote in this borough counted, brushed past the troopers and walked to the elderly guard with his hand outstretched.

"Pleased to meet you," Governor Henry Wolfington said as he firmly grasped the guard's hand. "How's it going?"

"Fine, Mr. Wolfington," the delighted guard said. "Just fine. And yourself?"

"You tell me," Wolfington said, feigning humility. "It's people like you who will decide how I'm doing on election day. I hope you think I'm doing a decent enough job."

The security guard beamed with self-importance and said, "Well, you got my vote, Gov. The missus too. By the way the name's Coogan. Danny Coogan."

Brideson was getting impatient standing at the opened elevator door. The two troopers remained expressionless, keeping their eyes on the guard and the front door simultaneously.

"Well, Danny," Wolfington blurted. "Thanks for your confidence in me. Tell your friends I could use their votes too."

Wolfington and Danny Coogan chuckled as Wolfington shook hands again and stepped aboard the elevator. When the doors shut Wolfington stared up at the floor indicators as the lift rose.

When the elevator came to a halt the troopers were out first, their eyes examining the corridors of the fourteenth floor. Empty. One trooper escorted Wolfington and Brideson down the hallway while the other went to check the men's room. The men's room door was locked.

"Hey, John," the trooper yelled. "Get a key to the men's room. Wanna check it out."

"Right," John said as he opened the door for the governor and Brideson.

Inside the men's room the Plumber moved with panicked alacrity. He gathered his tools and placed them in the toolbox. The silhouette of the state trooper hat on the other side of the smoked-glass panel was unmistakable. This wasn't in the plan at all. No one mentioned that a cop might inspect the men's room. There was nothing else to do but deal with the emergency. He placed the .38 into his belt and tiptoed to the door. As silently as possible he unbolted the three sliding latches, leaving just the regular catch lock on.

Now he made for the window, collecting the toolbox as he went. He climbed out onto the fire escape and softly shut the window. Now he pinned himself to the damp red brick wall as the rain continued to fall. The fire escape dripped with rain. He stood there perfectly silent with his hand on the handle of the pistol, listening for sounds from the men's room.

The state trooper put the key into the lock of the men's room door and stepped inside. There were three stalls and he checked each one. In the last stall there was a discarded *Playboy* magazine and he bent instinctively to pick it up. He studied the centerfold briefly, grinning, then dropped it back on the floor. Satisfied the room was empty, he walked toward the door to leave. He was about to go when he noticed the three latches on the inside of the door. He thought it curious that a public toilet would have such a security system. All right, maybe you don't want someone walking in on you when you're on the crapper, he thought. But three dead bolts? Something odd about that. He inspected the locks more closely now and could see they were quite new. The parings on the floor from where the screws had entered the wood looked moist and fresh. Something wrong here . . .

He looked around the room again and was about to make for the window to have a look outside when his partner called from the corridor. He opened the door instead of the window to let his partner in.

"The other guys are on their way up," the partner said. "We better get in there."

"But look at these locks here, John," the other trooper said.

"Screw the locks, Steve," John said. "Rule number one—stay with the governor. If we're with him nothing can happen. Come on."

Steve took one last hesitating look at the window, the locks, then shrugged his shoulders and let the door close behind him. The two troopers hurried for Be Be Gonzago's office as the whine of the ascending elevator echoed in the corridors.

A wrecking ball slammed the walls of his heart. The Plumber's face was soaking wet and he was no longer sure if it was rain or sweat. He waited until he heard the men's room door snap closed and hoisted himself back through the window with the agility of a squirrel. He was walking to the men's room door to fasten the latches when he heard the elevator doors snap open. Voices. A half dozen of them. Shoes scraping polished marble. Someone blowing their nose. Coughing. A silly deep baritone laugh. Then the knock. Three short taps, a heavy thud, two more taps. That was it. Almost time now. He wished he knew the face of the man who delivered the signal. Anything goes wrong and you can always throw one of these politicians to the dogs. Turn state's. But there was no way of knowing who it was.

The table was thirty feet long and highly polished, and the men sat in the red velvet cushioned chairs around it. A chandelier exploded with light above them. An ashtray sat on the table before each man. Governor Henry Wolfington sat at the foot of the table, nervously puffing on a Carlton cigarette. To his right was Brideson, a nonsmoker, still fidgeting with his papers and occasionally looking to the door of the conference room where the two state troopers stood mutely, their hands clasped behind their backs. Brideson was waiting for Be Be Gonzago's face to appear at the door. Part of his act—make the governor wait. Silly and anachronistic, Brideson thought. Things are just not done like this anymore. Not in most places anyway. But this was Brooklyn.

Seated to Brideson's right was the freshman United States senator from New York, David Hallahan, a man whose face looked more like a rump than a face, his cheeks bloated and hairless and as jiggly as his jowls, his unruly hair never quite clean looking and his eyes blinking too often. Moving right was Mayor Thomas Bailey, a pleasant sort who looked as if he washed his face with rye whiskey, the nose wired with purple vessels and his cheeks starting to go the same way, a man who could rise to the occasion on the campaign stump and still deliver a speech with verve and fire, but who privately was bored by the daily managerial chores of his office. Brooklyn district attorney Dermot Donnelly sat in the next chair, his face tanned from a recent Florida vacation, the tan bolstering an already overconfident demeanor. The chair at the head of the table and the one to its immediate right were empty, reserved for Be Be Gonzago and Johnny Quinn, respectively. Next to Quinn's empty chair sat

City Councilman Julio Garcia from the South Bronx who had come up through the Brooklyn machine but sprinted for the South Bronx when it became an Hispanic slum soon after the construction of Co-op City sent over a hundred thousand Jews from the South Bronx to the new housing development in a matter of two years, creating an instant poverty fiefdom that beckoned the likes of Garcia to step in and manipulate the federal poverty-program money. One chair to the right was Sam Stone, a councilman from Bedford Stuyvesant, a bony little man whose expensive tastes in clothes, jewelry, automobiles, and women could hardly be afforded by his council salary. On Stone's right was Sydney Weingarten, chatting with Wolfington, but Weingarten was the speaker of the New York state assembly and he took great pride in his office, even if he did see it as a springboard to a judgeship, preferably on the state supreme court.

Weingarten was a tall man with a stooped posture, but there was an aura of power emanating from him. His impatient eyes made underlings nervous, but Weingarten had a disarming smile that often made people divulge things they would later regret.

Finally Johnny Quinn appeared at the door like a bailiff announcing a judge. Be Be Gonzago followed directly behind him, allowing Johnny Quinn to lead the way to their chairs. The two state troopers stepped out of the way to let the two men pass. Johnny Quinn walked directly to Be Be's chair, pulled it out for Be Be, and then pushed it closer to the table after Be Be sat down. Johnny Quinn sat at his chair and immediately reached under the table and flicked a hidden switch to the on position. Only Johnny Quinn and Be Be knew this meeting, like all meetings held in this office, was being tape recorded.

Perhaps it was because of precautions like this that Be Be Gonzago had never been indicted, although there had been several grand jury investigations and press storms concerning some of his actions over the years. But nothing ever stuck.

Be Be sat at the front of the room pretending to look over the gathered. He squinted his eyes so no one could see they were unfocused. He and Johnny Quinn had gone over the seating plan by rote so that Be Be would be addressing the right person when he spoke. He placed his hands on the arms of the chair and directed his glare to where he knew Wolfington was sitting—dead ahead. He waited a full beat before motioning with his thumb toward the two state troopers.

"Hank, can you ask them to wait outside?" Be Be Gonzago said in a low, polite voice. "I don't like people standing behind me. I like to see everyone in the room. If you don't mind . . ."

Wolfington gestured for the two cops to wait outside. Before they left Be Be turned in their direction.

"No offense, fellas, but this is private business," Be Be said. The two troopers left quietly.

The room went quiet again for a moment and then Be Be Gonzago felt obliged to speak.

"We all know why we're here," Be Be said. "So let's not waste time. Hank, you told me on the phone you would like me to support you in this primary. I said we'd have to talk, there were things needed to be discussed. You suggested we all sit down and so here we are. The obvious question from me, Hank, is why do you think I should support you?"

Wolfington exhaled a weak puff from a Carlton and was about to speak when Brideson opened up.

"Well the obvious reason is that Hank—I mean the governor—will be the most effective candidate against any Republican in November, Mr. Gonzago. He has high visibility, a track record, and the best recognition quotient in the state."

Be Be looked at Brideson with distinct boredom and gently drummed his fingers on the polished mahogany before him.

"Hank," Be Be said. "With all due respect for your assistant, I'd like you to answer this question."

Brideson's face flushed as he watched Be Be Gonzago light the tip of a small ugly-looking cigar.

Wolfington scraped his voice together and looked directly at Be Be Gonzago as if he were a TV camera.

"Well, Be Be," Wolfington said. "I think there are a lot of good reasons for you to back me. We've worked together well in the past. Granted we've had our differences but we've ironed them out. I think in the past Brooklyn has fared well under my administration. The Brooklyn Navy Yard, for example, is now flourishing because of federal dollars I've helped get from Washington. HUD money has been coming in slowly, I admit, but no more slowly than to any other urban area in the country. A good deal of capable people from your organization are now holding important state jobs. Sure there have been some we've rejected, but we can't rubber-stamp every guy who ever licked an envelope in a Brooklyn campaign office into a state civil-service job."

"Come on, Hank," Be Be said. "I asked you a question and you're dancing around it like Fred Astaire. This isn't *Meet the Press.* This is me. You should know me better. I'm asking you, why the hell should I support you this time around when I've been screwed twice already?"

Sydney Weingarten spoke up for the first time, his elbows firmly planted on the tabletop, his head resting on his fisted hands.

"Let's be fair now, Be Be," Weingarten said. "We could have done a lot worse. I think sometimes you lose perspective down here in the city about just how Albany works these days. Hank and I have tried to get some pretty good bills through the assembly, and have succeeded on a lot of them, but some just never get out of committee in the senate. The Republicans aren't the greatest philanthropists when it comes to the city, you know."

"Sydney," Be Be said, matter-of-factly. "You know, I know, Hank knows that there's plenty wrong in New York City. Number one, crime. Number two, mass transit. Number three, highways. Housing, hospitals, welfare, Medicaid, schools, all these things are important too. But what I want to know is how a governor in his right mind can take twelve, count them, twelve, cops with him for security on a trip to Latin America? Wolfington takes twelve cops to South America when people are being killed on Nostrand Avenue because we don't have enough police protection. People scream about the potholes in the street and the West Side Highway being closed and our governor goes and paves half the back roads outside of Syracuse. Of course he comes from Syracuse, so I understand. But Buffalo, Elmira, and Poughkeepsie too? Come on, Sydney. Give me a break. And other people are crying about no housing in this city, I mean this is a real issue, not just some bullshit the blacks are yelling about for attention, and our illustrious governor decides to grab some guy's house next to his own summer mansion out there in the Hamptons under the eminent-domain scam because he wants to house his troopers in it and because it ruins his view of the bay. Meanwhile he wants me to ask people out in Coney Island, who will never see the Hamptons, and who live in hovels, to walk into a voting booth and select his name. Am I crazy or what?"

"Be Be, Be Be," Wolfington blurted. "Granted the thing in the Hamptons was a mistake. Okay, I admit that and already did in the papers. But you know as well as I do that mass transit money has to come from Washington."

"But, Hank," Be Be said, "mass transit money comes every year from Washington, and somehow all the tank towns upstate get more of it than the people of this city."

Be Be turned to Senator David Hallahan.

"David, how much federal highway money came into this state last year?" Be Be asked.

"Um, about one point three billion."

"Now, Hank, I happen to know this city received exactly one hundred and fifty million of that. The subways are our highways, Hank. The people in this city deserve more of the pie."

"The cities upstate need help too, Be Be," Wolfington said. "I represent the whole state. As for Medicaid, I've been thinking that over and I think it is about time the state absorbed more of that."

"We need more than that, Hank," Be Be said. "I'm not trying to be a prick here. Believe me. But there are a lot of my guys dangling by threads all over the place out there because when the citizens see them they want to know what the fuck is going on. They can't go on forever blaming the Republicans because we have a Democratic governor, a Democratic mayor, and a Democratic house speaker. So if anything, the Republicans can cut our nuts off this time around. And with good reason. We haven't done anything for the people and yet we like to call ourselves the people's party."

Dermot Donnelly, staring at his manicured nails, spoke up now, his manner distant and aloof.

"But that is exactly why we have to back Hank," Donnelly said. "Nominating this Kelly kid could be suicide. No one even knows him."

"Only ten percent of the polled Democrats know Hank better," Be Be said. "So that says something and I think Kelly is off and running. Who the hell ever heard of Alfonse D'Amato before the Republicans made him a U.S. senator?"

Wolfington was looking a little woozy and pulled out another Carlton. Brideson leaned over to light it. Johnny Quinn watched Brideson's move. A true lackey, he thought. The difference between him and me is that my boss is also my friend. Brideson looked up and held Johnny Quinn's glare for a moment and then broke it.

"Listen, Be Be," Wolfington said. "Next year will be a whole new ball of wax. And you know it is no secret that I do not intend to remain as a governor for the rest of my political career. The presidential primary is just two years away. I think, with your help now, I could be a strong candidate. I'm not saying I'm a candidate for sure yet, but I want you to consider that possibility before you make a rash decision. If we have a New Yorker in the Oval Office there will be more money to go around than ever. Something like that is crucial to the future of this city and state."

"So what you're really saying, Hank, is that you'd like me to endorse your presidential candidacy," Be Be said. "But see, I thought we were here to talk about you being the governor for the next four years. So, in effect, you're asking me to help get you elected so you can leave that office after two years to run for president. Well, I can't dance to that tune, Hank. I had heard that rumor, but now you're admitting this to my face. I think this state needs a full-time governor, not someone who will use that seat to get a more powerful one. That's the difference."

"Just who the hell do you think you are?" Wolfington exploded. "You can't sit here in your bullshit back room and think you can tell me how to run this state. How to run my career. You guys are over the hill, Be Be. This cigars and brandy and back-room horseshit went out with De Sapio . . ."

Brideson leaned over and tried to calm Wolfington down. He whispered in his ear as Wolfington turned the color of a stop light. Be Be Gonzago smiled thinly as Wolfington and Brideson powwowed.

"Be Be," Weingarten said. "Be reasonable. We can't endorse this Kelly kid. He's a knee-jerk liberal and the way he's running around on this nuclear issue we're likely to have another Jerry Brown on our hands, which would be all right except this is not California. This is New York and we don't do business that way here."

"Can't you at least hold off your decision for a week?" Brideson asked. "To give us time to come up with a sweeter package for you?"

"Sure," Be Be said. "I haven't announced anything yet. I haven't planned to announce my decision yet. Sure. The campaign is still young. Nothing is ever carved in stone."

"Can we get a picture outside the building with the governor?" Brideson asked.

"Of course, as long as he wants to be seen publicly with me, it's okay with me."

"Good," Brideson said. "I'll call the *Daily News.* They still have their Brooklyn office in this building, don't they?"

"Yeah, they do," Johnny Quinn said.

The meeting began to break up, men stood in pairs, Brideson on the phone, Garcia and Stone chatting briefly, Weingarten trying to comfort Wolfington as Donnelly stood at his side. Be Be Gonzago repaired to the toilet in his outer office. The men began collecting raincoats. The state troopers drifted toward the governor.

Soon all the men were shifting out of the office. Johnny Quinn and Be Be Gonzago were the last to leave. Johnny Quinn switched off the tape-recording apparatus.

"You got it all?" Be Be asked Johnny Quinn.

"Everything," Quinn said, "including that bit about running for president."

"Dumb prick," Be Be said.

The two men stepped out of the office and Johnny Quinn locked the door and they walked slowly down the hallway to join the others near the elevators.

The Plumber heard the coded knock once again. This was it. Sweat drooled from his armpits, collecting near his waistband. His body was itchy with fear. He listened to the many voices outside the door. Heard the gruff voice of Be Be Gonzago say, "Hey, Hank, hows about some lunch? We can still have lunch, right? I mean there's something left in the state coffers, isn't there?" The Plumber heard laughter and the governor of New York answer, "If you pay it's a deal, Be Be."

The Plumber stared at the cracked tile floor, the patterns playing tricks on his eyes. Sweat beaded on his scalp, he cocked the pistol, heard the approaching elevator. Heard feet shuffling and a nest of voices talking all at once. All fucking assholes, the Plumber thought. Should blow them all away. But there is just one. No more than that. Now he heard the doors of the elevator snap open with a loud snort. The Plumber yanked back each of the three dead-bolt latches. He gripped the door handle as tightly as the pistol.

Wolfington stepped into the elevator first, followed by the troopers. Weingarten stepped aboard and flattened himself against the far wall to make room for the rest of the men. Donnelly followed Weingarten. Now the rest piled in. Johnny Quinn and Be Be Gonzago last. Be Be was feeling pretty good, almost like the old days . . .

Be Be stared straight ahead, but he did not see the men's room door open. As soon as it did, most of the people in the elevator dropped to the ground and held their briefcases over their faces, shielding themselves from the coming impact. Johnny Quinn felt his heart catapult and leaped on Be Be Gonzago when he first saw the pistol. But it was too late. The sound of the explosions resounded off the high marble ceilings, a sound that had never been heard in this corridor before, deafening and filled with doom. The bullet slammed into Be Be's chest. There was supposed to be only one. But he did not go down so the Plumber fired a second bullet, blasting open the soft belly.

Be Be sank, ghosts dancing before his eyes, a smile on his face as the doors banged shut and the elevator hurtled down in the dark shaft.

"Is there blood on my shoes?" Be Be asked Johnny Quinn, who cradled him in his arms, crying profusely.

"No, they're fine," Johnny Quinn said.

Be Be smiled. He wished he could see. He thought of Joseph, throwing a football, eating a peanut butter and jelly sandwich, his dark eyes young and injured, not the same boy he was now . . .

"What a pain in the ass," Be Be Gonzago said.

The other men in the elevator were too astonished to speak. Mayor Bailey was whimpering with his hands clasped over the back of his head.

The elevator doors snapped open in the lobby and a scream went up from a woman awaiting the elevator. One reporter and one photographer were there. The wide-eyed photographer popped his flash over and over and over. One trooper stayed with the governor while the other jumped into another elevator with his pistol drawn and pressed floor number fourteen.

New York City policemen soon arrived and began to move the gawkers out of the lobby. Johnny Quinn was sobbing uncontrollably as he lowered his left ear closer to Be Be's mouth to hear what he was trying to say.

"I love him, Johnny. I love my boy . . ."

The hot breath on Johnny Quinn's ear went cold and now no sounds at all came from Be Be Gonzago. Screaming and pandemonium began to erupt in the lobby. An ambulance crew arrived. Someone shouted, "They tried to kill the governor but they got the wrong guy."

Johnny Quinn looked up in the direction of the voice and said softly under his breath, "You got it all wrong, fella . . ."

No one heard Johnny Quinn.

7

Joseph Gonzago remained standing in the front of the classroom, leaning his weight against the edge of his desk, as one student went on about city politics in Chicago.

"And when my father was out of work," the student named Jaszinski said, "the first person he turned to was the district leader. And he got my father a job. My father was out of work for almost nine months. He was in his fifties and the bank he worked for collapsed and he found himself out of work in a job market that was only looking for college-educated young people. But all his life my old man was a registered Democrat, did a little volunteer work, telephone canvassing, stuff like that for Richard Daley's machine. And after my father was turned down at a dozen different jobs he went to see the district leader. He explained his problem. The district leader remembered him and found him a job. Simple as that. So you can say what you want about machine politics, Mr. Gonzago, but when my old man was down and out they came through for him. I'm not saying machine politics isn't corrupt, but there's two sides to it, at least I think so."

Joseph brought his mind back into focus. "Good point, Jaszinski," Joseph conceded. "It's often true that a political machine takes care of its own. But what chance do you think your old man would have had if he was a registered Republican?"

Jaszinski thought for a moment, smiled, and leaned back in his chair.

"I never met one of them in my old neighborhood," Jaszinski said, and the class laughed along. Joseph smiled and lit another cigarette.

"Okay, look. There's two kinds of political machines," Joseph said. "On the one hand you have a guy like William Marcy Tweed, who was so greedy he chose to *bleed* the machine. Tweed was obviously more interested in how much money he could steal from the public coffers than the ultimate power it could have secured for him. As a result he died in a New York City jail called the Tombs. But that was also the late nineteenth century and things were an awful lot different then. Many people couldn't read then and there were fewer safeguards on taxpayers money. But then there is the other type of machine, like Richard Daley's in Chicago. Daley didn't bleed the machine strictly for personal profit but chose instead to *run* it. Daley recognized that power was more important than money. He did not die a pauper, but he wasn't a particularly wealthy man either. A good deal of his friends were though. And they got wealthy on scams like public-construction contracts, and from probate courts where Daley hand-picked the judges, who in turn handed out conservatorships, ward-of-the-court deals, trust funds, guardianships.

"Sure sometimes they might give a local citizen a job, or get the son of a friend off a criminal charge in the courts, but unless you do something for them they don't just walk around playing Santa Claus. And many times it's the poor who suffer the most. In New York City, for example, literally billions of dollars have poured in from the federal bureaucracy since Lyndon Johnson launched his war on poverty—which, coincidentally, he was waging at the same time he was at war with the people of Southeast Asia—and poverty has only gotten worse. Look at the South Bronx. Does it look to you when you see pictures of the South Bronx that billions have been spent on poverty there? Of course not. And the reason is that a few machine politicians moved in to manipulate that money. Poverticians, they call them in New York, and they are literally stealing food from the tables of the poor. There is one councilman up there by the name of Julio Garcia who on a salary of less than twenty-five thousand dollars a year has managed to buy a sugar plantation in Puerto Rico, who owns three homes in upstate New York and one in New York City, and drives a Mercedes-Benz. He also happens to be in charge of the local CETA program, two methadone clinics, and a local city hospital, all of which are largely funded by federal dollars. One of his right-hand men was sentenced last year for using federally funded CETA workers to firebomb the construction sites of those contractors who refused to hire only Garcia's hand-picked people, who in turn would be obliged to kick back a quarter of their earnings to Garcia.

"This is another kind of machine, Jaszinski. And when people go to Julio Garcia for a job, he expects them to do something for him. Sometimes that means arson. Garcia got his basic training in machine politics in Brooklyn, in the machine of Be Be Gonzago. Now, Gonzago is a special case. He's managed to both *bleed* and still *run* his machine. He has amassed a good deal of personal wealth from various forms of 'legal graft,' which have been legal since the days of Tammany Hall, and still has managed to keep his machine running."

Joseph saw a hand shoot up. "Yeah, Silverman," Joseph said, nodding to the tall bushy-headed kid in the first row.

"Can you tell me any form of government where the people in power do not take care of their friends first?" Silverman asked. "I don't care if it's totalitarian Communism, socialism, right-wing dictatorship, democracy, monarchy, or a theocracy. People take care of their own first. I mean the way the world is, people run governments. And people have this tendency to sometimes act like human beings, and I think it's basic human nature to take care of friends and family first. And I don't think anything anyone ever says about it will ever change that, do you?"

"Thank you, Mr. Silverman," Joseph said. "I mean that sounds very obvious, but you have put the ball right into the end zone. You're absolutely right. But, and there's always a but, the basic idea in this world is to get the guy in power who has the least friends in need, because a friend in need is a pest and sometimes a leech. Of course we'd all take care of our friends first if we were running the government, but there has to reach a time when all your friends have been taken care of. After all, how many friends can one person have? And then you have this obligation to take care of those people who are not your friends. Remember that not only friends pay taxes, not just your friends vote, not just friends need jobs, housing, medical care, education. But most machine hacks fail to realize this."

"Well, what do you see as the solution?" Jaszinski asked. Joseph looked at the clock and then at Jaszinski.

"That's what I want you to tell me," Joseph said with a smile. "If I told you what I thought the solution was I might be arrested for conspiracy. I want you all to think about Jaszinski's last question until we meet again on Wednesday, and we'll pick up from there. See you all then."

The students began collecting their books and belongings and filing from the room in a banter of chatter. Joseph was assembling his books at his desk when he realized the classroom was empty except for Jaszinski.

"Sorry," Jaszinski said. "I'm sorry you hate your father."

The student stood for a moment, swayed a little, awaiting Joseph Gonzago's response.

"Don't worry about it, Jaszinski," Joseph said, smiling. "Sometimes I am too. You were good in class today. I think you should consider doing your term paper on Daley. I mean you lived with his machine. You saw how it worked. And believe me, if you think it's a good form of government, that's okay. Just make your arguments good. Back them up with examples and facts. Don't be intimidated by my opinions on the subject. I won't judge you on your opinions. Just as long as you don't judge me on mine, okay, pal?"

"I used to think you were a mutt," Jaszinski said. "Conceited, stuck-up or something. But I admire the way you talk about your private feelings. Takes balls. Still, I bet somewhere you still love your old man. You gotta. He's blood. I think I'd like to meet him. And I think I will do that paper. Can you recommend any books?"

"Mike Royko wrote a book called *Boss* about Daley and Royko is a Polack like you so maybe you'll even understand it."

Jaszinski didn't realize Joseph was joking at first but when he saw Joseph laugh he laughed along.

"See, sometimes I am a mutt," Joseph said. "Want to grab some coffee—"

Joseph never finished the question. Before he could a small slight economics teacher named Flemming appeared at the door, his face white with horror. His shoulders were hunched forward as if he were standing in the freezing cold, and his short arms dangled lifelessly at his sides. Joseph thought Flemming was ready to keel over and made a move toward him. He saw the look in Flemming's eyes now, had seen it before, in the eyes of his boyhood friend Frank Donato the day Donato had learned that his father had been murdered on the Brooklyn waterfront. Donato had only been fifteen years old then and had promised someday he would run that waterfront, be the boss-man of the docks. Joseph thought it had just been young, macho talk. Joseph had been wrong. Donato had later become the president of the Longshoremen's Union. The look in his young friend's eyes on that long-gone day was like the glint from the polished oak of a casket. Flemming's eyes had that look now.

"What is it, Flemming?" Joseph said as Jaszinski strode with him toward the little man.

Flemming's face was glazed with perspiration, like something frozen left to thaw. A tremor seemed to be rattling him from within.

"Flemming," Joseph said. "What's wrong, man? You sick? Your heart? What?"

"Your father . . ."

Flemming was unable to finish the sentence without swallowing hard.

"What about my father?"

"The radio," Flemming said. "The radio news just said that your father was shot . . . murdered . . ."

Joseph stood very still, his legs feeling hollow and his head filling with air.

"They just announced it," Flemming said as Joseph felt himself reel. He knew then, right there, in the classroom of UCLA, that he was only eleven years old, but he wondered why he felt like a grown man and why he was so far away from home. "They said they were trying to kill Governor Wolfington but killed your dad by mistake. I'm so sorry, Joseph. I'm so damned sorry."

Flemming was on the verge of tears and Jaszinski stood mutely, looking from one man to the next, his Adam's apple moving up and down in his neck.

Joseph remained perfectly silent, feeling his body twitch, his eyes shimmering like gelatin.

"They can't do that," Joseph finally said, and realized how ridiculous it had sounded. Of course they could. And how come when a politician is killed in America everyone always speaks of the guilty in the plural? He sat in Silverman's chair, first row, first seat, and remembered a silly summer day when Be Be Gonzago had chased him around his back yard spraying him with a garden hose and laughing his deep, rich, tobacco-scratched laugh, and Joseph was running in circles, dressed only in underpants, Fruit of the Loom, no, Hanes, definitely Hanes, giggling his little high-pitched laugh. And later Be Be had dried him with the heavy, thick blue towel so vigorously that the shivering and the chills went right out of him. That night, the night of the same day Joseph had not recalled in twenty-five years, Be Be rocked him to sleep in his heavy hairy arms.

Flemming stood there as if awaiting instructions. Joseph looked up at him and tried to smile, but he felt as if his face would crack into a thousand little pieces.

"Thanks, Flemming," Joseph said. "Thanks for telling me . . ."

"I'm sorry it was me, Joseph . . ."

"It wasn't you, Flemming," Joseph said. "It was him. It was my father."

"Mr. Gonzago, if there's anything I can do," Jaszinski said.

"Do your paper, Jaszinski."

Joseph got up and walked past the two men, leaving his papers and books behind. He walked down the hallway of the large school, watching the hundreds, thousands, of students swarming to their classes. Their voices sounded unnecessarily loud, their feet hit the tiled floors too hard, music played softly somewhere, probably in the student lounge, and the smell of pot reeked through the air-conditioned building. A beautiful girl walked past Joseph Gonzago, said hello, and he thought he recognized her but did not return the greeting.

Joseph hit both glass exit doors with a bang and stepped out into the hot afternoon. The sky looked too far away; the sun looked like a cheap imitation of the real thing. His own car looked as if it should have belonged to someone else and his car keys felt too heavy. He opened the door, plopped into the seat. For some reason he readjusted the seat position as if his legs had shrunk since he had driven it last. Starting the ignition, he listened to the roar of the engine and felt the heat of the interior of the sun-baked automobile draw the water from his pores. He wondered if he sat here long enough he would dissolve into a pool of sweat. Joseph put the car in drive, snapped down the emergency brake, and sped off somewhere into Southern California.

The Plumber sat in the aisle seat in the coach section of the L-1011 as it flew west over the Rocky Mountains on the way to Los Angeles. Everything had proceeded according to plan, just as he was told it would. He had slammed the dead-bolt locks on the men's room door, made good his escape down the rusting fire escape, bolted from the parking lot without interference, and driven calmly to Coney Island. Here he dropped off the toolbox and the Oldsmobile car keys to the man who ran the Kewpie doll arcade stand. While the Plumber threw three darts at yellow balloons for a quarter, he was issued a plane ticket and a set of keys to a rented car. That was what you called winning from the top shelf. He had twenty minutes to drive out the Brooklyn-Queens Expressway to John F. Kennedy Airport, where he would catch the flight to Los Angeles.

The Plumber had expected a first-class ticket, but the man at the arcade said he knew nothing about that. The Plumber reasoned that perhaps the contractors did not want to draw undue attention by seating the Plumber in the conspicuousness of first class. That was okay, he thought. As soon as he arrived in L.A. he would be met by a man who would be holding a placard bearing the name of the new identity the contractors had given him—Maurice Keller. The Plumber hated the name Maurice, but it was so different from his own that it would keep him conscious of it and force him to remember it.

The Plumber leaned back in his seat, yanked it into the recline position, and sipped his Scotch on the rocks. Not too great a sacrifice, the Plumber thought. Two bullets squeezed from a pistol and now you're set for life. Too bad the guy you slammed is set for the pine box. He had his day at the top; now it's my turn. There's seventy-five large ones just waiting at the other end of this plane ride, and with that kind of dough you could even have broads like this stewardess walking down the aisle.

She was a tall, lithe blonde with small breasts, huge blue eyes, moist, full-bodied lips, and a pair of long, slender legs with well-rounded calf muscles. This is the kind of broad Maurice would have, the Plumber thought. This is something I should have done a long, long time ago, the Plumber thought. He summoned the Stewardess.

"May I kindly have another of these," the Plumber said, his mouth tripping on the contrived diction.

"Glenlivet?" the Stewardess asked with a smile.

"But of course," the Plumber said, and smiled.

The Stewardess moved up the aisle to get the drink. The Plumber watched her go, her long, sturdy legs bunching into fists of muscle at the calves as she walked. Some pair of earmuffs, the Plumber thought. There was a time when you only dreamed of women like that and now you can own one, rent one, lease one, trade one in after you put a full year of mileage on her.

The woman returned with the drink and a package of dry-roasted peanuts. The Plumber handed her a twenty-dollar bill.

"Do you have anything smaller, sir?"

"I'm afraid not," he said. "But the number of the hotel I'm staying at is written on the back of the bill. You can hold on to it and bring the change around to me tonight."

The Stewardess looked at the number on the back of the bill, smiled, and handed it back.

"I'm afraid we can't accept tips," she said. "But I have a pretty good memory and if I'm not doing anything later . . ."

She winked and moved on.

Ungrateful cunt, the Plumber thought. This time tomorrow Maurice will own the likes of you. He leaned back in his seat again, sipped his drink.

In the city of Albany in upstate New York there is an expression used by the lobbyists, assemblymen, state senators, executive lackeys, statehouse reporters, and high-level bureaucrats, that instantly brings to mind the center of power in the entire state.

"It depends on the second floor," the saying goes.

Of all the thousands of floors of every office building in the State of New York, probably no other floor affects the state's eighteen million citizens more than the second floor of the Senate Office Building in Albany. The executive chambers of the governor of New York are located on this floor.

Governor Henry Wolfington walked across the carpeted floor of his executive chambers exactly three hours following the assassination attempt on his life. He stopped before the large window that gave him a southwestern exposure of the city. Out there, he could see what some cynics felt was a fitting monument to former governor Nelson Rockefeller's great wealth and arrogance—the infamous Albany Mall, built for over a billion dollars during the Rockefeller regime.

Although most people from hot dog vendors to architecture critics for *The New York Times* thought of it as one of the most grotesque examples of modern urban planning ever created, Governor Wolfington found it inspiring. It looked the way a government should look—monolithic and antiseptic. Albany Mall was the image of detachment. Here, in the glass towers of the state government, you were to act as a cold, calculating professional. Compassion and pathos were for the newspaper columnists and the young pols on the make. Pragmatic, steely eyed management was for the truly devout public servant.

But today, not even the vision of the Albany Mall sprawling under a sheet-metal sky could help Governor Henry Wolfington from surrendering to the rule of his emotions. Someone had tried to kill him, take his life, and for the first time since the German 88s, called "Screamin' Mimis," pinned him and his infantry division to the beaches of Salerno during World War II, Henry Wolfington felt real, physical fear for his life.

As he looked out over the rain-pelted city of Albany, Governor Wolfington quaked visibly. The investigators from several law-enforcement agencies would soon be here for his debriefing. He would have to go over the details again and again and again. He took a seat behind the large glass-topped desk and mopped his brow and face with a damp right hand. Matthew Brideson, ever the epitome of tranquillity, sat in an arm chair facing the governor. Wolfington looked evenly at Brideson with the eyes of a frightened child.

"Do they hate me that much, Matt?"

Brideson drew his right leg up and propped his ankle on his left knee. "How are you feeling, Hank?"

Wolfington widened his eyes as if more light would illuminate his incredulity.

"How the hell do you think I feel," Wolfington snapped. "I've never felt better. Just a regular day except someone tried to kill the governor, which I wouldn't mind so much except that I am the goddamned governor. You don't look any worse for the wear, I can tell you that."

"All I'm concerned with is your safety," Brideson said. "And thank God you came out of this unhurt."

"I'm not sure if I'm unhurt," Wolfington said. "My heart has been racing all morning. My nerves are completely shot. Blood pressure's probably through the roof. And you sit there and ask how I'm feeling!"

"What I meant was, are you in the mood for talking?"

"Talking? Talking? If I could get it together I wouldn't be talking, I can tell you that. I'd be praying. I just threw Peggy out of here because she wanted to talk, and if I can't talk to my own wife, what do you think?"

"What I'm saying is that I think we should talk about how all this affects the campaign."

"Somebody tries to kill the governor and you want to talk about the campaign? What runs in your veins anyway, Matt, antifreeze?"

Brideson disliked the way Wolfington often referred to himself in the third person. As if he and the governor were two different people. Actually they were and perhaps that was the reason. Wolfington the *man* was often confused, lackadaisical, unable to grasp the political realities at hand. He also had small ideas—not that he did not have an ego, a monumental one, in fact, for only a man with a heavy dose of megalomania could expect a nation to elect him president one day—and the decisions he made in office were often myopic and predictable, a man afraid of taking chances. And yet Henry Wolfington *was* the governor of New York State in spite of his personal limits and his managerial and political shortcomings. It was as if he were aware of his limits and so created this alter ego to deal with them, and therefore referred to himself in the third person.

"But, Hank," Brideson said. "This greatly affects the entire makeup of the campaign. Don't you see that? One of our greatest worries has been this nuclear-energy debate with Kelly next week in Syracuse. Well, I think you should do what Jimmy Carter did when the Iran crisis and the Afghanistan invasion occurred. Claim that because of *events* you feel it would be inappropriate to go around politicking. You can say that because of the assassination attempt you feel it would be unwise to appear in a public forum. That you refuse to allow the campaign to encourage madmen with guns. Talk crime, law and order. Try to sway this thing away from nuclear energy. It could work. If the nuke nonsense comes up, you say it is most tragic, most regrettable, that six innocent citizens perished in the Indian Point accident, but that eighteen hundred people were murdered in New York City alone last year. And you were almost one of this year's crop. In Brooklyn—"

"Keep talking," Wolfington said. "I think I might like this. Go on, Matt."

"You could do your own version of Carter's Rose Garden act," Brideson said, his voice never rising an octave. "Meet with all the key people from the state right here. Kelly has to buy the TV time. You don't. You're news already. Use the office. You are the governor. Kelly is an assemblyman. Keep that in mind. You run the second floor. Remember that too. Kelly has one single little chair on the third floor, thrown in there with the rest of the legislators."

"Yeah," Wolfington said, his composure coming back now. "This is sounding pretty good."

"And you get the sympathy vote," Brideson said. "Like the time Moynihan got hit in the face with the cream pie? No one to this day knows how many fence sitters he got on that just because they felt sorry for him. But it sure as hell didn't lose him any votes, I can tell you that. And that was just a *pie.* Someone tried to *kill* you. Of course, you have to say you don't want to get any political mileage from Be Be Gonzago's death, so you'd rather not actively campaign until after the primary. Say this is no time for Democrats to fight amongst themselves. But of course you'll get all the mileage in the world out of it. This thing can help us enormously in another way too."

"I'm all ears, Matt, go on."

"Well," Brideson said, and sighed. "I hate to sound callous, but I think we have to be realistic here. Gonzago is dead. And with him gone, it's a cinch the Brooklyn county committee will vote Weingarten in to take his place as Brooklyn boss. So Gonzago is no longer a threat. And Brooklyn won't go for Kelly under Weingarten. Sydney has been looking for a seat on the state Court of Appeals for a long time. If you can deliver that for him, I'm sure he will deliver the borough of churches to us."

"It is callous," Wolfington said, frowning. "But hell, don't tell me anyone else wouldn't take the ball and run with it too.

"Yes, Matt. I think I like this whole scenario you've laid out here. As of today cancel all the governor's public appearances. No more nuclear-energy crap. Have the fellas down the hall prepare a major statement of some kind for the governor on crime, the courts, capital punishment. Let's change the face of this campaign; let's turn it right around."

"There is one last public appearance you must make," Brideson said. "We can't make the same mistake you made with the six people who died in the nuclear accident. I know you were afraid of the potential circus at that funeral, with the protesters and all of that, but you took much more flak from the editorial writers for failing to show up than you would have gotten from a bunch of ban-the-bomb hippies. This time you absolutely *must* attend Be Be Gonzago's funeral."

Wolfington drummed his fingers on the desk.

"Yes," Wolfington said. "The governor should be there by all means. But see to it that he has plenty of security, lots of troopers and some undercover fellas. The governor's life is at stake here. But I like it, Brideson. I like this idea a whole lot."

8

Sydney Weingarten inhaled deeply, so deeply it made his lungs ache and caused him to cough. He'd been pacing for hours in his wood-paneled office at the rear of the Nathan Hale Club in East Flatbush. He was still trembling from the sight of the puddles of blood, and the roar of the gun shots. My God, Sydney Weingarten thought. How could anyone ever know just how loud a gun shot is until one hears it? The sound of it had been so devastating, causing deep piercing pain in the inner ear, disturbing the equilibrium, and setting his whole mood and body off balance.

The sight of Be Be Gonzago, whom he had known for so many years, lying dead on the cold marble floor remained stamped in his mind. It was somehow so ugly and sad and unnecessary. How could it all have come to this?

He looked out the back window, through the protective bars that kept the thugs out, and saw a group of kids from nearby Erasmus Hall High School playing a game called "off-the-point" across the street. Sydney Weingarten vaguely understood the object of the game. He had never played any of those street games. Had never been coordinated enough to hit a ball with a bat, or catch a football on the fly, or hit a stone edge with a small pink ball in a game of off-the-point.

Sydney Weingarten had never been much of a street kid. After Yeshiva each day, his father, Sydney, would have tutors awaiting him at home where he was to learn classical piano, Latin, history, and mathematics. Sydney Weingarten wanted his son to follow in his path to the halls of government, to be an upstanding member of the community, a fine lawyer, and an elected man of the people. This was the destiny of Sydney Weingarten's son. He was not going to raise some street thug who hung around street corners smoking cigarettes and kissing young girls and getting into trouble. Sydney Weingarten, Sr. had seen enough of those kids wind up as clients as a criminal lawyer.

Sydney Weingarten was going to be a man whom people remembered, unlike his father, who had never risen above the title of

Chairman of Manhattan Beach Board of Trade. If that meant denying the child some of the secret desires all kids possess, so be it. The child would thank him when he became a successful adult.

The black policeman from the State Bureau of Investigation had left over an hour ago and Sydney Weingarten was still shaken by the experience. He had never been questioned by a law-enforcement official in his life. Most kids from Brooklyn learn how to deal with the cops before they reach their teens. Sydney Weingarten was now nearing his sixtieth year, and he had just had his first brush with the law. Not a brush, exactly. Just routine questioning. Sydney Weingarten had been one of eleven witnesses to the murder of Be Be Gonzago. But he had told the investigator that he had never really seen the killer because he was against the far wall of the crowded elevator and there were so many bodies obstructing his view. All he had heard was the deafening roar of the gun shots and later he witnessed the awful sight of Be Be Gonzago lying dead on the floor.

The black cop had asked no incriminating questions. The entire episode was still such a mystery. Came with no warning. Ended so quickly. Total madness, sheer horror. Sydney Weingarten had explained to the policeman that he'd had to cancel a scheduled meeting with a top Brooklyn rabbi afterward because he was too shaken to attend. The meeting with the rabbi concerned the racial violence between blacks and the Hasidim in Crown Heights. But any further talk of violence today would have been intolerable.

He explained what the meeting with the governor had been about—a solicitation of Be Be Gonzago's support in Wolfington's primary campaign. Weingarten said that the meeting had been inconclusive. Gonzago had not said yes and had not given an absolute no.

The black policeman had seemed satisfied with Sydney Weingarten's statement. Weingarten had asked that it be a short interview because he had to prepare the arrangements for Be Be Gonzago's funeral.

And now as Weingarten stood alone, looking down into the streets of Flatbush, a general malaise was set loose in his body. How had it all come to this? Sydney Weingarten asked himself. Violence and gun play and taking men's lives? For what? For a small chunk of power in a corner of the world called Brooklyn? It all seemed so misguided and ill-conceived in desperate greed. And yet it was over. Be Be Gonzago was now a dead man.

He stood there at the window looking into the streets of Flatbush, which were mostly populated by blacks now. Almost eighty percent of Erasmus Hall High School—the school he and Barbra Streisand, Neil Diamond, Dorothy Kilgallen, and so many other great people had graduated from—was now black. This, too, was a disturbing problem for Sydney Weingarten. Because it meant every year he had to gerrymander his district in such a way that he could hold on to the last strongholds of the Jewish voting block that had not yet moved to Miami and the suburbs.

But this was not paramount in Sydney Weingarten's mind right now. He was thinking instead of Be Be Gonzago. He had disliked Be Be in these final years, sometimes to the point of rage, but he knew he would miss him. There had been times when Be Be had been so generous to him. Times when they were almost like friends. But they never really had been friends of course. Both of them had wanted too many of the same things, not the least of which was Sylvia Stein.

Sydney Weingarten had greatly admired Be Be Gonzago and emulated many of the man's qualities and ruthless tactics. But Be Be had always had his own little circle of friends, his own clique upon whom he bequeathed the secrets and spoils of his power. Johnny Quinn, Frank Donato, a few select congressmen, assemblymen, councilmen.

Be Be had always been clever enough to spread the power around, Sydney Weingarten thought. It kept people from revolting against him. Be Be recognized that Sydney Weingarten was no fool—that he had ambition and was politically savvy. Sydney also still had some old-time ties from his father's glory days. Be Be knew better than to risk a direct confrontation with Sydney Weingarten. Instead he exiled him to Albany, even if it was to one of the most powerful jobs in the capital city. It kept him out of the way a good deal of the time. The speaker of the assembly had to have a good attendance record. And that meant Sydney Weingarten was gone sometimes for six to nine months of the year in the vacuum of Albany.

This was why Sydney Weingarten had to get out of the state assembly. There was no longer any way to maintain elective office in Flatbush, or most neighborhoods in Brooklyn anymore, because the entire face of the borough had changed. The streets in Flatbush were all still named after the Dutch. But it was the Jews who had really built Flatbush. Built it and made it world famous only to allow the blacks to come in and take it from them. But there were no streets in Flatbush named after the Jews—no Rabinowitz Lane, no Cohen Place, no Lipshitz Boulevard.

Time to get out, Sydney thought. Time to use the power now available to him, to get himself a fourteen-year appointment to the state appellate court where you could sit without having to face a malevolent electorate every two years, deal with nickel-and-dime problems like stop lights, slumlords, street crime, loud-mouthed community spokesmen.

He was still feeling uneasy and he knew it would take several weeks before the county committee could meet and vote to make official his position as chairman of the Kings County Democratic party. There was no need to rush or worry. It is time to try to forget the violent images that now pollute the mind. Go home and bathe and take a good long sleep.

Be Be Gonzago is dead, and that might be unfortunate, Sydney Weingarten thought. But you are alive and your time has finally come.

The Plumber moved to the front of the plane as the passengers began to exit. He had no luggage to collect. He had disposed of all of his clothing when he had moved out of the furnished room in Boerum Hill in Brooklyn the day before. The contractors had also made him destroy everything he owned indicating Jimmy Boyle had ever lived—driver's license, Social Security card, plumbers' union book, library card, Blue Cross card, and birth certificate. The contractors had given him two hundred dollars in cash and the suit on his back and told him that was all he would need until he collected his seventy-five thousand dollars and his new identity cards in Los Angeles.

The landing had been very smooth and the sun was spilling down on the city and the Plumber was enjoying the inner excitement of a new life as he moved toward the exit door to deplane. The Scotch had him feeling taller than he was, and it had eliminated the final tremors of anxiety. The Stewardess with the great legs stood at the nose of the plane saying good-bye to the departing passengers.

"Enjoy your stay in Los Angeles, Mr. Keller," she said as the Plumber approached her.

"You remember the phone number?"

The Stewardess tapped her temple with a painted fingernail and smiled. So did the Plumber. He stepped off the great jet and moved for the escalators, which took him down to the main center aisle of

LAX. The terminal was alive with scurrying people, dashing for planes, waving for sky caps, filling out rent-a-car forms, hauling overweight luggage, embracing loved ones, dashing for buses, taxis, limousines. A Hare Krishna approached the Plumber and tried to pin a flower on his lapel.

"Scram," the Plumber said, and pushed the bald-headed man's hand away. The Hare Krishna was persistent.

"It's time you returned to godhead," he said, and again tried to pin the flower on the Plumber.

The Plumber looked around, and certain no one was looking, twisted the Hare Krishna's wrist and stared at the painted red circle on the man's forehead.

"If you don't leave me alone, you fuckin' freak, I'll hammer a horseshoe nail through that dot on your knot," the Plumber said low and menacingly.

The Plumber kept walking and the Hare Krishna now approached a crew-cut soldier carrying a duffel bag. As the Plumber neared the front doors of the airport, he saw a man dressed in a chauffeur's uniform standing patiently bearing a placard in his hand. The name MAURICE KELLER was printed in block letters on the sign. The Plumber stood for several seconds just looking and smiling at his new name written on the card. The VIP treatment, he thought. He approached the chauffeur.

"Hello, I'm Maurice Keller," the Plumber said.

"Right this way, Mr. Keller."

The Plumber enjoyed the way he was addressed as Mister. Respect. He followed the chauffeur to the limousine, which was parked at the white zone in front of the terminal. The heavy, humid air sat down on him as soon as he stepped out of the air-conditioned terminal. He smiled at the sight of the palm trees, their fronds dueling in the lackadaisical breeze. The sky was the blue of butane flame and the hot sun sizzled at its center. The Plumber was very pleased with what he saw. This place was clean and warm and bright. Like a different planet.

A girl with skin-tight denim shorts and a deep toast-brown tan passed the limousine. She was blue-eyed, with dirty-blond hair with platinum highlights, and the Plumber liked the way the golden hair on her thin arms glistened in the sun. The Plumber did not even smile as he devoured the woman with his eyes, staring at her heavy breasts moving inside her red blouse. The girl, who was about nineteen, grinned thinly as she passed the Plumber. He was standing with his arm on the open back door of the large white Rolls-Royce. The girl walked with youthful confidence through the automatic doors into the terminal as the Plumber peered after her at the tight, round buttocks.

"She smiled at me," the Plumber said without looking at the tall, muscular driver.

"This is Los Angeles, Mr. Keller," the driver said. "She was smiling at the car."

"What's the hotel supposed to be like?" the Plumber asked as the driver tooled the Rolls onto the Sepulveda Boulevard North exit.

"It is a small hotel, but very nice," the driver said. "I'll drop you there and you can rest up, have a shower, change clothes, have a bite to eat, take a swim, whatever, until I pick you up tonight to bring you to meet your contact."

"I have no clothes to change into," the Plumber said.

"They are already in your room," said the driver. "Beautiful new clothes already selected for you."

The Plumber pushed a button on the control board in front of him and a small bar swung open, replete with ice, liquor, mixers, and polished glasses. The Plumber smiled as he mixed himself a Scotch. He pushed another button and a magazine rack folded down. He leafed through the magazines and saw they were all Nazi propaganda pamphlets, their covers bearing photographs of Adolf Hitler, swastikas, and white-power slogans.

"It's a good thing I'm not a Hebe," the Plumber said to the driver.

"Yes, it is," the driver agreed, perhaps a little sarcastically for the Plumber's liking.

Both men fell silent as the car swung onto Lincoln Boulevard and cruised slowly for seven miles to the city of Santa Monica, where it turned right on Santa Monica Boulevard.

"Do you always drive this slow?" the Plumber asked, annoyed. "This car could do a hundred without even trembling."

"Police cars in Los Angeles are capable of the same speed, Mr. Keller," the driver said. "I was instructed to take my time. There is no rush."

The car proceeded down Santa Monica Boulevard until it reached Yale Street. On the corner was a small motel called The Wayside. The driver handed the Plumber the key with the room number on it.

"This place looks like a real dump," the Plumber said. "I deserve better than this."

"I will pick you up at eight this evening, Mr. Keller," the driver said. "No need to check in. Everything is already arranged. You can go straight to your room."

The Plumber did not like this pompous chauffeur but decided not to argue with him. This was just a pit stop. Tonight you'll have your seventy-five large and tomorrow you can check into some swell joint.

The Plumber climbed the outdoor flight of stone steps to the second tier and stopped before room 236. He inserted the key into the lock and stepped into the darkened motel room. He flicked on the light and looked around—double bed, two lamps, arm chair, bureau, cheap art prints, writing table, clothes closet, night table, telephone.

He slowly began to undress and was standing in his shorts when he heard the sound. Made him jump, heart sink. At first he thought it was the sound of an animal, a cat spitting. He froze for a moment, trying to juggle the unknown fears. Then he recognized the sound. It was the shower. Someone had turned on the shower in the bathroom. His shower. His bathroom. The Plumber looked around for a weapon, thought about pulling his pants back on. But he did not have the time. He grabbed at the lamp and realized it was bolted down. Cheap fucking dump, he thought. There was nothing else even remotely resembling a weapon except for a plastic shoe tree at the bottom of the clothes closet. He snatched it up. Gouge his fucking eyes out, he thought. Slowly he opened the door to the bathroom, the sound of the shower grew much louder, steam billowed at him in gusts. His heart raced, pounding out a steady tattoo in his breast. Then as his eyes adjusted to the steamy room, he could see her through the foggy glass doors of the shower stall. Tall and pink and curvy and naked and perfect. Small breasts. Long wet blond hair, her face pushed up into the spray of the shower. Her hard buttocks in profile sloping out from an inturned back. His heart caught up with itself, his fear began to simmer. His penis began to enlarge. Now as she turned her back to him and he saw her lovely calves he knew who it was. He was going to have her . . .

"Come on in, Mr. Keller," the blond Stewardess said. "You did invite me, didn't you?"

The Plumber slowly slid open the glass doors of the shower stall and allowed his eyes to feast on the heat-reddened skin of the woman who had served him his drinks no more than an hour before.

"How the hell did you get here so fast?"

"Motivation," she said as she slipped a finger into the waistband of his shorts and pulled them down.

The Plumber stepped into the shower eagerly. The water was hot and forceful, and the Stewardess began to soap the Plumber with Vitabath. The green tingling foam overwhelmed the Plumber as it came to life at the urgings of the woman's deft fingers. The Plumber probed her body, clutching handfuls of buttocks, pinching the hot hard nipples, crushing his fingers against the wet coarse pubic hair, exploring hidden orifices, kissing the wet slippery mouth. Slowly the Stewardess began to stroke the Plumber's blood-engorged penis. He closed his eyes and leaned back against the hot tiled wall and reveled in the slow, skillful kneading of his penis. His low moans were swallowed by the rush of the hard spray of water.

The Plumber remained leaning against the wall with his eyes closed, and so he did not see her reach to the window ledge above them with her free hand. Did not see her take down the thin twelve-inch ice pick. As the water continued to run over his body, the Plumber felt himself climbing to the high, blurry region of orgasm. But he did not get quite that high. Before he did the Stewardess's hand slid down his shaft and her long, sharp painted nails stabbed into the flesh of his scrotum and she yanked down with all her might on his testicles. The Plumber tried to scream, but when his mouth opened wide in horror, it filled instantly with the gushing water. He bent in pain, and as he did the thin blade of the ice pick came up in one single motion, entering his body under the breast bone, perforating the tough little muscle of the heart.

There was little blood.

The Plumber slumped to the floor of the shower stall, and what little blood there was swirled down the drain like pink diluted mouthwash with the running water.

The Stewardess stepped out of the shower and towel dried her hair briskly. Then casually she took a hair dryer from a small overnight bag under the sink and placed the ice pick in the bag. When she was finished drying her hair, she carefully put on her eye makeup, rouge, and lipstick. Now she took the civilian clothes from her bag—a pair of faded tight jeans, a yellow halter top, and a pair of flat sandals. She shook her head so the hair would fall more naturally. She neatly placed the airline uniform in the bag and looked around. She wiped her fingerprints from the shower door handle.

She looked down at the fleshy heap of the Plumber in the shower and without emotion picked up a towel and wrapped it around the shower faucet and turned off the water. She wiped the faucets clean of fingerprints and was sure to do the same with the doorknobs—inside and out—as she stepped out of the bathroom.

She picked up the Do Not Disturb sign by the string and hung it on the knob outside the door as she left. She walked down the back stairs of the hotel to the parking lot and climbed into the front seat of the white Rolls-Royce. The driver reached over to kiss her but she pulled away, repulsed. He looked mildly offended but maintained his temper.

"Any problems?" he asked.

"Of course not."

The driver handed the Stewardess an envelope with cash. She ruffled the bills inside, bored.

"All here?"

"All twenty-five grand," the driver said.

"Who was he anyway?"

"Just some gambling debt, I think. Apparently he knew something somebody didn't want anyone else to know. Not even us."

"Who paid the money?"

"The envelope arrived by Federal Express. No names. No faces. No traces. Best way. Just a voice on the phone."

"That one was easy," she said. "Wish they were all that simple."

The Stewardess took out an emery board and began to file her nails as the limousine moved toward Wilshire Boulevard and east toward Beverly Hills. Now the Stewardess was annoyed. She realized she had broken a nail.

Brendan Kelly sat aboard the Cessna en route from Buffalo to Dutchess County airport for a speaking engagement in a town called Rhinebeck. The plane was a ten seater and Kelly was sitting with his campaign manager, Tim Harris, a balding, suety sixties radical gone legitimate in elective politics. Harris was thirty-seven years old now, a man with a keen, manipulative mind who understood that good old-fashioned grass-roots organizing coupled with media blitzing could put an underdog on top.

Harris had a gossip-column image of being a ladies' man who liked to frequent the "in" spots around New York City at night, dancing at discos and eating in the places where he knew the paparazzi would be sure to show up. Some of the people who disliked Harris, and they were many, were convinced that Harris would call the photographers and let them know where he would be eating with certain music, film, political, or media personalities. Harris, of course, always denied this, but his picture appeared on page seven of the *News* and the *Post* so often with different "newsmakers" that even the editors were starting to get suspicious that he was an incurable media hound.

But Brendan Kelly had known Harris for years, long before Kelly himself had entered elective politics. Kelly had never been a scruffy radical, but instead orbited the likes of Nader and other consumer advocates and antinuclear types. He knew Harris to be a superb organizer, who could recruit young go-get-'em politico kids who still believed licking campaign-literature envelopes was a political act.

Wolfington might have the backing of political machines like Be Be Gonzago's in Brooklyn, but if Harris could assemble enough young bloods who were willing to volunteer their services, it might be possible to match the manpower of the machine.

Kelly knew that his media man, Daniel Morse, was not exactly one of Harris's fans. But Morse's genius lay in television and newspaper publicity. Harris had a more acute political mind. He understood the issues better than Morse. Morse merely gift wrapped them. And did a hell of a job of it too.

Kelly and Harris were discussing the speaking engagement in the small upstate town.

"Rhinebeck is a strange little town, Brendan," Tim Harris was saying. "Conservative to the core in a lot of ways, but only a few miles from Woodstock, where we already have support. Bard University is just outside of Rhinebeck, and so there is something of an antinuke movement in the campus area. What you are going to find here is a mixture of farmers and college kids, and a lot of them are scared as hell of the power plants. You have to keep in mind the town is on the Hudson, and any contamination from another bad leak will almost certainly reach them through the underground streams. I think you better just stick to the antinuclear issue here. Don't hedge on it. Some of them will say it's all scare stuff. Some won't. If we can split in towns like this we're gonna have a horse race."

"If we split up here, Tim, and lose big districts like Brooklyn, it won't be much of a horse race." Brendan Kelly laughed. "They'll send me back to the glue factory."

"You'll still have support in the city, Manhattan anyway," Harris said. Harris was picking dried mustard from his tie, remnants of the foot-long hot dog he'd had for lunch.

"Has Dan saturated the local stations with the thirty-second spots, Tim?" Kelly asked.

"He keeps complaining about funds, funds, funds," Harris said. "Christ, if he can't get a little credit in the sticks . . ."

"Well, I told him I didn't want to run the debts too high," Kelly said. "As long as there were some spots aired we're okay. That one on the funeral of the six poor people who died at Indian Point, God is that effective. You know, if I didn't believe as deeply as I do about this issue, I might take some of the press criticism on that spot to heart. But when I go on there asking if we can afford to watch a scene like this again, I truly mean it. So I'm willing to take a little shellacking on that one. It's how I feel."

"Well, maybe a little less on the head on Dan's part might have been—"

Harris didn't get to finish the sentence, as Daniel Morse, a middle-aged man with a floury complexion, appeared from behind them, his right hand in his right trouser pocket jingling change in a habitual nervous fashion.

"How's this for a little less on the head," Daniel Morse snapped to Tim Harris. "Someone tried to kill Governor Wolfington but missed. They killed Be Be Gonzago instead."

Tim Harris looked up at Daniel Morse in mild shock. Brendan Kelly sat speechless, his mouth agape.

"When did it happen?" Tim Harris asked.

"Few hours ago," Morse said, running his hand through nickel-colored hair. Half moons of perspiration stained through the underarms of his light blue shirt. "Probably when we were trying to get the hell out of Buffalo in that storm."

"We were on the ground there for almost two hours," Kelly said. "No wonder we haven't heard. My God this is awful. What a mess. I might not have agreed with him, but murdered. Poor Joseph. He must be in terrible shape. You know Joseph Gonzago, don't you, Tim?"

"Yeah," Tim Harris said. "Haven't seen him for a few years, but he was a fellow traveler back in the good old days."

"What shall we do?" Morse asked, eager for direction.

Tim Harris, with a note of distaste in his voice, said, "We'll handle it, Dan. This isn't really up your alley. We're not going to make another funeral spot. Especially about Be Be Gonzago."

Morse's pale complexion reddened quickly, and he took a step closer to Tim Harris in the small plane. The sound of the engine grew louder as the plane pitched to the left and rain splattered the small windows.

"I resent that, you son of a bitch," Morse said. "Just who in the hell do you think you are?"

"Dan, Tim, please, calm down, for God's sake. A man has been murdered. Someone tried to murder the governor. Come on, guys, knock it off, will you."

Morse, seething, stared for a long moment at Harris, who refused to return the glare. Morse finally looked at Kelly and said, "Sorry, Brendan. Sorry." He shot one more fierce look at Harris, who sat picking the caked mustard from his tie, and walked back to his own seat. There was a long silence and finally Harris spoke to Kelly.

"We have to make a strong statement, Brendan," Harris said. "It's a chance to focus on the handgun issue as well. It's another clear choice on the issues between you and the governor. Could be real effective. Of course we'll couch it in our best condolences."

Kelly gave Harris a rather concerned look.

"Have the guys prepare something," Kelly finally said. "But I definitely want to see the statement before it goes out. I don't want it to look like we're going to cash in on this. I want that understood, Tim. No politics. This is a disgraceful thing. I don't like it. It's ugly and wrong and it makes me sick. If anything, I want to express my genuine outrage, Tim. This is not a broadside at the National Rifle Association, okay?"

Tim Harris nodded affirmatively. The plane dipped again and made for the runway.

9

Above him the helicopter gunships are spitting down tear-gas canisters. A wall of National Guardsmen are approaching, their carbines clenched tightly in double fists. The soldiers are wearing gas masks, making them look like an invading army of grasshoppers. The sound of the choppers is incessant, whack-a-whack-a-whack-whack-a-whack. The students race across the rollicking hills of the campus, stopping occasionally to pelt the soldiers with stones and bottles and bricks. Discarded placards are lying at his feet. His wet white handkerchief is coming loose. He tightens it around his nose and mouth to keep the tear gas from entering his lungs. The Vaseline smeared about his eyes is making everyone look distorted, as on a television with a weak tube.

The public-address system is blaring. It is the taped voice of Governor Ronald Reagan bellowing his earlier official remarks. "If they want a bloodbath, then let's get on with it. If they want a bloodbath, then let's get on with it. If they want a bloodbath . . ."

Standing next to him is an overweight woman in her twenties who is dancing in a crazy, silly circle, groping at her eyes, which are stinging from the tear gas and the blood leaking from a head wound. The soldier gives her a second hard, well-placed six-inch whack with his baton. He is watching all this. And now, as the soldier turns his back, he moves up behind him and delivers a double fist into his left lung. The rifle flies from the hands of the soldier and the uniformed man drops to the grass gasping for breath. Now he kicks the soldier violently in his kidney.

Around him dozens of members of SDS begin to pelt other soldiers, as the voice of the former Hollywood movie star talking of bloodshed continues to echo across the emerald green of the University of California at Berkeley. In his mind he is thinking that this is just a minor skirmish. Think of the people of Southeast Asia who are being burned daily by napalm, shredded by bombs, pierced by M-16s. It is 1969 and Nixon is spreading the war into three other countries now. And back home his father is supporting this war, sitting in the smug comfort of his cigars, brandy, and feudal power.

The country, hell, the world, is catching fire. Students everywhere are rising. The madness has to stop. He has no choice. He must participate. There is no time now for the past, for lost love and a family that never really was.

Other soldiers run at him and he begins to run, sprinting as fast as he can, outdistancing all of them. He uses all the ample speed in his body. He would never be here in the first place if it were not for the track scholarship. No one can catch him now as he continues to sprint, his lungs delighting in the fresh air as he moves out of the billows of gas into the sweet fresh air of the Bay area. The air is filled with spring and the bloodshed the governor had promised. He continues to run and run and run . . .

Joseph Gonzago awakened in his studio apartment in Santa Monica. He had not even bothered to fold out the Castro convertible the night before. He was sitting in an upright position and his pants were damp with brandy and the snifter glass was lying on its side on his lap. The empty Hennessy bottle stood on the floor next to the couch. Joseph's mouth was pasty and foul, and a slow, steady beat came from inside his head as if a very small man with a tack hammer was hanging pictures on the walls of his skull.

The phone was ringing. And ringing. And ringing. He didn't bother to answer. There was no one he cared to speak with. There was only one man Joseph Gonzago had ever really wished to speak with. Now he was dead. The late news the night before had carried the images in living color of his father bleeding his life onto the marble floors of the Brooklyn office building. Joseph had sat in the same position on the couch as he watched the film footage. He had remained unmoved. No tears. No screams. No outbursts. The bottle of Hennessy had been half full during the eleven-o'clock news and was almost empty by the time the one A.M. news repeated the same information.

The newscaster said that New York authorities had found a magazine in the bathroom from which the assassin fired the bullet. They were checking the fingerprints but had not come up with a suspect. There were no clues as to the gunman's identity or whereabouts yet.

He sat there with the sun blazing through his windows, the phone ringing for long periods of time, then stopping, then ringing again. Numb. He had tried to figure out what to do and had gotten drunk instead, and somehow the mind had twisted him into a dream about a time now gone.

The phone started ringing again. He did not even try to imagine who it might be. It did not matter. It wasn't his father. He knew now in the semisober light of morning that he could no longer put the decision off. The body of the man who had sired him was now cold and lifeless. There was no alternative but to go back. Back to the place where he had been born and raised. Back to strangers who had once been friends. To the part of the earth that held the remains of his mother and would soon hold the body of his father. Back to the great house in Flatbush. Back to Brooklyn. Back home.

Joseph Gonzago stood up from the couch and quickly undressed. He cautiously walked across the shag rug and caught a glimpse of himself in the full-length mirror on the inside of the opened bathroom door. His body was still strong and trim, the shoulders broad and the arms well-muscled.

When Joseph Gonzago had left Brooklyn on a track scholarship to Berkeley, the only thing he knew about politics was that it had deprived him of the father he wanted. He had gotten a father who saw his son as a new member of his machine, as a candidate, as a public figure who was to be loved in the spotlight instead of in the living room. There were times when Joseph felt his father was raising a thoroughbred foal instead of a son to adulthood, as if he were conceived and raised for the sole purpose of performance.

And the reason for this was that Be Be Gonzago did not lead an ordinary life. He was a politician and all his private moments were spent preparing for those he would spend in public. And Be Be saw his public performances as nothing more than groundwork for the position in life Joseph was intended to inherit.

There never seemed to be enough time in Be Be's schedule for Joseph's mother. Be Be was often away at public functions, testimonial dinners, organizing campaigns, making trips to Albany and Washington, lunching and dining with the politicians and the big businessmen. And there were always the whispers of other women. Be Be would disappear for weekends at a time, refusing to offer explanations for his absences. "I was out of town," was all he would say, and leave it at that. Then with whatever spare time he had, he would sit with Joseph, spinning wild dreams of power and success. Telling Joseph how important it was that he excel in school and in athletics, that it was imperative to steer clear of trouble with the law.

"How come you never spend time with Mom?" Joseph had asked him once. "I hear people say you have another woman, Dad, and that's where you go when you disappear."

Be Be had exploded and smacked Joseph's face. Told his son not to meddle in his affairs. Joseph had told him that his mother, Be Be's wife, Angela, was on the verge of a breakdown, that Dr. Licht had even said so.

When Joseph's mother swallowed the vial of Seconal on that fateful weekend when Be Be had once again disappeared without explanation, Joseph held his father responsible. There was talk of some note from a woman to Be Be that Angela had found. A love letter. Angela could no longer live in the halfway world of adultery, and so chose to remove one of the two women in Be Be's life—herself. Be Be had put on one of his best public performances after that one, tears and great grief. But Joseph had seen right through it. He knew that his father had caused the death of his mother, and if he had not cared for her in life, his tears at the wake were surely manufactured.

When the track scholarship from Berkeley came through, Joseph eagerly accepted it. Betrayal was in the Brooklyn air. When he arrived in California, Joseph finally discovered politics. But it was of a much different nature from the kind his father practiced. His association with the Students for a Democratic Society and the radical activities he got involved in became the substitute for love in his life. He fell in love with a cause, and this helped him to forget his past. His father became an enemy—both personally and politically.

As he looked back now he realized an awful lot of his idealistic rhetoric in those days was silly and naive. But his position on the war had been essentially correct. Yet, although he may not have been wrong about America, he had certainly been wrong about himself. Joseph knew that the person he had invented to bear his name in those important years of his life was basically a fraud. He was a young man running away from himself who found refuge and sanctuary in the company of so many others who were doing the same.

His politics had mellowed a good deal since, as had the politics of many of his contemporaries. Tom Hayden had made an unsuccessful run for the U.S. Senate, and Joseph had campaigned for him. Later he had worked for Hayden's new political organization in California, which formed grass-roots crusades for things like rent control, tenants' rights, farm workers' unions, and most importantly solar energy as an alternative to nuclear energy.

But Joseph Gonzago now believed that teaching was the most effective political forum to which he had access. If he could change the minds of even a few kids, who in turn might reach others, a slow but steady move toward a more progressive America might be feasible.

Joseph could not tolerate the former radicals who moved into the country for a life of camp fires, flannel shirts, horn-rimmed glasses, and corn-cob pipes filled with home-grown pot. Vegetarianism and canning your own food wasn't going to stop the MX missile.

Because Joseph still thought politics were important; because he knew politics directly affected the daily life of every single individual in the country; because he believed his political view of the world was just and democratic and feasible, he did not regret having been a part of the radical left in the sixties. Those days had been the boot camp for his more mature views today. It was no longer possible to support a country such as the Soviet Union, for example, but healthy skepticism also made you question the motives of some of the people who ran the country in which you lived. The lessons of those yesteryears kept him from ignorance today. This was important to Joseph Gonzago.

But right now Joseph Gonzago had no time for politics. Right now all he could think of was the murder of his father. He might not have been much of a father or a human being, but he was family, and Joseph had lived too long without any. As long as his father had remained alive, there had always been the remote possibility that somehow, someday, he might have been able to reach out and help him, reach out and tell him how much he wished he could love him, and hear his father say the same thing, genuinely, to Joseph.

He had often fantasized about his father lying very ill, dying a slow death, agonizing and painful, and in this reverie, Be Be would beckon Joseph to his side, plead in his final hour for the presence of his son, and Joseph would go to him and stand above him as he lay there, frail and helpless, and look down at him the way Be Be had looked down at so many others in his time. And there, while Be Be Gonzago was waiting for the end of his life, Joseph would reach for him and try to offer him some small comfort. Offer him the love and true affection that he had always wanted from Be Be.

Joseph scalded himself in the shower, regulating the water to the hottest temperature his flesh could tolerate without damage. After his shower he swallowed four aspirins, dry, wanting the bitter taste to eradicate the aftertaste of the brandy.

He dressed quickly, and phoned the airport to book himself on a two P.M. flight to New York. He threw some shoes, trousers, socks, underwear, shirts, sport jackets, toilet gear, into a large suitcase, and looked around the apartment. There was nothing else he really needed. After over a decade he didn't even own furniture.

He climbed into his Mustang, threw the suitcase in the backseat, and drove three blocks to the nearest branch of the Security Pacific Bank, where he withdrew three of the four thousand dollars he had stashed in a savings account. He left the bank and drove down Wilshire Boulevard toward the UCLA campus. It was only eleven A.M., so he had ample time to go to the school, have his talk with the dean, and still make the plane at two. As he drove down Wilshire he looked around at the surroundings that had been his home for more than a decade. Palm trees and fast-food joints, beautiful women, wide boulevards, and hot, feculent smog.

Joseph parked the Mustang in his assigned slot and walked toward the main building. He passed several students who knew him but none of them spoke. Joseph moved through the corridors of the school with his head held high, his eyes focused straight ahead. He stepped through the door of the dean's office, and the secretary looked up at him and tried to juggle the encounter with a combination of compassion and cool professionalism.

"He's been expecting you, Joseph," she said. "Sorry to hear about what happened."

Joseph nodded his head, pulled his lips into a sad grin, and stepped past her. She buzzed Joseph into the dean's office.

Dean Waters was a tall man with squinty little eyes.

"God, Joseph, what is there to say?" the dean said. "Anything. I mean anything I can do. Just name it."

"There's nothing anyone can do now, Mr. Waters," Joseph said, not bitterly, not sarcastically, just plainly.

"I've arranged for a sub to take over your classes for at least two weeks, Joe," Dean Waters said. "If you need more time, of course it's yours."

"I won't be coming back to teach at UCLA, Mr. Waters," Joseph said. "It's time for me to go back home."

The two men were still standing, the dean looking fidgety and concerned.

"Take a seat, Joe," Dean Waters said.

"I have a plane to catch," Joseph said, preferring to stand.

"Let's at least talk this through, Joe. I mean you're one of our most popular teachers. The students relate to you. They trust you. Students whose grades are low in almost every other subject excel in your classes. They see you as a friend. I realize you and I haven't always seen eye to eye, especially politically, but I have never once questioned your ability. You're up for tenure next year and I fully expect you'll receive it. I know the death of your father is horrifying for you. Especially under the circumstances. But just to chuck in your career, the roots you've laid here . . . No, Joe, I simply won't accept your resignation. This school needs you. The students need you. And, darngonit, I need you."

"I'm sorry, Mr. Waters, but I've already made up my mind," Joseph said. "I won't be coming back to UCLA. In fact, I don't think I'll be coming back to Los Angeles."

"Tell you what, Joe," Dean Waters said. "Take a six-month sabbatical. I know you're upset now. Give yourself time to think. Don't just throw it all away."

"There's nothing for me here, Mr. Waters. I want to go back to New York. I've never really liked L.A. I've enjoyed teaching here at UCLA, and I've met some great kids, good people. But I'm sorry. I have to go. There's a plane I have to catch."

Joseph extended his hand. Dean Waters looked at him sadly, clasped his hand.

"Sure you won't change your mind, Joseph?"

"I should have done that a long time ago," Joseph said, and turned and walked out of Dean Waters's office and started on his long journey back home to Brooklyn to bury his father.

Johnny Quinn had given a short statement to the state police. They asked about his association with Be Be Gonzago, his duties, and whether or not Be Be Gonzago had any enemies. This almost made Johnny Quinn laugh. A man like Be Be Gonzago had so many enemies the telephone company could have printed up a special phone book as thick as the Yellow Pages with just their names. Politics was a word synonymous with enemies, Johnny Quinn had told them. But usually not with murder. He couldn't think of anyone who would really want to kill Be Be Gonzago. That's what he told the cops anyway. But he could think of so many who would kill Be Be Gonzago; he knew he couldn't blow it open right now. Be Be had taught him many things in his life, but the most important thing

Johnny Quinn had learned from his boss was to think before you act. For the moment Johnny Quinn was going along with the theory that the assassin had been after the governor. The papers never even suggested that Be Be Gonzago was the intended target. So he went along for now. Until he had time to think.

The cops had left over an hour ago, and now it was time to remove the tape recording from the panel hidden in the wall and put it with all the other tapes Be Be Gonzago had made in his long political life. Thousands of little cassettes that could ruin a lot of people, not just Brooklyn big shots, but Washington sluggers as well. Be Be was a shaker and he knew it.

Johnny Quinn put the tape cassette in his jacket pocket and closed the sliding panel of the wall in the conference room. He looked at the chair at the head of the table, the chair where Be Be always sat, and it looked very empty. Johnny Quinn breathed in deeply, felt like breaking down and crying, and then snapped off the light and left to put the cassette where the others were kept, a place so safe almost no one even knew it existed.

10

Airports seldom change; passengers do. Joseph realized after he'd forked over $1.75 for a package of Vantage cigarettes that he had changed an awful lot since the last time he bought a pack of cigarettes at Kennedy Airport. He smoked Marlboros then and they cost about sixty cents. It was ten years later and Joseph Gonzago was now a man without a job, a home, a mother or father. He bought the *News* and the *Post.*

Folding the papers, he made for the escalator to go to the baggage claim. He breathed deeply, to see if the air of New York would awaken old feelings of allegiance to the city. It didn't.

He stepped on the escalator and realized the only contact he'd kept with New York in a decade was the renewing of his voter-registration card so that he could vote by absentee ballot against any of his father's candidates. It was a small, but terribly important personal gesture for Joseph.

As the escalator hummed down, he unfolded the newspapers and read the headlines he had deliberately not read when he bought them: BKLYN BOSS BLITZED! roared the *Post* in blood-red type. The *News* was more subtle: GOV OK GONZAGO SLAIN: SEEK UNKNOWN ASSASSIN. Each paper carried a gruesome page-one photograph of Be Be Gonzago lying in a pool of blood.

Inner turbulence shook his body. He quickly folded the papers and thought about what he should do. His first thought upon hearing the news of his father's death had been to go back to New York. He hadn't considered what to do when he got there.

Confusion overwhelmed him. He finally resolved to spend two days lost in the wilderness of New York. Fill up the senses with the things that have only been memories for so many years. Listen to people talk. Smell hot dogs sweating on iron grills. Listen to the war-movie soundtrack of the city—jackhammers, screeching tires, breaking glass, honking horns, loud music, subway trains roaring through black tunnels, flocks of pigeons taking wing, hawkers beckoning Johns into brothels, blind men playing accordions, dogs fighting, alley cats wailing in the night, people arguing behind doors, the whack of a mop handle on a Spaldeen as kids play stickball, pile drivers sending new foundations into the bowels of the city. Listen and look and smell and taste and feel all the things that were once normal to you.

You are a tourist here now, Joseph thought. See the sights and let the mind drift. Eat pizza and fresh bagels, soft pretzels, and egg creams, get a hot dog at Nathan's and a knish at Kirsh's at Brighton Beach.

And then slowly the murder of your father will take shape, will come into focus, will present itself in its entirety. Get all distraction out of your system, and then on the day your father is lowered into the earth you just make certain you are there so you can bear witness.

In these two days you will have to learn how you feel about your father. You know already that you do not like him. But you still are not certain whether or not you love him. And this is crucial. Because, as Jaszinski, your student, said, you are of your father's blood —you are the living son of this man who has been murdered. This is family, and you know that all your instincts beg you to act.

But how will you act?

This is the most essential decision. You must answer this question. But for now go ahead, turn to the sports pages and read. Feel free to look at the pretty girls in their spring fashions as they strut up Fifty-seventh Street instead of pulling up beside you on Sunset Boulevard in an MG. Meander through the streets of New York. Get lost, eat, drink, see movies and listen to music, sleep late, spend money, and eavesdrop on conversations at the next table.

Be a tourist in New York City. Have your picture taken at the Statue of Liberty, take the Circle Line around the great port, eat at Windows on the World, and get ripped off for a silly horse and carriage ride around Central Park.

But when you are done you must surrender everything else, acknowledge you are home and deal with the murder of your father.

Joseph had never heard of this new Transit Authority service called the Train to the Plane. It was a new feature in New York City. It had been established in Joseph's absence. He saw the posters for the airport train in the terminal as he waited for his single bag. It had been so long since he'd been on a subway train that he decided to take it instead of a cab.

The wait for the single suitcase was the usual twenty-five minutes. The terminal was swarming with police, both plainclothes and uniform. Joseph had a keen eye for plainclothes policemen from his radical days. All the arteries in the city were probably clogged with police, Joseph thought. The bus and train terminals, the tunnels and bridges and highways and piers, all looking for a man with a .38 caliber revolver matching the ballistics of the bullets pried from his father's body. When someone tries to kill the governor, the cops put on the full-court press.

After Joseph finally claimed his bag, he walked out of the terminal into an overcast afternoon where the misty rain collected on his face. He walked across to the traffic island and stepped aboard a Transit Authority bus. He paid his four dollars, took his ticket, and picked a window seat in the rear of the bus. When the bus was two thirds full, it pulled away from the terminal, made a few more terminal stops to collect more passengers, and then rumbled to the Howard Beach train station in Queens.

Joseph descended into the subway, carrying his suitcase and the two folded newspapers. A silver subway train was waiting at the platform. The train was crowded and the smell of wet clothing garroted the air. There were a few empty seats, but most consisted of a foot of barren plastic between fat women with six and seven pieces of luggage. On the floor of the train, trampled and muddy, was the front page of the *News* with his father's dead face staring up through the footprint of a sneaker. Joseph averted his eyes to the overhead advertisements, the loudest being for a hemorrhoid ointment. He decided to stand, leaning his back against one of the doors, as he always had years ago. It was the safest way of riding the subway—no one could sneak up from behind you, and if anyone approached you you were in an upright fighting position.

Joseph looked at page three of the *News.* There was a story by Beth Fallon, a political essay on machine politics. She wrote about how Be Be Gonzago's murder might be the end of an era, for machine politics were now going the way of the bald eagle. It was an endangered species, but she reminisced about some of its positive aspects.

"Regular politics gave you the machine," Beth Fallon wrote. "Reform politics gave you welfare. The thing about machine politics was that when you needed help, you didn't have to sell your soul in the bargain—just your vote. And a vote's a useful commodity, endlessly recyclable. You get to use (or withhold) it every two or four years.

" 'And when you sold it to them,' says a muckraker of my acquaintance who has taken a gloomier view of reform the past few years, 'at least you got something for it.'

"At its peak," Fallon continued, "the machine operated with such efficiency that it was off Ellis Island and onto the voter rolls without so much as a chance for a second beer. Saloons were the heart of the Democratic machine, so naturally the Republicans tried to limit or close them. 'Demon rum.' Ha. Demon votes, and not in their column."

Joseph flipped the page, unwilling to allow the pragmatic arguments of Beth Fallon to interfere with his own feelings on machine politics. Joseph picked up the *Post* and on page eight there was a story about Joseph Gonzago, the missing radical son who had not been heard from in years. There was a quote in there from the UCLA dean, who said Joseph Gonzago had resigned and was returning to New York. The reporter said that all efforts to track down Joseph Gonzago had been fruitless. Joseph was pleased. He was mildly amused by the photo they ran of him—headband, antiwar buttons, on a flatbed truck speaking through a bull horn. They probably got it from the FBI. The story included the political divisions between Joseph and Be Be Gonzago, and how Joseph had on several occasions publicly berated his father for his positions on issues such as the war, the draft, nuclear energy. It was unknown by press time if the boss's son would attend the funeral.

In the centerfold of the *Post* there was a collage of photographs of Be Be Gonzago's public life. Pictures of Be Be with Lyndon Johnson on the Johnson ranch eating ribs; a photo of Be Be with Carmine De Sapio at a fund-raising benefit for De Sapio's defense; Be Be at the ribbon-cutting ceremony for the Verrazano Bridge; Be Be with now-convicted Longshoremen's Union president Frank Donato at a Waterfront Commission hearing; Be Be Gonzago leaving a courtroom victoriously after being acquitted of a kickback scheme involving Brooklyn public-construction contracts.

All the pictures show the smiling, brazen, defiant tough-guy exterior, Joseph thought, as the train pulled into the West Fourth Street station. But they never captured the worried man behind the scenes. The man who fretted and suffered from insomnia when those trials and grand jury investigations hung above his head. Joseph remembered now that on those occasions, when Be Be would come under public scrutiny, he truly believed he had never done anything wrong.

The train thundered into Times Square, and Joseph hoisted up his suitcase and walked for the door. Joseph stepped off the train onto the suffocating, dirty platform.

Home, he thought.

Later he checked into the Mayflower Hotel on Central Park West, and went out as soon as he dropped his bag in the room. He walked through the streets, decided against the horse and buggy ride. But he did stroll down Fifty-seventh Street—the best walking street in New York. Beautiful girls—models, actresses, dancers—hurried along on their way to auditions. He paused and stared into several of the art galleries, didn't see anything he thought was worth the price tag. He dropped into the Russian Tea Room for lunch, had smoked salmon with Bermuda onion on delicious Russian black bread with a freezing-cold bottle of Heineken beer, and looked around the room and saw the faces of celebrities as they sat over the small tables making movie deals and book contracts.

Afterward he walked down to Times Square, staring at the marquees of the porn houses, the dirty-book stores, the topless bars. He ignored the hawkers's come-ons. At the corner of Forty-third and Broadway he let a black guy playing three-card monte take him for three twenty-dollar bills in a row even though he knew the game was rigged. He liked the way the guy talked in the singsong cadence of New York blacks.

He walked all the way down to Fourteenth Street, the Fifth Avenue of the city's poor, gave a wino five dollars and asked him for a quarter change. The wino looked at Joseph as if he were mad and hooked a passing citizen and begged a quarter, which he got and turned over to Joseph. Joseph then handed the quarter back to the wino and told him to buy coffee with the quarter. Joseph walked away, smiling. The wino watched him go, realizing he'd just panhandled $5.25 from a loony.

Joseph kept walking toward the Village and through Washington Square Park, realized the flower children of yesteryear had been replaced by malevolent-looking junkies who stared at him with ice picks in their eyes. Over on Sixth Avenue he grabbed a cab back to the Mayflower, went into the Conservatory Bar and drank until he was on the brink of drunkenness, excused himself from the company of a disappointed red-haired woman he'd been speaking to for over an hour, and went upstairs and fell on the bed and went instantly to sleep.

In the morning he took the A train to Jay Street and Borough Hall where he changed for the F train to Prospect Park.

In Brooklyn.

Joseph sat on a bench in the Eleventh Street playground of Prospect Park watching the young kids climb recklessly through the iron maze of the monkey bars. The sun was shining brightly through the overhanging trees, which were in leaf. This had always been his favorite playground as a child. And now he was sitting on the same bench where his mother and father used to sit when they watched him play in the sandbox more than twenty years before. Be Be had taken him there many times on his own. But mostly it was his mother. She would pack a picnic and they would spend two hours at the zoo, an hour in the playground, and then go across to the Long Meadow and spread a blanket on the grass—cold veal cutlet sandwiches on seeded Italian bread from Carmine's bakery on Ditmas Avenue. If Joseph was good and finished his sandwich, he would get a Devil Dog afterward and a container of Sun Dew. As Joseph sat there on that bench, he stared around the playground and saw himself on every swing, splashing with his pal Frank Donato in the sprinkler pool, racing Donato on the slides, bucking each other on the seesaws, and having races to the top of the monkey bars. Joseph always won.

When Be Be used to take Joseph and Frank Donato there he would sit at the stone checker tables with the old men and smoke the twisted Guinea Stinker cigars and make wagers on the checker games with the old pensioners. Be Be had always let them win. They played for pennies and nickels. Be Be truly enjoyed their company. Joseph remembered that. He would often bring them a bottle of anisette and paper cups and they would all sit around playing checkers for loose change and they would smoke the cigars Be Be handed out and sip his anisette and they would discuss the state of the world—which, of course, ended at the boundaries of Brooklyn. All of them were immigrants—Italians, Irish, Syrian. They were from the same kind of peasant stock from which Be Be had risen. Men of mettle who had chosen to live in this place called Brooklyn, and when Be Be came around they would always run off their litany of things that were wrong on their blocks—broken streetlights, traffic lights, leaky hydrants, uncollected trash, potholes, broken gas and sewer pipes, water fountains that did not work, hooligans hanging out on the corner ringing false alarms and breaking bottles.

Be Be would take out his fancy fountain pen and a small pad and write down the name of the man who was complaining and next to it his address and the nature of the complaint. He called these lists "contracts," and later, when he would go back to the office after taking Joseph and Frank Donato home, he would give the contracts to Johnny Quinn, who would immediately see to it that all the red tape of the bureaucracy became unstuck, and the problems would always be straightened out within forty-eight hours. The next time Be Be would come to play checkers with the old men they would thank him. Be Be would smile, let them win his pennies and nickels. When election day neared, he would ask them a small favor—tell your family and friends and your grocer and your mailman and your relatives to vote for Be Be's candidates, a list of which would arrive in the mail a week before the election.

They did.

Joseph stood and walked to the fenced-in checker tables and stared at the seat where Be Be had always sat—in the middle of all the rest of the old men, careful never to sit at the head of the table as if he were somehow more important than they. Joseph stared at that seat and he could almost smell the reek of the old De Nobile cigar and see the bottle of anisette standing upright on the table and hear the wooden clacking of checkers on the colored stone squares and the metallic scraping sound of nickels and pennies and Be Be promising he would win next time.

Christ, what a long, long time ago that was, Joseph thought.

Joseph found a taxi on Prospect Park West and took it out to Bay Ridge. He had told the driver that all he wanted to do was pass by the Walter B. Cooke Funeral Home on Fourth Avenue and Bay Ridge Avenue. He didn't want to get out, just drive by, maybe stop and have a look, maybe not even stop. After that he wanted to go back to Manhattan to the Mayflower Hotel.

The driver took Fourth Avenue all the way because the traffic-light sychronization was better than on any of the other boulevards in Brooklyn. It took less than twenty minutes. As the cab approached the Walter B. Cooke Funeral Home, Joseph asked the driver to slow down. As the cab slithered by the funeral parlor, Joseph leaned back and peered out the window in such a fashion that he could not be seen. A collection of reporters and photographers stood in a loose circle like numerals on an oblong clock.

Joseph saw there was a vacant length of curb across the street and down the block from the funeral home, and he asked the cabbie to make a U turn and push the big yellow machine into the space. The cabbie nodded and parked, lit a Pall Mall, and sat patiently as the meter chewed away the time. Joseph sat watching as limousines and taxis pulled in front of Cooke's and discharged men in suits and women in black dresses.

Joseph recognized Johnny Quinn first. Then the mayor, Bailey. The photographers aimed their black optical weapons at the pols while reporters buttonholed the pols for the predictable, obligatory quotes.

You should walk in there now, Joseph thought to himself. You should go in there and look at your father. These people are ornaments. They care nothing for the lifeless form that fills the expensive casket. To them Be Be was a meal ticket. Now someone else will dispense the jobs and the favors. Be Be is dead. And you sit here like a voyeur watching the ants carry away what little they can salvage from his carcass.

The cigarette smoke from the driver's cigarette was filling the cab in a pleasant way—strong, rich, seductive. Joseph found himself unconsciously reaching for his own cigarettes. He bit one out of the fresh pack. He took his eyes off the front doors of the funeral home to light his cigarette. When he looked back up he nearly choked on the first puff.

It was *her* and she looked beautiful. With a face that could stop or start a war, depending which side she was on. She wasn't on Joseph's. That was for sure. He ended the inner quarrel with himself about attending the wake.

"Okay, driver, we can go now," Joseph said. As the car slid by the entrance, Joseph watched her disappear into the vestibule of the funeral home. Then she was gone. He stared straight ahead, at the bulletproof plastic divider that separated him from the driver and took repeated pulls on his cigarette. But her face was now burned into his mind.

11

Joseph arrived at the cemetery early and aimlessly strolled the serpentine paths. He studied the tablets of the dead, most of them men who had left no real mark on the world except for the words chiseled into the heavy granite and marble stones. But then Joseph caught a glimpse of a large headstone, a name that registered in the way that names printed in bold letters pop out from gossip columns: ABNER DOUBLEDAY. Joseph wondered if this could indeed be the man who faked the world into believing he had invented baseball. And, yes, according to the words in the stone he was indeed the same man. Joseph knew of others buried here in Greenwood Cemetery, the graves of men Joseph would have liked to have seen. But he could not find them. He wanted to see Joey Gallo's grave and the resting place of Boss Tweed. Joseph smiled when he realized that this same part of the earth would be holding the bones of Boss Tweed and Be Be Gonzago. Both men had gotten an awful lot of votes out of this graveyard. The men and women who lay beneath the soil of Greenwood Cemetery always voted the straight ticket, he thought. Democratic. Joseph had always thought it was pure myth that political machines actually exhumed proxy votes from the boneyard. But he had been assured by many who would know that it was true. Be Be Gonzago would now be moving into one of his most loyal and reliable election districts.

The morning was bright, with sunlight lancing through the leaves of the trees. Up ahead, on a small knoll, Joseph could see two grave diggers leaning on their shovels, staring at Joseph. Joseph nodded, barely perceptibly. One of the diggers nodded back without comment or smile.

The other grave digger took out a pen and a pad and wrote something down. He looked back up at Joseph and jotted in his notepad again. Joseph didn't like the way the man was looking at him and the way the two men were now conversing with one another. But he shrugged it off. You dig graves for a living and you're liable to become a little loony.

Joseph could hear the motor procession now and walked in the direction of the sounds. He climbed a steep grassy hill and took a vantage above the scene where his father was soon to be buried. Long black limousines pulled up and discharged passengers. The women all wore hats and sensible shoes. The men had on their dark suits.

Joseph wished that it would rain. But there was no promise. He stood in the shade of a large maple and looked down. He saw them taking their places around the gash in the earth where his father would be placed. Sydney Weingarten, looking a little older, but basically the same. Frank Donato was there too, his wife clutching his arm. And there was Johnny Quinn, standing off to the side, alone, puffing on a cigarette, his thin body shivering even in the soft morning heat. Mayor Bailey, all the councilmen, the former mayor Sol Ross.

The Brooklyn DA Dermot Donnelly and Sam Stone, the black pol from Bed Stuy. Then Joseph saw gubernatorial candidate Brendan Kelly step out of a limo, looking taller and thinner and fresher than he looked in his photographs. Joseph found Kelly's presence rather curious. And next to Kelly Joseph recognized Tim Harris, the old student radical whose personal ambitions always seemed more important to him, in Joseph's estimation, than his politics.

Then Joseph saw *her.* He felt nervous, and uneasy. Then he heard the radio crackling from behind him. He spun, the two grave diggers were behind him, one with a walkie-talkie in his hand and the other training a revolver on him. Joseph's first instinct was to turn back and look at *her,* but he didn't see her; he saw instead Governor Wolfington stepping out of his limousine, followed by three state troopers and Matthew Brideson.

"What the fuck are you doing here?" the grave digger with the pistol demanded.

Joseph could not speak at first, then was about to when the man with the walkie-talkie flipped open a wallet, revealing a gold badge.

"I'm here to bury my father," Joseph Gonzago said.

"What's your father's name?" the man with the gun asked.

"Gonzago," Joseph said.

Both cops stared at each other. The one with the walkie-talkie shrugged. The man with the pistol stared back at Joseph.

"I'm sorry but I'll have to see some identification," the cop said.

Joseph handed over his wallet as the man with the walkie-talkie did a quick frisk of Joseph's body. Both men studied the identification cards in Joseph's wallet.

"Why are you standing up here?" asked the cop with the pistol, which he was now putting away.

"Why are you?" Joseph asked.

"Because someone tried to kill the governor this week and we're making sure that doesn't happen again."

"Why don't you go down and join them," the cop with the radio said.

Joseph nodded and turned back toward the crowd and slowly descended the hill for the grave site. He held his head high and threw his shoulders back.

Sydney Weingarten was delivering a eulogy, a verbose ode to the slain Brooklyn boss. Most everyone had their heads bowed except for the other plainclothes cops who stalked around in their obvious sunglasses, with earplugs in their ears. Joseph saw Johnny Quinn's head rise and his eyes met Joseph's. Quinn almost smiled but stifled it, yet he appeared to relax at the sight of Joseph Gonzago.

Joseph nodded expressionlessly to Johnny Quinn and then took his place in the circle around the grave. His eyes avoided *her,* avoided Gloria Weingarten, and instead focused on the coffin. The coffin was as powerful and broad and imposing looking as Be Be Gonzago had been.

Joseph surveyed the crowd, but was careful not to look at Gloria Weingarten. Be Be's old doctor, Leo Licht, was there. He was the man who had delivered Joseph into the world, a man who had survived the Warsaw ghetto and who lived a block away from the house where Joseph grew up. Frank Donato looked into Joseph's eyes now, a deep wound, bordering on tears, in his expression. Joseph winked at Donato, as he had always done as a child, and Donato winked back. The wink from Donato brought a thin tear over the lip of his eyelid. Donato quickly dabbed it with the back of his hand. As kids the two had pricked the skin of their right wrists and touched the blood together, an act of eternal blood brotherhood. Now Joseph's blood brother was facing a long sentence in prison for Waterfront racketeering. Joseph wished he could help him, but what was there he could do? Only an executive pardon could help him now.

Sydney Weingarten read on from sheets of white paper.

"What kind of man was Be Be Gonzago?" Sydney Weingarten asked rhetorically.

He was a bastard, Joseph thought. He was wonderful. He was a killer. He was gentle. He was wicked. He was strong and weak and miserable and delightful.

"Be Be Gonzago was the kind of man who comes along once in a lifetime. A man who sacrificed maybe too much of his life to his fellow citizens . . ."

Joseph did not hear the words. He knew they were being spoken, but the only image that filled his mind was the face of the woman he refused to acknowledge was there in front of him.

Joseph looked up at Sydney Weingarten.

Sydney Weingarten had paused to pull out a handkerchief to cough into. In this pause he took the time to make eye contact with the gathered. For the first time he saw Joseph Gonzago staring directly into his eyes. For a long, pregnant moment Sydney Weingarten's eyes appeared fake, like those of stuffed animals. Then his fingers began to rattle the crisp sheets of paper he was reading from and he continued.

"A selfless, generous man who gave his all for the good of all . . ."

A death merchant, a killer, a warmonger, Joseph thought. Say it. A bastard. A thief, a protector, a good father, an adulterer, a cheat. Your father. Your enemy. Your life . . .

Joseph looked away from Weingarten and saw Sylvia Stein, a once-attractive woman in her mid-forties with bleached blond hair, who looked as if she had had three or four face lifts. She was large breasted but with the body now going to spread. Joseph stared at her for a good long time, this woman whose crowning achievement in life was that she had once been Miss Manhattan Beach. That was at age nineteen. For this mound of jiggling flesh Be Be Gonzago had been unfaithful to Angela, to Joseph's mother. Because of her Mom took her life, Joseph thought. And now she has the audacity to stand here and offer her heartfelt condolences.

Joseph looked away from her for fear his anger would build too great. He saw Lou Moran, little Lou Moran, who owned the Straw Hat in Canarsie. Lou Moran was a decent man. Be Be had always loved little Lou Moran. One of the toughest sunsabitches Joseph had ever seen in his life. Won the bantamweight Golden Gloves championship twice and probably could have turned pro but for insisting on training in gin mills. When Lou Moran looked at Joseph he steepled his fingers and shook his head in sorrow and disbelief.

Joseph saw Gulatta and Rosario, his old fullback and halfback, respectively, from Madison High, standing near Sydney Weingarten. They had once been good friends. But their friendship had existed only on playing fields and in locker rooms. They did not look at Joseph, preferring instead to stare at their polished shoes.

Joseph nodded at a few aging pols and old acquaintances of Be Be's, showing no emotion, but he could feel himself running out of people to look at and knew that *she,* Gloria, daughter of Sydney Weingarten, was staring at him. To look at her now would be like reading his own obituary. One death was enough for today. He swept his eyes past her, unavoidably registering the smear of vision that included her as he panned his eyes to Ruth Weingarten, Gloria's mother. She had once been a truly stunning-looking woman, filled with vitality and stamina and kindness. Now she looked ravaged, with a face that only alcohol could twist into such a deformed visage. Her legs swayed and she was held steady by her son Bernie Weingarten, a young lawyer with hopes for a political future. Bernie looked a lot like his dad, tall and sort of gawky and pathetically unremarkable. All of his life Bernie had appeared to Joseph like a sentry on duty, patiently waiting in his box for further orders.

"If years from now, our grandchildren ask what Brooklyn was like at this time, they need only be reminded that our dear and great friend, Be Be Gonzago, lived here then, served his people with deep care and reverence, and they will know all they need to know. May God treat him as well as he treated all those he encountered before his tragic and untimely final day. May he rest here in peace, then, this great man of the people of Brooklyn, in the borough he loved and served so well, in his eternal home here in Brooklyn . . ."

Sydney Weingarten was now finished. He looked up as if expecting obligatory applause. Joseph picked up a handful of the damp earth and waited for the coffin to be lowered. When it came to rest at the bottom of the deep, mean pit, he dropped the dirt on top of it. Now flowers were tossed into the grave and Joseph turned his back and began to walk away.

He knew she was still looking at him.

"Joseph . . ."

Her voice, that one word, his name, hit him between the shoulder blades like a rifle shot. One word, the first in the rather banal obituary of Joseph Gonzago. Say no more please. I do not want to die. You are the ghost of the past. Don't show me my future . . .

"Joseph," Gloria Weingarten said again. "Can I just talk to you for a minute?"

Joseph straightened, his back still to her. He waited a moment, was about to turn, but she came up around his right flank and met him eye to eye. Gloria Weingarten looked at him and flicked an embarrassed smile. Joseph stared at her face. In womanhood she was truly stunning with large dark eyes that were almost overly intelligent, yet somehow very sad. Her face was not of the soft, rounded beauty of Southern Californian women. Gloria Weingarten's was a severe beauty, with high cheekbones that interlocked with a steep jawline. Her neck was thin and long and her lips were the color of half-ripened strawberries.

"Joseph, I just wanted to tell you how sorry I am," she said as she stared up into his eyes.

"You're—so—very—kind," Joseph said, each word pronounced almost as a separate statement. The sentence steamed like dry ice in the warm spring air. Gloria's eyes fielded the injury.

"I'm glad you came," Gloria said, thinking of nothing better to say. "I've thought about you, Joseph."

"I wish I could say the same," Joseph said. His body never moved; his eyes vented the icy wind that blew in concentric circles within him.

Gloria smiled, trying to illuminate the four-foot black void between them. It almost worked, and might have, had she held it even one more second. But Gloria Weingarten retreated, took a step back, then another.

"You look great, Joseph," Gloria said.

"Older," Joseph said.

"No, just great."

"Yeah. So do you. On the outside."

Gloria took it on the chin, with dignity.

Christ, grab her, right here, Joseph thought.

Gloria took three more steps backward and then she, too, grew colder, the black void widening.

"See you around," Gloria Weingarten said, and turned to walk toward the limousine. Joseph wanted to shout her name, run after her.

"Yeah, maybe," Joseph called after her. His scalp was very hot and he touched it and quickly withdrew his hand as if from a flame. Behind him he heard the sounds of the clods of soft earth being shoveled into the grave.

Frank Donato approached him, but Joseph was still staring after Gloria Weingarten, her scent hovering on the morning air. Then she stepped into the limousine with Sydney Weingarten; Bernie and

Ruth followed and the automobile drove toward the main gates. He saw her face once more as the limousine drove past; she was staring at him and he stared right back. Gloria broke the frigid stare first and the car drove on.

He turned to Frank Donato and the two men embraced. They said very little. Blood. Brothers. The blood spoke for them both. They patted each other's backs, and when they broke the embrace they stood at arm's length, grasping shoulders with hands they had never thought would grow so large and hairy and old.

"I have to get out of this place," Frank Donato said. "Call me. And be careful what you say. They still have the phones tapped."

Joseph nodded and Frank Donato walked down to his limousine, where his wife sat crying into a handkerchief.

Johnny Quinn now approached Joseph and extended his hand. Quinn's eyes were misty and hurt, the kind of eyes you could write a sad Irish song about. Joseph took his hand and shook it, grasped Johnny Quinn's wrist with his other hand. He patted Johnny Quinn's face softly and smiled for the first time.

"Hello, Johnny."

"Joseph," Johnny Quinn said. "Ah, Joseph. Good sweet beautiful Christ, what the hell have they done . . ."

Johnny Quinn burst into racking sobs and Joseph clamped an arm over his shoulder. With his free hand he took out his cigarettes and snapped one out of the pack. Johnny Quinn accepted it and Joseph lit it for him. Johnny Quinn dried his eyes on his sleeve.

"You just don't know, Joseph," Johnny Quinn said. "There's no way you could. He was the best man I've ever known . . ."

"I wish I had as good a friend as you were to my father, Johnny," Joseph said.

"Joseph, just before he died, I swear to God I held him in my arms, and he asked me to tell you that he loved you. That's what he asked me to tell you, Joseph."

"Ah, well, he was delirious, Johnny," Joseph said. "Stop worrying about it. It's done."

"No, Joseph, you don't understand," Johnny Quinn said. "He meant it. Every day in the office he picked up the picture of you he kept on his desk and ran his fingers over it. He was blind as a bat near the end, you know. No one knew that but me and Dr. Licht, but he couldn't see very much. But every day he picked up your picture and held it in his hand and just sort of felt the glass in front of your face. He always said how proud he was that you looked like him, Joseph. Always said that. Every day. He loved you, Joseph, more than you'll ever know. But he was, well, you know, Be Be wasn't too good at those kinds of things. Emotions, things like that. I don't know why. Maybe because no one ever told him things like that. Maybe—"

"Stop, Johnny," Joseph said. "Please. Today is a bad time for this."

"I'm sorry, Joseph," Johnny Quinn said. "I'm sorry. But I don't know if there'll be much more time."

Johnny Quinn took a deep drag on the cigarette, tore off the filter, and took another, deeper drag.

Joseph looked at Johnny Quinn inquisitively.

"Much time for what, Johnny?"

"I don't know, Joseph," Johnny Quinn said. "Like you say, today is a bad time. There's so much to go over. So much to tell you. So much you have to know. I want to talk to you about so many things. I want to tell you about Be Be, about your dad. I would, in a way, like to introduce you to him."

"It's a little late for that, isn't it, Johnny?"

"Maybe not. Can you meet me tonight?"

"I don't know . . ."

"Well, in the morning then?" Johnny Quinn said. "I don't know how much time we'll have. If you do get time tonight, I'll be in a bar in Canarsie called the Straw Hat."

"Lou Moran's place. I know it," Joseph said.

"I'll be there till closing," Johnny Quinn said. "I have no job to get up for in the morning anymore."

"I'll try to make it," Joseph said. "But listen, I want to ask you something, Johnny. I'm curious, is all. What the hell was Brendan Kelly doing at the funeral? Wolfington I can understand, Be Be has always supported him. But Kelly? He isn't exactly my father's kind of politician."

"That's one of the things I want to talk to you about," Johnny Quinn said. "Be Be was going to endorse Kelly."

Joseph narrowed his eyes, incredulous. Then he laughed.

"You don't really expect me to believe that, do you?"

Johnny Quinn placed a set of keys in Joseph's hand.

"Those are the keys to Be Be's Plymouth Fury," Johnny Quinn said as he pointed to a silver car parked below them on one of the winding cemetery roads. "The other keys there are for your house, the one in Flatbush. You still know where it is, I hope. You were born in it. They're both yours now. There's not much else. A few grand in a checking account, that's it. Some personal belongings, and I mean personal with a capital P. He left everything to you, naturally."

Joseph looked down at the ring of keys, rattled them.

"Come on," Joseph said. "I'll give you a ride home, Johnny."

"Nah, I think I'll walk, Joseph. I need to think. Besides, I'm in no rush and well, to tell you the truth, every time I get in that car now I can still smell Be Be's cigars, and every time I do I feel like crying my fucking eyes out. Please forgive my language."

Joseph watched Johnny Quinn put his hands in his trench coat pockets and start walking down the hill. He turned around once more.

"Oh," Johnny Quinn said. "I think you should use the Tenth Avenue exit. The reporters are all gathered at the Twenty-fifth Street exit. Most of the so-called mourners are leaving that way so they can get their pictures in the papers. If you want to avoid them, Joseph, go Tenth Avenue."

Joseph smiled as the gentle white-haired man waved good-bye.

"Sure I can't give you a ride home, Johnny?"

"Nah, just remember, Straw Hat till four A.M."

"I'll try but I can't promise."

"Good enough," Johnny Quinn said. "And by the way. Her number is in the book. Shore Road, she lives."

"Who?"

"I think you know who I mean."

12

Gloria Weingarten was looking at her father, Sydney Weingarten, who sat on the other side of her mother, Ruth. Sydney had already checked his watch three times in ten blocks as the limousine moved along Coney Island Avenue toward Church Avenue. Ruth Weingarten had her head on Gloria's shoulder and was soundly sleeping. Gloria did not bother to disturb her mother although the woman was drooling on her shoulder, staining the dark fabric of her dress. Instead Gloria gently stroked her mother's gray hair, pushing it up off her damp forehead. Only in sleep did her mother ever look in a state of peace anymore. And even then, peaceful sleep was sporadic. Most of her waking hours these days were dramatic vignettes, filled with rantings and skirmishes with Sydney. The alcohol and the Valium raged within her while Sydney supplied the outside antagonism.

Her father could not be blamed entirely, Gloria thought. He was a good man, a protective father, and had once been a more patient husband. Sydney had not forced the liquor into Ruth's mouth. Perhaps his erratic hours, the weeks away in Albany, and the pressures of his career had added to Ruth's frustrations, which inevitably led her to the bottle, but Sydney had certainly not wished it that way. Maybe if Ruth had been a stronger woman, she would have coped better, Gloria thought.

The limousine made the left onto Church Avenue, and Gloria saw Sydney check his watch again and tap with his Brooklyn College ring on the Plexiglas divider separating the front from the backseat. Gloria's brother, Bernie, turned around and Sydney indicated to Bernie to tell the chauffeur to drive faster. Then Sydney took a side glance at Ruth.

"Better get your mother into bed, flower," Sydney said to Gloria. "She's had a rather trying morning."

He checked his watch again.

"You sure must be in a hurry, Daddy," Gloria said.

"Yes."

They remained silent again for a while, with the sounds of Ruth's heavy, raspy breathing filling the automobile.

Sydney finally broke the silence, but kept staring out his window at the passing landscape of mom-and-pop stores on the half-busy boulevard.

"I saw you speaking with Joseph Gonzago after the eulogy," Sydney said.

"I just said hello, wanted to offer my condolences."

Why don't you tell him what you wanted to do was throw your arms around him? she thought.

"Gloria, flower, I know you're a grown woman now and I don't like to meddle in your affairs, your private life, but my advice to you is that you stay away from Joseph Gonzago. He's mean-spirited, selfish, and quite frankly, I've always felt he was a bit dangerous."

"Daddy, I haven't seen Joseph in over fifteen years," she said. "What makes you think he'd even want anything to do with me?"

Sydney faced her now, his eyes lit with anger.

"*Any* man would have you," he said. "But not just *any* man will. Especially him. Did you see him during the eulogy? He wasn't even listening to me."

Gloria thought, neither was I. I couldn't take my eyes off *him.* But he wouldn't even look at me.

"He was probably upset, Daddy."

"Look," Sydney said. "I'll do anything I can do to help the fellow. Maybe we can find him a job or something. Something that will straighten him out. He *is* the son of Be Be Gonzago, and the organization does take care of its own. But I can assure you he's not shedding any tears over his father. Remember, this is the same boy who upset your life, who publicly denounced his father on television, who burned American flags for the cameras. I'll not have him upset our life again."

"Daddy," Gloria said. "We were just kids. Stop getting yourself worked up."

Sydney looked at his watch again and cleared his throat and straightened his tie. A strained smile stretched his lips and he touched Gloria's hand.

"You're right," Sydney Weingarten said. "I suppose this dirty business, this needless violence, has us all a little edgy. I'm sorry, flower."

The limousine pulled up in front of a large twenty-room Tudor home on Ditmas Avenue. Sydney Weingarten remained seated in the car as Bernie and Gloria helped Ruth toward the house. The house had ten-foot iron gates surrounding it and burglar alarms taped in squares on the windows. Rosario and Gulatta were there to open the electronic gate and assist Bernie and Gloria in getting Ruth up the stoop. When Ruth was safely inside the house, David Gulatta came down the stoop, through the ten-foot iron gate, and up to the window of the limousine. Sydney moved over on the seat, rolled down the window, and handed Gulatta a folded sheet of paper.

"There are some instructions scribbled on there," Sydney Weingarten said. "I want them followed, David, and for heaven's sake try to be inconspicuous."

"Sure thing, Mr. Weingarten," Gulatta said.

With that, Sydney Weingarten pushed the little button that electronically filled the door with glass. Then he tapped his Brooklyn College ring on the Plexiglas divider again and the driver pulled away.

He checked his watch and was relieved he would be on time. Sylvia Stein did not like to be kept waiting.

Joseph Gonzago had not smelled the odor of a De Nobile cigar in a long, long time. The familiar smell of Be Be Gonzago's cigars clung to the inside of the car like an indelible memory. The aroma was that of Be Be in the early morning when the cigars were stale and heavy on his clothes and his breath.

He started the engine, which came almost silently to life, and then saw the stubs of the spent cigars in the ashtray. Joseph stared at them for almost a full minute, studying the bite marks at the tips made by the strong white teeth Be Be had always cared for so diligently. The perfect even tips had surely been snipped by the solid gold clipper Angela had bought him for Christmas when Joseph had been eleven years old. Joseph remembered which Christmas it had been because Mom had wrapped the gift and filled in the little tag on the outside of the present and said it was from Joseph to Dad. It was the first time Joseph had ever given Be Be an expensive Christmas gift, and he remembered now how proud he had been back then every time Be Be took the gold clipper out and used it in front of his friends. Be Be had never used it without remarking to his clubhouse pals that his son, Joseph, had gotten it for him for Christmas.

Then Joseph remembered a black day that he knew he would

never forget. Be Be had been angry with him because his school marks were not as high as he would have liked them to be. It was almost a year and a half after Be Be had gotten the gold cigar clipper. Joseph was to graduate from grammar school that coming June, and his midterm report card told Be Be that Joseph had only reached an eighty-five average. The month was April and there was still plenty of time to boost his average for the June finals, but Be Be was furious because it was the first time his son, his Joseph, the future president of the U.S. of A. had not gotten a ninety average to guarantee him a spot on the honor roll.

He remembered Be Be thundering at him, stalking after him through the house. Be Be told him that he couldn't be trusted to do anything on his own. That there were scholarships to think about, his future. He told Joseph that there was no place at the top of the world for people who refused to do things for themselves. And in his anger Be Be had pulled out a cigar, took out his gold clipper, and flung it to the floor when he looked at it.

"You can't even buy your own father a Christmas gift on your own without your mother's help," Be Be had said.

Joseph remembered the regret in Be Be's eyes after he'd said it. But Joseph also recalled the anger and embarrassment inside of himself. Joseph had locked the door to his room and cried for hours. Be Be kept whispering to him from the other side of the locked door, telling Joseph how sorry he was. But Joseph would not forgive. And Joseph realized now, as he sat staring at the small battlefield of Be Be's dead cigars, that he had also never forgotten. Joseph had promised himself that day he would get higher marks than anyone else in his class at Holy Family. And he did, finishing his finals with a ninety-seven average and three private-school scholarships offered to him. But Joseph did not accept any of the scholarships. When Be Be asked him why, Joseph icily replied that it was his *own* decision and *he* was making it, and went to a public high school instead.

Joseph remembered the defeated look on Be Be's face when he told him that.

Joseph thought now, as he shifted the car into gear, that it was probably after the incident of the gold cigar clipper that he started to lose some of his true love for his father.

He started driving the car with no particular destination in mind, but soon found himself heading toward his old house in Flatbush, almost as if the automobile, like a faithful old nag, was finding its own way home.

Sydney Weingarten reached over to embrace her again, but Sylvia Stein pulled away from his grip, and exhaled a cloud of cigarette smoke toward the ceiling.

"I'm all sweaty, Sydney, huh?"

"But we get to spend so little time together." Sydney was admiring the glow of her body as she lay in postcoital relaxation. He watched her heavy naked breasts heave with each breath, with each inhale and exhale of the cigarette.

"That's not my fault, Sydney honey," Sylvia Stein said, as she eyed his lax, nearly hairless body. "You're the one who's married. Not me."

Sydney leaned over to kiss her, but she nudged him away, feigning mild anger.

"I'm trying to enjoy the cigarette, huh?"

"Sometimes I wish I were the Marlboro man instead of the next chairman of the Brooklyn Democratic party," Sydney said. "Not to mention the next top judge in the State of New York."

"I've heard all this before, Sydney," Sylvia Stein said. "But instead all I get to be is your mistress you come to see once a week."

"You know I love you, Sylvia," Sydney said. "That I always have. Ever since college. And you know I want to marry you . . ."

Sylvia Stein broke out laughing and lit another cigarette from the butt of the other one.

"You've been handing me this line of shit for two years, Sydney. But you know you'll never divorce Ruth. You're afraid to because of the political consequences. You're married to politics, Sydney. And I'm getting sick and tired of being your side action. I was supposed to go to that play with you and now you tell me you have to bring Ruth. You'll never leave her."

"No, Sylvia, you've got it all wrong. Ruth is getting worse and worse. I'll be able to get her into an institution very soon. And then after a discreet period of time, I'll be able to divorce her without any gossip or innuendo. But right now she's just too dangerous. The drunken midnight calls to the newspapers, the public ranting and raving. I can't divorce her until after this election. But I promise, I swear to you, that as soon as it's over, and Ruth is out of the picture, I want you to be my wife."

Sylvia Stein moaned and sat up, and Sydney leaned over to kiss her again, but she turned her face to the side and allowed him only a peck on the cheek.

"You better get dressed," Sylvia Stein said as she checked her watch. "You'll miss your appointment."

Sydney glanced at his watch.

"To hell with the appointment," he said. "Let them wait."

Sylvia Stein was on her feet now and pulling on a robe. She picked up Sydney's underpants and held them out to him. He smiled and accepted them and began dressing. When he was finished dressing he embraced her and she kissed him closed mouthed on the lips. Sydney was about to leave when Sylvia Stein coyly called to him.

"Sydney, aren't you forgetting something?"

She held her right hand out, palm up. Sydney smiled and reached inside his jacket pocket and removed a white envelope.

"That time of the week already?" he said, smiling.

"Time really flies when you're in love, doesn't it, darling?"

He handed her the envelope and kissed her once more on the top of her head and hurried out the door. Sylvia Stein watched through the blinds until his car pulled away and then quickly rushed to the bathroom. She scoured her mouth with a toothbrush, scraping the ridges of her tongue and the crevices of the roof of her mouth with the hard bristles, spitting the sour taste from her mouth. Then she stepped into a hot shower and lathered herself almost violently and let herself turn pink under the boiling spray. She stepped out, towel dried, perfumed and powdered.

By the time she had the chance to pull her robe back on the doorbell was ringing. Sylvia Stein smiled and opened the front door. A handsome young man in his early twenties stood there dressed in tight jeans and a form-fitting knit sweater. He was tall and muscular and he strode into the house past Sylvia Stein. Sylvia Stein approached him immediately, looped her arms around his neck, kneading the muscles of his broad shoulders. She pushed herself up onto her tiptoes, plunged her tongue into his mouth, and let her hands drift down his back, grasping his arms and back muscles and cupping his buttocks. She crushed her right hand between his legs.

The young man stepped back and took her arms from his body.

"First things first, Sylvia," he said.

Sylvia Stein reached into the pocket of her robe, her breathing fast and frantic, and pulled out the white envelope Sydney Weingarten had given her. Impatiently she tore off the edge of the envelope and removed five crisp twenties from a thick wad of cash. She handed the bills to the young man and he placed them in his trouser pocket. Now he let Sylvia Stein yank loose the heavy silver buckle of his belt as she crouched before him.

Joseph spent most of the afternoon sitting in the living room of the house that had once been his home. He sat and thought for a long time, and then noticed there was a film projector set up. Joseph snapped it on and turned out the lights. The images came at him like artillery shells. He furrowed his brow, shaded his eyes with his right hand, and watched his father up there on the screen. Be Be was dressed in one of the expensive suits the Old Ginzo used to custom-make for him, beautifully cut of fine silks and cottons and wools. The shoes always had a shine, and no matter whom he stood with, it was Be Be you would notice first. As they're fond of saying about some actors in Hollywood, the camera liked Be Be Gonzago's face. There he was standing with Lyndon Johnson, that big-eared, big-mouthed liberal who talked about civil rights out of one side of his mouth, while authorizing the napalming of children out of the other.

And there were all the familiar New York figures—Wagner and Lindsay and Rockefeller and Wilson and the other collection of bankers, policymakers, and power brokers. Joseph watched a series of shots of Be Be with Robert Moses, the man who more than anyone else tore the heart out of the city.

He lit a cigarette and watched the newsreel unwind, most of the footage silly, stagy mugging for the camera. He looked at his father's eyes in the scratchy print on the screen. In none of the shots did he look really happy. How could he be happy? Somewhere inside of him, through all those years, he must have known he was destroying his family, killing his wife, looting the citizens who blindly loved him.

Joseph lit another cigarette and put on the other reel of film, figuring it was another collection of publicity footage the Democratic party had assembled for Be Be over the years.

Instead he saw himself up there on the screen, blowing out the candles of a birthday cake. He was very young. It must have been his fifth birthday because there were only five candles. He had two missing front teeth and he had on a cowboy hat and Fanner Fifty-six shooters. Be Be was not in the frame; he was taking the pictures. But Mom was in there, and so was Frank Donato and a few other children Joseph did not recognize. Then the film skipped over some faulty splices to several badly framed, hand-held camera shots.

First Holy Communion, Confirmation, Little League baseball. Some of them were humorous but most of them made Joseph feel old and very alone.

Then *she* came onto the screen, dressed exquisitely in a formal evening gown with Joseph by her side in a tuxedo. The prom. Joseph froze the frame and stared at it for a long time and then snapped the machine shut and sat in the half darkness of twilight in the living room for almost a half hour, smoking one cigarette after another.

Call *her.*

Call *her.*

He picked up the Brooklyn White Pages and found her number listed on Shore Road. He reached for a black desk-top phone and dialed the number. On the third ring she picked it up. He could almost see her, shifting her head in that special way of hers, swaying the long dark hair out of the way while she put the phone to her ear, and then the soft, Zephyrus voice:

"Hello?"

But he could not answer; found it impossible to talk.

"Hello," she said again. "Hell-oh."

There was a long pause this time, but she did not hang up. Joseph knew that she could see him, see his sweaty brow and his frightened little eyes as he sat alone there in the dark.

"Joseph," she said.

His heart pounded.

"Joseph, if this is you, I want you to know that I'd like to see you. I don't know who this is, but if it is you, Joseph, please come see me. You don't have to say anything now. Just come. Please . . ."

Joseph heard the gentle click from the other end and sat there with the receiver in his hand. He felt foolish, abashed. He hung up the phone.

An hour later Joseph Gonzago picked up his suitcase at the Mayflower Hotel, checked out, and drove back to Brooklyn. When he got off the Brooklyn Bridge he fully intended to head straight up the Flatbush Avenue Extension to Flatbush Avenue and back to the house. Instead he took the right from the bridge onto the Brooklyn-Queens Expressway out toward Shore Road. Night had just fallen and the Verrazano Bridge sparkled in the distance, and to the right the Statue of Liberty and the skyline of New York had come to life in the city that lives by night.

The car was taking him to see *her.* Gloria. Gloria Weingarten.

He stood in the vestibule of the apartment house, *her* apartment house, and stared at her name next to the little button. He pressed the button next to the name Gloria Weingarten. His finger touched the small, round, hard little button, and he withdrew it as if he had just touched a bare electrical socket. Then came her voice over the intercom.

"Yes." She sounded short of breath.

"Yes," he said. His throat was dry.

"Joseph?"

"Joseph." He felt like a myna bird. The buzzer bleeped and he hit the glass door with his right forearm.

The glass door rattled and the sound reverberated, and Joseph went through the door as if he were breaking through the line and heading for the end zone.

The elevator rose slowly. The cables sounded as if they needed oil and the car banged against the walls of the shaft. He glanced up at the floor-number indicator. He didn't see the floor number. He saw *her,* an apparition, up there on the ceiling, a red skirt pulled up around her bare hips, her eyes looking confused and trapped, her legs spread, her blouse intact, her lips parted but unable to move or speak, and they were in the living room of Sydney Weingarten's house, on the couch, and Joseph was above her, seventeen years old, his pants down around his muscular thighs and he was moving down to enter her. Then Bernie Weingarten burst into the living room. He wasn't supposed to be home. No one was. And Bernie started shouting. Shouting for his father.

The elevator doors snapped open. Bernie Weingarten was gone. Gloria Weingarten was still there, fully clothed, standing in front of the elevator, wearing tight designer jeans, flat tennis sneakers, and a yellow tube top revealing bare shoulders and arms.

"I won't say thanks for coming again." She smiled.

"Thanks for asking me." He stepped off the lift into the hallway. "Hard to find a parking spot around here."

She wore no makeup and this made her beauty even more intense than earlier in the day. She nervously led him down the corridor toward her apartment.

"It's not much, but I don't need a whole lot."

She walked a step ahead of him. Joseph had always loved the way she walked. As if she had a definite destination, a mission.

"You should have seen my place in L.A."

Stop the small talk, he thought. Grab her now.

He didn't.

She stopped and turned to him outside her door. "I wish I had." Joseph didn't comment on the remark. She led him into the small apartment. It was neat, smelled of *her.*

"Want a drink?" She didn't know what else to say, as if she were addressing a stranger.

"Scotch."

"Sorry."

He stared at her breasts beneath the tube top, a finger tug away. She noticed him staring and he quickly averted his eyes. He couldn't hold her stare and looked around the apartment at the eclectic collection of prints on the walls—Bosch, Rockwell, Lautrec.

"Vodka and grapefruit?" he asked.

"Sure."

He watched her walk that walk again as she went into the kitchen and fiddled with bottles and ice and glasses. She came out with two drinks and handed him his. He took two large gulps, not realizing he was almost finished already.

"You nervous?"

"I am *not* nervous." His voice crackled like cellophane.

"Well I sure as hell am." She sat on the couch, her body dissolving into it. He sat two cushions away.

He stared at her and could feel the glass growing warm in his hand. A scent came from her that brought back a thousand memories. Standing in a doorway kissing in the rain; walking in Prospect Park in the snow; the balcony of the Albemarle Theater touching her breast the first time—she didn't push his hand away; alone in a house together for the first time—that time she did push his hand away; the second time in a house alone together—they made love; her brother, Bernie, walking in—bedlam following.

"Penny for your thoughts," she said.

"Not worth much more," he said.

"Don't be so bitter, Joseph. Please. It wasn't my fault or your fault. Circumstances."

She moved closer to him and he squeezed the glass very hard, thought it would break in his hand.

"You had no right to do it," he said.

"He made me. I was a kid. I've had to live with that pain."

She touched his hand and he felt warmth course through his arm, up through his shoulder to the nape of his neck.

"You never gave me a chance to explain," she said.

"You weren't there to explain," Joseph said.

"I know. He took me away, and everything else away."

There was silence and he wanted her desperately. She leaned her head on the back of the couch, her eyes open wide, staring at him. He could feel her hot breath against his neck. His blood began to burn, he wanted her so badly. She clutched his hand harder and he turned and looked into her fragile eyes.

"You don't exist anymore," he said.

"I'm sorry to hear that."

She ran her hand up his arm, caressed his neck, making everything in his body twitch. She turned his head to her and drew him closer. He allowed himself to be inched toward her as she lay against the arm and the back of the couch, propped upon pillows, her covered breasts pronounced and her hair shining and lovely, her face filled with honesty and need and regret.

"Joseph, I thought I would never see you again."

She tried to draw him even closer, but abruptly Joseph stood up from the couch, looked down at the injured Gloria, who stared back into his eyes.

"I shouldn't have come here, Gloria."

"I'm sorry for taking you for granted."

"You didn't. I want you more than anything I can think of."

"Then why are you leaving? Stay with me."

"Gloria, if I don't know why, I can't expect you to. Let's just leave it alone. Good-bye."

Joseph softly put down his glass and walked toward the door.

"Where will you go? What will you do now?"

"Forget."

Joseph opened the door, and as he closed it he could hear Gloria Weingarten say very softly, "I love you."

He stood for a long moment in the street outside her apartment building looking at the long black animal with the small incandescent eyes across the harbor. That was Staten Island. Or was it Jersey? What difference did it make. *She's* upstairs. Traffic buzzed over the bridge like giant metal bees. A water-chilled wind blew through the trees along the water. A Cadillac with its headlights off slithered by, the two men in the front seat shrouded in darkness. But Joseph knew they were looking at him. One of them appeared very familiar, the shape of the head like a vague, incomplete memory. The car stopped briefly and he was sure now he knew the man in the passenger seat. But he thought he must be imagining it. The car began moving again and took off very fast. Joseph threw a half-smoked butt to the ground and walked like a man half finished with an important mission to his car and headed for the highway.

13

The Straw Hat was a saloon on Rockaway Parkway in Canarsie. Be Be Gonzago had started his political career in Canarsie, working for candidates in the 11th congressional district and the 39th assembly district. Every day for years Be Be Gonzago had walked the tree-shaded streets that make up Canarsie, knocking on the doors of the one- and two-family dwellings, chatting with the registered Democrats, asking them if there was anything the clubhouse could do to help them. Election district by election district, Be Be Gonzago had made his way, greeting as many people as he could on a first-name basis. The blue-haired old ladies playing Mah-Jongg on the pier would wave to a young Be Be Gonzago as he strolled from Canarsie Beach Park, across the overpass of Shore Parkway to watch the old men fish and the young kids dive for coins in the waters of Jamaica Bay.

It was almost midnight when Joseph Gonzago squeezed into a parking space on Rockaway Parkway, a few doors down the block from the Straw Hat. He was about to get out of the Plymouth when he saw a Cadillac that looked familiar slide by. There were two men in the front seat, and Joseph thought it might have been the same car he'd seen outside Gloria Weingarten's building. Paranoia, he assured himself, and got out of the car.

The red neon of the Miller and Rheingold signs blinked on and off in the window of the Straw Hat. It didn't look like much of a saloon. Strictly a neighborhood haunt. Lou Moran, the ex-amateur fighter, ran the Straw Hat. When Joseph had seen Lou Moran earlier in the day, he had estimated that he must be in his fifties now. Lou Moran was one of those Irish-Americans who really should have been born Italian. He used all the Italian slang and curse words, had a Brooklyn-Italian accent, dressed in Italian fashions, wore a solid gold Saint Anthony medal around his neck, and he talked, of course, with his hands. In Brooklyn, in neighborhoods like Canarsie, you were a good risk if you talked with your hands. This was because a man like Lou Moran turned mute when handcuffs were shackled on him.

Joseph stepped into the Straw Hat and surveyed the bar. There were campaign posters from bygone elections on the walls, some of them so camp they must have been worth money. ALL THE WAY WITH WALLACE–LEMAY. There was an old Abe Beame poster too: BEAME KNOWS THE BUCK. Sure he did, Joseph thought. He only misplaced a few billion of them back in 1975. MAILER AND BRESLIN—VOTE THE RASCALS IN. WIN WITH WEINGARTEN. There's a slogan for you, Joseph thought. It was on a wall just outside the back room of the Straw Hat, the place where drunks went to sleep it off. In most Brooklyn saloons the room where you slept one off was usually called Pier Six. In the Straw Hat they called it Albany. In Albany, the city, the most exciting thing you could do was sleep.

Lou Moran was behind the bar, bent over a copy of the *Daily News*, that carried the coverage of the Be Be Gonzago funeral. Most of the stools at the bar were empty. Sydney Weingarten was sitting in a booth with Dermot Donnelly and Sam Stone. Joseph couldn't see Johnny Quinn anywhere and so he walked to the bar, his peripheral vision taking in the men in the booth, watching their reactions. He grasped the brass railing of the bar and finally Lou Moran looked up, his face at first startled, then flourishing a broad, tobacco-stained smile before retreating to the *proper* grimace of mourning. He hitched up his pants, which hung below his ample gut on the rack of his narrow hips. Lou Moran reached across the bar and took Joseph Gonzago's head in his broad, thick hands like a man testing the ripeness of a cantaloupe. He cupped his hands over Joseph's ears and pulled him closer so he could kiss him on the cheekbones.

"Joseph, so what does a mameluke like me say to you?" Lou said. "I'm sorry but I just wanted to express this condolence to you even though out of the blue you walk into my joint after exactly ten or eleven years. And so what are you drinking? Because Joseph Gonzago drinks free on the house in my store. I won't take no money from a Gonzago."

"Scotch, Lou. And thanks."

"You don't thank me in my store because my store is your store when you're in my store."

Joseph smiled and looked at the reflection of Sydney Weingarten and Dermot Donnelly and Sam Stone in the smoked mirror. Lou Moran free-poured the amber whisky over a cluster of crackling clear ice. Lou Moran could read saloon gestures like a card sharp at a poker table. He stole Joseph's attention for a moment and nodded with a snort toward the men at the table.

"Un gotz." Lou Moran was matter-of-fact. "In them days when their mothers were alive, they say it was in the war, the first one, the rubber was inferior. Living proof right there. First time any of them come here. To see what they could see, you ast me. Club soda."

Joseph smiled and looked back in the mirror. The three men were leaning over the table in a huddle, occasionally stealing a glance at Joseph. They were out of earshot so Joseph felt comfortable talking softly with Lou Moran.

"Is Johnny Quinn here?" Joseph swirled the Scotch in the glass.

"Albany. Had a pretty good lump on too. Was talking crazy shit. Thinks they were trying to kill your old man and not the other potato."

"They?"

"Yeah, thinks maybe it was guys outta the machine. Talking something about diaries or something. Him and Weingarten, they ain't exactly like Bogart and Bacall, you know. Johnny don't like him. Thinks . . . well fuck it, Joseph, Johnny was triple teamed with the booze. You know you drink enough of that shit at his age and it starts drinking you."

"How long has he been asleep?"

"Hour a half. Maybe a deuce. I hadda ast him to go back to Albany there to catch a snap because he was railing away."

Joseph picked up his drink and swiveled on his stool and walked toward the back room, passing Sydney Weingarten's table and looking at the three men.

"Hello, Joseph." Sydney Weingarten's voice was unemotional. "I'm very sorry about your dad. If there's anything at all I can do . . ."

"No, I don't think so," Joseph said, his voice cold. "Thanks just the same."

Dermot Donnelly nodded, distractedly stirring his swizzle stick through his drink. "Sorry, Joseph."

"Terrible shame," said Sam Stone. Stone's suit looked as if it were still on the padded hanger, his slight body barely obvious beneath it. "I'm deeply regretful, Joseph. Truly."

"You're all very kind," Joseph said. The front door opened and Joseph saw Rosario and Gulatta thump through.

Both men approached Joseph, ready to greet him, but Gulatta looked sideways toward Sydney Weingarten, as if for permission. Joseph saw Weingarten's lips tighten and relax, and Gulatta picked up the sign and went ahead and shook hands with Joseph.

"Cheese, Joe, what do I say? I mean everybody was so shocked."

"Yeah," said Rosario. "Unbelievable. One day he's here and the next . . . bang, kaput!"

Weingarten shot Rosario a cold look to admonish him for his insensitivity. Rosario shrugged, looked uneasy, and quickly fumbled for Joseph's hand.

"Anyways, good ta see ya, Joe. Long time no see."

He always was a little ridiculous, Joseph thought. Until you banged a football into his belly and told him to run straight ahead. He never looked ridiculous then. In fact he made *you* look like a genius.

"Thanks, fellas," Joseph said. "See you around, huh?"

All the men said good-bye and uttered small pleasantries Joseph did not bother to field. He walked toward the back room to awaken Johnny Quinn.

Joseph found Johnny Quinn sleeping with his head on a Formica table in the back room. In the old days, before they passed the sex-discrimination law in New York, this was the place the wizened old pols took the campaign groupies for a little postelection celebrating on the sly. Now with the new laws Lou Moran was compelled to allow women into the bar through the front door. So this often meant the wives accompanied their politician husbands there.

But the back room still offered more than just a place to sleep off a drunk. You could talk safely back there with little fear of being bugged. If one of the special prosecutors had managed to put electronic listening devices back there, it would be difficult for them to glean anything over the blare of the six wall-mounted box-shaped juke boxes above each of the half dozen tables. When you needed to discuss serious business in Albany, the back room, you simply put a quarter into the juke box and let Jimmy Rosselli run interference for you at top volume.

A silver dollar of saliva had formed on the table under Johnny Quinn's mouth. He was snoring and his hair was damp with sweat.

Joseph placed his drink on the tabletop and gently brushed the hair from Johnny Quinn's forehead. His skin was hot and beaded with perspiration. He looked sadly ugly in sleep, his nose too fleshy and his lips thick and moist.

"Johnny, Johnny, wake up. Come on, slugger, get up."

Joseph was gentle with Johnny Quinn, patted his face lightly and lifted him by the bony shoulders to an upright sitting position.

Johnny Quinn opened his eyes, but they had the spooky dead look of a mannequin.

"Want coffee, Be Be?" Johnny Quinn wiped his wet lips with the back of his hand.

"Come on, Johnny. Be Be is dead. You know that."

Now the eyes came into focus. He looked into Joseph's eyes and shook his head and raked his fingers through his tousled hair.

"Joseph," Johnny Quinn said. "Ah, Joseph. What the hell have they done?"

He closed his eyes and shook his hanging head. Joseph lifted his head up by the stubbly chin and looked Johnny Quinn in the eyes again.

"Come on, Johnny, no more soap suds, huh? You asked me to come out here and what do I find? You look like you went swimming in the Seagram's River."

Johnny Quinn laughed. "Bushmills."

"Even worse," Joseph said. "More polluted."

"You're not kidding, Joseph. Polluted."

"So here I am, Johnny. Just like you asked me. I came all the way out here to Canarsie to find you, and so what is it you want to talk about?"

Johnny Quinn put his fingers to his lips, took a quarter from his pants pocket, and put it into the juke box. Bing Crosby came on singing "Danny Boy." Joseph grimaced as Johnny Quinn raised the volume.

"Okay," Johnny Quinn said, his speech still staggered from the booze. "There's things you have to know. Things you have to see. I don't know how long I'm going to be around to show you." He handed Joseph a set of keys. "Those are for a special room down in the Municipal Building. I'll take you there tomorrow if I have time. There's records, files, tapes, diaries. Everything. Those are the keys to Brooklyn in your hand."

"What the hell are you talking about, Johnny?"

"I found me a nice plot today, Joseph. It's not too far from Be Be's. Nice. On a hill. Lotta sun. A big maple next to it but still a lot of morning sun. I got all the information today when I was at Greenwood. It's small but that's okay because my will stipulates cremation. Just enough room for an urn and a small headstone. It's just a little down the road from Be Be. Nice."

"Johnny, knock this nonsense off. Quit blabbering. This is drunk talk, Johnny. Buying a grave. You're young, have lots of years left in you. Come on, I'll take you home. You need some sleep."

Joseph reached for Johnny Quinn's arm but the elderly man yanked it away.

"No, Joseph, you listen to me. I'm serious here. Someone has to know what to do with all the stuff Be Be left behind. You see, he fully intended for you to have it. He knew I didn't have the mettle to run this county. He knew I wasn't ruthless. That's why Be Be knew he needed someone else to take over for him when he left. He wanted you to do that, Joseph. He knew you were the only one. He loved you so much it was alarming. But he knew he'd lost you. That ate at him. It would have killed him too if *they* didn't . . ."

Joseph held up his hands as Der Bingle ran out of grooves. Tony Bennett came on now singing about San Francisco.

"Johnny, stop . . ."

"No, you stop!" Johnny Quinn spoke with as much authority as his timid demeanor could muster. "Just listen to me. Let me talk. That's all I ask. Be Be never really trusted anyone. Oh, there were a few. He trusted me. He trusted Lou Moran, and Jack Coohill and Frank Donato. And Dr. Licht, of course. He tolerated a lot more because he owned them. But he knew the only person he could pass his chairmanship on to was you, Joseph, but he knew he would never live to see the day you would accept it."

"You have that correct," Joseph assured him.

"You're interrupting again," Johnny Quinn snapped. "I know you hold your father responsible for a lot of things. For your mother. For the Vietnam war, although that's really a little ludicrous. You didn't like his politics and how he used his power. But you know nothing about how he really used that power. I can tell you that. Sure he was an opportunist—he wore nice clothes, always had a few bucks in his pockets, got invited to the best parties. But the guy, for all that, had compassion that wouldn't quit. You should learn that while you were out burning flags and smoking the reefers and bad-mouthing your old man that you could have been home, you could have been here, and you could have learned to love him. And god damn it, I might not have much time left in this world, but I'm going to give you that opportunity right now. I'm gonna see to it, for your sake and Be Be's, you get that shot. Because even though your father is dead I don't think it's too late to learn to understand him, to pity him, to laugh with him, to cry for him, to bloody well learn how to *love* him. Now, I'm finished for the moment and you can give me a ride home."

Joseph sat there, open-mouthed, staring at Johnny Quinn, this gentle old man whom he'd never heard raise his voice much over a whisper, sitting there flushed red with anger and emotion. He was going to answer Johnny Quinn, but for some reason, at that moment, he felt it would be an awful hard act to follow. He looked at the set of keys Johnny Quinn had handed him and he pocketed them. Joseph stood up, grasped the old pol by his elbow, and helped him to his feet.

"Come on, Johnny, let's go."

Johnny Quinn walked ahead of Joseph toward the door. He paused momentarily at Sydney Weingarten's table and stared down at the speaker of the assembly and gathered the white froth that was left in his dry mouth and spit it at the floor near Weingarten's table. Sammy Rosario made a move toward Johnny Quinn, but Sydney Weingarten grasped his arm and smiled and made him sit back down. Joseph stared at Rosario with narrowed eyes. What the hell is going on here, he thought.

"It's all in black and white, Sydney," Johnny Quinn said. "Just for the next of kin."

Johnny Quinn turned to Lou Moran, who was behind the bar.

"I'm sorry if I caused any trouble, Lou," Johnny Quinn said.

"Johnny, you could drive a Buick through the winda and you could call this a drive-in and you'll always get served in my store," Lou Moran said. "And, Joseph, don'tcha make yourself a stranger here."

Joseph Gonzago nodded, smiled, and followed Johnny Quinn out the front door.

Outside the night was balmy, with a salty breeze from Jamaica Bay drifting down the boulevard. Cars cruised by in both directions and a single dilapidated bus puffed by like a fat man climbing stairs. Most of the stores were shut, but red neon winked from dozens of windows. Joseph helped Johnny Quinn into the Plymouth, shut the door, and climbed in the driver's side.

"The cigars," Johnny Quinn said.

"I know." Joseph pulled out of the parking space into light traffic.

"Why don't you throw them out?" Johnny Quinn stared at the ashtray.

"Someday I will."

Joseph reached the corner and stopped for a red light. He draped his arm over the seat and yawned and then noticed the Cadillac he'd seen earlier parked at the corner. It made him straighten his spine, and he looked into the rearview mirror. From the door of the Straw Hat he saw Rosario and Gulatta step out onto the sidewalk. Joseph banged a quick right through the red light and drilled the Plymouth into an alley behind the corner tenement. He killed the headlights and sat there in silence.

"You're beginning to understand," Johnny Quinn said.

"Understand what?" Joseph was slouched down in the seat, his rearview mirror adjusted so he could see anything that moved behind him. The gold iridescent eyes of a startled cat came into view—blinding light illuminating its eyes. Headlights. And then the sleek Cadillac zipped by, and visible under the light of a streetlamp Joseph saw Rosario and Gulatta in the front seat.

He was certain now that they were the men he'd seen in the same car outside Gloria's apartment building earlier in the night. The Cadillac vanished from sight and Joseph started the engine and moved in reverse. He passed the streetlamp and saw WOLFINGTON FOR GOVERNOR posters plastered all over it. In smaller print on the same poster was another legend below Wolfington's name. RE-ELECT WEINGARTEN—HE SPEAKS FOR BROOKLYN IN ALBANY. Same slate, Joseph thought.

Johnny Quinn dozed during most of the trip to Sunset Park. Joseph led him into the apartment and sat him on his couch. It was one of those hard plaid jobs shaped like a park bench. The edges of the arms were all clawed up, the fabric unruly with pulls. Joseph looked around for the cat who'd done it but did not see one. Couldn't smell one either.

"Where's the cat?" Joseph took a seat on the coffee table facing Johnny Quinn.

"Pixie died on me two years ago."

Joseph looked around the apartment. A few old campaign posters were tacked to the living room walls. A clear candy jar was packed to the top with old campaign buttons. A badly focused black-and-white print of Be Be with Johnny Quinn was in a five-and-dime frame on top of the black-and-white Philco television set.

This was the legacy of a man who had spent his life working for other men without ever receiving their notoriety, money, or power. This was one of the real back rooms of American big-city politics. Little men leading little lives so that bigger men could grow even bigger.

"Johnny, when you were talking before you used the word *they* when you referred to whoever killed my dad."

"You just used the word dad in referring to your father," Johnny Quinn said, and smiled. "That's at least a start."

"I did, didn't I?" Joseph smiled too.

"I used *they* because I think there's a group of people in on this," Johnny Quinn said. "They wanted Be Be out of the way. They thought he had seen his day. People kept telling Be Be that things had changed since Watergate. That machine politics were dying. On their way out. Be Be told them Brooklyn was different. That if his organization wasn't still worth something, why did all the big game court him? He made them listen to him when he told them that Brooklyn was still the biggest Democratic county in the state and that he ran it. They knew he could still deliver Brooklyn, especially in a statewide election."

Johnny Quinn yawned again, his open mouth revealing the cobalt clamps of his dentures.

"But, Johnny, even if it was a group of people, a conspiracy, they were gunning for the governor. For Wolfington. Not Be Be."

"Nah, Joseph. You don't understand what's at stake here. These people have their eye on the country. Not just Brooklyn or New York. They want to run the *whole* nation. When Carter got into the White House he took half of Georgia with him. Well, these people know Wolfington desperately needs to win this election because in two years when the presidential election comes up he must look like a winner. And they know he'll reward those guys who helped him win this time. Presidential power, Joseph. Access to a president. Cabinet posts. Big time! But you can't run a guy who lost his own state the last time out."

"You mean you think they were trying to kill Be Be because indirectly he might have stood between Wolfington and the White House two years from now? That this election was just a dress rehearsal for the Oval Office?"

"Now you sound like a Gonzago." Johnny Quinn smiled.

"You're really convinced about this, aren't you, Johnny?"

"Yup." Johnny Quinn was yawning again and this time his head sagged to the side.

"Don't fade on me, Johnny. Not now. I have to know what is going on here." Joseph nudged Johnny Quinn without response.

"I find it really hard to believe that Be Be was going to support

Kelly," Joseph said. Johnny Quinn was snoring now. Joseph shook him again and Johnny Quinn came momentarily to life.

"Meet me tomorrow at the Municipal Building," Johnny Quinn said. "One o'clock, Joseph. Sleep. I need sleep. I can't think. I'll show you everything you need to know."

"Johnny, please, talk to me. Who are these people you're talking about? Is Wolfington behind this himself? Who? Johnny?"

It was no use. Johnny Quinn was fast asleep and snoring very loudly. Joseph searched through a wall closet and came up with a frayed bedspread, made of cheap terry cloth, and placed it over Johnny Quinn. He switched off the bare overhead light and walked out the door, which spring-locked automatically behind him.

14

The doorbell would not stop ringing and the Victrola needle was hitting the same clatter of static about every two seconds. Joseph sat up with a start. Something ugly and hard and sweaty was in the palm of his right hand, which was under the pillow. He slowly withdrew his hand from beneath the pillow. In it was a .38 Smith and Wesson revolver.

Joseph stared, bleary-eyed, at the pistol. He tried to piece together the final events of the night before. He had visited Gloria. It had gone badly. He drove to the Straw Hat, took Johnny Quinn home. Johnny had ranted on about some conspiracy against Be Be before falling asleep. When Joseph had come back to the house, this house, the house where he had grown up, he had sat in his father's car parked across the street for almost an hour trying to work up the courage to go in.

Then he had seen a car, a Lincoln, pull abreast of the house with two very mysterious-looking black men in the front seat. One was bald, the other had a bushy Afro. They sat staring at the house for almost fifteen minutes as if waiting for someone before a private security patrol car approached them and they sped off.

But the gun?

Now he remembered. When he had finally come into the house, a museum of mixed memories, he had gone to the refrigerator and eaten cold meatballs from a pot until he realized he was eating a meal his father had prepared while still alive, just a few days before. It had spooked him. The taste of his father's spicy peasant sauce, which Joseph had always loved as a child, made him feel eerily close to his father, as if his apparition were there in the room. You do not eat a dead man's meal, Joseph remembered thinking. But he had continued eating until it was all gone.

Then he had roamed through the house, put his mother's favorite Mario Lanza album on the old RCA Victor. He then went into his own room. Nothing had changed since he'd last left—the football and track trophies still polished and dusted; the clothes hanging neatly in the closets; the album cover of Bob Dylan's *Blonde on*

Blonde tacked to the wall; the famous poster of Che—all there, intact, making Joseph feel very silly and grown-up.

When he went into the master bedroom he switched on the TV and put on Be Be's favorite silk bathrobe, the smell of his father's perspiration and after-shave still fresh on the cloth. Joseph had clutched it, held it to his face, and sobbed while the television set next to the bed delivered news about his father's death and what it would mean to the gubernatorial campaign. He vaguely remembered Wolfington's voice saying he would not be making any more personal appearances, was canceling the scheduled debates with Kelly, and was extending his deep condolences regarding Be Be Gonzago and expressing his sadness to Be Be's son, Joseph.

Kelly had come on too, registering his shock and regret and calling for gun control and saying that although this was a great tragedy, he thought Wolfington was now trying to gain political mileage from it.

At that time Joseph remembered pushing his sweaty hand toward the coolness beneath the large down pillow and his hand reacting to the special coldness of steel. He recognized the pistol as his father's, the one he'd always slept with. Joseph had always called Be Be a paranoid because he slept with a pistol. But, in the end even his paranoia had failed to save him.

Now the doorbell would not stop and the scratched record was starting to annoy him. He could not remember when sleep had come, but he hated to be awakened this way. He walked to his mother's old sewing room, switched off the Victrola, and furtively walked down the stairs and peeked through the curtains on the door. When he realized he still had the gun in his hand, he slipped it into the pocket of his father's silk robe. He had to squint to make out the form outside the door because the spring sun was blinding. But it did not take long to recognize *her*. She had on tight kelly green corduroys and a soft white turtleneck blouse. He hesitated a moment but then unlocked the door and stood looking at her, face to face. She had a brown paper bag in her hand and two newspapers tucked under her left arm. She smiled, embarrassed.

"Hot bagels," she said. "Lox, cream cheese. And I remembered the Bermuda onion, the way you like them. Hope you're hungry."

Joseph didn't say anything, his eyes were still adjusting to the sunlight.

"You alone?" Gloria asked.

"Not now. Why'd you come here?"

"I thought you'd be here. One of us has to put pride in the pocket. I wanted to see you. Badly. So I volunteered. Even if it is a suicide mission." She smiled, trying to get Joseph to do the same. He didn't.

"Bagels still hot?"

"Just bought 'em."

Joseph pushed the door open wider and Gloria walked by him into the house. She strode directly to the kitchen and put down the paper bag and the papers and turned to the sink, where a saucepan sat with Italian sauce congealing on the sides. Almost instinctively she turned on the water and picked up a bottle of detergent and a sponge.

"Leave that. I'll do it."

"It's okay," Gloria said.

"Leave it, Gloria!" She sensed a note of abruptness in his voice and shrugged and shut off the water.

"I'm sorry," Joseph said, softening. "I'm used to living alone I suppose."

"Me too."

They ate in the dining room, each crunching into the toasted bagels overloaded with lox, onion, and cream cheese.

"Do you know why you left last night?" she asked, pausing between bites.

"The right thing to do," he said, and took another bite, staring at the bagel instead of her.

"God Almighty, Joseph. Fifteen years is a long time."

"Yeah, the kid would have been in tenth grade by now."

Gloria stopped chewing, put the sandwich down on her plate, took a slug of coffee, and stared narrow-eyed at Joseph Gonzago.

"You want to throw me out, fine. But I'm going to say what I have to say, Joseph. We were kids. We were in love the way only kids know how to be. We got jammed up. My brother, Bernie, caught us. He told Sydney. Sydney and your father were the Brooklyn version of the Hatfields and McCoys. Those were different times, Joseph. My father had influence over me. I was a JAP, for Christ sakes. There was no way he was going to let me have Be Be Gonzago's grandchild. He made me have the damned operation. I didn't want it. You know that. He took me away, kept me there, sent me to a private school in Switzerland."

"Yeah, I saved all the stamps."

"I didn't write because I knew you hated me, and I didn't want you to hate me anymore because I loved you. I loved you even more. After what I went through I had no one. My mom snapped, had a breakdown which she still hasn't recovered from. I became a woman overnight. You knew a little girl. There's a big difference, fella, in case you didn't know it, between being sixteen and a half years old and losing your virginity to a boy and making a baby and having it yanked out of your belly. *I* had to live and die through that. So forgive me if I sound a little bitter too. But I didn't come here to listen to a grown man talk like the boy I used to love. I'm sorry I bothered you. Especially now, because I know you are going through one of the roughest times of *your* life."

Gloria had spoken in a near whisper, as if in respect for the dead. She now stood and picked up her purse and made for the door, head high. Joseph looked at her, the words still four-walling off the inside of his head.

"Sit down," Joseph said. Gloria kept walking.

"I said sit down!" He was shouting now. She grabbed the doorknob.

"Please," he said softly. When she turned back to him, her eyes were strong and good.

"I want you to know that there have been others. There had to be."

"If you don't want me to talk like the little boy you used to love, don't talk to me like one," he said.

"Does it bother you?"

"Yes."

"Good."

"Why's it good?" he asked.

"Because it didn't bother me until I saw you again. Then it bothered me."

"Anyone now?"

"Yeah." She smiled.

"Who?"

"I'm trying to seduce him right now."

Joseph smiled. "Try harder."

He spilled her onto the king-size bed and lay on top of her. Their laughter died down and she stared up at him. Their mouths met and she closed her eyes. He did not. He watched her and agilely began to undress her and himself. She had to help him with her trousers because they were so tight. She stood, pulled them off, her underwear coming off with them as he lay naked and nervous and erect on the bed. She looked more beautiful than even he remembered her, with a soft film of perspiration gleaming on her taut skin. She slid on top of him, slowly, gently, coaxing him in. Then he rolled her over, mounting her, and she wrapped her arms and legs around him and clung to him as if he were a secure girder at a very great height.

"You are worth every minute of it," she said, and said nothing more until they were finished.

Later they lay propped on the bed under the damp sheets, and Joseph slugged from a bottle of Peroni beer and Gloria ran her fingernails through the glistening hair on his flat plank of belly.

"Do you still love your father?" Joseph asked as he stared at the ceiling.

Gloria was propped on her elbow, staring at Joseph, trying to register the question.

"I'm not sure. Not the way I used to anyway. But I guess so."

"What's it like, Gloria?"

"You loved your father. You don't need to ask."

"At one time."

"When he died you came back."

"Maybe so I could stop hating him."

"Maybe because you were guilty of not loving him more. No?"

"Maybe."

"Weird conversation."

"Weird father."

"I don't think Be Be was weird. I thought he was cute."

"Cute?" Joseph turned to her and laughed.

"Yeah, cute. Silk suits, walked like a rooster, the way he growled at people, charmed the ladies . . ."

"Charmed one very special lady into the grave."

Gloria brushed the hair from his forehead and kissed him. "Don't say that."

"She's gone and he helped."

"So's he now, Joseph. Bitterness won't help."

He turned to her and smiled, put his arm around her and kissed her.

"You do."

"Yeah, I helped myself to you."

They laughed.

"Gloria, let me ask you something," Joseph said, his mood growing more serious. "Did Sydney and Be Be get along the last few years?"

"Politically I don't think they saw eye to eye since Be Be beat my father for the chairmanship in sixty-three. But they were both pragmatists. They were civil to each other. They talked and went to the same functions and bartered with each other. Hell, they were politicians, they saw things differently, but they compromised. I guess."

"The guilt is that there is no guilt," Joseph said. Then he took her in his arms, ran his hands over her soft, yet firm, body.

"Who said that?"

"The names have been changed to protect the innocent."

"Half the time I don't know what you're talking about," Gloria said, smiling.

"That means half the time you do," he said. "That's not bad."

"Neither are you," she said. She was smiling and her eyes were shining. She kissed his body, lower and lower, her breath startling his skin. He lay there helpless, Gloria taking him prisoner, an act of surrender that hardly felt like defeat.

Joseph parked the car in front of a saloon called Duffy's on Court Street and made for the Brooklyn Municipal Building. This was the bureaucratic pacemaker of the borough of Brooklyn. From this nine-story pile of filthy brick the citizens of Brooklyn were regulated. There was the probation department, the sewer department, traffic control, the property-tax offices, the district attorney's office, the highway commission, the parks department, the sanitation department, rent control, the building department, zoning, the power department, the Environmental Protection Agency, and forty or fifty other esoteric bureaucracies that included something called the Water Board.

Joseph Gonzago checked his watch and it was almost one P.M. Johnny Quinn was waiting in front of the building, his eyes cast to the bright sky. Joseph approached him and he and Johnny Quinn shook hands. Johnny Quinn's hands trembled and Joseph figured it was the booze.

Johnny Quinn looked both ways up and down the street to see if anyone was watching. The street was mostly empty except for a few citizens making their appointed Saturday rounds of shopping.

"Anyone follow you, Joseph?" Johnny Quinn asked.

"You're still pushing this conspiracy theory," Joseph said. "I thought maybe a few cups of coffee would have ended that."

"I remember what I said," Johnny Quinn said. "And I intend to prove it. Come on."

Johnny Quinn unlocked a door to the Municipal Building with a large key on a heavy ring.

"Where are we going?" Joseph asked.

"To Be Be's real tomb," Johnny Quinn said.

Joseph looked at Johnny Quinn strangely, a smirk tugging the corners of his mouth. Joseph figured there was no use asking any more questions because all he'd get was more cryptic answers.

The office building was old and smelled of too many decades of cigarettes and ammonia and dust. The floors were a dull marble and had not been polished in a long time. There was a bank of elevators in the lobby and Joseph instinctively walked to them. But Johnny Quinn summoned Joseph to follow him to the fire stairs. Quinn pushed open the heavy fire door, which led to a cavern of steps and damp cinder-block walls. Wet newspapers were clumped in the corners of each landing as Johnny Quinn led Joseph down four flights of crumbling steps.

"Johnny, where are you taking me?"

"I'm taking you to meet your father."

Johnny Quinn moved on, kicked an old cardboard box out of the way, and hoisted open the fire door leading to the sub-basement. Joseph stepped into the sub-basement. The loud mechanical whirr of machinery tickled the hairs in Joseph's ears. A boiler kicked on with a loud metallic clatter, which sounded like men shoveling coal into a steam engine.

"Come on, Johnny, what is this?" Joseph said, his breath short.

"Don't worry," Johnny said. "It's perfectly safe."

Johnny Quinn splashed through the puddles and Joseph followed. They turned a corner and twenty feet in front of them was a solid brick wall resting on long foot-thick slabs of cement. There was a solid metal door in the middle of the wall with a legend, WATER BOARD: JOHN QUINN, COMMISSIONER. The room number on the door was B-0001.

Johnny Quinn opened the door and Joseph stepped inside. The room was bright with fluorescent light and the carpet was a light champagne shag. There was a small couch, a large desk, a liquor cabinet, a small refrigerator, a desk, and a row of filing cabinets. The telephone on the desk was off the hook. There were no windows.

"Christ Almighty," Joseph said. "I bet they don't line up at the door to see you around here."

Johnny Quinn smiled again and filled two glasses with ice and splashed Dewar's Scotch over the cubes. He handed a glass to Joseph.

"Have a seat," Johnny Quinn said. "I suppose I owe you an explanation. As you saw on the door, I'm the commissioner of the Water Board. I get fifty thousand dollars a year for the job. I'm also the secretary to the county organization. It isn't a job really. It's a title. As commissioner I have never dealt with a single citizen. Be Be created the job specifically for me. It serves no *public* function, and that's why the phone is always off the hook. Very few people even know it exists."

Johnny Quinn paused and took a sip of his Scotch.

"You mean this is your plum?" Joseph said. "Fifty grand of taxpayer money for absolutely zilch? I mean that's your patronage for loyal services to Be Be?"

"Yes," Johnny Quinn said. "But it's not really for zilch. It serves a purpose. I'll get to that later. Here no one works above me or below me. I am the Water Board. As far as I know there isn't even another politician in the city who knows the Water Board exists. Be Be could just as easily have given me a fifty-thousand-dollar job in any other agency without creating this," Johnny Quinn said. "But he wanted to have a place that absolutely no one else knew anything about. Be Be realized that if you want to keep things like tapes, you better make sure you keep them in a place no one will find. No one ever knew Be Be tape recorded any of the deal-making patronage sessions. But he did and the reason he did was that he knew there were a lot of people who wanted his job. No one ever openly opposed Be Be after he won, but he always kept his guard high. If someone was gonna take him down, an awful lot of people were gonna go with him."

"Be Be had more in common with J. Edgar Hoover than I thought," Joseph said.

"It isn't easy to get where Be Be got," Johnny Quinn explained. "I bet you don't even know that story, Joseph, because he never told too many people. I bet you don't even know how Be Be went from the gutter to run Brooklyn. Do you?"

"Not really," Joseph said. "It's not really important how he got there. It's the filthy schemes he pulled when he did."

"Ah, you think you know it all," Johnny Quinn said. "You don't know the story, so how can you make judgments like that?"

"All right," Joseph said. "Go ahead, tell me."

"From the beginning?"

"Yeah," Joseph said, curious now. "Yeah, from the beginning."

"Be Be was, well, how would I put it, poor," Johnny Quinn said. "Big deal, so were a lot of people. When he came back from World War Two he had a few medals. A silver star. I guess you know that. This made him a pretty hot shot in Canarsie back then. The girls loved him, the bartenders gave him free drinks, the usual hero malarkey. But you know, that stuff starts to wear off. So he needed a job. The local Democratic club from the Thirty-ninth A.D., the Benjamin Franklin Club, figuring they could cash in on a little of Be Be's hero status, gave him a job as an election-district captain. No big deal. They paid him about two grand a year. His job was to take complaints from any registered Democrat in the four square blocks of his election district. You know, the usual nonsense, somebody wants a traffic light, somebody needs a streetlight, the garbage men aren't picking up the trash, some kid in a jam with the police needs a fix down the courts. That kind of thing. Well Be Be did that job for two years.

"And in two years as an election-district captain, Be Be's people never went one night without a lamp post, never had a leaky fire hydrant, never had a pothole wasn't filled the day after it appeared. Most of the other guys did nothing for their E.D.'s. They treated the job as a no-show plum. Be Be worked every day. From nine till five. From six to midnight he shaped up down the docks for extra money. He fell in love with your mom and wanted to get married but he needed money. He saved almost every dime he got. After two years, when there was a close election for the assembly seat where his E.D. was, it was Be Be's four square blocks that swung it for the Ben Franklin Club candidate. He canvassed all the people he helped over those two years and he got a ninety-five-percent turnout in his E.D. The other E.D. captains didn't fare so well. The head mummies of the club couldn't thank Be Be enough. So they gave him a thousand-dollar raise and three more election districts to run. Remember now that turf, and not money, means power. But Be Be also needed money. He took on the other election districts and worked his butt off. Some days he got two, three hours of sleep because he'd still be shaping down the docks."

Joseph sat mesmerized, his Scotch glass idle on his lap. Johnny Quinn paused to take a drink of his Scotch and Joseph followed suit.

Johnny Quinn said, "Some seventy-seven-year-old district leader, who had a twelve-thousand-dollar-a-year job, was retiring. He was a member of the Benjamin Franklin Club and the club was gonna replace him with another one of their guys. Be Be went to the men running the club and asked if he could be considered. They laughed at him. Told him he was just a kid, a newcomer, that there were a lot of guys who had seniority who deserved it a lot more than Be Be. Be Be argued that he worked harder, that he delivered services to the citizens in his election districts, and in return they delivered their votes to the club. The club hacks told Be Be they were grateful for that, and that maybe in five or six years they'd let him have something a little bigger. But they told him he was too young to be a district leader. Be Be was really furious.

"He said he'd never forget them laughing at him when he walked out of the room," Johnny Quinn said. "He told me then and there he made up his mind that someday he would put himself in the position of laughing at them. He vowed someday to take over that club. Anyway, he had about five grand in the bank now. He had been saving almost everything he could spare for four years. He also got a hell of an education on how the system worked in those four years. Be Be only had a seventh-grade education, but he was a genius. He read Socrates, Sartre, Camus, Machiavelli, Tom Paine, Jefferson. He had natural gifts for sizing up a situation. He came to me. I was an election-district captain in the same district where this vacancy for district leader was gonna come up. He told me he was gonna go down to the board of elections and put his name on the ballot, but that he needed a few hundred signatures. Would I help him?"

Johnny Quinn paused in the story here and looked Joseph in the eye and took a quick gulp of liquor.

"Be Be was the only man I ever trusted with what I thought was the most horrible secret in my life back then," Johnny Quinn said. "Be Be was the only man I ever admitted to that I was a homosexual. Once when I was drunk at some function I even told him I loved him. You couldn't believe how beautiful he was—"

"Johnny," Joseph broke in, embarrassed. "You don't have to tell me all this, you know."

"Oh, Joseph, I don't mind," Johnny Quinn said, his face reflecting some sweeter time. "And I'll tell you why. Because it was Be Be who told me even back then that being a faggot was okay with him. He made me feel like a human being. You don't know what that meant. Especially back then. He treated me as a friend.

"I had three E.D.'s of my own," Johnny Quinn said. "I could pull them pretty good too. I didn't even think it over. I just told him I'd do anything I could do for him. So we went out and we started collecting signatures together. And I couldn't figure out what the hell Be Be was up to. Every goddamned registered Democrat we went to Be Be would ask them if they had any parking tickets that needed to be taken care of. Now everybody who has a car has tickets, and people were really starting to buy cars then because the war's over almost five years now. Somebody in every family has tickets. So Be Be starts accumulating all these tickets. And I'm thinking to myself, 'How the heck is he gonna fix these many tickets? Even the mayor doesn't fix that many tickets.' The tickets ranged from like a two to five dollars too."

Joseph was smiling now and leaning forward on the edge of the couch.

"But I couldn't figure it out," Johnny Quinn said. "He didn't collect parking tickets from any of the voters in his own E.D.'s or mine. He would just ask them if they remembered the time he had helped them out, and they'd say yeah, and he'd say, well, now he needs their help. That he's running for district leader and he can really do a lot more for them in that position. And he gets all these promises from these people to go out and vote for him and no other candidate. In my E.D.'s he has me cashing in all my markers for him too.

"But in all the other E.D.'s in the district where he's running for district leader—which takes in maybe twenty-five E.D.'s then—he's collecting parking tickets like they were baseball cards. I ask him about it and he just smiles. I figure he's got some con going. Anyway, the Benjamin Franklin Club goes ape when they find out Be Be has his name on the ballot opposing their guy. They bar him from the club. Be Be smiles through it all. Election day comes and he has me and him still knocking on doors. He has all the promises from all the people he knows and I know, and he goes back to the people with the parking tickets and asks them if they've heard anything from the Department of Motor Vehicles. They all say yes, that they got receipts from the traffic people saying everything is taken care of. They're all pledging support. I mean he must have collected at least a thousand of those tickets, which if there's a couple of Democrats in every family means thousands of votes. I still don't know what he's up to, because I know that all the people down at the Department of Motor Vehicles are clubhouse appointments and they're not gonna help out a guy who's challenging the clubhouse.

"Anyway around ten that night the results start coming in," Johnny Quinn said. "Be Be's got the clubhouse mummy by two lengths. It was a walk in the park. All of a sudden he's a district leader. And then there's juice. Patronage, clout, muscle. Me and Be Be and your mom went out to Coney Island to have clams and beer and to celebrate. Finally, I say to him, 'Hey, Be Be, how did you fix all those tickets?' He looks at me and smiles and says, 'What fix? I paid for them fuckin' tickets.' Excuse my language, but that's exactly what he said. Your mom almost chokes when she hears this, but then he tells her that his position as district leader will get him a good patronage job with the city. Which he does get. As head of the agency that controls the streetlights. He makes some pretty good money from helping a certain company get the maintenance contract for the city. You can call it a kickback if you want. Be Be always called it cash flow. It always flowed through him, to others, helping him build friendships, favors owed, until he was in a position to broker for the job of party boss.

"He started a small insurance business, a bail-bonds office, a printing company. The money helped him to get in a good position with other district leaders. If a kid in another district leader's community got jammed up with the law, a simple call to Be Be's bail-bonds office had the kid home in time for supper. Someone needed insurance, they went to see Be Be and they knew they'd get a fair deal. A district leader or assemblyman was running a campaign and they needed literature printed up, they went to Be Be. If he liked them he did all their printing for free. In the end all Be Be needed to win the chairmanship was the majority of votes from the other district leaders from each assembly district in Brooklyn. By the time 1963 rolled around Be Be also had a big piece of a bank. He had all the financing he needed and enough favors owed to him to steal that vote from right under Sydney Weingarten's nose. Once Be Be got into the chair of Brooklyn party boss, he vowed never to be unseated. The one way to insure that was to get the goods on those who might try to unseat him. That's what's here, in this room. The goods. But enjoy your drink before we go into all that."

Johnny freshened Joseph's drink and Joseph looked him in the eye. Joseph swirled the ice in his glass, watching it spin in the small whirlpool and slowly disintegrate.

"What was Mom like in those days, Johnny?"

"They were both mad about each other," Johnny Quinn said. "I don't think I've ever seen two people more in love. Happy as hell. Angela was a saint. She was the only other person back then who knew my secret besides Be Be. She understood me even more than Be Be did. She'd have to." Johnny Quinn beamed a broad grin. "We had the same interests."

Joseph laughed heartily and took a slug of his Scotch, which was beginning to loosen him up.

"Be Be treated her well?" Joseph had a look in his eye that an archaeologist might have when getting his glimpse of a lost city.

"He lived for her and her only. She lived for him. But there was always the politics. This did not present a great strain until after you were born. Angela thought Be Be should spend more time with you. This put a strain on your mother. You would know better than me what kind of a strain it put on you. I imagine it was substantial.

"But I can tell you this. There was never a day in Be Be's life that he wasn't totally dedicated and in love with your mom. After she died he realized he might not have been as good a husband and father as he could have been. He insisted there could have been more time. But he liked to do everything himself. He believed in himself. He regretted that afterward he hadn't been more devoted to Angela. And, of course, to you."

Joseph thought for a moment and then looked evenly at Johnny Quinn.

"You know it's not that simple, Johnny," Joseph said. "There's plenty of people who have demanding jobs who still spend time with their families."

"How many of them have jobs as demanding as taking care of the largest Democratic district in the country? Three million people, Joseph!"

"One of whom was named Sylvia Stein, who Be Be found enough time for on long weekends. That's what sent Mom over the edge."

Johnny Quinn stood up, shaking, grasping the edge of a filing cabinet for balance. He placed his glass down and peered down at Joseph Gonzago with fury in his eyes.

"That is a monstrous, ugly lie," Johnny Quinn said. "I know Be Be spent weekends away an awful lot, but I can tell you right now that it wasn't in the bed of that little slut. Don't ever say a thing like that in my company again. It's scurrilous, lousy, filthy gossip. Lies!"

Joseph was surprised at Johnny Quinn's reaction. Johnny Quinn was still shaking and drained his glass to steady himself.

"But Mom got all those letters in the mail and—"

"Mudslinging, dirty tricks, slander. There was a good reason for Be Be being away for those long periods of time. He would never tell me the reason. All he told me was that it was unavoidable. That's all I know. But I can tell you he was never with that slutty bitch Sylvia Stein, because when Be Be was gone on those trips, she was exactly where she's always been for the past dozen or so years—between Sydney Weingarten's legs. God forgive me, but it's true."

"Anyone can walk on water when it is frozen, Johnny."

"Have it your way, but it's the wrong way. I swear to you."

Joseph held his head in his hands. All the years he had taken pleasure in resenting his father; all the dark and ugly things he'd said of and felt about and done to Be Be Gonzago might actually have been false and unwarranted and wrong. And if that was the case, he'd lived a decade of lies and had lost the love of a father to a misunderstanding that could no longer be reconciled.

Johnny Quinn walked to the desk, placed the empty glass down, picked up the off-the-hook telephone receiver, and unscrewed the transmitter cap. Inside the cap was a small brass key. Johnny Quinn took this key and walked to the file cabinets and opened the master lock that unbolted all three cabinets. He handed the key to Joseph.

"This belongs to you now, Joseph," Johnny Quinn said. "In those files you'll find out more than you've ever known about Be Be. The people who owe him favors are in there. There's an enemies list. There's dossiers on almost every politician and bureaucrat of substance in the city. And state. You'll find out who owes him money, who came to him with deals. There are tape recordings in there so explosive that if you aired them publicly, they'd have to build a new jail just for the people speaking on them. I want you to know if there's anything you need explained, anything you want me to do, you just call me. I think you should listen to some of these tapes, read the files and the diaries. Take your time. I'll leave you here alone. He asked me to be sure if anything ever happened to him that you get all of this. I've done that now. The rest is up to you. I think your father was murdered. I think the motives are in there. Stick to the enemies list. Forget *my* conspiracy theories. You make your own decisions. If you feel that I'm a paranoid old coot, so be it. If you decide you want to do something about his murder, please talk to me first. You'll be going up against some of the most powerful people in this city, state—hell, in the country. But I'll leave you alone now. You know where to find me. I'll either be in the Straw Hat or at home or traveling between one of the two. Just one last thing. I think you should listen to that last tape, made just before your dad was murdered, first. Then work your way back. They're all dated. The files are alphabetized. Good luck, Joseph."

Johnny Quinn walked out the door without either of them saying good-bye. Joseph sat there in the small office with the small brass key in his hand.

It felt as if it weighed a thousand pounds.

15

There was no longer any time for tears. Joseph Gonzago had cried enough. He'd listened to numerous tape recordings from Be Be Gonzago's private files. He'd looked through many file folders: Some were very simple documentation of extortion and kickback rackets involving members of the Brooklyn Democratic machine; others were more cryptic, written in the jigsaw lingo of graduates of the Harvard Business School, replete with tables, charts, graphs. These Joseph did not understand. He was impressed that his father had been able to decipher them.

He'd listened to the final tape recording his father had made in his office on that morning he was shot to death. Wolfington had just about confirmed his plans to make a run for the White House two years hence. Joseph knew this gubernatorial race was crucial to those plans. He would not want to toss his hat in the presidential ring as citizen Wolfington. But to do so as the thrice-elected governor of one of the most important states in the union made him a serious candidate.

Still, Joseph thought, was this motivation enough for murder? Would Governor Henry Wolfington actually kill a machine boss so that he might one day sleep in presidential pajamas?

Of course he might, Joseph knew. People killed for a lot less. But was there any real proof? And if the conspiracy theory was true, who were the others involved? Johnny Quinn said the answers were all in this room. But there was just so much territory to cover. Reams of papers, some of which he did not understand. Reels of tape of people he could not even identify. They talked in political shorthand, referring to people by initials and code names and even numbers.

And then there were the private diaries. Joseph had read through some of them. The majority of the entries were mundane, banal jottings about sporting events, meals Be Be had eaten, a joke he'd heard that day. The diaries were leather-bound, beautifully tooled, with gold clasps; the entries were all written in Be Be's lovely script, with a fountain pen and the gold nibs he had always used to sign Joseph's homework.

There were a few entries that gave Joseph pause. There was the one about himself.

I could hardly keep from laughing. Joseph had his first fight today. He won! Like he will win everything in his life. He defended the honor of his mother. The boy he fought made fun of Angela's Italian accent. Someday my boy will be the President of this country. Maybe the first Italian American in the White House. Nobody will laugh then. Today he fought for his mother's honor. Someday for his party, his heritage, his country. I must live to see this.

Joseph vaguely remembered the fight. A boy had made fun of his mother as she sang along with Mario Lanza, and Joseph had punched him as hard as he could in the face. The boy's laughter had turned to tears. Joseph shook his head and lit a cigarette and turned to another diary. It was from the Vietnam war years and the entry came the day after a massive march on Washington by the peace movement.

Big march in Washington yesterday. Joseph was there. Norman Mailer was arrested. As usual. At least they say what they feel. I have to support this Humphrey guy now no matter what. Who else we got? Nixon? The war is wrong. But what happens if I come out and say that? What happens to jobs here? Federal money goes out the window. I'm losing my Joseph because of this shitty war. What do I know about foreign policy anyway? Foreign policy for me is getting money from Albany and promises from Manhattan. I can't stop the crime on Nostrand Avenue so how can I stop the war in Vietnam? My job is Brooklyn. My people are Brooklyn. My war is in Brooklyn. I have to fight it here.

"Jesus Christ, Dad," Joseph said aloud. "You lost! You never told me any of this."

He poured another Scotch and sat back on the couch, his mind reeling. You never told me how you felt about the goddamn war. You wore a white hat and I painted it black. You never told me any of this stuff, Dad. None of it. These other diaries, these things you wrote. These are the things a father is supposed to tell his son. Why? Were you afraid if I loved you I would have known you as more than the Boss? I didn't want a boss, Dad, I wanted a father. And the father I wanted was there all along, but you were imprisoned by what you had become in other people's eyes.

And what now, Joseph thought. Do I go to these people and make them pay? Do I talk to Johnny Quinn? What about this decision to get involved with your life now that you are dead? Do I become a part of the things I hate? Politics? Machine politics? Talk to me. Make me love you, you bastard. You never had the decency to do it when you were alive. Do it now. No one can embarrass you now. No one can beat you or outpolitick you. Talk to me, for God's sake. Tell me about my mother. About you and Sylvia Stein. Tell me . . .

. . . *what a goddamned town this is. You come here for tests and you could die of the fucking cold! Minnesota has got to be the worst place on the entire planet to die besides Albany. Tests, tests, tests. When you're a kid they send you to school for tests. You get old they send you to the doctor's. No break. I miss my Angela terribly. When I am frightened, I always do. She is more important to me than anything. I want to tell her all about this. But she doesn't look good these days. I would make it worse. Joseph wouldn't understand either. Boy, would Sydney like to know about this one. I know that snake-in-the-grass is behind these silly letters from this Stein broad. Sydney thinks he can get me through my family. He doesn't even know what family is. Poor Ruth. Poor Gloria! I already told these doctors I want no treatments. My hair falls out and I look like Weingarten. Like Phil Silvers! Never! Must call Angela in* A.M. *Miss my boy too. This isn't fair. This is a trick. People with family should live forever! And vote early and often. Ha.*

They killed a dead man, Joseph thought.

They murdered you when you were already dead. You and your stupid, pig-headed, Guinea pride. You killed yourself, let them kill Mom, and then they dug you up and killed you again. You never let Mom know. The letters from Sylvia Stein were meant to hurt *you.* Instead they took away your wife and sent away your son. Why did you go there alone to the clinic? You should have told *us* about it, for Christ sakes. Joseph stood and flung the diary against the wall and then shattered the glass against the file cabinet.

Mom would still be alive, you would still be alive! But no! You had to stay the big shot. Big Boss with the Big Casino. Can't let anybody know. And now it's too fucking late! You had your shot and blew it! I don't care what else you have to say!

He let the convulsive sobs rack his body, and then he walked over and picked up the diary and leafed through it once more. There was a date he was looking for, a date he would never forget.

Angela. Today they have taken you from me with their schemes. I will never rest until I get even. I promise you on the memory of the day I met you, when you were wearing the blue chiffon dress and I asked you to dance. You were the best dancer on the floor and the best wife any man ever had and the best mother God ever gave the gift of a child. I should have told you about those silly letters. But I never thought you would believe them. I was so blind that now I will never see you in this life again. The people responsible for this will wish they were dead instead of you, my love. I should kill them all with my bare hands right now. But no. I will watch them suffer humiliation and pain and embarrassment as they did to you. Let them publicly be made into scandals, mocked, ruined in the name of history. I will live until this happens and then I will join you in heaven, with the help of your prayers.

There was a large ink stain at the bottom of the page, incongruous with the meticulous care that characterized all the other entries. Joseph sat numb, rereading the entry again. His mouth was dry and his fingers trembled as he slowly closed the diary and fastened the snap.

He looked around the room, very silent, composed. He stared at all the files and tape recordings and diaries. There was a startling ringing in his ears, as if he had just heard the deep, menacing voice of his father shouting at him. The ringing would not stop. Joseph Gonzago did not want it to stop.

"You are not yet dead, Dad," he said aloud as he continued to look around the room.

16

Joseph stepped out of the shower towel drying his hair and checked the digital clock next to the bed, which indicated it was 8:45 A.M. Gloria had left a note saying she had to rush to work, was late, had considered waking Joseph up but knew if she did she would never get to work at all. Compliments will get you anywhere, Joseph thought.

Gloria had written that she left the house at 8:15. She must have just missed the phone call from Special Agent Francis X. Cunningham from the State Bureau of Investigation. Joseph had exchanged unpleasant words with the state cop, demanding to know where he had obtained the phone number. Joseph had felt very foolish when Cunningham said in the Brooklyn White Pages. The cop wanted to see Joseph at his office at 10 A.M. Joseph said no at first, but the cop was insistent. Said he had some very important information about his father's death. Finally Joseph agreed to go see him at his office in the World Trade Center at ten sharp.

On the drive to the meeting Joseph put Cunningham together in his mind. Irish, face the color of Bazooka Joe gum, jowly, beer belly, busted veins in his nose, his head the size of a sniper's dream, fifty-two probably, an alumnus of St. John's, a bigot, right-wing, smokes Camels or Chesterfields unfiltered, lives in the burbs with a German shepherd, three kids in parochial school, a fat wife, two cars, a weather vane and an American flag on the roof of the two-story thirty-year-at-seven-and-a-half-percent house, where he kept bowling balls, golf clubs, a gun collection, and a full bar in the finished basement, and where he also played seven-card stud with the guys on Tuesday nights.

"Pleased to meet you, Joseph," said the tall black man dressed in the Cardin suit. He was at least six-four, built for hoops, wearing Gucci loafers and an open-necked shirt with a few hundred dollars worth of gold around his neck. "Francis Xavier Cunningham."

Joseph stared at the man, who was in his early thirties, somewhat dumbfounded. They were in the waiting room of the State Bureau of Investigation on the eighty-third floor of the East Tower. An

American flag and the New York State flag stood on either side of a receptionist's desk. Cunningham extended a hand, which Joseph stared at for one beat on the awkward side of cordiality.

"It doesn't run," Cunningham said, smiling. Joseph realized he was behaving a bit ridiculous. He shook Cunningham's hand.

"Nice to meet you. Sorry."

"Come on, we'll talk in my office."

Joseph followed Cunningham past the reception desk, down a long corridor of doors that led to small cubicles on either side. Cunningham walked with athletic grace, his legs strong and the stride long. Change rattled in his pants pocket as he walked, with Joseph trying to keep pace. They turned into a small, tidy cube with a desk, two file cabinets, two visitors' chairs, and a fair view of the harbor through a window that did not open. Cunningham sat behind the desk and Joseph sat on a plastic chair facing him.

"Thanks for coming," Cunningham said, as he stared even-eyed at Joseph Gonzago. "I'm sorry I was so abrupt with you on the phone, but this case is top priority around here. The feds are starting to get itchy noses and we would sort of like to hand-launder this ourselves. Are you able to discuss your father's murder yet?"

"I think so, yeah. Listen, I'm sorry about the way I gaped at you out there, but I was expecting—"

"Officer Joe Bolton, don't worry. The name throws everybody off. Difference between SBI and FBI is we're all New Yorkers here. None of us look like we're from Oz. Anyway, we have some information I'd like to share with you, but I have to get a promise from you that it doesn't make page one. A deal?"

"Sure." Joseph could not believe he felt so relaxed with a cop. He'd spent the better part of his life learning how to sniff them out, mistrust them, and dislike them.

"Cops in L.A. found a guy, a plumber, dead in some motel room. Stabbed with an ice pick. We have reason to believe he might, and, Joseph, I emphasize *might,* be connected to the shooting. He's an ex-con. Worked on ships sometimes, doing steam fitting, plumbing. He had ties with the Brooklyn piers. We know you and Frank Donato used to be good pals, and he ran the dockers' union before he was busted for stealing seventy-five thou . . .

Joseph cut Cunningham off, the mistrust starting to rise: "Are you insinuating that Frank Donato—"

"Let me finish, please. I'm not insinuating anything. I'm trying to lay the facts out here. I want to nail whoever is responsible for killing your father. I want to nail him to a park bench. I think you can help me do it."

"What did Be Be Gonzago ever do for you?"

"I'll be honest with you. I never met your father. But between me you and the wall he was influential in getting me into this job. I'm from Brooklyn. I applied for this job and realized less-qualified white guys were getting in in front of me. I went to a councilman named Sam Stone. He talked to your dad. Be Be made a call. I got a badge. But even if he wasn't responsible for getting me my badge, that badge says I gotta catch bad guys."

Joseph stared at Cunningham queerly.

"Are you kidding me? Be Be Gonzago never went out of his way for a black guy in his life as far as I remember."

"For this one he did, Joseph. He's no fool. I'm a registered Democrat. Stone delivers votes. But look, fuck all that noise, I'm talking here about a guy they found in L.A. You going to listen or what?"

"I'm listening."

"Well, this guy, as far as we can ascertain, did some leg breaking for shies and graduated to small-time contracts. Bumped off shellfish for loan sharks. Strictly five-and-dime time. Anyway he arrived in L.A. on the first flight out of New York following the shooting. He died quite suddenly when an ice pick hit his heart about an hour after arriving in L.A. We have no weapon, but they're sure it was an ice pick. A car with his fingerprints on it was found in a long-term lot out in JFK and the tires match the skid marks left in the parking lot behind the building where your father was killed. Not exactly much to go on, but who knows."

Joseph was intrigued.

"Guy have a name?"

"Boyle, James. Yellow sheet has more entries than the New York marathon."

"Blank."

"Thought maybe you might have known him. Maybe Donato knew him. He'd be more willing to tell you than me. His paychecks on the Brooklyn docks were signed by a guy named Avakian. You know him?"

"No."

"Will you ask Donato about all this?"

"I'll think about it. Let me ask you a question. What do you think about my father's murder? Theories?"

"We're still going on the wrong-guy theory. They were gunning for the governor and Be Be got in the way."

"Yeah."

"You have any theories?"

"Be Be Gonzago always had a knack for getting in the way."

Cunningham rose and extended his hand toward Joseph. "Thanks for coming over. I appreciate it. I know you don't have much love for the heat, but I hope you're on my side this time around."

"What school did you play for?"

"Ruined my right knee playing for St. John's."

Joseph and Cunningham shook hands.

"Were you any good?"

Cunningham smiled. "I'm better at this. See ya."

"So long."

17

The taxi was caught in stop-and-go traffic. Sydney Weingarten grew angry every time he traveled Ocean Parkway. Once it had been one of the most splendid boulevards in all of New York. The word "parkway" had been coined by the two men who had designed this boulevard. Their names were Frederick Law Olmsted and Calvert Vaux, the same men who had designed Central Park and Prospect Park, and their intention had been to create a wide boulevard with tree-shaded lanes for horses and carriages, bicyclists, and strollers that delivered you from the inner city to the banks of the Atlantic in an atmosphere of bucolic tranquillity.

Now Ocean Parkway took you from the crime of Flatbush to the slums of Coney Island where en route old people could be picked off like grazing buffalo by the savages who had claimed it in the name of affirmative action, he thought. The blight of Ocean Parkway infuriated Sydney Weingarten more than the clogged traffic.

He remembered it in better times. In those days he rode a bicycle along it with Sylvia Stein. She was then the most beautiful girl in all of Brooklyn. She was seventeen that summer, she had been crowned Miss Manhattan Beach, which, oddly enough, is in Brooklyn. Sydney remembered seeing her photograph in the *Brooklyn Eagle* when they ran a group shot of all the contestants. She was easily the most beautiful.

Sydney had gone to Manhattan Beach the day of that contest to see her in person. He was twenty years old and a junior at Brooklyn College. Sydney's father, Sydney, Sr., was Chairman of the Board of Trade in Manhattan Beach, and therefore he was the master of ceremonies. Sydney had begged his father all week to introduce him to this girl Sylvia Stein. Sydney, Sr., had assured his son that he would introduce him to the girl. But he warned him that she was younger than he was and he should be careful with any girl if he intended to enter into politics as Sydney, Sr. insisted.

"Wives get you elected," his father had told him. "Girl friends get you indicted."

Sydney, Jr., swore that he would be honorable. He would do

nothing more than take the girl to the movies, a picnic in Prospect Park, swimming at Manhattan Beach. The father had smiled and told his son he would do what he could.

The day of the contest Sydney Weingarten saw Sylvia Stein in person and his life would never be quite the same. She wore an orange bathing suit and her body was magnificent and tanned. When she was introduced by Sydney, Sr., a great roar went up from the crowd, catcalls and whistling, and it was apparent even before it was announced that Sylvia Stein would be the winner. There might have been a riot had the title gone to anyone else. Sydney, Jr., stood there in the front of the crowd, staring up at Sylvia Stein, who walked with perfect confidence and grace on the stage, and he knew that he, out of all these hundreds of other boys, would have the privilege of a formal introduction after the contest was over. It had filled him with a great sense of power and confidence and worthiness.

The taxi driver had to skid to a halt when traffic opened up as a young black boy dashed across the boulevard kicking a soccer ball, oblivious to traffic. The driver cursed and stomped on the gas as soon as the boy was out of the way.

Afterward, when Sydney Weingarten, Sr., had presented Miss Sylvia Stein with her bouquet of roses and her crown as Miss Manhattan Beach, she had posed and smiled for the photographers from the *News* and *Mirror* and *Eagle.* Sylvia Stein stood up there above Sydney Weingarten, Jr., goodness and excellence oozing from her face and the sun shimmering on the orange bathing suit.

This must be my woman, Sydney now remembered thinking to himself. This must be my wife.

Sydney Weingarten remembered how beautiful Sylvia Stein's eyes were and how perfect her teeth were when she smiled at him at the luncheon buffet following the beauty contest. His father had introduced Sydney, Jr., to Sylvia Stein and the two of them sat at the same table and chatted away. Sylvia was very impressed with sitting with the son of the contest judge, who had ambitions of entering politics as soon as he finished college. Sydney was a perfect gentleman that afternoon, dazzled Sylvia with his knowledge of local politics and world affairs.

Sydney Weingarten knew he was in love with Sylvia Stein when she had remarked to him near the end of the luncheon, "I have never met a more intelligent, mature young man in my life. Will I see you again?"

Sydney had been trying to work up the courage to ask Sylvia for a date, but you didn't just blurt things like that out in those days—especially to a beauty queen who was coveted by most men his age in New York. They made arrangements to go bicycling the next Sunday, and after the bike ride they would have dinner and see a movie.

That summer Sydney Weingarten and Sylvia Stein saw each other almost every single day. Sydney had remained a perfect gentleman even in those moments of summer passion when Sylvia became most vulnerable. Sydney had remembered what his father had said about girl friends getting you into trouble.

Sydney was the absolute envy of his friends and of many others he did not even know because he was Sylvia Stein's boyfriend. Boys all over New York had tacked to their walls the color photograph of Sylvia Stein that had run in the *Sunday News* Coloroto Magazine section. Sydney's wallet, though, contained personal photos of him and Sylvia at Coney Island, at Radio City Music Hall, at the Statue of Liberty. Sydney knew he was not a physically attractive young man, but he carried himself with distinguished grace and pride. When he walked into a room, people noticed him. He had *charisma.*

Other young women began to take a keen interest in this young man who went out with the girl all their boyfriends drooled over. They knew all about his very promising future as a lawyer and a politician. Everyone said so—Sydney Weingarten was a man of destiny.

Then at the end of that great summer Sylvia Stein packed her bags to go away to college in Miami. She had won a scholarship and she had cried when Sydney said good-bye to her at the Port Authority bus terminal. They both promised to write and pledged their undying love and loyalty to one another.

Through the first half of the semester they exchanged letters every other day. Then Sylvia's letters started trailing off to one every week, one a month, and then even less frequently. Sydney was depressed. At a dance at Brooklyn College one night a very pretty young woman named Ruth Soloman approached Sydney Weingarten, who was standing by himself sipping sweet wine. She introduced herself, said she had recognized him and was very impressed by his skill on the debating team. Sydney had been aching for Sylvia, but his loneliness was only compounded by this attractive young woman who was so obviously attracted to him.

Ruth Soloman was nineteen years old and lived alone in an apartment on Nostrand Avenue. After the dance she invited Sydney back to her apartment for coffee and innocent chitchat. Sydney grew very nervous. He did not want word to get back to Sylvia that he was with another girl. But he was, after all, a healthy young man, and he was lonely and in need of female companionship.

Sydney began to slug the wine to ease his tension. Sydney was not much of a drinker, but when he did drink all his inhibitions were drowned. He did go with Ruth Soloman that night to her place. And when he got there she asked him to read some of the term papers she had been working on to see if he could be of any help. But Sydney was not in the mood for term papers and guidance counseling. He made the first advances. Ruth Soloman tried to fight him off, at one point smacking Sydney Weingarten across the face. But he insisted. And finally Ruth Soloman surrendered to the advances of this very popular, promising young man. It was just one of those things, Sydney had tried to explain to his disappointed father later.

Eight months and three weeks after that night Ruth Weingarten gave birth to a daughter called Gloria. It was Ruth's seventh month of marriage to Sydney Weingarten, Jr., law student, man of destiny.

Ruth Weingarten would give Sydney a son named Bernard two years later. Sylvia Stein became a sad memory and Sydney Weingarten became a councilman and would have become the chairman of the Kings County Democratic party in 1963 had it not been for the underhanded tricks of a man named Be Be Gonzago, who snatched victory from Sydney Weingarten's grasp. At first the two men became bitter enemies. But later, as they matured both politically and with age, they came to a compromise. Be Be Gonzago would support Sydney Weingarten, who had since won an assembly seat, in his move for assembly speaker of New York in return for his support from Albany. This accomplished, these two powerful men mended political fences. But neither was very fond of the other.

There had been times over the years when the memory of Sylvia Stein would keep Sydney Weingarten awake nights. The image of her in the orange bathing suit—her skin tight and tanned, her firm young buttocks and her ample breasts and startling eyes and perfect smile—haunted Sydney Weingarten.

But Sydney Weingarten had learned to accept Ruth over the years. This was no blazing, urgent love like the one with Sylvia Stein. Still it was solid and cordial and, most important, *presentable* to the public whose continued support every two years was crucial to his career.

But there were too many days and nights away in Albany, too many public functions, too many false public poses for Ruth Weingarten. She had slept with just this one man in her life and he had become an enigma. A face on a poster. A man without a home. She had married a job. A career. Ruth Weingarten began drinking. She made several public scenes while intoxicated. She had become sloppy and incoherent and once even ranted at Sydney over dinner at a fund raiser. She made late night phone calls to the press.

Then Sydney Weingarten insisted Gloria Weingarten have an abortion. He sent her away to boarding school in Switzerland. Sydney insisted that his daughter would not be forced into marriage the way he had been to Ruth. Especially to the son of Be Be Gonzago. When confronted with the loss of her daughter's loving company and the realization that her life was in the shadow of a man who filled the spotlight, her lights dimmed and the breakdown followed.

Then from out of the past Sylvia Stein showed up at a political function one night in Canarsie. She was with a much older man, a former judge now a widower. The function was a fund raiser for Sydney Weingarten's re-election campaign. Sydney Weingarten was on stage, speaking at the podium, when Sylvia Stein caught his eye. Sydney Weingarten could not speak for several seconds. The passion that had lay dormant for so many years erupted again within him. She was wearing a low-cut orange dress. She had aged, but she was still the most beautiful woman he had ever seen.

Since that night, Sydney Weingarten knew he must finally have her totally. Ruth would have to be placed in a sanitorium and a quiet, discreet divorce could be arranged later.

The taxi finally pulled up in front of Sylvia Stein's house on a quiet tree-lined street near Manhattan Beach. Sydney paid the driver, tipped him two dollars, and stepped out. Sylvia Stein opened the door and leaned on the door frame, filing her nails with an emery board. A cigarette dangled from her lips. The backs of her hands and elbows and knees betrayed her real age. Otherwise she was a voluptuous, handsome woman. Sydney Weingarten did not notice any of time's insults. Sylvia Stein was wearing an orange bathing suit.

There were two men strolling no more than one hundred yards behind Joseph Gonzago and Frank Donato. When Joseph and Frank Donato quickened their pace, so did the two men behind them. If they slowed, the other two men slowed. But always they remained a hundred yards behind.

"How do you put up with that shit?" Joseph asked Frank Donato.

"After fifteen years you get used to it," Donato said. "The Waterfront Commission guys never give up. They already got me nailed, as you know. I'm facing seven years, Joey. The appeals will take up maybe another year and a half. But they got me. What can I say? It was bullshit, but it was also stupid on my part. They hauled more papers and tapes into court than the *Times* prints on a Sunday. A lousy ten grand somewhere along the way is what I took. That's it."

"Why, Frank?" Joseph asked. "Why'd you do it? You had to know they'd get you."

"Part of it was to see if I could get away with it, Joey. To try to prove to those assholes my life was my own. Pride. It was idiotic. I think maybe if they would have just left me alone all my life, I wouldn't have done it. But your pride makes you want to fuck 'em, Joey. I was the asshole. Somebody got pinched on some extortion racket and dropped a dime on me to get state's evidence immunity." But they claim I took seventy-five from the pension fund. That is a fucking lie, Joey. I don't rob my own."

The two men were walking along the Brooklyn Heights Promenade near the Brooklyn Bridge. Below them the dock workers were unloading ships.

"But it's wrong, Frank, man," Joseph said. "Dead fuckin' wrong. You just can't go around using your political clout for your own greed."

"Grow up, Joey, will ya," Donato said. "My fuckin' guys get sixteen G's guaranteed every year, work or no work. You think you get that playing straight pool? Every longshoreman on the Brooklyn waterfront is guaranteed sixteen thou a year whether he picks up a sack of grain or not. That's what I got for my guys. Not just me. I'm a good fuckin' labor boss. I'm no millionaire."

"Be Be got you the job," Joseph said. "You got all those dumb ideas from him. He handed you this job and you ran the docks like he ran the rest of Brooklyn. Dumb. Dumb and wrong, man."

"Be Be did a lot for his people," Donato said.

"Spare me another epitaph," Joseph said.

Donato laughed. Joseph looked over his shoulder and the Waterfront Commission agents were still a hundred yards behind.

Frank Donato paused and leaned over the railing. "My family will be taken care of though. I have a lot of friends. One of the things that really bothers me is that when I go, that mother humper Weingarten will put a guy named Avakian in my job. You ain't seen nothin' till you seen that guy in action. At least I took from the fuckin' ship owners. Weingarten's guys will definitely fleece the rank and file. There already is seventy-five grand gone I never touched. You watch. Campaign contributions. Dinners. Ringin' doorbells for votes."

"How did Be Be get along with Sydney in the last few years?" Joseph asked.

Frank Donato looked down the hundred yards of railing to where the Waterfront Commission agents were standing.

"Like me and them guys down there," Frank Donato said. "Worse. I don't hold it against them guys personal. They got a job, they do it. Their kids eat too. It's the guys who run it I hate. Be Be and Sydney got along like me and the head of the commission. They fuckin' hated each other. Everyone knows that."

"Why?"

"Why," Donato said. "Because Weingarten resented Be Be's power. Why else? Be Be marooned Sydney in Albany. He couldn't move without Be Be's support. And he has ambition like you can't believe."

"Who do you think killed my father, Frank?"

Frank Donato did not answer right away. He looked out at the harbor as a tug led a long dirty barge out to sea. From below came the sounds of automobiles rushing along the Brooklyn-Queens Expressway toward the Brooklyn Bridge. The sound of a pile driver echoed in the distance.

"Joey," Frank Donato said. "You been gone a long time. Things change. Be Be was getting old. They got special prosecutors now for politicians. The only deals you can make now are with Washington, because if you own the attorney general nobody is gonna nail you."

"That didn't help Nixon," Joseph said.

"Nothing could help Nixon," Frank Donato said. "You kidding me. He left himself wide open. He had tapes and didn't burn them. You think if I got my hands on the tapes that hung me they would've lasted five minutes? Not on your life."

"So who do you think killed my father?"

"The guy they said tried to kill the governor, only I don't think they were trying to kill the governor."

"You think they were trying to kill Be Be?"

"From eight feet away who could miss?"

"But why?" Joseph asked. "Why'd they wanna kill Be Be?"

"The Democratic gubernatorial nomination could be decided in Brooklyn, Joey. Brooklyn is New York's biggest democratic district. In a close race, whoever takes Brooklyn gets the nomination."

"You don't think Wolfington—"

"Maybe not him," Frank Donato said. "If he knew about it, I don't think he would have put himself that close to a bullet. I mean who would? But maybe someone who could benefit from Wolfington's re-election."

"You mean somebody from Brooklyn?" Joseph asked.

"Maybe."

"Like Weingarten?"

"You said it," Frank Donato said. "Not me."

"Who was Be Be backing in the primary?"

"He told me he was going for Kelly," Frank Donato said. "Be Be changed his mind sometimes. But he hated Wolfington. That I know."

"And what about Weingarten?"

"He was backing Wolfington," Frank Donato said. "Said he was a good Democrat. That Kelly's campaign was dividing the party. That he was too liberal. But all that's bullshit. Weingarten wants a supreme court seat so bad he already looks like a judge. But first he'll go for Be Be's seat so he can deliver Brooklyn. He'll run unopposed."

"Why unopposed?"

"Who else is there? It's an interparty election. Just Brooklyn Dems."

"Somebody gotta oppose him, Frank."

"Don't look at me, Joey. I'm a convicted felon, remember."

"But you're still president of the union."

"I got one year left. I wanna see my kids a lot. Nobody would vote for me after this anyway."

"But you still got friends, clout, power."

"There's nobody to throw it behind, Joey."

"What if there was somebody, who knew where all the bodies were buried, I mean knew every deal, had it on tape, on paper, on file? What then?"

"Then you might be able to beat him," Donato said. "It would be hard. But blackmail still works pretty good. It would still be tough though, cause Weingarten knows a few closets with skeletons too."

"Would he know as many as Be Be might have?"

"Nah," Frank said. "Be Be knew where they all were."

"When will the interparty vote be?" Joseph asked.

"Two weeks or so," Frank said. "They have to let the corpse get cold. Have a memorial dinner in Albany where a lot of the brokering will take place. You assemble people. The unofficial vote will take place at Be Be's dinner I'd say."

"If I found a candidate, would you back him?"

"Does a bear shit in the zoo?"

Joseph laughed and shook Frank's hand.

"Who are you talking about anyway, Joey?" Frank asked.

"Just somebody, Frank," Joseph said. "I'm not sure he can be convinced to do it. I'll have to talk it over with him."

"I got maybe two hundred fifty guys who'll knock on doors or kneecaps if you need 'em," Frank said.

"I'll let you know," Joseph said, and walked away from Frank Donato, who stood looking out over the harbor.

18

Gloria boarded the Brooklyn-bound D train at Rockefeller Center, her mind filled with private anxiety. She had left work early after speaking with her mother on the phone. Ruth Weingarten had called and she was intoxicated and rambled on about Sydney and brother Bernie. She made little sense. She had told Gloria that Sydney was planning to murder her, and that he was capable of it because he had killed before. She said she had heard him talking about it with friends when they did not know she was listening. Ruth said she also knew Sydney had a mistress because she could smell the perfume on his clothes on those rare nights when he did come home. A very expensive perfume, Ruth said.

Gloria knew this was the alcohol and the Valium speaking. Sydney Weingarten might have his shortcomings as a husband and a father, and maybe even as a public servant, but he was still a moral man. He might have a peculiar vision of right and wrong, mostly old-fashioned and iron-fisted, but Sydney Weingarten always did what he thought was right and proper.

Gloria had even learned to forgive Sydney Weingarten for the unforgivable. It had taken almost fifteen years, but she had learned to absolve him for pressuring her into that operation so long ago, for driving an ax through her love with Joseph. As she got older she understood. Sydney had acted out of love for her. Misguided as that love might have been, it was still love. He thought he was doing the thing that would save his daughter from shame and disgrace. He had been wrong but not evil.

She understood this years later when her mother had confessed to her that Gloria was conceived out of wedlock, that Sydney had married Ruth because it was the proper thing to do. He had tried to love this woman that circumstance had made his wife. Gloria respected that. And she knew that her father had tried to save his daughter from the same fate.

Ruth's raving on the phone had upset Gloria. Ruth was now talking of murder and conspiracies. Before it had just been the "other woman." Even that was absurd. Sydney Weingarten was incapable of risking his true love—his career—for the comforts of a woman on the side. Gloria was certain of this. Murder was something so completely ridiculous that Gloria worried that Ruth might be on the verge of something drastic. Her mother did have a severe drinking problem. She was also a manic-depressive. She took too many tranquilizers. She was emotionally unstable.

Ruth Weingarten really should have married a banker or a professor, a man who left for work in the morning with a good-bye kiss and returned with the evening paper at dinnertime, had a cocktail, and went to bed. Instead she had married a politician, a man in the public eye, and Ruth was supposed to be a prop at his side during campaigns and political soirees. Ruth had cracked under the pressure of lonely nights while Sydney was away in Albany. She could not take the constant public scrutiny, reading about her husband, and sometimes even herself and her children, in newspaper stories. She was a shy, private woman living in a glass house.

Gloria was also aware that when Sydney sent her away to boarding school after the operation, Ruth had lost something crucial. Gloria knew that Ruth lived vicariously through her daughter, that she wanted Gloria to live the life she had been denied. She encouraged Gloria to be a free spirit, to choose what she wanted in life instead of having those choices thrust upon her.

The subway train was stuffy and getting crowded as it moved toward Brooklyn. As it began to cross the Manhattan Bridge, Gloria's mind filled with early images of her mother and herself: her mother putting her hair in banana curls; dressing her in red ribbons and chiffon dresses and patent-leather shoes; learning to peel potatoes; walks by the Canarsie Bay; listening to her mother hum the "Blue Danube" as she ironed her father's shirts.

Gloria smiled. Silly, early, yet indelible memories, she thought.

Then there was the memory of her mother on that night when she first explained womanhood to Gloria. She explained why her body was changing and expanding and told her that womanhood was the greatest gift she would ever have. She taught Gloria to treasure this gift and made her promise never to squander it.

Funny, Gloria thought as the train entered the dark tunnel and roared into DeKalb Avenue, how those simple lessons still went with her. Almost everything she did in life she had learned from her mother. She might not always be conscious of it, but Ruth Weingarten was always with her. When she shopped, she always picked fruit the way she had watched her mother choose it. When she cooked, she used Ruth's recipes. When she bought clothing, she always checked the zippers and inner seams carefully as Ruth had taught her. When she worked, she did it with the same zeal with which her mother used to do housework. When she made love, she took those things mother had told her about womanhood with her to bed.

Ruth Weingarten was everything to Gloria Weingarten. And now her mother was losing her mind and Gloria needed to be with her to hold her and hug her and love her the way her mother had always done for her.

At Church Avenue Gloria stepped off the D train and walked to her mother's house on a tree-shaded street in Flatbush.

"Who was it, Ruth?" Sydney Weingarten asked in a very soft, patronizing voice. He was sitting at the dining room table across from Ruth Weingarten, who sat bleary-eyed with a glass of rye and soda jammed with ice before her. "You made two phone calls today, Ruth darling. One was to our flower, Gloria. But Bernie said you made another and you hung up the phone quite abruptly when he came into the room. Who was it, darling?"

"I think it was to the slob at *The Village Voice,"* Bernie said as he sat at the end of the table sipping coffee. "She likes calling him. That Gotbaum animal."

Sydney turned to Bernie and put his fingers to his lips, ordering him to be quiet. No one had noticed that Gloria had come into the house and was standing in the living room, listening to the conversation.

"Please try to remember, darling," Sydney said. "Was it Mr. Gotbaum you called?"

"Well, it was a man's voice," Ruth said. "He had a very nice voice. I don't know if it was a village voice."

Ruth laughed dryly and then dissolved into a phlegmy fit of coughing. Sydney was growing impatient. "Ruth, let me try to explain something to you. You are not a well woman. You have problems. The doctor wants to put you into an institution. I've resisted that, darling, because you are my wife and the mother of my children. I don't want to see you institutionalized. But I can't have you making phone calls to newspaper reporters and blabbering away about things you know nothing about."

"What does she know about anymore, Dad?" Bernie said. "She

knows three numbers. Gloria's, Gotbaum's, and the liquor store. She needs help. I think we should have her committed."

Ruth turned to Bernie and her eyes narrowed. "I am committed, Bernard, son of mine. I am committed to life in this house. I am never allowed out without a chaperon. I am told whom I may and may not speak to. There are locks on the telephones, but I found the keys. I am committed to having to live this life. So don't threaten me with an institution. What the hell do you call this?"

Ruth was growing angry and her eyes were flashing and her complexion was reddening. Sydney put his hand on top of hers to try to soothe her. She grasped his hand and lifted it to her face as if to kiss it. Instead she smelled it.

"She uses lovely perfume, Sydney," Ruth said as she stared him in the eye. "More expensive than anything you ever bought me."

Sydney withdrew his hand, furious, but he contained the outburst he wanted to unleash.

"Ruth, please let me try to explain something to you. I know your life has been a difficult one. Being married to a man in public service is never easy. It has shattered the dreams of the best of women. And once you were a strong woman. I understand those strains. But I must implore you to stop this needless, selfish blabbering to the press about our personal lives. There is a very crucial campaign coming up. I must face the voters every two years. If I am re-elected this time out, I stand a very good chance of getting a judgeship. This would mean I would not have to be away so often. We could spend more time together."

"You mean you'll have more time to spend with your fancy woman, Sydney," Ruth said. "I know you intend to kill me. I told the man on the phone you intended to kill me, Sydney."

Sydney slammed his fist on the tabletop, splashing Bernie's coffee all over the tablecloth. Ruth grasped her teetering glass and took a deep drink.

"I am reaching the end of my rope with you, Ruth," Sydney shouted.

"Hang yourself with it, Sydney," Ruth said.

"She's mad, Dad. Nuts. Dangerously nuts. I think—"

Bernie was cut off by Gloria, who stepped into the dining room.

"Hello, Mother," Gloria said. Ruth looked up at Gloria and smiled. Tears welled in her eyes as she got up from the table and moved swiftly across the floor to her daughter and threw her arms around her.

"Gloria, Gloria, I know you won't let them do it," Ruth said, and buried her head against Gloria's shoulder. Gloria hugged her mother as she stared at her father and brother sitting at the table. Bernie looked uneasy as Gloria stared at him, bitterness in her eyes.

"Hello, flower," Sydney said.

"Poison ivy," Bernie said.

"I'll ignore that silly remark, Bernie," Gloria said. "But I will not ignore your remarks about our mother."

"He didn't mean anything by it, flower," Sydney said. "Bernie is just worried about your mother, as I am. She's sicker than you know."

"Do you want her to talk to reporters in her state about our family?" Bernie asked. "Dad is up for re-election. We can't have her talking to this reporter, an avowed socialist at that, about what goes on behind these doors."

"Has it ever occurred to you that the solution might be to change what goes on behind these doors?" Gloria asked, steel in her voice as her mother clung to her. "Perhaps if Mother was treated as the woman of this house, a woman with dignity and intelligence and purpose, there would be nothing to say to anyone that couldn't *help* both of you in your campaigns."

"Aren't we exaggerating just a little, flower?" Sydney asked with a gentle smile. "Your mother gets everything she wants."

"When was the last time either of you told her you loved her? When was the last time you took her out, Father, just to a movie or a play or a walk by the sea? Without the TV cameras and the rubber chicken, and speeches and glad-handing with men you despise but who give money to your campaigns? When was the last time you took her on a vacation or took her shopping or swept her off her feet on a dance floor? Be honest, Father."

Sydney listened and then answered, annoyance creeping into his voice.

"Ruth and I did all those things in our halcyon days, Gloria. We're both a bit old for courting and costume parties. I'm a very busy man. I have responsibilities."

"What about your responsibilities to *her*, Father? What about Mother? She's a goddamned constituent too, you know. She's a registered Democrat. She lives in your district under your roof and she wears a lump of gold on her finger that says she's your wife. Come on, Father, be fair."

"Give it a break, will ya, Gloria," Bernie said. "Who died and made you Dear Abby? You should talk."

Gloria led Ruth to an arm chair and sat her down. Ruth lay her head on the back of the chair and slowly rotated it, trying her best to control herself. Gloria walked directly to Bernie, her eyes flashing.

"What is that supposed to mean, counselor?"

"Christ, Gloria, you come in here giving Dad a Miss Lonelyhearts routine when your life isn't exactly what I'd call wholesome."

"Bernie," Sydney snapped. "Leave it out. Stop all this bickering."

"I wonder if Gloria would like Mother to give the press the scoop about her new—or should I say renewed—romance," Bernie said, smiling and sipping his coffee.

"You foul-minded son of a bitch," Gloria said with venom. "What I do in my private life is of no concern to you. At least I don't chase little groupies who are obviously only after your petty power from your father's notoriety. No, sir. I choose my men because they mean something to me. You are pathetic, Bernie, and most times I am embarrassed even to admit you are my brother. You're a lousy brother, a wicked son, and as a lawyer you are a laughingstock and an ambulance chaser. My advice to you is to keep your mouth shut unless you are pushing food into it."

Sydney Weingarten stood up as Bernie made a move toward Gloria, who defiantly stood her ground. He grasped Bernie's arm and looked from his daughter to his son.

"I won't have this. You are brother and sister, joined by my blood."

"My blood, too, Sydney," Ruth said. "I still have a little left in case you have forgotten."

"I'm sorry about this, Mother," Gloria said.

"Don't be," Ruth said, smiling. "It feels like all the windows are open, letting out years of stale air."

"Gloria, I had intended to bring this up with you alone, but since we are making this a round-table family discussion, I will say it now. Bernie might have been a bit indiscreet in the way he addressed you, but I must say I have to agree with him. This business of you and Joseph Gonzago is sheer madness."

Gloria stared into Sydney's eyes, shock registering in her face.

"I must be hearing things," Gloria said. "Am I about to get one of your famous lectures on morality, Father? Because if I am, I'd like first to remind you that I am no longer the frightened little girl you manipulated once—"

"No, you're an old whore now where you used to be jailbait," Bernie said. Sydney spun and smacked Bernie across the face. Bernie stood in astonishment, his face the color of a Chinese apple, his eyes bulging from their sockets.

"Never, never again speak to your sister in that manner. Do you understand me? No one in the Weingarten family will ever be addressed in such a manner while I have a breath left in me. Do you understand me?"

Bernie stood numb, speechless, staring at his father in bewilderment. He grabbed a jacket from the back of a chair and stormed from the room and seconds later the sound of the slamming front door echoed through the house. Sydney stood trembling, watching him go.

"I'm sorry, Father," Gloria said.

"For a moment there I thought I saw the Sydney Weingarten I was once proud to be married to," Ruth said.

"Mom, please."

Sydney placed his hands on Gloria's shoulders and looked lovingly into her eyes and tried to smile, but it seemed forced. Gloria returned his gaze, but as she did an aroma emanated that was flowery and very strong from her father. It was the scent of a very expensive woman's perfume, and as she smelled it, she looked at her father with concern and incredulity.

"Gloria, my flower, please forgive Bernie," Sydney said. "He's still very young, and he's very nervous about my campaign and perhaps not yet emotionally equipped for his job. But he'll learn. He has a fine legal mind, he is a good speaker. Perhaps he is lacking in compassion what he makes up for in effort."

"I really don't care what he says to or about me, Father," Gloria said. "But I won't tolerate him speaking to Mother as if she were some kind of frozen vegetable."

"Make me into a potato and I'll live underground where they want me," Ruth said, as she walked back to the table and picked up her drink and drank from it.

"Mom, enough, please," Gloria said.

"I'm going to bed," Ruth said.

"I'll be up in a minute to say good night."

Ruth carried her drink with her as she climbed the stairs to the second landing, and went past the telephone with the lock on the rotary dial, which stood on a table in the hallway, into her bedroom, and shut the door.

Gloria watched her go, and when Ruth closed the door, she turned back to her father, who still had his hands on her shoulders. Sydney was smiling now, his eyes almost twinkling.

"An awful lot of the things you said tonight were true," Sydney said. "Perhaps as a couple grows older they start taking one another for granted and slowly grow apart. I'm not saying I'm not partly to blame for your mother's condition. But she makes little effort on her part either, Gloria. So I'll tell you what, when this campaign is over, I will take your mom away, just the two of us, to a place where she can be treated perhaps as an outpatient, somewhere in the sun, where we can have dinners by the sea, and maybe I can even sweep her off her feet on a dance floor, if anyone still knows how to play real music anymore. I'll shower her with flowers and chocolates and tell her I love her."

Gloria wanted desperately to smile, but the scent of the perfume coming from her father hung like a dark lie between his words and the truth. Gloria said nothing but kept staring at Sydney Weingarten, emotionless.

"If I do that, if I do everything in my power to cure and save your mother, will you do something for me?"

Gloria knew what was coming and girded herself for the request.

"What's that, Father?"

"Will you end this nonsensical interlude with Joseph Gonzago?" He looked for surrender in Gloria's eyes, but instead saw angry determination.

"Let me ask you a very important question, Father?" Sydney nodded. "Just what the hell makes you think I am having this so-called interlude with Joseph Gonzago?"

Sydney withdrew his hands from Gloria's shoulders and tried to gather the words that would constitute a viable answer.

"Well by now it's common knowledge that . . ." He couldn't continue because he knew it would mean admitting something ugly.

"Common knowledge, Father? I find that hard to believe. I haven't seen any items in the gossip pages. I haven't heard this on the rumor circuit. What makes you think I am seeing Joseph Gonzago, Father? Please tell me."

"It was brought to my attention, leave it at that."

"By whom? One of your spies? Did you have someone watching and following me? Or were they watching and following Joseph? That's the only way you could know, Father. Because yes, I have seen Joseph. But we have not been in public together even once. He came to my house once and left. I went to his house once. We might as well get all this out in the open. I'll spare you the intimate details because I don't think they are anyone's business but mine and Joseph's. But no, Father, I do not intend to stop seeing him. I am a grown woman. I make my own decisions. And I do not need your permission or consent or your secret agents trailing me, thank you."

"Gloria, it wasn't like that. I only worry about you. Joseph is not a very stable young man. Look at his past. Working with militant groups. Denouncing his country. Criticizing his own father in print . . ."

"Oh, I'm sure that really upset you, Father, seeing as how you and Be Be were such kissing cousins and all that."

"Gloria, stop this right now. I must insist you put an end to this dangerous affair. It could be damaging to me and your brother to have you associated with him."

"The answer is no, Father. I love and respect you, but I must ask you to butt out of my personal life."

Sydney's eyes went wide with ire. "I am a very resourceful man, young lady. I do not want you to suffer any consequences."

"Will you please stop and listen to how ridiculous you sound?" Gloria said with mock laughter. "What are you going to do? Pass a law? Call an emergency session of the legislature? Please, Father, stop all this. Sometimes I wonder whether I know you at all. I mean, you say you'll do everything in your power to help Mother, to show her you truly love her. But there has to be a proviso attached. It's as if you're brokering with some political enemy. You'll love Mother if I stop loving Joseph. How ridiculous can you be? This isn't a floor debate or a committee hearing. We're talking about people's lives and emotions here. Filibusters and amendments and back-room deals don't work when you're talking about two people loving each other. There is no chairman of the Romance Committee, Father. So please, leave the brokering for politics and let me live my life. And if you can find the time and conscience, let Mother have a life too."

Sydney Weingarten looked Gloria over from head to toe in disgust, and when his eyes met hers he held the stare.

"I asked you nicely, Gloria," Sydney Weingarten said. "Now I am telling you, I want an end put to this Joseph Gonzago affair."

Sydney Weingarten turned and grabbed his briefcase and his suit jacket from a chair and began walking out of the room. Gloria was bristling as Sydney walked toward the front door.

"I like your new after-shave, Father," she said, and turned and began walking up the stairs. Sydney Weingarten paused by the door, the words hitting him like poison darts. He turned with his eyes blazing, but Gloria was gone up the stairs to her mother's room. He opened the door and gently closed it behind him.

19

Joseph Gonzago ate lunch at a restaurant called Charlie's on Flatbush Avenue near Grand Army Plaza. He mopped up the last of his chicken diavolo with a large hunk of crusty French bread and watched the traffic limp along Flatbush Avenue from his window table. The Willamsburg Bank Building was in clear view and the large clock at the top showed it was nearing four P.M. His appointment with Brooklyn district attorney Dermot Donnelly was at four thirty.

Joseph was curious about Donnelly. Be Be had him listed as an enemy in the Water Board files, but as far as Joseph could recall Donnelly owed his entire career to Be Be. It was Be Be who had taken him into the club when Donnelly was a young fireball spouting a lot of reform rhetoric. Be Be understood from the beginning that Donnelly had a certain appeal—he was good with the media—but thought he was a little limited in his scope.

So Be Be sat young Dermot Donnelly down and talked him into accepting a position as a traffic court judge. Be Be explained to Dermot Donnelly that if he stayed there a year, there would be a civil court judgeship coming up. But he had to stop hammering away at the machine as the reason for the rise in crime. Donnelly thought it over, accepted Be Be's offer, and took the traffic court position. As Be Be had promised, Donnelly wound up on the civil bench a year later.

After three years in the courts Be Be offered him a chance at one of the most important positions in the Brooklyn machine—Brooklyn DA. Donnelly told Be Be he really had bigger plans. He wanted to run for Congress, maybe even the U.S. Senate. Be Be told him that his chances of ever getting elected to a congressional seat or the Senate were next to nil. He explained what a truly powerful position Brooklyn DA was, and Donnelly finally accepted Be Be's backing.

After two years as district attorney, Donnelly went after a congressional seat anyway. He did not have to give up his DA position to do so. He was furious with Be Be for not throwing full support behind him. Be Be was equally furious that Donnelly had run against his wishes. This led to a cooling in their relationship. Donnelly was trounced at the polls and he went back to the DA's office, smarting and embarrassed.

After Donnelly lost his race for Congress, he did settle into the district attorney's office. He realized his future was in law enforcement. But still he had national designs in his head. Attorney general of the United States of America had the kind of ring Donnelly liked. But that was an awfully big ambition. Donnelly knew that even to reach the status of consideration for such a job he had to make headlines. Something he knew how to do pretty well. He would also have to ride the coattails of some potential presidential candidate. That candidate would have to come from his home state. When Donnelly looked around, there was only one man with presidential stature in New York State, and that was Henry Wolfington. Donnelly knew that to fall in with Wolfington would cause a deeper rift between Be Be and himself. This frightened him, but his personal ambitions were great enough to give him the courage to do it.

In Brooklyn there was one man law enforcement had been trying to put away for over fifteen years. If Donnelly succeeded where others had failed, the political mileage would be tremendous. The people would look at Dermot Donnelly as the man with enough courage to buck the machine in the name of law and order. With this kind of publicity, Wolfington would offer him his backing for the job of state attorney general. And if Wolfington made it to Washington, he could take Attorney General Donnelly with him.

Dermot Donnelly knew the man he must indict and convict if his career was ever to go national was Frank Donato, president of the dock workers' union. Frank Donato was Be Be Gonzago's godson. Be Be Gonzago would not be pleased with Dermot Donnelly's plans to jail Donato, who was not only a personal protégé, but a political ally as well.

With the help of wiretaps and informants, Donnelly was successful in getting Frank Donato indicted, convicted, and sentenced. The trial lasted weeks, with Donnelly's name in the news every day as the flinty prosecutor who turned around and indicted a favorite son of the very machine that gave him his start.

After the Donato conviction, and as he began to hand down major indictments of nursing-home operators and other labor leaders, Dermot Donnelly approached Henry Wolfington, asking him if he'd like his support. Wolfington was more than willing to accept. Donnelly asked Wolfington if there was a place in Wolfington's future for him, and Wolfington said there was. Wolfington agreed to run on the same slate as Donnelly for the attorney general's office in the upcoming primary.

Donnelly was someone Joseph really wanted to talk to. He finished up his brandy and coffee and paid the check. He drove the Plymouth down Flatbush Avenue, and as he passed the Brooklyn Academy of Music, he saw a large billboard advertising a production of *Hamlet*, which would open the night after next. Joseph had always loved that play. Among other things it was a pretty good murder mystery. He would remember to pick up some tickets and take someone very special to see it.

The Brooklyn district attorney's office was located on the fourth floor of the Brooklyn Municipal Building.

Joseph bought a *New York Post* from the blind news dealer in the lobby. The headline was seventy-point pica: KELLY CLOSES GAP IN NEW POLL. In thirty-point pica underneath: WOLFINGTON CAMP DISPUTES RESULT. Joseph rode the elevator to the fourth floor as he started to read the headline story on the new election poll. The story said that Kelly had pulled within five percentage points of Governor Wolfington in the primary race. The election was three weeks away. Wolfington's camp disputed the poll, saying it was taken in a climate of political hysteria over the attempt on the governor's life. Deeper into the story both sides said that Brooklyn, which still counted for ten percent of the statewide vote, could very well sway the election one way or the other. But since Brooklyn was temporarily left leaderless, it was anybody's guess which way the entrenched machine might swing. Joseph knew Donnelly needed Wolfington to win in order to get the state attorney general's seat, and he was curious to see just how heavily the news of this latest poll weighed with Dermot Donnelly.

The room was large with wood burnished walls, and the solid oak desk Dermot Donnelly sat behind was at least ten feet long. On the walls hung portraits of former district attorneys, and an American flag and the flag of Brooklyn stood together between two large bay windows overlooking Brooklyn Borough Hall. Dermot Donnelly was talking on the telephone when Joseph Gonzago walked in and sat down in the chair in front of the desk. Donnelly looped the coiled telephone cord through his fingers nervously.

". . . I don't care if it's pot roast or boiled ham, Joan. Whatever you want. Whatever's easiest for you. I don't even feel like talking about food now. I was on the stump this morning and ate two Nathan's hot dogs, a knish, pizza, a dill pickle on Essex Street, a pretzel. Ask the kids what they want . . ."

Donnelly popped a Tums into his mouth and rolled his eyes toward the ceiling. "Chicken's fine, Joan, sure. Any goddamned thing at all."

Finally Donnelly cradled the phone, looked at Joseph, and ate another Tums.

Dermot Donnelly was fifty-two years old, and his hair was silver with a bright pink scalp peeking through it. He stood from his swivel chair with great effort, walked around the desk to where Joseph was sitting, and leaned his rump against the edge of the great desk. He reached out his hand and Joseph shook it, and then Donnelly folded his arms and rested them on his middle-aged paunch. He cocked his eyes in concern and beamed down at Joseph.

"How're you feeling, Joseph?" Dermot Donnelly's tone was one of understanding and quiet reverence, like a priest's.

"Alone," Joseph said.

Dermot Donnelly nodded his head in devout sadness.

"I know how you must feel," Dermot Donnelly said. "If there's anything I can do . . ."

"There is," Joseph said. "Maybe you can explain to me why my father is dead."

Joseph's voice was as soft as Donnelly's. He wanted to play this straight. Donnelly looked perplexed as to how to answer.

"Well, Joseph, we're all shocked. These things . . . I mean, Lord, how do I answer this? Last year there were two thousand murders in this city. I can show you videotapes of kids, no more than twelve and thirteen, confessing to these brutal murders. Most of them don't even know why they do it, and they're the only ones who could know. Obviously, in Be Be's case there was motivation. Someone was trying to kill the governor and missed. Be Be was a victim of circumstance. He was in the wrong place at the wrong time. I wish I could give you a better answer. But murder is something that rarely makes any sense. Just a nut with a gun is my guess."

"What do you think of the new Kelly poll?" Joseph asked, shifting gears purposefully to try to break Donnelly out of his confession-booth tone.

Donnelly was momentarily stunned. He unfolded his arms, walked back around his desk, sat in his swivel chair, leaned back, and pushed away a copy of the *Post* on his desktop.

"You mean this? Well, it'll make it interesting anyway. But right now I'm more interested in how you're feeling and doing than the damned primary. Win or lose, life goes on anyway."

"They didn't shoot the governor though, they killed my father," Joseph said. Donnelly didn't like the transitions.

"They? You're talking in the plural, Joseph. As far as anyone knows so far, we are dealing with a lone gunman, still at large. Ever since Jack Kennedy the whole country talks in the plural, as if automatically there's a conspiracy if a politician is the victim of a crime. Politicians can be the victims of lone nuts. Look at Reagan. One guy, one gun, one disturbed mind. Besides, if it was a conspiracy, why would the conspirators hire an amateur who couldn't hit his target at eight feet."

"Maybe he did."

Dermot Donnelly sat up straight in his chair, unfolded his arms.

"You mean you think they were aiming for your father?"

"Now you're using the plural, Mr. Donnelly," Joseph said.

Donnelly flicked a weak smile.

"Well, I thought you were speaking hypothetically, Joseph."

"All right," Joseph said. "Let's talk hypothetically for a moment. You're a prosecutor. Some say a very tough one. You have to look at all the angles, all the possibilities. Let's say, maybe, someone had a lot to gain from killing a guy like Be Be because he still had a lot of clout in Brooklyn. Maybe not as much as he used to, but enough to make the difference in a very important election. Suppose, for example, as the story in the *Post* says today, that Brooklyn on its own might determine the outcome of a Kelly-Wolfington election. And suppose a guy like Wolfington had aspirations for the White House and desperately needed to get re-elected in order to have a base of power when he wanted to run for president two years from now. Only problem is that Wolfington is in a very close election and could even lose his governorship, never mind ever getting elected to the White House. And so he needed a man like Be Be who just might have enough clout left to deliver Brooklyn. Only problem here is that Be Be liked the other candidate, was going to back Kelly. But Be Be's decision is not popular with some other prominent Brooklyn politicians who stand to get good patronage jobs from Wolfington if he's re-elected, or better still great patronage jobs if he ever makes it to the White House. I mean this is not unrealistic. Jimmy Carter brought in all his Georgia friends. Ronald Reagan took California east with him. Why wouldn't Wolfington take New Yorkers with him, especially ones who stood by him when the going got rough? Now these people who stand someday to have direct access to the president of the United States, with all the power that goes with it, wouldn't they be just a little bit upset with Be Be Gonzago, who was going to try to put a damper on these grand plans? Wouldn't something like that be motive enough for murder? And wouldn't the best way to take suspicion away from you be to put your candidate in the midst of the danger, to make it look like he was the target and a man like Be Be an innocent victim? This is just hypothetically speaking, of course."

Dermot Donnelly's lips were chalky white from the Tums. He kept his hands on his lap, out of Joseph's line of sight.

"Hypothetically speaking?" Dermot Donnelly said. "Hypothetically speaking, I think that is the most paranoid concoction I've ever heard in my life. I don't think, from my experience behind this desk, that motive is even remotely credible."

"But you just said before that you could show me films of kids who don't even know why they kill. People have certainly killed for less than the White House and power."

"If you want you can find a conspiracy in a game of solitaire," Donnelly said.

"Enough people have been known to cheat at that too."

Donnelly stood up again, the politician in him swelling and overwhelming the man who lived beneath that veneer.

"Joseph," he said. "You know what I think? I'm no doctor, but I think you need a good rest. Go to Europe. Or South America. Cuba or China. Get away from the states awhile. Once you see some of those governments, you'll come to appreciate this one a little more. We don't go around shooting our way into the White House here, Joseph."

"Enough people have been shot out of it, Mr. Donnelly," Joseph said as he stood up. "But maybe it is a good idea to get away awhile."

Joseph held out his hand to shake Dermot Donnelly's. The Brooklyn district attorney's hand was damp. Joseph held his hand about ten seconds longer than Dermot Donnelly had expected he would, and stared into the red face, into the alarmed blue eyes. There were scribbles of anxiety there—perhaps from the frustration of a tough campaign. It wasn't panic, more like the eyes of a man with chronic insomnia.

"But I have some things to take care of in this great democracy first," Joseph said softly.

"Leave it to the State Bureau of Investigation," Donnelly said. "They know what they're doing."

"Yeah," Joseph said. "The SBI. Just who do they answer to, Mr. Donnelly?"

"Well, to the state attorney general, of course."

Joseph smiled.

"That's what I thought," Joseph said as he made for the door. "Good luck in your campaign." Joseph stepped out the door. Donnelly watched the door close. Then he sat back down at his desk, ate another Tums, and picked up his telephone.

Business was slow at the Straw Hat, so Lou Moran came from behind the bar to sit with Joseph, Johnny Quinn, and a middle-aged man named Jack Coohill. Coohill was the quintessential political flack. He'd worked for so many politicians over the years as a press agent that his normal speech sounded like a press release.

Jack Coohill also ran a poster business. He plastered posters anywhere he could find a blank wall in the city. He literally knew every single politician in the City of New York, and almost all of them statewide. Every one of them had at one time or another employed the services of Jack Coohill. When you hired Coohill, you got a package—the poster distribution, the sound trucks, and the best press releases in town. He had been a reporter once for the now-defunct *Daily Mirror,* and so he knew most of the reporters around town. He knew their watering holes—the Lion's Head in the Village, Costello's up near the *Daily News,* Runyon's in midtown, and for the few who could afford it Elaine's on the Upper East Side.

Johnny Quinn had brought Jack Coohill around to meet Joseph because Coohill had long been a good friend of Be Be's. Be Be had literally given him permission to work Brooklyn. The money he made in Brooklyn usually came out of the general funds of the Brooklyn Regular Democratic party.

The four men had been drinking a good three hours together. Jack Coohill could drink bourbon all night with no visible effect, and he was into his eighth Wild Turkey on the rocks when the subject of Sydney Weingarten finally came up.

"Sydney Weingarten," Jack Coohill said, his head cocked as if reading from the *Almanac of American Politics.* "Fifty-two years old, speaker of the New York state assembly for the past eight years. Climbed the ranks of the Brooklyn machine first as coffee boy, later as city councilman, then ran unsuccessfully for Congress in Canarsie before finding his natural home in the state assembly. Voting record is schizophrenic. Ranging from ultra-right to ultra-left. Favors capital punishment and abortion. Opposes casino gambling, but backed both the state lottery and Off Track Betting. Carries substantial weight in Albany. Ambitious. Looking to get a seat on the supreme court. Son Bernie, city councilman, notorious nincompoop. Sydney has in recent years broadened his base of political support to include blacks and Hispanics, which is hard to understand on the one hand because his voting record will tell you he has opposed almost every single piece of affirmative-action legislation. But makes sense on the other hand since the black and Hispanic leaders he has allied himself with are notorious poverticians such as Julio Garcia from the South Bronx and Sam Stone from Bedford Stuyvesant. Overall political definition—low-life motherfucker."

Jack Coohill drained his Wild Turkey and Lou Moran, who was chuckling, replenished it with the bottle that sat on the table.

"Just how influential was Be Be in Sydney's rise to power?" Joseph asked.

"Dumb question, with all due respect, Joseph," Jack Coohill said. "Be Be was responsible for Sydney rising to speaker of the house. But a better question would be: Just how influential was Be Be in insuring Sydney never went any farther than that? Be Be made Sydney and Sydney knew it. I suspect the reason Be Be never tore him down from speaker is that he was harmless there. Be Be didn't hate Sydney. But Sydney hated Be Be all right."

"Enough to kill him?"

Jack Coohill stared at Joseph for a long time before answering and took another good belt of the booze.

"Joseph," Jack Coohill said. "I worked for Sydney Weingarten in just one campaign. I told Be Be after that I'd rather lose the entire Brooklyn contract than ever have to work for him again. Be Be asked me why. I told Be Be that I would not work for any candidate that was willing to kill his own wife to get into office. I saw that man literally slap the shit out of Ruth Weingarten because she was late for a luncheon appointment."

"You didn't answer my question, Jack," Joseph said.

"It isn't a question anyone is gonna answer directly, Joseph," Johnny Quinn said.

"You want for me to answer the question," Lou Moran said. "I'll answer it. Sydney Weingarten would kill his mother for a plate of baccala if baccala could vote. Yeah, I think he hated Be Be enough to kill him. Me, I think so. He's a pedigree mutt that they should cut off his balls and sauté them with capers."

"I think Lou has put it much more eloquently than I ever could," Jack Coohill said.

"Elegant my stamingya," Lou Moran said. "I'll give him elegant right up his heinie hole with his old man's cuff links. Joseph, you need any help, you know what to do?"

Lou Moran reached in his pocket and took out a dime and handed it to Joseph.

"You put that dime inna phone and you call me up with your hands and you tell me with your mouth and I'm there."

Joseph looked at the dime in the center of his palm and smiled. Jack Coohill dropped a dime on top of Lou Moran's dime. Johnny Quinn made it thirty cents.

"Something is rotten in Denmark," Joseph said.

"Fuck Denmark," Lou Moran said. "The fish stinks from the head over here in Brooklyn."

"That, Lou, is the difference between elegance and eloquence," Jack Coohill said.

"Fuck the big words, I got a fungo bat behind the bar I been dyin' to use for five years."

"You might get your chance," said Johnny Quinn. "The decision is Joseph's."

"I say let's lay for the weasel and crack open his skull with the fungo bat and leave it at that," Lou Moran said.

"I'm afraid this affair is a little more complicated than that," Jack Coohill said.

"Well, you let me know when the uncomplicated part comes and I'll be there," Lou Moran said. "The last time I used that fungo I went four for four. All Greeks in a diner."

Joseph checked his watch. It was getting on for eleven o'clock. Gloria would be waiting at the house for him and he was tired. He also had a lot of serious thinking to do. He said good night to the three men and headed out of the Straw Hat.

There was no parking spots on Albemarle Road. Joseph circled the block twice in search of a place to park his car. The streets were inky black. The overhanging trees that had now reached full spring leaf cast deep, long shadows and smothered the light from the streetlights. Finally Joseph gave up looking for a parking spot and parked the car at a fire hydrant.

He locked the driver's door and began walking the block and a half toward his house. His hard leather heels cracked off the gray slate sidewalk. There were no other sounds in the street except the distant moan of a tomcat. Then Joseph thought he heard footsteps behind him. He turned but there was no one in sight. He guessed it must be the branches of the trees slapping against each other. He kept walking, quickening the pace. Now he was certain he heard footfalls. Branches do not slap against each other in rhythm. Especially not two different sets of branches. Because now it was the sound of two sets of feet. But Joseph could not see them, could not locate the people making those sounds. He stopped, turned completely around. Saw nothing, just headlights moving along distant Church Avenue.

And finally he realized why he could not see anyone behind him. The footsteps were not coming from his rear. They were coming *at* him, the footfalls made by two men who were approaching him from the front, but in crouched strides in the gutter, shielded from view by the bumper-to-bumper caravan of parked cars. But Joseph realized too late.

The thick girder that slammed against his windpipe was the arm of a large black man. Joseph's head snapped back, his mouth sucking for air. All he could see was the black tapestry of leaves above him. A fist slammed into his belly, followed by another to the solar plexus. There was no air. In panic Joseph slammed his elbow into the midsection of the man holding him from the rear. The vise on his neck loosened a few threads, enough for Joseph to grab a finger and chomp it between his teeth. His bite was ferocious, muscles bunching in his jaw. Joseph felt a warm, salty liquid leak into his mouth as the man who belonged to the finger let out a wail of pain. The man loosened his grip completely now, and Joseph took the bleeding finger and bent it backward as far as it would go. The bone cracked like rock candy, and the man staggered in disoriented anguish.

Joseph turned to the other man in time to catch the flat delivery of a sap across the cheekbone. Joseph staggered, and as he began to fall, he grabbed the man between the legs and gripped his testicles. He twisted the man's testicles like a wet shirt. The man screamed in the high-pitched report of a woman under attack. As he twisted, Joseph pulled himself up from his kneeling position. The sap hit him repeatedly on the skull. He could feel the blood running down over his ears and down his forehead and neck. Joseph yanked down on the man's testicles as hard as he could.

"Please . . ." the man begged. Joseph let go for a second, just long enough to deliver a left uppercut into the groin. The man fell. Joseph saw his face. He was a black man in his forties. Now Joseph felt his right lung coming through his chest. The large man behind him had delivered a kick to Joseph's back, and the wind left Joseph in a single gust.

"You muthuh fuckuh," Joseph heard the large man say as he kicked Joseph in the ear. "You Guinefied scumbag. You won't be goin' roun' askin' no more questions, my man. You gone to stay out of biness that don't concern you. I'm gonna put my knife right in your heart, peckerwood."

Joseph was facedown on the ground. He wished he had Be Be's .38. Suddenly a man in a short-sleeved bathrobe emerged from his house and pointed a hunting rifle at Joseph and the two black men, who were dragging Joseph up the street toward their car.

The man in the bathrobe shouted and fired a single shot into the air. The two black men looked at each other and dropped Joseph and began sprinting up the street.

Joseph finally managed to get to his feet, and when he did he was looking into the barrel of the rifle held by the man in the short-sleeved bathrobe. There was a tattoo on his right arm. It was a series of numbers. He stared at Joseph, who was leaking blood. Joseph stared back. He recognized the man with the gun immediately. It was Dr. Licht, the doctor Joseph had gone to as a child. Dr. Licht was a man who had lived through the Warsaw Ghetto to talk about it. He did not recognize Joseph at first because of Joseph's age and all the blood running down his face.

"Dr. Licht," Joseph said.

"Who are you?" the doctor snapped.

"Joseph Gonzago."

"My God," Dr. Licht said. "Let me help you into my house."

The good doctor soon had all of Joseph's wounds irrigated and bandaged. Butterfly Band-Aids would suffice, the doctor told him. Joseph told the doctor that he had been mugged. He did not elaborate.

"I supervised the autopsy on your father," Dr. Licht said. "It was very hard for me because we were such good friends. Be Be came to me all his life he lived on this street. Since I came out of medical school. He was a good man, your father. You should only be half the man he was and you'll be a fine man. Believe me. You don't know good until you've seen the devil himself. I have seen the devil. In

Warsaw and in Auschwitz. I saw the devil as a young boy. You should only be half the man your father was. A great man."

Joseph thanked the doctor. Dr. Licht told Joseph he would stand on his stoop and watch to make sure Joseph got home safe. As he walked the block to his house, Joseph realized that there was no longer any time for procrastination. He had intended to go home and think about what he should do about the death of his father. He wanted to think things through, try to sort out the guesswork from the facts. Had Be Be been murdered intentionally? Or was it an accident as others claimed? There was no longer any doubt. Those men tonight wanted to hurt me badly—maybe even kill me, he thought. There was no reason anyone would want to do either except that he had asked questions about the murder of his father. There were several ways of approaching this nasty business. But the approach Joseph Gonzago decided upon was to carry out the plans that had probably gotten his father killed. For if he could acquire the necessary power to influence the election, his adversaries would emerge. No hunches, theories, or suspicions would suffice. Joseph Gonzago wanted hard evidence in front of him—evidence he could see and touch. Just as he wished he could see and touch his father. He wanted those responsible for murdering his father to live to understand that their plans were not good enough. Their killing Be Be Gonzago was not sufficient. They had overlooked a major flaw in their plan. Be Be Gonzago's son still lived. And now his son, Joseph Gonzago, would carry out the plans that led to his murder. Be Be Gonzago's son would exact the sweetest of all vengeance. He would bring back the spirit of Be Be Gonzago—his ghost if you will—and let him reign in death as in life.

20

Governor Wolfington was a mess. His nerves were as frayed as wires after an electrical fire. He paced his Albany office, walking frequently to the seal of the state on the wall, his fingers studying it as if he were reading braille. There was something almost nervously erotic in the action.

On rare occasions like this, when his mind and body were weak, Henry Wolfington succumbed to the medicinal comfort of a bottle of champagne. It helped him to bubble away his anxiety.

Brideson poured the governor another glass of champagne.

"It looks like the assassination attempt backfired, sir."

"But how the heck can the citizens blame me for getting shot at? What did I do? I almost got killed! Do they blame me for almost getting killed, for God's sake? I'm a nervous wreck. I haven't been the same since this thing happened."

Wolfington drank up the second glass of champagne and Brideson filled the glass immediately and placed the towel-wrapped bottle back into the ice bucket.

"I'm simply dumbfounded as well," Brideson said. "I never thought a thing like that could work against you. I thought the opposite would be true."

"What's happening down in the city?"

"Well, better news there," Brideson said. "It may sound callous to say, but the absence of Gonzago puts us in a better position. It looks as though Weingarten will replace him. If he can deliver the borough, and I have no reason to believe he can't, we'll be in very good shape. The machine might have been weakened in the past few years, but there are still some very loyal people down there. I think the machine pulling for us can make the difference. We can outspend Kelly and use the office of the governor to help too."

"I still can't believe we have to depend on Brooklyn to win this thing," Wolfington said.

"It's still the largest Democratic district in the state. It has always been important, but the margins have never been this close for us before. I'm convinced we need Brooklyn to win."

Wolfington shot Brideson a grim look and finished his glass of champagne. Then he walked to the state seal emblazoned on the wall and touched it with his fingertips.

Joseph had waited across from the Nathan Hale most of the morning. His head ached from the beating. He'd told Gloria on the phone that he loved her but could not see her for a few days because of family business. The first order of business was to follow the Lincoln with the two black men from the night before to this street. Ahead of him now he saw the black Lincoln Continental double-parked outside Sylvia Stein's house. Joesph pulled to the curb, at a hydrant, killed the motor, and watched as Sydney Weingarten climbed out of the backseat and closed the door. The Lincoln, drove off. Joseph saw the license plate—STONE 1. Sydney Weingarten climbed the stoop to Sylvia Stein's house and rang the doorbell. Sylvia Stein answered the door and let Sydney Weingarten in.

Joseph sat in the car for a little over an hour. At least he thought it was an hour or more. He wasn't sure. He never bothered to look at his watch. Now the black Lincoln appeared again and double-parked outside the house and honked. Sydney appeared in the doorway, tieless, his suit jacket draped over his arm. Sylvia Stein appeared too, and Sydney kissed her on the cheek. She wore a long beautiful silk robe. Sydney got into the Lincoln and it drove off.

Joseph got out of his car and walked to Sylvia Stein's house. He rang the doorbell and waited. Sylvia answered the door, obviously expecting to find someone else.

"Oh," she said, a little startled. "Hello. My God, you're Joseph Gonzago. I recognize you from the pictures in the papers."

"Hello, Miss Stein," Joseph said almost sheepishly.

Sylvia looked both ways on the street, saw no one, and looked back at Joseph.

"Please come in, Joseph."

"Oh, no, Miss Stein, I don't want to disturb you."

"No trouble at all, Joseph."

"Actually, I'm sort of in a rush."

"Well, come in for a minute anyway."

Joseph nodded and stepped inside but did not sit down. Sylvia fell into a lounge chair and looked up at Joseph.

"You sure did grow up to be a fine-looking man, Joseph."

"Well, thank you, ma'am. You're a lovely-looking woman, if you don't mind me saying so."

"Not at all. Come on. Sit down."

"No, Miss Stein, what I have to say won't take long. You see, for years I had partially blamed you for the death of my mother. I thought you and my father had had an affair, and that you wrote him all kinds of love letters which my mother discovered. This caused her to commit suicide, Miss Stein. But lately I have found evidence that indicates you and my father never had an affair. I just want to clear this up. Is it true or untrue that you and Be Be Gonzago were lovers?"

Sylvia Stein looked at Joseph Gonzago in silence for a long time. She puffed on a cigarette and finally stood up and walked close to him. Her perfume was expensive and lovely. She looked so deeply into his eyes that she might have been trying to look at the back of his head.

"Untrue," Sylvia Stein said. "And I never wrote him any letters. I've heard about these letters but never saw them. They are forgeries, and if you produce them, I can prove it if we go to a handwriting specialist. Don't get me wrong, Joseph. In my time I have sort of gotten any man I wanted when I wanted. I would have liked nothing better than to have been Be Be Gonzago's lover, and if that sounds vulgar or disrespectful, so be it and I'm sorry. But Be Be was a beautiful man. He was good-looking, made of stone, in body and character. I would have parked my shoes under his bed anytime. In fact, I tried to several times. Be Be turned me down. He loved your mother something fierce. She must have really been something because half the broads in Brooklyn would have liked to nail Be Be Gonzago. Sort of like taking a scalp. But no. I never had an affair with Be Be Gonzago. Unfortunately."

"Thank you, Miss Stein."

"Sylvia's the name. Want a drink?"

"No, thank you. But I would like to take a rain check. Say, tomorrow night? I have two tickets for the Brooklyn Academy of Music, where they're staging *Hamlet.* Would you like to go with me?"

Sylvia Stein smiled brightly. "Yeah," she said suddenly. "Yeah, I'd sort of really like that. I was supposed to go with someone else but, well, you know how it is. He's taking his wife instead."

Joseph laughed and so did she.

"I'll pick you up at seven then?" Joseph was smiling.

"That'd be fine. Later we can have a drink maybe?"

"Sure thing," Joseph said. Joseph turned to leave when Sylvia spoke again.

"Hey, Joseph. Why'd you come here in person? Why not just call up on the phone?"

"Because I wanted to see your face when you told me about my father. I had to see your face before I could believe you."

"Do you, Joseph?"

"Yes. Yes, I do."

21

Brendan Kelly sat aboard the chartered airplane somewhere over the Adirondack Mountains. Sitting next to him was his campaign manager, Tim Harris, thirty-five years old with a politically checkered past. In the sixties Harris had helped found the Students for a Democratic Society, became a firebrand campus hero, and later a defendant in one of the most bizarre trials in American history. The trial involved a conspiracy to bomb the printing plants of every American publisher who put out textbooks on American history.

Of the eleven people indicted in the conspiracy, Harris was the only one to win an all-out acquittal. He had defended himself in court, sometimes spellbinding the judge, jury, and United States attorney prosecuting the case with his almost unlimited knowledge of the law. Harris had been a law student when the conspiracy indictments came in. The government claimed that the SDS people wanted to bomb the printing plants to gain publicity in their crusade to show that American students, especially in the elementary and high school levels, were being brainwashed by textbooks that were essentially propaganda for the capitalist establishment and big business. None of the defendants received jail terms in the trial, but Tim Harris walked away without even probation and with a national reputation that became the envy of his colleagues. After the trial his radical buddies, including people like Joseph Gonzago at Berkeley, ostracized him from their circles, claiming that he had recognized the court, which was a violation of their revolutionary code. Some, Joseph not among them, also said that Tim Harris had sold out, because he denounced the violence of the Black Panthers and the Young Lords and similar groups, and instead advised that the system should be changed from within. In short, he had become just another liberal in the eyes of his boy-revolutionary peers.

This didn't much bother Tim Harris. He had seen the activism of the sixties fizzle and went the pragmatic route. One did not have to live in gunnysack all one's life to prove that you identified with the plight of the workers of the world. It would be much better to try to work within the system and accomplish real change. Tim Harris had never so much as tossed a firecracker during his revolutionary days. He saw himself as the one who had matured while the others still wanted to build bombs with daddy's allowance.

He was the logical choice as campaign manager for Brendan Kelly. Harris had been associated with the anti-nuclear-energy issue for years, long before Three Mile Island or the major disaster upstate. He was bright, tireless, and worked the press with savvy, having once been a darling of theirs. He could also write well, having published two books on his ideas for a new America, which little by little were being incorporated into Kelly's stump speeches.

"New York City is bothering me greatly, Tim," Brendan Kelly said in the privacy of the rear of the plane, out of earshot of the accompanying reporters. "I think we might have had a shot with Gonzago in Brooklyn. At least the man listened before telling you to go to hell. But my dealings with Weingarten over the years have been like dealing with a Neanderthal."

"Our pollsters say Staten Island will probably go Wolfington, but in the general election always tips Republican anyway," Harris said. "Queens, well that could be a toss-up. There isn't a whole lot left to the Bronx, and what there is doesn't vote much, but still Weingarten has struck up a neat little partnership with a certain Julio Garcia from the South Bronx. This guy is an out-and-out extortionist. I mean he bombs construction sites which refuse to hire the kids from his poverty programs. Then when they do hire the kids, he gets a fifty percent kickback of all wages from the kids. As you know, the farmers upstate are about split. Some get major tax breaks from the revenue of the nuclear power plants. Others get their jobs from there. Still others fear another accident. That's why in an election this close, Brooklyn and her ten percent are so damned important."

"And you don't think, Tim, there's any chance of negotiating with Weingarten?" Kelly had his fingers steepled.

"Not a prayer, Brendan," Tim Harris said. "The man wants to be the top judge in the state. He wants to sit as the head of the state Court of Appeals. Are you aware of just how dangerous a man like that could be in that position? In essence, he tells every other judge in the entire state what to do and how to do it. Not only that, but scuttlebutt has it he has designs on the Supreme Court of the land, in the event Wolfington ever makes it to the White House. No, Brendan, we can't talk to Sydney Weingarten. No way."

Kelly laughed and stared out at the mountains below.

"What about Gonzago's son?" Kelly said. "You said you knew him back in your louder days."

"I knew him. Not very well. Very intense guy. Wanted to be an actor. Then a revolutionary. As soon as Jerry and Abbie showed the world you could run a network without owning stock, he started rising. He's not bad in front of a camera. Good training. Probably could have been a hell of an actor. Good-looking, as you know. Athletic. Also very, very smart. Street smart as well as politically. But I don't see him having much influence with his father's old cronies in Brooklyn. He despised his father. Publicly ridiculed him. I don't see him being much help to us, Brendan."

"Still, I don't think it could hurt to give him a call one of these days. Just to say hello, feel him out, see what he's up to. Maybe some of his father's old friends will listen to him. Hell, if nothing else he's still one vote."

"Okay, I'll give him a call," Harris said.

"Can't hurt anyway," candidate Kelly said.

Joseph chose a file folder from the third file cabinet. The folder was labeled, STONE, SAM, COUNCILMAN. Joseph sat on the couch in the Water Board and began leafing through the folder. There were three separate lists of Sam Stone's campaign contributions from three separate campaigns. Coinciding with these lists was a record of Sam Stone's very influential votes as president of the city council and a member of the board of estimate. These votes were limited to building contracts. The way the list read you did not have to be Carl Bernstein to figure out that Stone was voting in favor of awarding city-funded construction contracts to firms that contributed to his campaigns.

This was heady stuff. But it was really just a conflict of interest and might not necessarily be illegal. What could put Stone in the can was a transcript of a conversation between Stone and Be Be Gonzago that was also in the file. This transcript, backed up by the actual tape, which was in the other file cabinet, could probably have landed Be Be in jail too. But Be Be was dead. He had kept all this stuff so that if he had ever gone to the can, he'd have taken along a few cell mates.

Joseph read parts of the transcript.

STONE: Apex Development gets two million to build the new day-care center, and they've promised to backhand at least one fifty.

BE BE: Too much. Make it no more than seventy-five. Don't get greedy. That's what sends these guys to the special prosecutors.
STONE: But they've already agreed, Be Be.
BE BE: Then you knock it down, God damn it. I don't like this greedy shit. It's way too much. Seventy-five is plenty. We can spread it around in a few campaigns. You don't even need that much for your own. You're running virtually unopposed.
STONE: Still, there's expenses from the last one.
BE BE: For what? Hookers, Cadillacs, dope? You pay that out of your own pocket, Sam. That has nothing to do with the party. You wanna run a campaign like it was a Don King promotion, then you foot the fuckin' bill. You could have run your last one on fifteen G's. Instead you went eighty-five thou. That's what some folks in places like Bensonhurst might call nigger rich, Sam Stone.
STONE: (Laughter) I won it though.
BE BE: No, Sam, I won it. I won it for you. Always remember that and you'll always win. Forget it, even once, and I'll see you never win so much as a Kewpie doll in this borough again. Now remember. Seventy-five grand, Sam. Not one fifty. Understand?
STONE: Whatever you say, Be Be.
BE BE: All right, now get out of here. Go polish your jewelry or something. I got work to do.

Joseph grinned and replaced the file folder. He picked up another folder. This one was labeled: BAILEY, TOM, MAYOR. Joseph leafed through it and realized that it was almost identical in nature to the one on Sam Stone. The stakes were smaller and involved kickbacks for things like milk deliveries to municipal hospitals. If a certain milk company wanted a contract to sell milk and eggs to public schools and hospitals, it would have to pay a percentage of its vast profits to Bailey, who would use what he needed for his campaign, take some for pin money and maybe a European vacation for him and the missus. The rest went to the Brooklyn machine that made him mayor. Small potatoes maybe by the standards of big business, but put all the little kickback operations together and count the assets and you could join the Fortune 500. Joseph felt the weight of the file folder. It wasn't much. A term paper, maybe. Tax records for a working man. But in the case of Mayor Tom Bailey it was worth its weight in prison years.

Joseph spent several hours looking through these files. Many he did not understand; the transcripts were often cryptic and vague, or filled with code names for people, places, firms. But for a person familiar with all the players, the files would represent unlimited power. The names were incredible—Senator David Hallahan, Congressman Gentile from Flatbush, O'Connor from Bay Ridge, borough president Victor Lupo and councilmen and assemblymen, commissioners and treasurers of municipalities from Gravesend to Red Hook.

Joseph knew a couple of people who could decode and interpret and evaluate the potential of these files. Johnny Quinn and Jack Coohill were just the men to hold the fourth-largest city in America hostage with such information. All they awaited was a green light from Joseph. Who would serve as governor of the State of New York —and possibly even who might be the next president of the United States—might be determined by how, if at all, those files were manipulated. There were some names missing from the files. Dermot Donnelly was not in there. Sydney Weingarten was also missing. And some of the cronies who answered directly to Weingarten. But there were certainly enough names to blow the town apart.

Joseph put the files away, locked the cabinets, put his key into the phone receiver, and left the Water Board.

The next day, after he awoke, Joseph left the house. He had some phone calls to make and did not want to make them from his house, where the phones might have been tapped. He walked to a pay phone on Flatbush Avenue. He reached into his left-hand pants pocket, where he never kept change, and took out the three dimes given him by Johnny Quinn, Jack Coohill, and Lou Moran. Lou Moran answered. Joseph told him he was calling with Lou's dime and that it was crucial that he meet him in the lobby of the Municipal Building the next evening. When he reached Jack Coohill, he told him the same thing. Joseph told Jack Coohill that Lou Moran was going to meet him there and that he was going to call Johnny Quinn with his dime to ask him to do likewise. Jack Coohill told Joseph he didn't think Quinn would be home. He'd spoken to him earlier and Quinn had said he was going to Greenwood Cemetery to visit Be Be's grave and to see about some other business. He hadn't said what the other business was. Joseph knew it was about buying the little plot of land down the slope from Be Be's grave. Joseph tried Johnny's number anyway but there was no answer.

He tried calling Johnny Quinn several more times during the day, but there was no response. Finally Joseph realized it was almost five o'clock. He'd get Johnny Quinn early in the morning. Right now he had to get ready for his date with Sylvia Stein at the Brooklyn Academy of Music. He placed Johnny Quinn's lone dime in his left-hand pocket and headed home to get dressed.

Sydney Weingarten joined Gloria and Ruth Weingarten and walked slowly down the aisle to the third row. He did not rush because Ruth walked unsteadily. He hated theater but this was protocol because it was a fund raiser for the Brooklyn Arts and Culture Association. All the major Brooklyn pols would have to attend.

The Brooklyn Academy of Music was a three-tiered affair with wonderful acoustics and constructed so that viewing was excellent from almost any seat in the house. The stage was large and deep, with red velvet curtains on either side. Massive chandeliers hung from the great domed ceiling. The seats were comfortable and covered with crushed red velour.

Gloria entered the row first and took the fifth seat. Ruth followed her and took the fourth seat. Sydney took the third seat, even though he was quite sure no one would be sitting at the aisle seats. Those two seats had been reserved by Be Be Gonzago. He wouldn't be coming.

The powerful overhead lights burned through the riot of prismatic glass. Ruth looked at Sydney Weingarten and smiled weakly.

"Shakespeare is wonderful," she said.

"How would you know?" Sydney said in an aside.

"Oh, I know a lot of things you don't think I know, Sydney," she said with a quiet certainty.

Sydney turned to her, his eyes suspicious as the lights started going out.

"Such as?" he whispered.

Ruth smiled to herself and let the silent darkness protect her. She grasped Gloria's hand and patted it. Sydney was annoyed with Ruth and slouched lower in his seat. He, too, found comfort in the darkness—perhaps he could doze inconspicuously, which was one reason he did not sit at the aisle where people might notice. The other reason was that it would not be proper to sit in Be Be's seat before the county committee voted it to him.

The play began and Sydney Weingarten made himself as comfortable as possible in the total darkness. Just as Bernardo and Francisco struck up their conversation on stage, Sydney Weingarten realized the two aisle seats were being taken. A man sat next to him and a woman occupied the aisle seat. Sydney Weingarten did not turn to see who it was. The theater was totally silent and dark save for the lights and dialogue from the stage.

Sydney watched the play distractedly for the first fifteen minutes. He thought about Ruth and what she had said about knowing things he did not think she knew. What could they be? Was she putting him on? Bluffing? Or was it just more of her delirious chatter? Whatever, the woman was a constant burden. He could not wait to unhinge himself from her so that he could be with Sylvia Stein. He thought of Sylvia Stein for several moments.

By the end of Act Two, scene 1, when Ophelia is frightened and goes to Polonius to tell him she thinks Hamlet is mad, Sydney Weingarten was still thinking of Sylvia Stein. Her image was so clear in his mind's eye now that he could almost swear he could smell her expensive perfume. The perfume he had given her.

Then he heard her cough. And knew it was her cough.

Sydney Weingarten sat perfectly still. He stared straight ahead, terrified of the possible public embarrassment this situation could cause. He was sandwiched between his wife, his daughter, his mistress, and some escort of hers. Then, his embarrassment turned to jealous anger. Who the hell did she think she was, going out with another man? After the presents and money he had given her. After the promises she had made to him.

Slowly he turned. Incredulous, he saw her sitting there, engrossed in the play, staring straight ahead. She looked beautiful. And then his focus drew back to see who this man was.

Joseph Gonzago stared Sydney Weingarten in the eye, with an expression of wry amusement.

"You wouldn't want to miss this next scene, Sydney," Joseph whispered. Sydney turned his attention back to the stage when someone behind them shhhed them.

Sydney Weingarten sat rigidly next to Joseph Gonzago as they both watched Hamlet and Claudius on the stage. Sydney began to feel nauseous, unable to get his breath.

"This is the best part of the play, Sydney," Joseph Gonzago whispered. Sydney began really to perspire.

As the lights went on for the intermission, Joseph could see that Sydney Weingarten was trying to mutter something. But, in fact, he seemed to be choking. The commotion disturbed the people around them, and then like ripples, people turned to look. Sydney Weingarten began to claw his way out of his seat.

"Must have eaten a bad goober, Sydney," Joseph was saying with a smile. "Just sit still and Joseph will fix everything."

People gathered around. Gloria moved past Ruth and Sylvia Stein into the aisle as Sydney Weingarten pushed his way to his feet.

"I just need some air," Sydney said to Joseph, his eyes smoldering, brushing off his suit. He stared at Joseph, who grinned maliciously. Then Sydney Weingarten shot a long, hard look at Sylvia Stein. Sylvia Stein stared at him, expressionless. Ruth now made her way down the row and stood for a moment next to Sylvia Stein.

"That's very lovely perfume you are wearing, Miss Stein," Ruth said.

Sylvia Stein did not say one word. She simply rose from her seat, stared for a long moment at Sydney Weingarten, who looked back with ferocity, then she turned and threw her head back and walked up the aisle to the exit like a woman striding to a coronation. Sydney stared after her.

Sydney Weingarten then looked at Ruth.

"Like I said, I know more than you think I know, Sydney," Ruth said.

"Gloria," Sydney said. "Take your mother home."

But Gloria was staring at Joseph Gonzago, tears welling in her eyes.

"Joseph, why are you doing this?"

"Because he's a goddamn maniac," Sydney Weingarten snapped. "Now take your mother home."

The crowd was still looking on as if at a traffic accident.

"It's all over," Sydney announced. "I'm sorry for the commotion. My apologies. I was just feeling faint."

Several moments later the lights began to blink on and off again to signal that the performance was once again about to get under way. Gloria kept staring at Joseph as people took their seats.

"Why, Joseph?" she asked again.

Joseph walked over to Gloria and whispered in her ear, "Take your mother home, Gloria. Your father is right. Forget about me."

Joseph walked up the aisle as the lights began to dim. Sydney Weingarten walked ahead of Gloria and Ruth, behind Joseph. Joseph saw Sam Stone and Dermot Donnelly standing at the top of the aisle, awaiting Sydney Weingarten.

"Good evening, gentlemen," Joseph said. "I have to try to get this tux back early or they'll charge me for overtime."

"That little spectacle was uncalled for, Joseph," Donnelly said.

"Hypothetically speaking perhaps," Joseph said, and kept walking. Sydney joined Donnelly and Stone at the entrance to the lobby, and the three men watched Joseph Gonzago disappear into the night.

As the play continued in the Brooklyn Academy of Music, a knock came upon the door of Johnny Quinn's apartment. Quinn had been having himself a few private drinks, his phone off the hook, the radio playing, looking around his room, thinking about his lot in life.

Johnny Quinn opened the door and saw the two familiar faces. He thought he might still have enough time to slam the door in their faces, make a quick phone call, or make a run for it through the window. But then he simply opened the door a little wider.

"I was wondering when you guys would get around to me," he said. "What is it you want?"

"We just want you to sign a paper, Johnny, and that's the last thing we'll ever ask of you."

"Absolutely the last thing," said the second man.

"Sure," Johnny Quinn said. "Just show me the dotted line."

Johnny Quinn signed his name on the paper he did not even bother to read. The radio was playing a song called "Pack up Your Troubles," and Johnny Quinn smiled and listened to the silly old lyrics. Then he couldn't hear the music anymore.

22

Gloria Weingarten had stayed by her mother's bed for over an hour, comforting her to sleep. Ruth Weingarten had sobbed for a long while, having finally come face to face with the woman she was certain was Sydney's mistress.

Gloria then left the house and walked for a long time. Down to Coney Island Avenue, past the new influx of antique shops and the shuttered auto parts stores and the nursing homes toward Park Circle. She crossed the circle and strolled down the park side of Prospect Park Southwest toward Bartel-Pritchard Square, where she hoped she might find a taxi to take her home to Shore Road. As she strolled along the park side, she thought deeply about Joseph Gonzago. Had she waited fifteen years in the prime of her life to get him back and then lose him? What was wrong with him? He acted so crazy? Why was he at the theater with that horrible woman, Sylvia Stein, who her mother swore was Sydney's mistress? Had the things they said to each other just a few nights before as they made love been for nothing?

She stood in the center of Bartel-Pritchard Square and finally hailed a taxi. She climbed into the backseat and told the driver where she wanted to go. As the cab moved toward Bay Ridge, Gloria Weingarten leaned back in the seat and finally smiled. She'd made up her mind she was going to win and that was half the battle. Already she was tasting the spoils.

The apartment was cordoned off as forensic dusted for prints. A police photographer popped his flash over and over, snapping Johnny Quinn's body from every angle.

The cleaning lady was sitting on a chair in the kitchen, her body ticking and jerking and shrugging. She was a nervous wreck. A cop handed her a glass of straight Scotch. She sipped it. She'd found Johnny Quinn a half hour earlier when she'd let herself in with her key. She explained she came twice a week to clean the apartment, mostly just dusting and a little laundry and a few dirty dishes. She said Johnny Quinn was a very neat bachelor, and she suspected he kept her in his employ as much for company a couple of mornings a week as for her cleaning services. She said he was so lonely and gentlemanly.

The police found the suicide note on the coffee table when they arrived. The note was a short typewritten message that was signed in ballpoint pen at the bottom. The message was spare and simple:

TO WHOM IT MAY CONCERN: DYING IS BETTER THAN LIFE WITHOUT BE BE. SINCE THAT DAY WHEN HE DIED IN AN ACCIDENT OF FATE I KNEW WHAT MY FATE WOULD BE. THERE ISN'T MUCH TO LEAVE BEHIND, SO NO WILL IS NECESSARY. MY APOLOGIES TO THE NEIGHBORS AND FAREWELL TO MY FRIENDS. REGRETFULLY, Johnny Quinn.

The signature was in Johnny Quinn's handwriting. The pistol that had killed him lay loosely in his right hand. Dermot Donnelly arrived with an investigator from the district attorney's office. A uniformed detective from NYPD brought the suicide note to the district attorney.

"Looks like he was some kind of a gay, Mr. Donnelly," the cop said. "He had those funny kind of magazines here. Not the porno stuff, but you know about gay rights and things like that. Political magazines."

Dermot Donnelly read the suicide note and looked up at the cop and handed it back.

"I understand, Officer." Donnelly looked quickly at Johnny Quinn, then turned his back. The face was distorted and appeared to be smiling and winking at him—one eye was closed, the other was open, and his jaw was twisted into a ghoulish grin.

"The only reason I'm here is because I knew the man. I wanted to be sure it was suicide."

"No doubt about that, sir," the cop said. "The note explains the whole thing. Only one thing troubles me."

"What's that, Officer?"

"The note is typewritten, but there's no typewriter in the house. And he signed it in ball-point pen, but we can't find a ball-point pen anywhere. What papers he does have here are all written in fountain pen, like the one we found in his jacket pocket."

Dermot Donnelly did not look concerned about these details.

"He could have written the note somewhere else, Officer."

The cop rubbed his eyes. "I suppose. But a guy is gonna zap himself, he usually doesn't write the note, take a subway home, then do it. Suicide, from my experience with it, is something you do on the spur of the moment. But who knows? I mean it takes all kinds."

"Thank you"—Donnelly looked at the cop's name plate—"Lenihan. But do me a favor, will you. I don't think it's necessary to include all that stuff in your report. I knew the man. He was a friend. We have a suicide note. I'd just like to close the case as fast as possible. The political situation in this city is bad enough without raising new questions. And don't talk to the press, please. Stay away from them. They'll blow the whole thing out of proportion as usual."

"That's fine with me, Mr. Donnelly," Lenihan said. "I mean it's a suicide from the looks of it. But there will be a coroner's inquest. They'll bring him out to Kings County where the autopsy will be performed. Then they'll just plant the poor old guy. Oh, yeah, that's the other thing. He had this in his jacket pocket too. It's some kind of purchase slip for a plot in Greenwood Cemetery. I mean, that really wraps it up. The day he kills himself he buys a cemetery plot. Thoughtful of him. Saves the city from putting him in potter's."

Lenihan handed Donnelly the purchase slip. Donnelly studied it with concern. Something uneasy rose and fell in Donnelly's stomach. A man so meticulous about his own impending doom was certainly capable of taking care of a lot of other business before he died.

SBI agent Francis X. Cunningham stepped through the door and panned the room. He had his gold shield pinned to his jacket. His face registered no emotion. Dermot Donnelly saw him and looked disgusted.

"This isn't state business," Donnelly said. "Just a simple suicide, Cunningham."

"If it's just a simple suicide, what are you doing here?"

"I knew the man. I wanted to see for myself. Leave it alone."

"I don't know if I can, Donnelly. At least I have to check it out."

"The guy left a note. He was distraught over Gonzago's death. He was a homosexual. Maybe he loved Be Be. Who knows? Please, just leave it alone. It's just a tragic, sad affair."

"Can I see the note?" Cunningham was staring at Johnny Quinn without any discernible change of expression.

"That cop over there, name's Lenihan, has it. You'll have a copy of my full report by tomorrow."

"I certainly hope so, Donnelly."

"So long, Cunningham."

Dermot Donnelly stepped out into the hallway, through the huddles of alarmed tenants, past demanding reporters whom he did not answer, and out to his car, where his driver sat patiently reading the morning *Times.*

Joseph Gonzago was about to get out of his car, which he'd just parked across the street from Johnny Quinn's apartment building. He stopped when he saw Dermot Donnelly walking out of the building past a herd of onlookers and patrol cars and police barricades. He waited until Donnelly's car moved away from the scene before he proceeded to Johnny Quinn's apartment. He was stopped by a uniformed cop at the entrance to the building. Joseph explained that he was a friend of Johnny Quinn's, that he was here to see him. The cop led him into the apartment. Francis Xavier Cunningham looked at Joseph as he entered the room. Joseph did not return the stare. His eyes were affixed on Johnny Quinn's body.

"You knew him, didn't you?" Cunningham said, his voice soft in deference to the scene.

"I knew him," Joseph said. "He was a nice man. A hell of a nice man."

"Why would he kill himself?"

"Is that what they're saying?" Joseph said, his reaction steady. He looked at the telephone, which was off the hook. Joseph had tried calling earlier in the morning, but all he got was busy signals and so he drove out to see Johnny.

"Why don't they hang up the phone?" Joseph asked, feeling foolish for asking such a banal question under these circumstances.

"They won't change anything from the way they found it until all the prints and photographs and evidence are gathered."

"Why are they calling it a suicide?"

"He left a note. One cop says he also found a receipt for a grave site he bought yesterday in Greenwood Cemetery."

"Oh, God Almighty," Joseph said. "The poor old lonely bastard."

"Guess he was pretty upset about your father, huh?"

"Yeah," Joseph said as he watched the police move around the apartment, their expressions nonchalant. "He loved Be Be. His death broke him up, I guess."

"Yeah, that's what he says in the note."

Joseph looked up at Cunningham, eagerness flickering in his eyes. "Can I see this note?"

"I'll ask." Cunningham went over to the homicide detective, and the two men exchanged words in a direct, professional manner. Finally the detective produced the note and handed it to Cunningham, who brought it over to Joseph. Joseph almost snatched it from Cunningham's hand. He read the brief message and knew right away that Johnny Quinn had never written it. He did not let his face reveal what he was thinking.

Joseph handed the note back to Cunningham, who returned it to the homicide detective.

"What do you think?" Cunningham asked.

"It's there in black and white," Joseph said.

"Suicides have been faked before, you know."

"Yeah."

"Hey," Cunningham said. "You think you can give me a ride? I took a taxi over here."

Joseph was still staring at Johnny Quinn, as if drawing strength from the gruesome vision before him. He wanted to make an indelible impression of that vision on his mind.

"Yeah," Joseph said. "Sure, come on. I guess there's nothing to do here. I'll have to take care of the funeral and all."

"That'll have to wait until after the autopsy. There's plenty of time."

The two men left the killing ground and climbed into Joseph's car.

Joseph took Fifth Avenue to Flatbush Avenue. Flatbush Avenue was his favorite street in Brooklyn, a long spine that ran from one end of the borough to the other. As they passed Erasmus Hall High School, Cunningham struck up a conversation.

"You know something, Joseph," Cunningham said, lighting a cigarette. "I know you know something I don't know."

Joseph looked over at him, smiled, and said, "Yeah?"

"Yeah? I'll tell you how I know. Main reason is that your phone is tapped. I know it's tapped because I ordered it tapped. The only problem is that you don't do much talking on it. And in my business we interpret silence as a shout. You understand, don't you?"

"Who gives you the right to tap my goddamned phone?" Joseph was truly angry. "You people think you can just march over people's lives, do what you want. That the ends justify any means. You are disgusting. You ought to be ashamed of yourself, Cunningham."

Cunningham blew a smoke ring that shattered on the windshield.

"Let's not get ourselves all worked up, Joseph," he said. "This isn't 1968. If it weren't for tape recordings and things like that Nixon might still be around."

"Is that what tax dollars are used for?" Joseph asked.

"We are talking about murder, friend. Your father's murder. I know his murder might not bother you, fella, but to me it's bad business."

The car was humming over the steel ribs of the Brooklyn Bridge now.

Joseph diverted his eyes from the road just often enough to get Cunningham nervous. The speed increased and the car began to swerve into the other lanes. Joseph's voice grew in volume almost in synch with the speed of the car.

"Cunningham, let me tell you something. You are starting to get me angry. I don't like it when I get angry. You wouldn't either. You see, if you mention one more word about my father, I might just forget my college education and my good manners and really deal with you like the kid from Brooklyn I used to be. You understand?"

Joseph was doing eighty now, and Cunningham had his feet propped against the dashboard, his hands in front of his face, his eyes were terrified. Joseph was still staring at him instead of the road, and Cunningham began to swallow hard and finally managed to speak.

"I understand. Now slow down."

"That's good, Cunningham. That's really fucking good." Joseph made a screeching turn onto Chambers Street and finally began to decrease the speed of the car. His anger began to drop along with the speed.

"You crazy son of a bitch," Cunningham said. "Don't you understand that all I'm trying to do is find out who killed your father? Granted, sometimes I might say things to get people angry so they open up. But you have a death wish, Joseph. We could have died back there."

Joseph looked at him and smiled.

"That's the difference between anger and fear, Cunningham," Joseph said. "You get frightened and I get angry. Anger *might* get you killed, sure. Fear *always* will. You see, I don't really care. But I'm not going to let anyone frighten me anymore. And if people make me angry and I die angry, at least it will be painless. And the one thing better than getting angry is getting even, Cunningham."

"I'm afraid I can't let you do that, Joseph."

"See, you're afraid again."

Joseph pulled up in front of the World Trade Center, where SBI headquarters were located. Cunningham opened the door and climbed out. He leaned on the open door and stared in at Joseph Gonzago, who sat calmly behind the steering wheel, as businessmen passed them on the busy street.

"Do you think Johnny Quinn committed suicide?" Cunningham asked.

"Do you think my father's murder was accidental?"

"I don't know," Cunningham said. "I know this much—there's no typewriter in Johnny Quinn's apartment. I looked."

Joseph tried not to register any reaction. Cunningham extended his hand for Joseph to shake. Joseph looked at it a few moments and then decided to shake it.

"You really think you could kick my ass?" Cunningham asked.

"Yes," Joseph said.

"Me too. See you around and be careful. Crazy man."

Cunningham slammed the door and started walking toward the massive building. Joseph watched him a few moments and then drove back toward the Brooklyn Bridge.

23

Sydney Weingarten slammed his fist onto the bold-face type at the top of page six of the *New York Post.* It was the lead item of the day. A hundred and twenty-five words of moral hangover. The item mentioned Sydney Weingarten and the bizarre scene at the Brooklyn Academy of Music.

Something had to be done about Ruth. And quickly. She might not be as out of it as you think, Sydney thought to himself. Those mumblings about knowing more than he thought she knew made him anxious every time he thought of it.

The intercom buzzed on his desk at the Nathan Hale Club. The receptionist told Sydney that Mayor Tom Bailey and Dermot Donnelly were there to see him. Sydney told her to send them right in. In less than a minute the two men entered the room. Tom Bailey's face was puffy and pale. Dermot Donnelly looked grave but in total control of himself. Sydney motioned for both men to sit down and they did.

"We have to hold some sort of dinner in Be Be's honor," Sydney said. "Do it under the pretense of one of his favorite charities. Cancer or the blind or something like that. Donate the proceeds to it. But the dinner should be a dress rehearsal for the vote of the county committee. I know only forty odd of them vote for the chairmanship. But we have to show these district leaders that I have the support of the organization. Get the old Gonzago loyalists to see that the majority of the Brooklyn organization is behind me. I don't want to wait until the actual vote. That would be dangerous. Anything can happen. We'll make up some unofficial ballots to accompany each plate. It's been done before. But it has to be done under the auspices of a memorial tribute to Be Be and some charity.

Weingarten laughed and held up page six. He was trying to break out of his depression and scoffed at the item, which troubled him, in front of his friends.

Donnelly did not join Sydney and Bailey in the chuckle.

"Don't take this young man too lightly," Donnelly warned. "The kind of mental state he's in now might very well be temporary. It happens all the time. A mild nervous breakdown—postshock trauma. He is forging guilt with vengeance. And he's very—hell, extremely—bright. This man is clever and irrational, which makes him very dangerous, Sydney. You see, it's obvious after last night that he does not care a hoot what people think, say, or feel about him. His father's been killed. He wants to know who did it. His mind is filled with conspiracies and conspirators. A sane man, a rational man, might not act without proof. But a disturbed, troubled, irrational man like Joseph Gonzago is likely to act to get the proof."

Sydney Weingarten looked at Dermot Donnelly, poker-faced.

"Thank you so much, Sigmund, for your diagnosis," Sydney said. "Since when are you the house shrink?"

"Laugh if you want, Sydney, but I've read volumes on the human mind in the criminology courses I've taken over the years," Dermot Donnelly answered. "A violent crime very often has a severe, damaging effect on the relatives and loved ones of the victim. It is not unusual. It goes beyond revenge. It becomes obsession. High-salaried executives chuck their entire careers out the window while avenging the death of a son or daughter or wife. They hire private detectives. They go on violent rampages. They don't see the world even as rationally as the murderer who killed their relative. In a subconscious way, they know they must become like their prey—think, act, live like the person they are after—in order to corner him. They no longer care about their own lives. They figure they lost a good deal of that when their loved one was killed, so they throw caution to the wind and work on impulse. They live in body only, and for one reason only, to get even. So laugh if you want, but Joseph Gonzago is not going to give up until he finds out who killed his dad. I believe this totally."

Sydney Weingarten shifted his weight on his seat, leaned back, and stared at Dermot Donnelly. The eye contact indicated to Donnelly that they would further discuss Joseph Gonzago later, when they were alone. Mayor Bailey fidgeted in his chair. He changed the subject.

"I heard on WINS that John Quinn killed himself last night," Bailey said. "Poor old Johnny. I sort of liked the old fella. Gentle sort of guy. Loyal. Smart. Good worker."

"Pity," Sydney said, "yes, a pity."

"I was there this morning. Was awful." Donnelly shook his head.

"Mind if I help myself?" Bailey asked, nodding toward the liquor rack. Sydney nodded his permission. "Anyone care to join me? All this nasty business has my nerves frazzled."

Donnelly and Weingarten waved their hands in denial. Bailey poured himself a triple shot of Bushmills Irish without ice or mix and walked back and sat down. He took a sip and Sydney watched him retch, his body jumping. Finally Bailey managed to get down the first sip of the day. He coughed a deep, wheezy fit that sounded like an engine that would not start.

"Tom," Sydney said softly. "You're not looking too well. Maybe you should give the bottle a rest for a while."

"No, I'm fine, Sydney. It's just this nasty business has me up nights. A few nips help me sleep."

"But this is the morning," Sydney said. "It's not on, Tom. You're the mayor of the greatest city on Earth. Don't forget that. I don't think it's fair to you or the city. Forgive me for dumping my advice on you, but we're going through a critical period here. We all have to be on our toes."

Bailey nodded sheepishly and placed the drink on the desk and waved his hands at it.

"You're right, Sydney," Bailey said. "It's just the goddamned pressure. Running this city is enough of a headache without watching friends get murdered or killing themselves. But you are right. I'm glad you pointed it out. Sometimes I think I drink just to forget how much I've been drinking."

Bailey chuckled. The others smiled along with him.

"That's good, Tom," Sydney said pleasantly. "Now listen, I'm going to ask you a favor. I'd really like you to host this dinner for Be Be. I want everybody there. I want all those votes sealed that night. It shouldn't be hard. A goose here, a kiss and a promise there. A real shindig. Keep the press out but well informed about it. Get some entertainment, maybe one of those Italian crooners Be Be used to like. Keep the speeches short and the speakers at a minimum. Introduce me as the only man who can fill Be Be's shoes, blah, blah, blah. You know how to handle it. Will you do that for me, Tom?"

Tom Bailey smiled. "Of course, Sydney. With pleasure. And I know just the guy to handle all the incidentals. Jack Coohill. He was Be Be's friend. He'll make sure everything goes all right."

Sydney nodded his head. "I can't stand that unctuous son of a bitch, but I think you're right about him being the most appropriate. He's the guy Be Be would have hired. Let's not look like grave robbers here. Let's do it in grand fashion, like Be Be would have.

Yeah, use Coohill. Five hundred a plate. Black tie. And get some decent food. Call Coohill this afternoon and get it rolling. I'd like to have the invitations out by the day after tomorrow."

Bailey said good-bye to Sydney and Donnelly and left, trying his best to look like the man who ran New York, with long, confident strides and his head held high. But he looked like a man running an errand.

When he was gone, Sydney Weingarten looked at Dermot Donnelly and rolled his eyes in his head and drew his face into an expression of pity.

"Poor old guy," Sydney said. "He could have been a good one too. Good manager. Speaks well. But drinks better than he does anything else. I don't think we can let him go another term."

"He's the least of our problems right now," Dermot Donnelly said. "There's something more important here that we have to deal with and his name is Joseph Gonzago."

"How can you be sure it isn't an act? Last night you had your doubts as to whether he was crazy or not." Sydney toyed with the cord of the telephone, pondering deeply.

"That was before he behaved like that in public," Donnelly said. "What I saw last night was a deranged young man in my opinion."

"But suppose it is just an act? To embarrass us? Maybe keep us off guard?"

"Well, even if it is, he's a dangerous man," Dermot Donnelly said. "For example, I don't know how he was let in, but he was out to Johnny Quinn's apartment this morning after I left. That black detective, Cunningham, even showed him the typed suicide note."

"So?"

"So, Johnny Quinn doesn't even have a typewriter."

"Oh, for God's sake, Dermot, you're starting to act paranoid. You act as if this kid is a sleuth or something. But I have an idea to settle this business. If he is crazy, something will have to be done about him."

"Also if he isn't . . ."

"Well maybe not," Sydney said. "If he isn't nuts, he'll get over it and everything will go just fine. I'm convinced of that. These things fade away. But Rosario and Gulatta were boyhood chums of his. They played sports together, palled around with him. I'll have them spend some time with him. They know him better than you or I. Who knows, maybe the kid is acting the way he's always acted. I mean, look at some of the things he's done over the years. You wouldn't call associating with the Black Panthers exactly an exercise in sanity, would you? Or running around burning down flags and cheering the blowing up of ROTC buildings? So maybe we think he's crazy now—that he's changed since his father's death. But maybe this is the way he always acts. Let Rosario and Gulatta decide. They knew him better than anyone."

"Not a bad idea," Dermot Donnelly said. "I never knew him that well myself."

"Good then, I call them this afternoon. And stop, for God's sake, worrying so much, will you? I'm the one with my name muddied in the paper."

Sydney smiled to make Donnelly relax. Donnelly returned a smile as genuine as a butcher with his finger on the scale.

"Don't forget," Sydney Weingarten assured him. "We're in charge here now."

An hour earlier Joseph had called Dr. Licht and asked if it were possible to supervise the autopsy on Johnny Quinn. The doctor had said that since he had been Johnny Quinn's doctor for as long as he could remember, he could swing the official permission with no problem. Joseph said he was most interested in Dr. Licht's opinion as to whether or not it was a suicide. Dr. Licht promised to get in touch with Joseph as soon as the autopsy was completed.

Joseph had hung up and sifted through more of the files in the Water Board. It was now almost seven o'clock, and Jack Coohill and Lou Moran sat on the small couch in the cell-like office, each sipping a Scotch. Coohill was sifting through the secret files, engrossed, amazed. Joseph was awaiting Coohill's reaction to the documents, but the old flack had not yet spoken. Lou Moran was fidgeting.

"Poor old Johnny," Lou Moran said, uncrossing his legs and crossing them the other way. "Christ Almighty nailed to the boards, I still can't believe it."

Joseph looked at Lou Moran and said, "You think Johnny killed himself, Lou? You knew him well."

Lou Moran rolled his head around in circles, trying to relieve the tension in his shoulders. His eyes took on a dusty, sad look.

"Johnny was always a lonely sort of guy, Joseph. Some people, they say he was queer. I don't mean disrespect for the dead. But I never cared one way or the other and I never once asked him about it. If he was queer, he never, you know, threw his ass around. The man acted with respect in my saloon. He was a gentleman. He was a loner and he drank pretty good and he tipped my bartenders and waiters like they were *people.* He could sleep with talkin' Mister Ed, and as long as he don't do it in the Straw Hat I don't care. But I know this much, Johnny Quinn would never deep six himself if he thought he could find out and prove who did Be Be first. It's bullshit. You heard him like I heard him that he didn't think it was an accident, so I don't buy this suicide shit any more than I shop at Tiffany's for bar glasses."

"So you think he was murdered?"

"I don't think he fell on a bullet."

Jack Coohill spoke up for the first time. "I tend to agree with Lou, Joseph. But the logical question is, why?"

"Because they knew he could dime on them, that's the why." Lou Moran was angry now, and drained his glass.

"Who's 'they,' Lou?" Joseph asked.

"Whoever. You want names? I give you names. I can give you more names than they got in a Chinese phone book. Wolfington, Weingarten, Donnelly . . ."

"Now hold on, Lou," Jack Coohill said. "It's all right to throw those names around in here. But if you do that in public, you'll be in court so fast you'll never know what happened."

"I been to court before. Worse things too. I bit off an ear doctor's ear once because I find out he's the one selling the goof balls to the kids in the school where my kids used to go before they dropped out. He was the neighborhood connection. An *ear* doctor! I says, 'Okay, I'm gonna give you a new name. From now on everybody is gonna call you Dr. van Gogh, motherfucker.' Right in his office I bit off his ear. They call that poetic justice, now he can hear poetry outta just one ear. I went to court. You know what the judge says to me? He says I did the right thing. Of course, the judge, he was a friend of Be Be's. The doctor they busted. He did time, standin' on his ear."

Joseph and Jack Coohill laughed, but Lou Moran didn't laugh. He was dead serious. He was angry. He was the kind of man who believed in what he did and when he did it, didn't think it was funny.

"I think we have a fair idea of who some of the people are," Jack Coohill said. "Just how far-reaching this crew of people goes remains to be seen. But I'll tell you one thing, this stuff in these files is political doomsday for an awful lot of people. All you have to do is mail some of this stuff to the proper authorities."

"The problem, Jack, is that there are no proper authorities," Joseph said. "Most of the people in those files are supposed to be the proper authorities, and we can't expect them to prosecute themselves. I don't think it's paranoid to say that there could easily be a cover-up."

"What about the newspapers?" Coohill said. "You can try people in the court of public opinion. You can embarrass people into prosecutions. Remember that John Mitchell was the attorney general during Watergate and he went to the slammer."

"But there's more at stake here," Joseph said as he poured fresh Scotch over half-melted cubes in all three glasses. "I know something about politics. Maybe not in the practical way you guys do. But I know this. If this stuff doesn't taint Wolfington, it'll help him. It could backfire. He could come up looking like he was the target of a bunch of guys in New York who were trying to hijack the state. Sympathy could go out for him. And I know it'll be damned hard to connect Wolfington to any of this. And besides, I don't want to ruin these people so much as I want to try to fulfill the plans that they killed Be Be for. I want to show them that killing Be Be Gonzago was not good enough. Then I want to ruin them. I want to bury them, then dig them up and kill them again. Follow?"

"Can we do it with the fungo bat the second time around?" Lou Moran was smiling now.

"I follow," Jack Coohill said. "You want Kelly to win, so we can get the proper authorities to prosecute them all after they've lost?"

"Yeah," Joseph said. "Yeah."

"There's only one way to do that, Joseph," Jack Coohill said. "And that's for you to take Be Be's seat."

Joseph stared at Jack Coohill for a long, steady beat. The idea both disgusted and intrigued him. It would mean becoming a boss of a political machine.

"How is it done?" Joseph was nervous now.

"You kick ass and take names," Lou Moran said.

"Actually that's pretty much the answer," Jack Coohill said. "The names are here." He slammed his fist against a file cabinet. "You have these files. You want the votes, you get them with these. Those you can't get with the files or those not included in the files, you get other ways. Promises, coercion, cashing in on favors due your father. There are also a bunch of files in here that don't come under a criminal classification, Joseph. Loans your father made which were never paid back. Guys he got jobs for. People whose court cases he helped out with. Patronage. A lot of guys owe your father more than a wreath of flowers, Joseph. Make them pay *you.* We need people, lots of them; money, lots of it; ruthlessness, more of that than anything else."

"Can it be done in two weeks?"

"Your name is Gonzago," Lou Moran said. Jack Coohill nodded his head in agreement with Lou Moran.

"Tough, very tough, but maybe," Jack Coohill said.

"How? Be more specific. Sell it to me, Jack." Joseph was nervous, his stomach muscles bunching.

"Okay, here's an example. Mayor Bailey called me today. He wants me to organize a big memorial dinner in honor of Be Be. I've handled dozens of these things. There is always an engraved card in a large envelope under each dinner plate from the person who stands to gain the most from the corpse they are honoring. We could slip Xerox copies of some of these files into those envelopes along with Sydney Weingarten's greeting. Incriminating documents, outstanding loans, old favors past due."

"Could I come out as a surprise guest speaker? I'd like to look down at those people."

Jack Coohill smiled. "No problem, nothing could be better."

"How much money would we need?" Joseph was getting excited.

"Say five thousand, seed. I'll see how much of it I can embezzle from Weingarten's funds."

"Perfect," Joseph said.

"It won't be easy," Coohill said. "I want you to know, that if you decide to do it, and I think your becoming boss is the only way it'll work, that this will be the toughest fight of your life. No offense, Joseph, but this isn't a march on Washington to protest the war, or some demo outside a courthouse to free the Indianapolis Five Hundred. Weingarten will do everything in his power to stop you. He will stop short of nothing, and he is ruthless and resourceful and smart as hell. He has money, clout, people. It'll be close at best, and scary and dirty and dangerous."

"But you think we can win?" Joseph was coming back to Earth now.

"Yes, I think we can," Jack Coohill said.

Joseph thought it over for a few moments. "I'll let you know by tomorrow," Joseph Gonzago said.

"Good enough," Jack Coohill said.

Coohill and Lou Moran rose, shook Joseph's hand enthusiastically, and said good-bye. Lou Moran paused before leaving, his face troubled.

"Joseph, could I ask a question over here?"

"Sure, Lou."

"If you say yes, if you decide to do this very important thing, and you become the boss, you know, like your father, and you help this Kelly get elected and all, after all that, are you still gonna go afta whoever it was who got Be Be? You know, the ones who phoned it in? Or are we just gonna let it go at that and forget it, yes or no?"

Joseph stretched his head back and examined the low ceiling. Then he lowered his head and stared directly at Lou Moran, with Jack Coohill behind him. Joseph's eyes seemed to look very far away. "No, Lou, if we do this, if we go ahead, we don't let it go at that. That will only be the beginning."

Lou Moran smiled as Jack Coohill looked on, his face rigid in acceptance and understanding. They left and Joseph Gonzago sat there alone for a long time thinking about his father.

24

Sydney Weingarten had taken a two-o'clock plane to Albany. At the airport he grabbed a taxi to a Howard Johnson's hotel on the outskirts of the capital city. It was a short ride from the airport, one of those simple hotels where airline pilots, and especially stewardesses, helped to perpetuate their reputations of promiscuity. Sydney gave the taxi driver three dollars on a $2.40 fare because he was feeling good. The headache was gone. The page-six item had been dismissed by most as silly gossip unworthy of newsprint. Sydney triumphantly told the cabbie to keep the change. The cabbie grunted and Sydney stepped out of the cab and carried his small briefcase with his change of underwear and socks and toiletries and some papers with him into the hotel. He did not have to check in. The man who had rented this suite for him kept it on a permanent basis for important visitors whom he did not want anyone to recognize. The press never hung around this hotel, and the airline transients hardly knew who the movers, shakers, and players of Albany were, even if they had bedded them down.

Sydney Weingarten walked across the small lobby and entered the elevator and rode it to the top floor, where the largest suite in the hotel was located. He stepped off the elevator and walked to the door and knocked softly. The door opened an inch and an eyeball appeared in the crack. Then the door closed again, the clatter of a chain lock being unfastened were audible, and it swung open to let Sydney Weingarten in. Sydney Weingarten put down his briefcase and shook hands with Matthew Brideson, top aide to Governor Henry Wolfington. Another man stood with his back to Sydney and Brideson, a drink in his hand, looking out over the capital city of New York State. He turned and smiled thinly and walked to Sydney Weingarten.

"I don't think you two have ever been formally introduced," Matthew Brideson said cheerfully. "Sydney Weingarten, meet Daniel Morse."

Sydney Weingarten recognized Daniel Morse from photographs

and television. He was the press secretary and media wizard of the Kelly campaign. He looked heavier and older than his pictures.

"Now, time to talk turkey," Brideson said. "You brought the gratuity I hope."

Sydney Weingarten nodded. Sydney Weingarten placed an envelope in Daniel Morse's left hand and shook his right hand. The two men chuckled for a few moments as Sydney peered across the room toward the window and out over the sun-splashed skyline of Albany.

Joseph Gonzago dropped back, faked the handoff to Rosario, and as Gulatta ran a straight fly pattern down the sideline, Joseph threaded the needle perfectly.

The ball landed squarely in Gulatta's hands, then popped out and bounded along Madison High School's playing field and Gulatta skidded five feet on his face.

"Two, four, six, eight, who do we assassinate—Gulatta, Gulatta, Gulatta!"

Joseph shouted and jumped up and down. Then he walked on his hands down the playing field. Rosario stood puffing in the center of the field and Gulatta rose groaning to his feet.

"I'm telling the coach," Joseph said in a childish whine. "Wait'll Coach Magno finds out you been out of trainin'."

Joseph was talking to the two former members of his backfield as if he were still a teen-ager. The two men were no longer in very good shape, the muscle tone long ago exchanged for cold beers slipped across a thousand saloons. Joseph was still in excellent condition, his throwing arm accurate, his wind strong, his stamina overwhelming for a man his age.

He had agreed to meet them at three o'clock, but showed up an hour early so he could have a real look at the old school. When he had arrived, kids stood outside the gates of the school smoking cigarettes. A few sucked on joints.

The playing field was in bad shape now—rocky and dusty and splotched with strangled brown grass. He walked through the field with his hands in his pockets, looking up at the crumbling wooden stands, remembering afternoons when great roars came from the throat of the crowd. And when he would look to the sidelines, there would be Gloria, her face beautiful and her teeth white, jumping high into the air after Joseph had thrown for another touchdown or even run one in on his own.

His father had seen very few of those games in his senior year, after Joseph and Be Be had a major falling out over the Vietnam war. Joseph remembered a young reporter asking him once why his father rarely came to the games anymore, remembered grabbing the young reporter by the collar and threatening to kick his ass if he printed a word about that. The reporter never did. Joseph had called him a few days later and apologized for threatening him and thanked the reporter for keeping it out of print. The reporter said he wasn't a sports writer anyway, that he covered the political beat for the *Flatbush News.* Joseph remembered the reporter's name now because the guy had gone on to become one of the best political writers in the city. His name was Jason Gotbaum and he was working for *The Village Voice.*

Joseph had even run into Gotbaum in Chicago years later during a protest of the Tim Harris trial, and they talked for a few minutes. Joseph had told Gotbaum he was there with SDS and Gotbaum was impressed. He was the first reporter to write about Joseph Gonzago's attitude toward his father. Joseph remembered as he walked along the playing field now how when that story had first appeared, he had sat and wished it would hurt Be Be Gonzago—hurt him deeply, politically and personally. He had hoped it would make him squirm. And then how that same night he had gone to bed, still thinking about the things he had said about his father, the bitterness suddenly mixing with remorse into some sappy stew of emotion that made him leak tears onto his pillow in the crash pad where he was living, and all the other boy revolutionaries asking him what was the matter and Joseph telling them all just to leave him alone.

That ached inside of him now. Because Joseph had read the diary entry in one of Be Be's leather-bound books pertaining to that particular article and the diary was self-abusive. Be Be had held no animosity for Joseph. He had said that Joseph was probably correct and that he had every right to say such things about a father who had never been able to show his son honest love.

The urge to cry erupted in him again now, but he controlled it. He stood and inhaled deeply as the school emptied of students who made for their cars and the buses and the subways to go home. He had spent so many days of his life here on this ball field, trying to find the adulation he could never get from his father at home. He had found it, but it was a pale substitute, emotional saccharine. It only had made him lonelier. Except for Gloria.

Rosario and Gulatta arrived, and soon they were tossing around a football which Joseph took from his car and the two out-of-shape men were soon winded and exhausted.

Every time one of them tried to engage Joseph in a serious conversation, Joseph would point to an imaginary player on the line and call him a name from the old Madison High roster, and he would carry on halfhearted conversations with them. Gulatta was getting fed up trying to talk to Joseph, but Rosario wasn't convinced it was for real. So when Rosario would pepper Joseph with serious questions about what he was doing with himself these days, Joseph would slam the ball into Rosario's bread basket and then tackle him or drop back and hit him with a fiercely thrown jump pass.

Now as Gulatta got up from his five-foot skid Joseph insisted they go for some pizza.

"Let's go to Avenue U and get a sausage pie and a cream soda from Dirty Jim," Joseph said.

"Dirty Jim's been dead seven years," Rosario said. "Some fuckin' eggplant walked in one night, shot him dead for thirty-six and change."

"Nah," Joseph said. "Dirty Jim can't be dead. We'll call him at home and tell him to put up a sausage with extra cheese and a bottle of Hoffman cream."

"Joey," Gulatta said to the smiling Joseph. "Dirty Jim is dead, just like Rosario says. Seven years."

Joseph knew now that it was time for the tears. Because now they would either buy the performance or walk out on it. In acting school they taught you a technique called emotional recall. If the scene at hand called for tears and you needed them you had to concentrate on some dark, terrible memory from your past. So to bring tears right now for poor old Dirty Jim, all Joseph needed to do was to recall the tears he had almost shed an hour ago for Be Be.

When Joseph took his hands away from his face, his two old school friends stood looking at him in astonishment. Gulatta backed away a little more, his eyes accepting the lunacy written in Joseph's. Rosario studied him closer, as Joseph stood in a Quasimodo half crouch, his teeth gnashing.

"It was only an old pizza maker," Rosario said. "Dirty Jim. What's he to you?"

"I said he isn't dead," Joseph screamed. "Stop saying it." Joseph sprang out of his crouch and his fist caught Rosario high on the temple, causing the large old halfback to lose his balance, which made his leather heels slide out from under him.

Gulatta had his arms wrapped around Joseph now as Joseph groaned animal noises.

"Calm down, Joseph," Gulatta said. "Calm down."

And now Joseph closed his eyes and leveled his concentration, forcing his body to switch tracks, to move over into laughter. He thought about Sydney Weingarten's face at the Brooklyn Academy of Music after being confronted by Sylvia Stein and his wife. And soon he was overcome with laughter, so much so that Gulatta let Joseph go.

Rosario stood for a long moment, his hands balled in fists, wanting to retaliate for the sneak punch. But Gulatta grasped his shoulder, led him to the side.

"Come on," Gulatta said. "The fuckin' guy is a total space shot. Be a Moonie or something in a month. You watch."

"I'd like to kick his fuckin' ass," Rosario said. "I always wanted to kick his ass. The big star on the field. The big mouth Commie asshole."

"Come on," Gulatta said, and led Rosario to their car.

Joseph watched them leave and recomposed himself. He looked at his right hand, which smarted from the impact of knuckle hitting skull. It felt just wonderful and Joseph picked up his football, plopped it in his trunk, and climbed into his car.

He allowed himself one small smile and drove toward home.

25

"I do not think it was suicide," Dr. Licht said as he handed Joseph Gonzago a stinger and sat across from him in his living room.

Joseph had stopped by Dr. Licht's house on his way home. He did not want to talk on the telephone about the matter and Dr. Licht was only a block from home anyway.

"Why do you say that?" Joseph asked, and took a drink of the brandy mixed with crème de menthe.

"Even if I did not know John Quinn well, and I knew him as well as any doctor knows a patient, I would not believe he had killed himself," Dr. Licht said, and he, too, now took a deep slug from his stinger. "It is very obvious. I simply reviewed the coroner's report. They determined it was, in fact, a suicide. But they were led to that conclusion based upon more than mere medical facts. I think there might have been official pressure to clear the matter up very quickly.

"But if you studied the hands of the man, of Johnny Quinn, you would have to come up with some doubts. Johnny Quinn was left-handed. So naturally his left hand bore more old scars and stains and evidence of use than his right hand. Nicotine stains on the left hand. Scars from household accidents, paper cuts, bones that were broken in the left hand a long time ago. The hand a person favors in life always has more calluses, more telltale signs of wear and tear. That's why I know Johnny Quinn did not kill himself."

Joseph Gonzago sat across from Dr. Licht and looked puzzled.

"I don't think I'm following," Joseph said.

"Well," Dr. Licht said, "the hand you favor would be the hand you would naturally use if you were to kill yourself. Because the hand you favor is stronger than the hand you do not favor. You see, Joseph, Johnny Quinn died from a bullet that entered his right temple. Which means he would have used his right hand. If you are going to shoot yourself, you use your favored hand. That's why I think Johnny Quinn was killed by someone else."

"You're certain?"

"Certain, no. Convinced, yes."

"Thank you, Doctor."

Joseph stood up from the arm chair in Dr. Licht's comfortable, old-fashioned living room. He placed his stinger on the coffee table and shook the doctor's hand.

"Oh, Dr. Licht," Joseph said. "Maybe you can answer me something. I've been reading through Be Be's old diaries. And he has many entries from Minnesota. Do you have any idea why my father would go to Minnesota?"

Dr. Licht inhaled deeply and freshened Joseph's drink and told him to sit back down.

"I was never allowed to tell anyone this before," the doctor said. "Be Be swore me to secrecy. But now that he is gone, I can't see the harm in letting you know. You're his son. I suppose you have the right to know. Your father went to Minnesota because I sent him there. Many times, as you say."

"You sent him there?"

"Yes," Dr. Licht said.

"Why?"

"To try to postpone the inevitable. Be Be Gonzago was a very sick man. When he was killed he was dying of a very advanced terminal cancer. He would probably have lived only a few more months. Maybe a year, because he was tough. But he lasted eleven years. I sent him for treatments at the Mayo Clinic in Minnesota. The Mayo Clinic is one of the best, but also so that he could keep his condition a secret. Once they thought he had licked it. But it came back three years later. It always does. He did not want his political enemies to know about this because they might have tried to use it against him. He also did not want Angela or you to know because he did not want pity, and he did not want to strain further the tense family situation. I advised him to tell you and Angela but he refused. Very stubborn."

Joseph sat in the stuffy old chair. My God, he thought. What have I done? I hated a man for so many years and his only crime was trying to save his own life. All those weekends away, when Mom and I were convinced he was out whoring, he was in some hospital having needles jammed into his body, chemotherapy blasted into his tissues. The man was dying and would not allow anyone to know. What have I done? Joseph asked himself again. Be Be Gonzago was a good man. He was my father.

"Joseph," Dr. Licht said with concern. "Try to understand. Be Be was a very cantankerous man. He felt that his sickness was a form of abandonment of his family. He did not want you to know about his condition because he felt it would burden you. He wanted to fight the monster himself. That's the way he was. I hate to say this, but the way he died was much less painful than what was in store for him. He also could not see very well. Glaucoma, cataracts. I feel better now that you know."

But I don't, Joseph thought. No matter how long I live I will never be able to undo what I have done to my own father. I helped kill this man, this man I should have loved.

Joseph left Dr. Licht's house in a stupor. He did not want emotions to cloud his goals now. Guilt was blinding, made you stumble and try to work from hindsight. Joseph knew he needed foresight, to be one step ahead of those people who were now his enemies, just as they had been Be Be's.

He walked slowly down the street from the doctor's house toward his own. He spotted the man sitting on the beat-up Volvo parked in front of his house. He did not recognize him at first, but as he drew closer he could see that under ten years of aging Jason Gotbaum from *The Village Voice* hadn't really changed much.

"What the hell are you doing here?" Joseph asked testily.

"I wanted to talk about your father."

"I'm not talking to anyone about my father. If I do, you'll be first. Okay? Good-bye, Jason."

Joseph moved toward the stoop and Gotbaum followed.

"How come you're not talking now? You always did before."

"That's a cheap shot, Jason."

"You're right. I'm sorry." Joseph paused on the first step and faced the reporter.

"It's a personal sort of time for me, Jason. I found out things about my father that . . . well, never mind."

"Look, I know you must be upset. When all's said and done he was your father. I understand. I always hate these assignments. Ever since I was a copy boy at the *Trib.* Interviewing the relatives of the dead is grave robbery. I'm sorry. I tried. I'll leave you alone. How are you anyway?"

"I'm okay."

Gotbaum was feeling clumsy and stared up at the leaves of the maple in front of the house. A row of sparrows sat close together on a single branch as if they were waiting for a bus. Twilight began to dim the sky.

"Look, I want you to know something. I made a pretty good living busting Be Be's chops over the years. But I felt terrible when he died. I really did. I don't know why. Maybe because he was generous to his friends. He was loyal. He was never a hypocrite. He was funny and charming. I didn't like his politics a whole lot, but I guess if I were a drinking man I would have liked to have had a beer with him rather than with some of these boring reformers. I don't know, maybe I'm getting soft in middle age."

"And gray." Joseph grinned.

Gotbaum laughed. "Noticed, hah? And *bald* too. But I think you know what I mean."

"Yeah, I guess I do," Joseph said.

"I also don't think we know all there is to know about the murder." Gotbaum was a shrewd, cunning bastard, Joseph thought. Coming through the back door now.

"Oh?"

"I'm not so sure I believe the story the way the police and witnesses tell it, that's all."

"You're beating around the bush, Jason. Say what's on your mind."

"What if the gunman wasn't trying to kill Wolfington?"

"What of it?"

"That means he was trying to kill Be Be. I'd like to know why, if that's true."

"Look, Jason, my father is dead. Nothing is going to change that. Theories don't interest me." He wasn't a very convincing liar right now. Gotbaum saw through him and Joseph knew it.

"They always did before," Jason said.

"Now's now, Jason. You're gray, I'm older too."

"I think I like the old you better," Gotbaum said as he pulled open the front door of the Volvo. "You made better copy."

"I don't even like rock and roll anymore."

"You know something," Gotbaum said as he climbed into his car. "I don't either. I have kids now too. And I can't stand the smell of pot. Long hair looks sloppy so I make my kids cut it short. I'm exactly what I always hated. And fatter and balder and grayer. Thank God I never went into television."

Joseph laughed as Gotbaum started the engine.

"So long, old timer," Joseph said.

"Listen. My instinct tells me something bigger is going on. I don't know why. I always trust my first instinct because in my business I have to. It's history in a hurry. Someone said that once. My first instinct tells me you know something no one else knows. That's why you're tight-lipped and hard to find. If you ever want to talk about it, give me a call. You know I'll write it the right way. I'm not *that* old."

"I already told you you'd be the first one I'd talk to if I ever decide to talk," Joseph said.

"Thanks," Gotbaum said. "And hey, do me a favor, will you? Get a haircut."

Gotbaum pulled away. Joseph smiled after him. Joseph Gonzago climbed the steps to his house two at a time. He wanted to get to bed early and get up early. It would be a long day tomorrow.

26

Lou Moran had not been woken up this early in more than three years. The phone rang and rang and rang. The night before he had ruined himself with espresso and Sambucca and cigarettes. He lay in the king-size bed in the apartment on top of the Straw Hat and the dream was about killing. The dream had started with him beating a liquor salesman to death with a bottle of Fleischmann's, but somehow it had changed gears and the liquor salesman became an inspector from the Board of Health and he was force-feeding paper towels to the health inspector in the bathroom of the Straw Hat and finally it ended up with Lou Moran rocking a mop down the throat of his ex-wife, Madeline, who, three years before, had betrayed him for a sanitation worker.

The phone sounded again. Lou snatched up the phone and snarled into the receiver, "Listen, whoever the fuck this is, you wouldn't like it if I make my dreams come true."

"Lou," Joseph Gonzago said. "It's Joseph."

Lou Moran sat up, leaned against the headboard, lit a cigarette, cleared his throat.

"Jesus, Joseph. What's the time?"

"Six A.M. I made up my mind." Joseph sounded bright, cheerful, his voice shored with confidence.

"Yeah?"

"It's on."

"If you were here right now I would kiss you on your lips," Lou Moran said. "Well, maybe I should make that your cheek. Put it this way, I love you for this. I'm gonna hit the rain locker, wash my body, and where should I meet you after?"

"Water Board, as soon as possible."

"Do I bring the bat?"

"Not yet, but keep it handy."

"I want Sam Stone first," Joseph said as he passed around mimosas to celebrate his decision to go for his father's chair. "I want to smoke at least one of these guys out. I think since we really have the goods on Stone maybe we can make him crack and talk. Besides, the two torpedoes that jacked me up outside my house were in Sam Stone's car. He must fear me. I want to know why. I think we should just send him a copy of his file. Especially those Xerox copies of the kickback checks. I guarantee he'll invest a dime in a phone call to me. I want to see this son of bitch come out of his cage."

Joseph was not aware that his speech patterns and his vocabulary were changing. He'd spent many years trying to bury his Brooklyn accent, ridding his speech of colloquialisms, trying to sound somehow "American," and he had succeeded. People he'd met in Los Angeles could never pinpoint his background from his speech. Now he felt comfortable in reverting to what came natural to him. He wanted to sound Brooklyn.

"Yeah, and?" Lou Moran looked at his empty glass, his face pleased with the taste of the champagne laced with orange juice.

"And what?" Joseph asked.

"What about me? What do I do?"

"Have you ever run a Xerox machine?" Jack Coohill asked.

"Of course not." Lou Moran looked almost offended.

"Then now you're going to learn, Lou." Jack Coohill pointed at the file cabinets. "We need three copies of everything in these cabinets."

Lou Moran looked at the cabinets.

"You need an experienced colored woman for that, Jack. Tell him, Joseph."

"Lou, you have to eighty-six the racist remarks."

"What racist remarks? I'm talking about giving a colored woman a job. I'm no bigot, Joseph. You know that. I just don't trust most people. I don't dislike minorities. I dislike the *majority* of the human race. Ninety-nine percent of human beings are disappointing. Right or wrong?"

"You might have a point, but if Jack says you have to learn how to run a Xerox machine, I'm counting on you to learn."

"I thought this was gonna be fun," Lou Moran said. "All right. Whadda I gotta do over here? And don't go pointing to six million buttons because they brought a cash register like that into the Straw Hat and I wound up beating it with a hammer because I couldn't figure out how to ring up a Piels."

"You can do it, Lou. Come on, I'll show you." Jack Coohill began placing papers from file folders into the self-feeding Xerox machine. Lou Moran watched the papers zip through the machine, which collated them with precision. Lou was impressed.

"Sort of like feeding these mutts into a meat grinder," he said.

"That's the idea," Joseph said. "Think positive, Lou."

"Joseph, I've prepared a list of people I think you should see," Jack Coohill said. "These are all people who owe Be Be in one way or another. I don't think it would be a good idea to let any of them know what we're up to. I think you should just make some social calls. Some you can even just phone. Let them know you're around. Ask them what they think of the gubernatorial race. Ask who they're going to support. Don't mention anything about Weingarten unless they bring it up. Do it as a sort of thank you for the mass cards and those who signed the funeral parlor book. You know. Bereaved son. I'm sorry to sound callous, but I don't think there's any more room for manners here. We have to be even more ruthless on ourselves than we are on the other side. If we can cash in on your father's death, we have to do it."

Joseph was momentarily silent and felt an ache in his chest cavity. Then he gathered his determination again and cleared his throat.

"Jack, I'm ready to do anything. Don't worry about me."

He took the list Jack Coohill had prepared for him and looked it over. The names were familiar but in a vague way, like the names of old classmates. Jack Coohill placed a pair of headphones on his head and sat next to a reel-to-reel tape recorder with an electric typewriter before him.

"Transcribing tapes is probably the main reason I left the damn newspaper business," Coohill said. "Well, that and getting caught publishing press releases under my byline."

Coohill laughed. "But, here we go." Soon the Xerox machine was whirring and Lou Moran was getting the knack of it. The staccato clatter of the typewriter seemed to harmonize with it. Joseph Gonzago smiled and walked toward the door. The typewriter and the Xerox paused for a moment.

"See you later, Boss." Lou Moran said the word boss as if it came naturally to him when speaking to Joseph. Joseph cringed, then he let his shoulders ease and smiled.

"Yeah," Joseph said, and left.

Joseph connected the telephone answering machine with little difficulty. He'd had one in Los Angeles. Everyone seemed to have one in L.A. After he hooked up the machine, he started making the calls to the people on Jack Coohill's list. By three P.M. he had spoken to twelve of the men on the list. There were no women. Ten of the men got on the phone with Joseph straight away, two called him back within a half hour. They all exchanged cordial chatter, grievances, promises to get together for a drink.

Now he was in the waiting room of Senator David Hallahan's New York office. Joseph was amazed at how easy it was to get the appointment with a United States senator. The Gonzago name was a skeleton key in New York. Joseph intended to open as many doors as he could with it.

As he sat waiting to visit Hallahan, he was seized by a terrible descent of the spirit. It was the recall of the voice of Gloria Weingarten on the phone, talking to the tape machine, as Joseph awaited a call from an assemblyman from Dyker Heights.

"Joseph, please, please call me. I need to talk to you. Please don't make me beg you."

She had not left her name or number. She knew she did not have to. She sounded wrecked. Drunk, drugged, or hungover. Heartbroken? Oh, Christ, what am I doing to her? I'm going to lose her again, he thought. After all these years, wanting her more than anything else imaginable, and now I won't even take her phone call. But I can't talk to her, I can't let her know that I think her father might be somehow responsible for my father's murder.

If I must lose her to avenge my father, I will.

He kept repeating this in his mind, trying to steel his aching heart.

"The senator will see you now, Mr. Gonzago."

Joseph walked into the inner office.

The senator walked toward him with feet as big as the boxes others buy their shoes in. He had a loping, gawky stride. Although he spoke with a quick, bubbly confidence, his pronunciation was terrible, as if he swallowed his words.

"Joseph, Joseph, so nice of you to drop by," Senator Hallahan said. "You look very fit indeed, and I want personally to express my shock, horror, and sadness over the death of your father."

"Your secretary is very beautiful."

Hallahan had expected at least a thank you, or a nodding acceptance of his words of deep regret and sorrow.

"Lucy, yes, fine-looking gal. But how have you been, Joseph?"

"You boffing her?"

"Excuse me?"

Why the hell did I ask him that?

"Just kidding, Senator. Me, oh I'm fine. I just dropped by to thank you personally for stopping by my dad's wake."

"You are welcome, but I'd like to ask you to repeat that smarmy little question you asked me before that." Hallahan was smoldering. Joseph picked it up, and all at once decided to run with it, fuck this fat pig, run him around in circles. You have him by the balls, remember that. You own this man. You are his boss.

"I asked you if you were boffing that beautiful little girl out there. Because if you are, you should be locked up for impersonating a man. You're nothing but a backhander, a take artist, and a low life, Hallahan. I know things about you you probably don't even remember you ever did, that's how corrupt you are."

"Get the hell out of this office, you scurrilous little rodent," Hallahan growled. "I don't know if you realize who you are talking to. And I don't care what mental or emotional shape you're in. I never liked you. Never liked what you stood for. And I like you even less now."

Hallahan was on his feet now. Joseph smiled at him and stood up and beamed into his eyes.

"David Hallahan, the old newsboy from Red Hook, Brooklyn, made it to the top all on his own, poor boy made good. If I look hard enough I'll probably find your balls in a jar of formaldehyde in my father's trophy room, the price of admission to the United States Senate."

"Get out."

"When was the last time somebody kicked your fat two-car-garage ass, Hallahan?"

"Shall I get the police?"

"Nah, I'm leaving. I'll see you around though."

Joseph walked out of Hallahan's office, leaving the senator almost breathless with anger. Joseph had not felt as good about himself in weeks. Coohill might think he had overreacted, but Joseph felt wonderful. He had always had a particular loathing for Hallahan. Hated him for his righteous public posturing, hated him for his dismissive, patronizing attitude toward the poor, hated him for his chameleonlike waffling, hated him for his selfishness and his conceit. It did not bother him one iota that Hallahan was a very powerful man. Joseph had the goods on him now, held him in the palm of his hand, and he could talk to him any damned way he saw fit. I am the fucking boss, he thought as he winked at the secretary on the way out. It felt tremendous. No wonder people thirsted for power. Power was wings.

Sam Stone glided down the corridor of his one-story office building in Bedford Stuyvesant. The room was decorated in wood, leather, suede, chrome, and glass with flourishing ferns hanging tastefully. He examined the plain manila envelope. There was no return address, so he dropped it on his desk and walked across the Persian carpet to the ebony bar, where he mixed himself a rum and Coke with a twist of lime in a tall glass jammed with tiny cubes of ice.

He walked back to his desk, sat behind it, opened a drawer, and took out a small square mirror and a straight-edged razor blade and tamped some cocaine from a four-gram bottle onto the glass and cut it up into four even lines. With a four-inch sterling silver cylinder, given him as a gift by Carla last Christmas, he took two lines up alternate nostrils.

Now he slid a gold letter opener under the flap of the manila envelope. He blew into the envelope as if to sanitize the contents with his breath. He took out the enclosed papers, which did not seem very important to him at first. He put the silver straw up his right nostril and snorted another line, tears forming in his right eye. He leafed through the papers, waiting for the burning sensation to subside and his vision to clear. Suddenly everything came clear at once. He saw the Xerox copies of checks from various construction companies made out to him, or one of his dummy corporations that listed him as president. Then he madly riffled through the transcript of his conversation with Be Be Gonzago.

He stood up, walked to the back of his chair, grasped the Rhodesian chrome bar with both hands, and leaned over to read the words on the paper again as if expecting them to have changed.

Sam Stone's instinct told him to pick up the phone. He did not know right away whom it was he should call. But there had to be someone who could help him. The cocaine spun around his head like a hail storm, scattering all thoughts in circles. He fumbled for his Rolodex, looking for a certain name. He finally found the card with the phone number.

The receptionist at the Nathan Hale Club told Sam Stone that Mr. Weingarten would be out of town for three days.

"Where out of town?" Buttons of sweat formed on his high chocolate-brown forehead.

"He didn't say. My guess is Albany."

"Was he going to see a Mr. Morse?"

"I have no idea, Mr. Stone."

He did not say good-bye. He hung up quickly and called Sydney Weingarten's home in Flatbush.

Ruth Weingarten heard the phone ring, and ring, and ring. She was lying on her bed in her bedroom, a room she had not shared with Sydney Weingarten for many years. Ruth got out of bed and looked out the back window from which she saw Bernie sleeping in a hammock in the yard.

Ruth Weingarten walked to the telephone and picked it up but did not say anything. She looked down at the lock on the phone dial and thought of Sydney Weingarten.

"Hello," Sam Stone shouted into the phone. "Hello. Is anyone there? This is Sam Stone."

"Everybody is going to die," Ruth Weingarten said. "They told us that in grammar school. Did they tell you that, Sam?"

"Ruth," Sam Stone said. "I need to talk to Sydney."

"Sydney? Oh, Sydney doesn't live here anymore. He must be with his fancy woman, Sam."

"Do you know where to reach him, Ruth?"

"No one has ever reached Sydney, Sam."

"Is Bernie there, Ruth?" Sam asked, exasperated.

"Bernie eats and sleeps too much, Sam."

"Ruth," Sam said, "it is very important that I find Sydney. Do you know if he went to see a man named Daniel Morse? Please, Ruth, try to remember. Daniel Morse?"

"Is he the one from the *Price Is Right?*"

"Ruth," Sam said. "Please, Ruth, try to listen to me."

"I'm not allowed to listen, Sam," Ruth said. "Sydney said so."

Ruth Weingarten hung up the telephone and went back into her bedroom and looked for her Valium.

Sam Stone heard the phone click. He looked at the earpiece and slammed the receiver down. Then he snatched it up again. He knew that he would have to act on his own. He couldn't afford to wait to clear it with Sydney Weingarten.

Only one person could have had access to these papers, Sam Stone thought. Everyone knew Be Be kept files, but the ones that were taken from his office were innocuous and almost silly. Nothing damaging in them. If there were secret files kept by Be Be

Gonzago, only one person would have access to them, and that was his son, Joseph Gonzago.

Sam Stone dialed another number.

"I need you two here right away," he said. "I can't talk about it on the phone. Come right away. Something has to be taken care of right away. Tonight."

27

Joseph Gonzago opened the front door of his house and saw the envelope on the floor of the vestibule. A plain white envelope with just his name typewritten on the front of it. Joseph immediately spun around, sensing for some reason that there was someone standing behind him. There wasn't, just the branches of the trees clicking against one another in the soft overture to dusk.

He picked up the envelope and quickly closed the door, locked it, and stepped into the house. He tore open the envelope and removed the small white sheet of paper inside. There was no greeting, no salutation, just a simple note.

> I want the tapes and the checks.
> What do you want? Call me from a safe phone.

Nothing more. Joseph smiled. The power and potential of the secret files had not really registered until now. Sam Stone was obviously shaken. He had responded in a matter of hours and anonymously, so that the note could not be traced to him. Stone knew that if Joseph Gonzago had sent the file to him, he would understand the reply.

Joseph walked to Flatbush Avenue and found a working pay phone on the corner of Church. Joseph dialed Sam Stone's number with Johnny Quinn's unused dime. It was a private line that Joseph found the number to in his father's private phone book. Sam Stone answered himself.

"Yeah." Stone did not sound nervous and Joseph knew this meant he was, like the smile of a fighter just before he kisses the canvas.

"I got your note."

"I got your package. What do you want?"

"Names."

"What names?"

"The names connected to my father's extended vacation."

"Is that all you want?"

"No, I want money."

"Cash flow is dry."

"Then I want a snowstorm. I think you know what I mean."

"That's possible."

"And I don't mean flurries. I'm talking about the kind of blizzard that still gives John Lindsay nightmares when he thinks about Queens." Joseph listened to a long pause.

"We're singing in the same key." Sam Stone's voice was soft.

Joseph knew that Sam Stone understood he wanted the names of some of the people connected to the murder of his father and, in addition, a kilo of cocaine thrown into the bargain.

"If what you bring me isn't stepped on, my stuff will be original. Are we connecting?"

"Yeah. Where? When?"

"Tomorrow night."

"No, has to be tonight."

Joseph thought it over for a moment. "All right. You ever go skating in the park at midnight?"

"No, but my associates will."

"Are we straight?" Joseph asked Sam Stone.

"Absolutely."

Joseph hung up the telephone and listened to the giddy metallic jingle of the dime drop, almost like Johnny Quinn's last laugh.

Lou Moran thought he would go blind. For the past seven hours all he had done was to make Xerox copies of files. The big blinking light from the machine kept popping into his eyes, but Lou Moran did not close the lid because he found it was faster with it open. When it was closed the papers often got stuck.

Jack Coohill had been at the typewriter all day. He had transcribed dozens of tapes. Also typed out little invitations and the envelopes they would go in. These were for the memorial dinner Mayor Bailey would host in honor of Be Be Gonzago. Coohill had tried on several occasions to explain what the contents of the papers in the files meant, but Lou Moran gave up trying to understand what he was talking about.

Then the call came. Lou snatched it up. He heard Joseph Gonzago's voice say hello on the other end.

"Listen, Joseph, no offense with the minorities or anything, but don't you think we can at least get a rabbinical student or somebody to do this copying shit?"

There was a long pause. Lou listened and suddenly a smile began to spread like prairie fire across his face.

"Yeah, sure. Are you kidding me or what? Tonight. Already? Yeah, of course, you can bet your cannolis I'll be there. I wouldn't miss this if Tony Bennett had reservations at the Straw Hat. I'll put on my best suit."

Jack Coohill looked at Lou Moran after he had hung up.

"What's cooking?"

"Pigs' knuckles."

Lou Moran was evasive, and instead of saying any more he started whistling as he sped the papers through the Xerox machine.

"This ain't really such bad work," he said.

The moon was full and the lot was empty. The parking lot of the Wollman Skating Rink in Prospect Park had the capacity for more than a thousand vehicles, but the only one parked there was Joseph Gonzago's Plymouth, sitting dead center, with no other vehicle in sight.

The lot was dimly lit by far-off fluorescent lamp posts. The floodlights that ordinarily lit the tarmac were not on now because the rink was closed for the season. In the near distance the hypnotic disk of moon was reflected in the mirror-topped waters of the lake. Occasionally a bird would flutter in the trees. The sounds of cars moving on the Prospect Park roadway were distant and remote. From the other side of the lake came the sounds of youth. Boys. Girls. A radio. The noise carried on the lake like electricity. Joseph heard the sound of an approaching engine and saw a set of headlights. The car moved toward him. Joseph felt his heart climbing as if for escape. He straightened his spine. Felt for the pistol. The sweat poured freely down his body. The car approached and then Joseph saw the people inside. Teen-agers, a guy with manicured hair and an open-necked collar and a girl, looking nervous, young, very pretty. The driver saw Joseph in the car and swept a U turn. Someone is definitely going to lose her virginity tonight, Joseph thought as the car left the parking lot and rolled back onto the circular park road. Just not here. Too bad, because there was moonlight and still water on a lovely warm night.

He heard what he thought was a scrape of leather on asphalt coming from behind him. Then he didn't hear it anymore. His eyes focused on the rearview mirror, but he could see nothing except the solid licorice blackness of the park.

Then all at once both doors of his car were yanked open and a pistol was pressed to his head. They had come on foot! They had not approached by car as expected. The two black men were instantly recognizable to Joseph. The tall one still had a splint on his finger. The other one was looking on the floor of the backseat to be certain no one was with him.

"This time your ass is mine, motherfucker," said the tall one. "I think maybe I'll piss on your face before I blow it off your skull."

"Get the tape and papers and blow his fuckin' head off and let's split," said the second man nervously. He started rummaging in the glove compartment, found nothing. He put his pistol into his belt and searched the front seat.

"The tape, motherfucker," the big man said. Joseph looked into the big man's face. The smaller man was bent over the backseat now; he had removed the cushion and was rummaging inside the seat foundation. The big man grabbed Joseph by the front of his shirt, pulling him to an inch of his face. "Open your mouth so I can piss in it."

Joseph smiled at the big man. The big man was momentarily flabbergasted. "You think this is funny, motherfuck—"

He never got to finish the sentence. Lou Moran's fungo bat whammed down with double-fisted impact on the nape of the big man's neck. The smaller man looked up. "Hey, what the—" Joseph had his pistol in the smaller man's petrified face. Now Lou Moran slammed him with the bat across his spine, hearing something pop. The little man's eyes sunk and his tongue lumped over his lower lip. Lou Moran dragged him by the seat of his pants and sprawled him on the tarmac. He whacked each knee once, then each ankle and did a finale with a golf shot to the right temple.

Lou Moran adjusted his beautifully tailored three-piece pin-striped suit and walked back around to the other side of the car where the larger man was struggling to a kneeling position.

"Inside slider," Lou Moran said as he detonated the fungo bat off the large man's right jawbone, sending the jaw swinging like a gate before he thumped to the ground in a heap.

"Lou, enough, man, enough."

"Nah."

Lou Moran crushed both kneecaps and then seemed satisfied and hitched up his pants. He motioned toward the open hood of the trunk from where he had come.

"Fuckin' breathing in there stinks." He took out a pocket comb and ran it straight back through his hair and looked at the teeth of the comb before putting it away. "Lost the crease in my right pants leg. These two fuckin' pineapples were useless. The Greeks at least put up a fight."

Lou Moran slammed the trunk of the car.

"Gimme the envelope with the Xerox copies I put in there and I'll leave it in their car," Lou Moran said.

"Where is their car?"

"Must be around the other side of the skating ring."

"Rink."

He searched the fallen men for car keys, found them, and walked around and found the concealed Lincoln. Joseph followed him. Lou Moran opened the car, careful to use his handkerchief to avoid leaving fingerprints, and looked inside. It was clean.

He walked to the back of the Lincoln and opened the trunk. It, too, looked clean. But Lou Moran took out a stiletto and ripped open the spare tire. Inside were three large plastic bags filled with white powder.

"That's the coke, I guess, but I don't know. I never put nothing stronger than my pinkie up my nose."

Joseph tasted the white powder. It was crystal cocaine.

He dropped the manila envelope with another Xerox copy of the Sam Stone file into the trunk in plain sight. Lou Moran then pulled on a pair of gloves, got in the Lincoln, and drove it in reverse to the center of the parking lot and got out. Joseph followed on foot. Both black men were still unconscious. Joseph felt both of them for a pulse.

"Don't worry, they're alive, they'll just be playing marbles with dice for a while. Let's go."

Joseph climbed into the Plymouth, took a last look at the two men sprawled beneath the full moon as Lou Moran drove out onto the park road.

"Why'd you have to hit him the last shot?" Joseph asked.

"What are you kiddin' me? He said he was gonna piss in your mouth! Nobody gets away with saying something like that to the boss of Brooklyn, I don't give a fuck who he is. Besides, they were sneaks. They come on foot."

"You enjoyed doing that, didn't you, Lou?"

"It was all right. I done better. I'm outta shape. My wind is gone. Fuckin' cigarettes. I could use a drink. What about you?"

"Till the sun comes up."

28

"Two goddamned days I'm gone and you guys can't handle a simple silly little thing like this!" Sydney Weingarten was shouting at the top of his lungs at Sam Stone, who sat abashedly before him. Dermot Donnelly sat off to the side, but Sydney's tirade was not directed at him.

"I'm sorry, Sydney," Sam Stone said. "No one knew where you were."

"No one was supposed to know where I was."

"Well, I thought this matter needed to be seen to immediately," Sam Stone said. He was a nervous mishmash of tics.

"Sam, do you realize you have just ruined your whole career?" Weingarten stood up and began pacing. "You could have been the first black chairman of the Brooklyn Democratic party after I left for the Court of Appeals. I would have given it to you. All for yourself, for your people, Sam. But now, how do you think it would look for a drug dealer to be running the party?"

"I told them not to take the drugs, not to use my car. I told them to rent one. It was supposed to be simple."

"It was simple. You used two simpletons. And the transcript! Christ Almighty, Sam, how did you ever allow that to get taped in the first place. How many times over the years did I tell you and all my friends to be careful what you say in Be Be's office. I always suspected he used tape machines. But no, everybody told me I was paranoid. You can bet your ass there's nothing like that on me up there."

"It was three years ago, Sydney. I trusted Be Be then. I'm sorry."

Weingarten picked up a ringing phone. It was the receptionist telling him that Rosario and Gulatta were outside. Sydney told her to tell them to wait a few minutes.

"What am I going to do, Sydney?" Sam Stone appeared on the verge of tears.

"Time, probably. But we'll see what Dermot can do for you. But this involves the state too. We can't keep the whole lid on this, Sam. I mean we don't even know if Joseph Gonzago ever showed up there in the park. These two bozos of yours were stupid enough before they had their heads bashed in. What the hell could be left upstairs now? How can you be sure it was Joseph Gonzago who you talked to on the phone?"

"I never thought of that."

"Never thought of that. Wonderful. It might have been a cop, for Christ sakes, trying to get me through you."

Sydney paced another few minutes, thinking.

"Okay, look, lie low. Don't talk to reporters. Don't leave the state or you'll be in violation of bail if you do. Stay home, don't move around. Don't answer the phone. We'll work out some other kind of communication, but don't answer the phone and stay at home. Low profile this thing. That's all you can do for now. The transcript is mostly useless without the tape. Let's hope to God that doesn't turn up. I'll try to keep you out of jail. That's the best I can do."

"Thank you, Sydney."

Sam Stone rose from his chair and walked to the door and went out the back door into a waiting limousine to avoid reporters.

"A real mess," Donnelly said. He had been quiet throughout the meeting.

"Just how bad?"

"The worst. Do you know how much a kilo of pure cocaine is? You could keep ten square blocks of Brownsville awake for a week with that much cocaine. And the transcript. Just how much of this garbage are Stone and Garcia into? Garcia must be getting it out of Washington Hospital up in the Bronx. He's the chairman of the board there, you know. Pure cocaine isn't easy to come by. This is pharmaceutical."

"I had no idea how deep in they were. I thought they just dabbled in it. I had no idea it was this big. I thought it was for kicks. But what can we do? Can we smother it?"

"Smother my Irish ass," Donnelly said. "The narcotics division was on the phone to reporters before I even got out of bed this morning. Do you have any idea what the *New York Post* is going to do with this? And to tell you the truth, I don't blame them. This is big news. And I am going to respond to it. I am going to convene a grand jury. I am going to prosecute the dumb son of a bitch. I have to. There's no way around it."

"Can we postpone it until after the primary?"

"I guess so. Maybe. As long as I convene a grand jury right away I can call witnesses over a period of months. But Jesus, Sydney, how the hell could he do this to us? You know what that grand jury is going to do? They are going to indict. They have to. Because I will have to make sure they do. And then I will have to prosecute, and unless he gets those two zombies of his to take the fall, I will have to try for a conviction. I simply refuse to bungle this case. I can't come in looking like a shithole prosecutor, taking care of my friends. I can't. How can anyone ever appoint me to a higher law-enforcement position if I screw up an open-and-shut case like this one? It would ruin my reputation, and I refuse to destroy myself to save that goddamned idiot. I'm sorry but I've worked too hard, taken too many risks."

"What if we convince Sam to leave the country, like Adam Clayton Powell?"

"Of course that's a possibility."

"But for the time being stretch it along a little until we can arrange it. You never know, he might decide to leave right away. That would clear up an awful lot of problems. You could beat your breast and call for his blood and all things would be square."

"Only one problem with that," Donnelly said. "He would always be somewhere knowing things we wouldn't want him to know."

"It'll work for the time being anyway. We'll have to start making some arrangements right away, I think. Let's just make him disappear."

"I never heard that," Donnelly said, and walked out of the room, still furious and shaken.

Rosario and Gulatta came in about a minute after Donnelly left. The two men sat down without speaking.

"I've thought over what you two told me about the Joseph Gonzago matter," Sydney said. "I'll leave the incidentals to you. Just make cotton picking sure it doesn't come into this office. But I think your proposal has merit."

"Then the answer is yes." Rosario looked eager.

"I never said yes. I said it was meritorious, I never, ever, want to hear another word about it again. And remember that this dinner is two weeks from today. Now if you don't mind, I have to ask you to excuse yourselves. I have enough troubles as it is. So long."

Both men stood, looked at each other, nodded, and left Sydney Weingarten on his own in his office. Sydney looked down at the *Post* headline and shook his head. You idiot, Sam, he thought. You made the pants too short.

It was the tenth door Lou Moran had knocked on that day. This work was better than making Xerox copies. The man he was seeing was the publisher of a newspaper called the *Flatbush News,* a Brooklyn weekly with substantial clout and readership in the community. The paper made a pretty good profit by paying reporters minimum wages and printing lots of press releases and church and synagogue bulletins along with political advertisements. The legal notices brought in an awful lot of revenue too. The "legals," as they were called in the newspaper business, and the campaign ads during election time helped out the paper enormously. The man who delegated the public legal advertising had been Be Be Gonzago. Be Be had always given the legal notices to local papers that agreed to endorse regularly the candidates of Be Be's choice. Be Be kept a dozen such newspapers afloat with the legal advertisements from the civil courts, listing name changes, custody claims, guardianships, conservatorships, ward-of-the-court cases, auctions, and the other nonsense from the probate and civil and traffic courts that by law had to be published in a newspaper for public perusal. Which newspaper, the law did not specify, so Be Be had given these ads, paid for with public funds, to newspapers that were friendly to him. It was an important network of influence for the machine.

Arthur Gould greeted Lou Moran warmly. Gould occasionally stopped into the Straw Hat for a drink because Lou Moran was an advertiser in the *Flatbush News.* Lou Moran had seen nine other publishers from Bay Ridge, Fort Greene, Greenpoint, Sunset Park, Brooklyn Heights, Park Slope, Bensonhurst, and Red Hook already today, and so his spiel was down pat by the time he got to Arthur Gould. All the other publishers had agreed to respect Joseph Gonzago if he became the chairman of the Brooklyn Democratic party. They were all rather surprised that such a move was in the works since everyone thought that Sydney Weingarten was the obvious successor to Be Be's vacant seat. Lou Moran told each publisher that he was being given this information in the strictest confidence, that absolutely no one else knew about Joseph Gonzago's plans but Lou Moran, Joseph Gonzago, and whoever the particular publisher in the room happened to be at the time. Lou Moran told each publisher that theirs was the only newspaper being informed because it was apparent that their particular paper was the best in Brooklyn.

"Joseph Gonzago?" Arthur Gould said, flabbergasted.

"Yup," said Lou Moran. "Now I don't have to remind you, Arthur, that Be Be was generous to you over the years. This paper done good by the regular Democrats in Brooklyn. It wasn't Sydney Weingarten who gave you legals from up in Albany. It was Be Be down here in Brooklyn from Court Street. Be Be never forgot any a you guys at Christmas either."

"Chanukah, Lou, not Christmas."

"Same deal, Arthur. The legals will still come to you and a pretty good bonus if you stick with us if Joseph gets his father's seat. I want you to endorse our candidates in the primary. Use the family angle, anything you want. But if Joseph becomes chairman and Sydney Weingarten runs his own group, a split might come in the party for a while. But remember, it's the chairman who hands out the legal ads, not the speaker of the assembly."

"Why would Sydney form a separate group?" Arthur asked.

"The gubernatorial primary," Lou Moran said. "Joseph and Sydney, they don't see eye to eye on who should get the nomination. Whoever's gonna get it needs Brooklyn. You could help us with that with the *News.*"

"Who is Joseph going to endorse if he becomes chairman?"

"I can't say yet, but it was the guy who Be Be wanted," Lou Moran said. "What the hell difference it make who it is?"

"All right, Lou," Arthur Gould said. "But only because he's Be Be's son. I owe Be Be a lot and I'll respect his blood. You can count on the *News,* Lou."

"Good," said Lou Moran. "And don't let Weingarten's people harass you. If they threaten you, gimme a call and we'll take care of it. One hand washes the other, Arthur."

"Deal," said Arthur Gould, and Lou Moran walked out the door. He had only two more papers to go. That would take care of that. Tomorrow he would start talking to the big campaign contributors. To the lawyers who got the best appointments down at the probate court in return for a contribution later on; to the bail bondsmen who got the most references from the courts; to the real estate speculators who were marched past the red tape for building permits and zoning changes; to the contractors who got the best contracts on the worst bids for publicly funded building in Brooklyn. There were a lot of people to see tomorrow. But they could all be easily convinced.

Be Be Gonzago had kept a file on every one of them.

When she arrived at her mother's house at five o'clock that evening Gloria Weingarten felt very tired. One minute a great euphoria would bubble through her, making her very pores seem to tingle. A minute later she was nose-diving back to reality. Joseph is gone, she would say. But he'll be back. There is a reason and method to his madness. Then her spirits would sink again. He's gone again and this time forever, she would admit to herself. He does not phone me, does not accept my calls, he does not want me.

Gloria Weingarten needed her mother. Mother always forgave, consoled, and made the most sense.

Bernie was in the living room watching television and Ruth was probably upstairs having her afternoon nap. Gloria said nothing to Bernie, just breezed by him and hurried up the stairs. She went in to look at her mother, wanting to see her sleeping, peaceful face. Instead she found her mother wide awake and standing at the back window staring out at the big old oak tree that grew in the yard. When Gloria entered the room, Ruth slowly turned around, a beatific smile on her face, her fingers joined in front.

"Hello, darling," Ruth Weingarten said. She looked almost sanctified, her face in a state of grace and clarity, her eyes smiling as well.

"Mother," Gloria Weingarten said. She felt her throat constrict; her eyes were filled with despair.

"What is it, darling?" Ruth still smiled, but it was an expression of reassurance.

"Mother, I'm scared."

Ruth held out her arms, and suddenly Gloria Weingarten was a little girl, alone and terrified. Gloria dropped her handbag to the floor and walked slowly to her mother, who took her in her arms and held her to her breast.

"Mother, what is happening to all of us?"

"Only the things we let happen, darling. I'm so glad you came to me. Look at me."

Gloria looked up at her mother, who was smiling.

"Look at me? Do you see anything different?"

"Yes."

"What?"

"I see who you used to be."

Ruth Weingarten laughed and took a deep sigh and patted her daughter's cheek.

"Well, not quite. But I'll show you something."

She took Gloria by the hand and led her to her bureau and

opened a drawer. In the drawer were four pint bottles of whiskey, the seals intact, full.

"Five days. Not a drop. And do you know why?"

"Why?"

"Because I refuse to kill myself. Not for my sake. But for yours and even that big lump downstairs, who is still and always will be my son no matter what. But mainly because your father wants me dead and I refuse to do him any more favors."

Ruth Weingarten's speech was full and clear, she did not slur a single syllable.

"Oh, Mother, I'm so proud of you. I am so damned proud."

"Hey, don't get too excited. It's only five days. And believe me it isn't easy. Do you know how many times I wanted to get out of that bed last night to open one of those bottles? About once every fifteen minutes. But you know what I did instead? Every time I got the urge for a drink I either picked up an emery board and did my nails, or put on nail polish, or dabbled around with makeup and eye shadow. For goodness sakes, I even shaved my legs and plucked my eyebrows. Last night was the worst. I've cut down on the pills. Cut them in half."

Ruth wiped away tears from Gloria's eyes with beautifully manicured fingers. Gloria hugged her and smiled. She smelled like Mother, the Mother of yesteryear, a smell of cleanliness and safety and truthfulness. She was very warm and very soft to Gloria's touch.

"I'm dying for a drink right now," Ruth said. "I was going to remove the nail polish and paint them again. I don't know what else to do."

She held her daughter at arm's length, her soft hands cupping Gloria's shoulders. She looked at Gloria's face and smiled and then glanced over at a photograph of Gloria taken when she was ten years old. The old photo was in a brass frame on the teakwood dresser, and her hair was in banana curls.

"Will you let me do your hair?"

Gloria laughed, looked at the old picture, and pointed. "Not like that, Mother?"

"Oh, come on, give an old souse a break. Hell, girl, I'm still your mother, and I'm not asking I'm telling you. Now sit you down there and keep your head straight."

Gloria was laughing now, her spirits soaring and staying there.

"Anything you say, Mother."

Ruth Weingarten went and got a spray bottle and setting lotion and a bag of rollers from her bathroom, which was connected to the bedroom. Soon she was wetting down Gloria's hair, and combing it straight as she hummed the "Blue Danube." Gloria was laughing hysterically as her mother began setting her hair in banana curls.

"Gloria, I need help," Ruth said, fastening a curler in her daughter's hair. "I'm not sure I can fight this all alone. Will you help me?"

"Of course, Mother."

"I need to see a doctor. Not one of Sydney's doctors. I need to see someone who is going to save my life."

"I'll do anything I can, Mother, you know that."

"Now, what's wrong with *you?* You came here to see your mother because you're frightened and confused. Tell me."

Gloria was silent for several moments.

"It's Joseph, Mother."

"I always liked Joseph the best of all your boyfriends, and God knows you've had enough of them."

"That's my problem. I not only like him best. I love him. I am absolutely head-over-heels fall-down-on-the-floor in love with him and have been for more than fifteen years."

Ruth chuckled. "That's a problem? I wish I had your problem. I wish I had that problem even once in my life."

"I can't sleep, I walk around in a stupor, I can't even do my work."

"That sounds like fun. It sounds wonderful to me."

"But he doesn't love me, Mother."

"Oh, well, that's not so bad. At least you love him. That's half the battle. Besides, you don't really know if he doesn't love you."

"He's told me so."

"Don't ever go believing everything a man tells you. As you know I haven't had that much experience with men, but I watch them and I've looked at a few. More than a few."

"Mother!" Gloria chuckled.

"What's the matter? I'm not supposed to be human? When I see an attractive man I'm not allowed to look?"

Gloria laughed.

"And I'll tell you something about what I've noticed about them. They're all babies. Growing up terrifies them because they know that at some point in their lives they must tell the truth. Babies don't have to."

"But he changes all the time. I'm afraid he might have emotional problems, mental problems."

"Hey, little girl, that boy's father was just shot to death. He has no mother, no father, and he's a baby. And you expect him to find time in all of that for you? I'll tell you something. If men are babies then women are spoiled brats. But tell me, and don't be embarrassed, have you slept with him since he's been back?"

Gloria turned to her mother, her eyes wide, her mouth agape. "I don't believe this. I just don't believe this. Come on!"

"Well have you?"

"Yes. All right. Yes. I feel like hiding in the closet."

Gloria began laughing but tried to hold it in.

"Was it good?"

"Are you sure you're my mother and not some impostor?"

"Then it was good. Well, after fifteen years it didn't have to be. And I bet it was more than just once."

"For God's sake, Mother, you're going to make me die. Yes, more than once and it was good every time. But I had to practically drag him there."

"Then he loves you."

"What?"

"It's obvious he wasn't just after your body, little girl," Ruth Weingarten said, smiling. "If you had to coax him and he did it, well, that means he wanted who you are not just what you are. I mean you only have to take one look at Joseph Gonzago to know that he could have his pick. He's not handsome, he's beautiful."

"Son of a bitch, Mom," Gloria said. "But then all at once he changed, sort of acted real cold, aloof. It started at the *Hamlet* play. He said Sydney was right, that I shouldn't see him any more.

"Then I'm sure he loves you, because he wouldn't have bothered saying anything at all if he didn't feel anything at all for you."

"Do you really think so, Mom?"

"Yes. But Joseph's father's been killed. Murdered. Don't you understand that? Love is an emotion that's always there, darling, but anger, guilt, vengeance are things you have to deal with right away. Love goes on the back burner. You know what I mean?"

"But I want to help him through this. I know he's hurt, Mom. I want to help him."

"Then stay out of his way. He'll get around to you. Don't you dare get jealous of the love he had for his father or you'll lose him forever. He knows what he's doing."

"What do you think he was doing with Sylvia Stein at the play then?"

"Believe me, not everyone has the same bad taste as your father, my dear. Joseph Gonzago is up to something, but it certainly isn't Sylvia Stein's knickers."

Gloria gasped, and then laughed.

Ruth was finished with the banana curls now. "Let it dry," she said. "You'll look beautiful. Maybe you should write Joseph a note. A short note. Tell him you know he's troubled. Tell him you'll wait. Tell him you love him. Let him know you'll stay out of his way."

"You think so, Mom?"

"That's what I'd do. And I've been thinking an awful lot about what I would do if I were a single woman again in these past few days."

Ruth took a step backward and with a flourish flaunted herself in front of Gloria.

"Not too bad, am I?"

"You're beautiful, Mom. Beautiful."

"Good, then get ahold of a lawyer too. I want a divorce."

Gloria stood up and looked at her mother in disbelief.

"A divorce!"

"You don't think I'm going to save my life to throw it away, do you?"

Gloria felt a sudden pang of sadness.

"Are you sure? I mean, don't you think you should think it over?"

"I have, darling. For over fifteen years."

"Have you told Sydney?"

"We don't talk, you know that. He's too busy with his fancy woman, with his career and his friends. Like that Sam Stone. He called here yesterday in a panic. I understand why now. Did you see the news?"

"Yes, I did. Scoundrel. I hope he rots in jail."

"He called looking for Sydney. But Sydney's been away. I don't know where. I guessed at his fancy woman's house. But Sam Stone asked me if he went to see someone, someone named Daniel Morse. Do you know who that is?"

"Sure. He works for the Kelly campaign."

"Oh, well, then I must have had the wrong name. Sydney is working for the other one, Wolfington."

"But why would you remember that name?"

"I'm not sure. I was very bad yesterday. I think I was half delirious. The withdrawal pains are horrifying, Gloria."

"Daniel Morse is a media consultant with Kelly."

"I'm sure I've heard his name mentioned before too. By Sydney.

With Donnelly and Stone. But I was drinking heavily then. They were always talking about his gratuity. But maybe I'm wrong, it might have been a different name. I'm not sure."

Ruth plugged in a hair dryer and blew the hot air over Gloria's hair. It took less than two minutes to dry it and the two did not talk while the machine buzzed. Then Ruth took out the curlers, one by one; the long cylinders of hair hung from Gloria's head in perfect proportions. When she was done, Gloria looked beautiful, more beautiful than her mother had seen her since she was a child.

"Now, little girl, aren't you just the bee's knees?"

Gloria laughed at herself in the mirror.

"Not bad. Now I'll just have to watch out for child molesters."

They both laughed and then they embraced.

"Thanks, Mom."

"Thank *you* for coming to see me and for talking and helping me. Please don't tell Sydney anything about this. As far as he's concerned I'm still a lush, all right? He's a very spiteful man, and if he thought I was trying to help myself, I think he might try to have me institutionalized. He has the doctors on his side, you know. He could do it easily."

"Don't worry, Mom." Gloria kissed her mother. "I love you and won't let anything happen to you."

"I love you too, darling. And I'll bet so does Joseph. If he has any brains at all."

Gloria left her mother in her bedroom, looking out the window at the oak, humming the "Blue Danube" and smiling.

Lou Moran had convinced Joseph Gonzago to get fitted for the suit by the Old Ginzo, the tailor in Bensonhurst who had always made Be Be's suits. It was three nights ago, the night Lou Moran had taken his fungo bat out of retirement.

"You have to have a fuckin' suit," Lou Moran had said, just before he belted back a double Sambucca. "You wanna be a boss, you gotta look boss." Joseph chuckled. He hadn't heard that expression since the early sixties.

Joseph had promised Lou Moran to go to the old tailor. And now he was standing in front of the wizened old man's shop on Eighty-sixth Street near Eighteenth Avenue, a small, narrow shop, the front of which was not much bigger than a kiosk. The sewing machine was planted in front of the dusty old window where the simple, peeling paint legend read: SCARPETTA—HAND TAILOR.

Joseph walked into the old shop, saw the old man sewing a fine silk jacket by hand with a pair of bifocals nesting on the tip of his long, bony nose. The Old Ginzo must have been seventy-five or more, his face a checkerboard of creases and wrinkles, with the soft blue eyes of a turtle fisherman, his hair still remarkably dark, his shirt collar frayed and gray. His fingernails were long and the color of butterscotch. A cigarette idled in a tin ashtray. The sun lanced through the dusty window and silvery dust particles twirled in the light. The store was jammed, packed, overstuffed with material, suits, pants, jackets, vests, trench coats.

Joseph nodded to the old man, but the old man did not nod back. He stared at Joseph Gonzago with an awe that older men usually reserve for younger athletes. He placed his needle and thread down on the linoleum-lined ledge of the window and stood up. He was not much taller than five feet, but his upper torso was still broad and powerful.

"Hello," Joseph said, feeling a little uncomfortable with the manner in which the Old Ginzo stared at him. "I'd like to get fitted for a suit."

The Old Ginzo said nothing, walked around his small, cluttered counter, and took Joseph Gonzago's right hand in both his veiny hands. He stared up into Joseph's eyes.

"You are the son of Be Be Gonzago," the Old Ginzo said.

Joseph was momentarily speechless.

"Yes."

"Yo do-a me great honor coming to my store. Sit down, I get the grappa and we drink to the soul of your father."

The Old Ginzo shuffled off toward the back of his shop, pulled aside a dingy single curtain that revealed small living quarters in the rear of the shop—a single bed, a table and two chairs, a couch, a television set, and a bathroom. The old man returned in a moment with two smudgy glasses and a bottle of grappa. He placed the two glasses on the counter, half filled each one, and handed one to Joseph.

"To the eternal rest of the soul of your father."

The Old Ginzo clicked glasses with Joseph Gonzago and the grappa slid down his throat. Joseph followed his lead. The Old Man then took each glass, wiped the inside dry with the tail of his white shirt, and shuffled off to the back room to put them away. He returned quickly.

"How did you know I was Be Be's son?"

"Because he gave you his face. And because every time he came to my store he showed me your pictures. He was a very great man. A very kind man. A very proud man. Proud mostly of his son."

Joseph looked at the small man and smiled softly.

"Thank you very much, signor."

"No, I thank you for coming to me. I make you the best suit of your life. I put everything else away. This suit is for Gonzago, I tell everybody they must wait. Come here."

He stood Joseph on a stepping stool and measured his leg length.

"Your father was my best customer for thirty-five year. Nothing but the silk. I make maybe two hundred suits for Be Be Gonzago, and every time I see him on the television or the newspaper he's wearing Scarpetta's suit. This always make me very proud. But mostly to know this man. He wear a suit maybe two or three times, and he give them away. He gives them to the winos on the Bowery sometimes. Imagine! Fine silk suits on the Bowery. This is the kind of man he was. So wonderful. Sometimes he just give them back to me—like new—and I sell them. He tells me to keep the money. I cry my eyes out when he gets shot. I'm telling you, like my brother was killed. A very great man. I make you the same kind of suit he wear allatime. The very best. Silk. So it fits your body like the skin of leopard."

"Mr. Scarpetta," Joseph said, "I want this to be exactly like the kind of suit my father would wear on the most important night of his life. I need it in one week. I'll pay you whatever it costs."

The Old Ginzo looked up at Joseph and took several straight pins from his lips. The yellow measuring tape was looped around his thick old neck.

"Your name is Joseph, I know because Be Be tells me this. So I want you to do me a favor, Joseph. Don't call me Mr. Scarpetta. Your father, he always call me Old Ginzo. I like this name better. Because there is affection in this name. I have your suit in less than a week, because I tell everybody else, the mafiosos, everybody, to go and fuck themselves. You Be Be Gonzago's boy. When my brother and sister and my nephews and my cousins needed a green card to come into this country I call up Be Be. He gets me the green card or the visa faster than I make him a suit and they take the next plane to America. Be Be Gonzago came to the wedding of my daughter, to the funeral of my wife. You think you can pay me your money? You want to pay money you go to Barney's and pay your money. You want a suit from Old Ginzo, you accept it with affection as a gift. For free this suit."

"No, with all respect to you, Old Ginzo, I must pay you for this suit. Your offer is accepted with affection and I thank you for your kind words for my father. But if my father ever taught me anything, it was to respect the old people. I'm a young man, you're an old man, and you work hard and must get paid. All right?"

The Old Ginzo smiled, shook his head joyously.

"Same like your father. He makes the favor but he not take the favor. You're just like your father. This must mean you will also be a very great man."

The Old Ginzo looked up at Joseph, who towered over him. The man's eyes fastened on Joseph's and he spoke with an inner authority of peasant wisdom. He held a piece of white tailor's chalk in his right hand and emphasized his words with it.

"See, I'm just an old tailor, but I know this much," he said. "You come from the blood and balls of Be Be Gonzago, you gonna be the boss just like your father."

Joseph held the stare of the old man. His words were simple, but they set Joseph's blood afire.

"You mark my words, Joseph Gonzago," the old man said softly. "I make this suit for the Boss."

Joseph's lips parted in a self-assured grin.

29

It had taken Joseph two days to figure out a way to get to see Frank Donato on his own. The Waterfront Commission guys were pros and they knew every one of Donato's moves. They were not easy to shake. But on this bright Wednesday morning Frank Donato left his office at the ILA and walked downstairs and stepped into his white Mercedes 450 and started the engine. At almost precisely the same moment the two agents assigned to tail Frank Donato wherever he went started their car.

Frank Donato was smiling to himself. He didn't know if Joseph's cockamamy idea would work, but even if it didn't it would be good for a few laughs. Frank Donato put a gray Stetson fedora on his head and jimmied the gear shift into drive and slowly cruised along Court Street to Union Street and headed up toward Grand Army Plaza. He checked his rearview mirror occasionally to be sure his shadows were with him. They were.

At Fifth Avenue he stopped for a light and the tail car rolled up close behind him. Frank waved to the two men in the tail car through the rearview mirror. The two shadows waved back with mock curled fingers. The light turned green and Donato proceeded up Union Street past a group of Puerto Ricans who stood looking under the hood of a Pontiac in front of a store called FLAT FIX. All the Puerto Ricans were pointing at the motor of the car and holding bottles of beer wrapped in one-pound brown paper bags.

Frank Donato smiled and kept driving. At Seventh Avenue he stopped for another light and again waved to the two men behind him in the same fashion. The agents smiled too and waved back. The light changed and Frank Donato proceeded up Union Street toward Grand Army Plaza at the mouth of Prospect Park. He waited for a light here too and the three men waved at each other once more. It was a common game.

Then this light turned green and Donato proceeded to the massive traffic circle. As he did, one dozen white Mercedes 450s exited Prospect Park and began honking horns loudly. Each driver wore a gray fedora hat. Soon there were Mercedeses everywhere and the two Waterfront Commission agents drove and watched in confusion because the cars all looked the same. The man on the passenger side of the tail car jumped out and started looking into the windows of the many Mercedes as they sped past him, but none of the men he saw was Frank Donato.

Frank Donato was on the other side of the circle now, watching the scene in his rearview mirror as the two Waterfront Commission men scrambled in the middle of the circle of white Mercedes like desperate contestants in a game show, screaming at the men who sat idly behind the many steering wheels. The Waterfront Commission car could not move; it was surrounded by the expensive German automobiles. Frank Donato looked at all of this through the rearview mirror, and as he took Eastern Parkway down past the Botanic Garden, he waved his curled fingers at the mirror and laughed aloud.

He got to the Straw Hat a half hour later, certain he had not been followed. Joseph Gonzago sat alone in a rear booth with a cold beer in front of him and a second beer for his old boyhood pal. Frank Donato, dressed splendidly in a cream-colored suit, said hello to Lou Moran, who was behind the stick, and Lou indicated that Frank should walk to the rear. Joseph had the juke box playing at the booth because they were going to talk.

Frank had a grin on his face when he sat down, and Lou Moran came over with shots of Irish whiskey. Frank Donato took a sip of the beer as Lou Moran left the booth and smiled again.

"You should have seen their faces, Joey," Frank Donato said. Frank Donato was the only person who had ever called him Joey, privilege of friendship because Joseph did not like the name. "They simply couldn't believe it. That was a funny idea of yours to rent all those Mercedes. I just hope those guys bring them right back before it runs your bill through the roof. I got twelve of the craziest bastards off the docks to drive them. Worked like a charm, Joey. Christ, I haven't had a laugh like that since my trial started."

Frank Donato was chattering nervously and laughed when he finished and took a sip of beer. He noticed Joseph was not laughing and that Joseph had not spoken. Frank Donato stopped when he noticed the intensity in Joseph's eyes.

"Who is Jimmy Boyle, Frank?" Joseph said in a low voice.

"Jimmy Boyle? The only Jimmy Boyle I know of is a two-bit wise guy from the waterfront."

"Friend of yours, Frank?" Joseph was deadly serious. He sat erect in his seat and glared into the suds of his beer as Tony Bennett sang about leaving his heart in San Francisco.

Frank Donato looked directly at Joseph, his fingers joined around the mug of beer. "Joey, I've been taking interrogations on the stand for the last seven months from men who want to lock me in a cage. Men who want to break up my family and disgrace my children. I don't need that kind of attitude from you, Joey. You are supposed to be my friend. If you have something you want to know, ask me directly. Don't play horseshit games with me, Joey. I know you too long, love you too long for that. Give me at least that."

Joseph took a silent gulp of beer.

"Jimmy Boyle is the man who shot my father." Joseph looked into Frank Donato's narrowed dark eyes.

"How do you know this?" Frank Donato spoke in very sober tones.

"I just know. Tell me what you know about him, Frank. I'm sorry I spoke to you that way, but I wanted to see your reaction. Forgive me."

"It's all right, Joey. Jimmy Boyle, the Jimmy Boyle I know, is a two-bit enforcer for small-time racket guys. He's Lionel trying to be Amtrak. I find it almost incredible to believe someone would hire him to kill Be Be. No one takes him serious."

"Who's Avakian?"

"Doug Avakian is the lowest species on the evolutionary scale. He's the treasurer of the union. Weingarten got him in there with some pressure on the Waterfront Commission to leave their hands off him. I'm no saint, believe me, but if you want to meet a thief, introduce yourself to Doug Avakian and you'll think I'm Saint Francis. Joey, they have me taking seventy-five thousand dollars that I never so much as smelled. I never saw seventy-five thousand dollars in my life, Joey. That's the truth. But they hung that on me. They had fancy tailors, stevedores, ship owners, shoe salesmen, car dealers, all kinds of assholes come up to the stand to say how much money I spent. Of course I spent a lot of money over the years. I make a good wage. I have taken from ship owners, but I swear on the lives of my children I never took one cent from the men, never touched their pension fund. You know what I took from the men, Joey? Favors. That's all. Like that one today. I need a few screwballs to drive a dozen Mercedes and they're glad to do it. If I'm building a new shed in my yard, maybe I ask a few guys to come out to the house and give me a hand. But I cook them steaks, give them cold beers, I go to bat for them when they're in trouble. Maybe it's wrong, maybe it's a misuse of influence, but it was never meant as slave trading, Joey. Sure they got me on tape saying things I should never have said. A grand here, three, maybe four hundred there. But seventy-five thousand dollars, Joey. That isn't me. But somehow or other when Avakian opened the books he made it look like I took seventy-five thousand dollars from the pension fund. I don't know how he did it. I probably signed things I never read or signed things I thought were legitimate expenses that were going in his pocket and looking like they were going into mine. I'm not really sure.

"But I know why. Because Sydney Weingarten has been trying to get Avakian my job for a very long time. Because if you have the docks, sure there's a little money in campaign contributions, and there's a few votes, but mainly because there's bodies to push doorbells when they're canvassing and pulling votes. Now with me out of the way there's a hell of a good chance he'll be elected president of the union. He'll probably be spending the seventy-five grand I got nailed for on campaign literature, posters, and Christmas bottles for the rank and file. I have never killed a man, Joey, but Doug Avakian I would kill with my shoes if I could get away with it. But I'm in enough trouble as it is."

Frank Donato paused and took a sip of beer.

"Jimmy Boyle and Doug Avakian did business together?"

"Yeah, but Boyle was always such a roach I never paid attention to what kind of business. That was my problem. I should have watched every move Avakian made but I didn't. I really didn't think he had the balls to move on me. I really didn't. I figured if Avakian and Boyle were doing business together, it had to be some great grandiose plan to knock over a gynecologist in Boys' Town."

"But what if Weingarten was one of the guys they were doing business with?" Joseph was calm, unemotional.

"That would be different, then I would have paid attention . . . Hey, wait a minute, Joey, are you suggesting Weingarten might have gotten Avakian to hire Jimmy Boyle to kill Be Be? Is that what you're saying?"

"I'm supposing for the moment."

"Holy Christ." Frank Donato looked amazed. "You think maybe we should find this guy Boyle and have a sort of loud chat?"

"He's dead. But I'm well informed Boyle killed my dad. What I don't know is who killed Boyle. He was murdered in Los Angeles the same day my father was killed."

"What you are saying to me is almost too incredible to believe, Joey. You're saying that maybe Weingarten—"

"I'm not sure Weingarten is involved. I suspect him but I'm not sure he has the balls."

"He doesn't need the balls, Joey. All you need to do is hire someone who has them. I'm convinced I wouldn't be in the jam I'm in now if it weren't for Weingarten. I hate to say this, especially to you, Joey, but Be Be didn't pay much attention to small details the last couple of years. He was getting older, tired. He took care of major things, like judgeships and elections. But he started to forget that taking care of the small things is just as important. It was what made him different, special, so damned powerful. But he hated dealing with Weingarten anymore. Weingarten, for Be Be, was such a pain in the fucking ass to deal with. Weingarten was always whining and it drove Be Be nuts, so he just let him do things he ordinarily wouldn't have let him do and then stopped him when he thought he was going too far. But in the old days Be Be would never have allowed a guy like Weingarten to get a weasel like Avakian in as treasurer of the International Longshoremen's Association. Don't get me wrong, Joey, I'm not saying it's Be Be's fault I'm in the crap I'm in now. No one has ever been as good and generous to me as your father. You know how I felt and still feel about him. But when Be Be saw Weingarten getting Avakian in, I went to him and he said he couldn't be bothered dealing with it because Sydney was such a pain in the ass. He felt as long as I was still president of the local it didn't matter who the treasurer was. He said, 'Sometimes you have to throw the birds some crumbs, Frank.' Little did he know he was feeding Rodan. Once Weingarten got his foot in the door, he was like a Fuller brush man. He wasn't satisfied until he sold his entire line, and all of a sudden I'm facing seven to ten for walking away with seventy-five thousand dollars I never so much as laid eyes on."

"Part of which might have been used to pay Boyle. And whoever killed Boyle. And so forth and so on," Joseph said.

Frank Donato's face grew hard and livid.

"That would be the ultimate fucking insult!" Frank Donato slammed his fist on the table. "Could you imagine if the money I'm going to the slammer for was used to kill Be Be? Doing time for somebody's contract money!"

"Sounds probable to me, Frank."

Donato put his face in his hands and kept it there for a few minutes. When he raised his head his eyes were shiny with tears.

"I'm going to miss my children so damned much, Joey. I miss them already and I'm not even gone. I look at them when they're asleep and I know they'll have to live with the stigma of having a father who's an ex-con. I feel like I failed them, Joey. And my wife. I destroyed her life real good. Seven to ten, Joey, without my wife and kids. The appeal has no chance. It's just a way to say a long goodbye. I found out I'm a coward, Joey. I'm afraid of going to jail. I'm afraid my kids will resent me. I'm afraid my wife will be human and find someone else at night to keep her company. How did it ever happen, Joey? When we were kids, we had such big plans and none of them were about going to the joint."

Joseph leaned across the table and tenderly patted Frank Donato on the cheek. There was a granite block of certainty in Joseph's voice when he spoke to him.

"Trust me," Joseph said. "I'm not going to let you go to prison."

Frank Donato looked up at Joseph Gonzago, and for a moment he thought he was looking at Be Be. The same calm look of determination in the face, the same reassuring voice.

"That's what Be Be told me, but with him gone . . . ."

"Then trust me now, Frank. Be Be is not as gone as you might think. There is a lot of work to do. I'm going to need your help. I am not going to let them put you in jail. Will you trust me? That's all I ask of you right now."

Frank Donato stared at Joseph again, and he felt an eerie tingle. He was certain that Joseph Gonzago could not possibly be wrong. Gonzago sat erect and in control. It suddenly seemed to Donato that there was no matter, no problem, Joseph could not solve.

"I trust you, Joey," Frank Donato said. "I will do anything you ask me to do."

"Thank you, Frank," Joseph said. "Now I want you to go home to your wife and your children. Buy them presents and flowers. Take them out for dinner. I especially want you to pick up your children and kiss them and hug them and tell them you love them. Promise me that. Promise me that you won't act like a condemned man, that you will act like a husband and a father who will never let them down. Okay, Frank? Will you do that?"

Frank Donato was smiling again now, wiping away tears.

"Yes, Joey. I'll do that. I'll do anything you ask me. You're the boss, Joey. You're the boss."

"And just one more thing," Joseph said. "Don't ever tell me again that you are a coward because you are afraid. There is nothing wrong with being afraid, Frank. I've known you all my life and I have never seen you act like a coward. You are a good man, a good husband, a fine father. That takes balls, believe me. Now go home."

Frank Donato stood and looked down at Joseph Gonzago to say good-bye, but Joseph was not looking at him. He was staring at his glass of beer and beyond, to a place only Joseph Gonzago could see.

Gloria Weingarten was working on her seventeenth draft of a letter to Joseph Gonzago. She could not get the letter correct, no matter how long she worked on it. Then she remembered a story one of the senior editors at her publishing company had once told her about a friend who had sent him a letter, a very long letter, trying to put into words some jumbled, long-simmering emotions. At the end of the letter the man had written: "I'm sorry this letter is so long. It would have been much shorter if I had had the time."

She picked up her pen again and wrote these words:

Dear Joseph:
I love you. I will not apologize for that. I think you love me too. I'm convinced you are involved in something you don't want to involve me in. That's fine. I'll wait for you. Not forever, but for a while. I might have some information that is useful to you involving a man named Daniel Morse. Go lightly, my love, and be careful.

Love,
Gloria

She reread the note. It was just what she wanted to say. She sealed it in an envelope, addressed it to Joseph Gonzago's house, and placed a stamp on it. She walked out of the house, and dropped it into a mailbox.

Gloria took a deep breath and exhaled deeply. The letter would take a day or two to reach him. She would not stay in and wait by the phone anymore. She felt like having a good stiff drink. She had money in her wallet. She had a good appetite. There was an Italian movie playing in Manhattan she had been meaning to see. She felt comfortable with her own company. She stood on Fourth Avenue in Brooklyn and flagged a taxi and climbed in and told the man to take her to the Palm steak house. She was going to have a martini, a medium-rare sirloin, a half bottle of red wine and see a movie. Gloria Weingarten was feeling much better.

Two days earlier Rosario and Gulatta had called Joseph Gonzago and asked him if he'd like to go camping. Both men spoke to Joseph on separate extensions at the same time. Joseph told them he was busy. They asked what could be so pressing that he didn't have the time to spend a weekend up at Breakabeen, where they used to go camping, with old friends.

"Come on, Joseph," Gulatta had said. "We'll bring a couple of cases of beer, maybe a little reefer, some steaks. We can fish in the stream, swim in the waterfalls. For old times' sake. We have a lot of catching up to do, pal."

"But I have so much work to do," Joseph said.

"What kind of work?" Rosario asked. "I thought you said you quit your job. Come on, it'll be good for you. Get away from it all. I bet our names are still written on the big rock at the very top of the falls, the place where Donato got stuck that time and you had to carry him down. Come on, you can't be like one of the old Guinea women in black, mourning for the rest of your life. Let's go up. We'll bring some fishing poles, drink beer, talk about old times. Hell, we might even pick up a few of those hayseed chicks from the town and bring them back to the woods like we used to. Whadda you say?"

"I don't know, it's kind of sudden." Joseph was trying to get everything clear in his head. There was a purpose behind all this. They either wanted to pick his brains or get him out of the way for a few days while Sydney Weingarten organized all his moves for Be Be's seat. But he knew he was smarter than both of them. He could probably pick their brains easier than they could pick his.

"Why not?" Joseph said in commitment. "Sure. The city is getting me down anyway. You guys have the equipment? Tents, sleeping bags, all that stuff?"

"Sure, we have everything we need," Rosario said. "We'll pick you up Saturday morning. Six A.M. Get a jump on the traffic."

"It's a deal," Joseph said.

Now, on Saturday morning, at quarter to six, Joseph Gonzago pressed a fresh cassette into the pocket-size Sony tape recorder, turned it on, and counted to ten to test it. The condenser microphone picked him up loud and clear. He walked to the other side of the room, leaving the tape recorder on the bed, and talked at a normal level. When he played this back his voice came through with perfect clarity. The condenser microphone was built into the body of the tape recorder so there would be no problems with loose wires.

He took a bottle of clear nail polish and began applying it to the fingers and palms of his hands. It was a trick he had learned from one of the meetings he had attended on guerrilla warfare back in the sixties. With the nail polish on your hands you would not leave fingerprints, and it was not as conspicuous as a pair of gloves. He then pushed the .38 into his jacket pocket and the small Sony tape recorder which was no bigger than a cigarette pack into his shirt pocket. He was dressed in a rugged flannel shirt, a pair of hiking boots, and dungarees.

He heard the horn honking outside his house and knew it was them. He grabbed his small knapsack and hoisted it over his shoulders and quickly left the house.

Joseph Gonzago sat in the backseat of the station wagon drinking a bottle of Heineken as the car, packed with camping gear, sped north on the New York State Thruway. He did not worry about leaving fingerprints on the bottle, the nail polish would prevent any from adhering there. His hands felt scaly and unnatural, but it was a necessary precaution.

Three empty bottles of Heineken lay at his feet, and he felt the building need to urinate. Rosario was doing the driving and was not drinking.

"Come on, have a fucking beer," Gulatta said, shoving a bottle into his face. Rosario pulled his face away, snapped, "I'm having enough trouble with the goddamn car as it is. There's something wrong with the gears. You put the goddamn thing in reverse and it leaps forward a few feet before it catches into reverse. That means the whole gear shift must be stripped. I don't want to drink and drive on top of that. We have all weekend to drink and it's only seven thirty in the morning. Besides, these troopers up here are cocksuckers. They put you right in the can for drunken driving."

"Pussy," Gulatta said. "How's about you, Joseph? Want another one?"

"I have to piss bad," Joseph said. "I better wait until after we stop at a gas station."

"You guys are a bore," Gulatta said.

"I gotta stop anyway to see if they can do anything about the goddamn gears," Rosario said. "There was a sign back there that said there was a gas station in three miles. I'll stop there."

Joseph knew this was the right time. He eased the tape recorder out of his pocket, switched it on, and in about a minute they pulled into the gas station. Joseph obscured the tape recorder under his knapsack on the backseat, but in such a way that the condenser mike was exposed. Rosario pulled up to the gas pumps and a greasy kid of about seventeen with bad acne approached.

"Help ya?"

"Fill it up," Rosario said. "And listen, you know anything about cars?"

"I know everything about cars. What's your problem?"

"When I put this car in reverse it leaps forward about three or four feet. I've been banging out people's tail lights for a week. Will you have a look at it?"

"Demonstrate it for me," the kid said. Rosario put the car in reverse, stepped on the gas, and the car jumped a good five feet forward before catching and spinning into reverse.

"You got a real problem, fella, let me take a look under the hood."

"Where's your john?" Joseph asked. The kid pointed and Joseph got out, leaving the tape recorder running as the kid with the acne rummaged under the hood of the station wagon. Joseph walked to the bathroom and relieved himself of the beer. He idled for a few moments, then took his wallet out and placed it on the floor behind the toilet bowl in the small stall. He gave himself a full five minutes and then went back out to the car and climbed in the backseat and closed the door.

Rosario and Gulatta looked as if a conversation had just been interrupted and sat silently. Joseph picked up the tape recorder and switched it off and put it back in his shirt pocket. Rosario looked at Gulatta nervously and Joseph realized that Gulatta was now behind the wheel, with Rosario in the passenger's seat. Rosario looked very tense, anxious, as the acned kid kept playing under the hood. Joseph noticed that his companions were too quiet, almost as if their privacy had been invaded.

"Jesus," Joseph said. "I think I dropped my wallet in there."

"Take your time," Gulatta said. "This dumbbell isn't nearly finished yet."

Joseph stepped back out of the car and walked to the men's room again. His mouth was dry now, his breath short. His heart was beating fast. His fingers itched but he did not scratch them for fear of rubbing off the protective coating. Joseph went into the toilet stall and sat down on the closed seat. He switched on the tape deck and hit the rewind button. He listened to it whirr. He stopped it and hit the play button. Rosario's voice came on: "Fill it up. And listen, you know anything about cars?" The gas station attendant came on saying, "I know everything about cars. What's your problem?"

Joseph was getting impatient so he hit the fast forward button and let the tape whiz through the machine. He hit stop and then play. Gulatta's voice was clear as a bell: "He ain't so fuckin' crazy if you ask me."

"You might be right. I don't know." It was Rosario answering.

"It's your turn," Gulatta said.

"Why's it have to be me?" Rosario's voice asked Gulatta. "I like the guy. I have nothing personal against him."

"I didn't have nothing personal against Johnny Quinn either," came Gulatta's reply. "It's just your turn is all. It comes with the money, pal."

"I'm not so sure this is the right thing to do," Rosario said.

"Look, accidents happen," Gulatta answered. "Don't worry. Besides, it isn't our decision anyway. After he goes over we can head up to Montreal like the man said to do. Get out of town for a week. Let it blow away. Montreal is a dynamite town."

"If it was somebody else . . . Ah, what the fuck, if I have to do it, I'll do it. I wish this kid would hurry up under the hood. I don't think he knows what he's doing."

"Cool it, here comes Joseph. Be cool."

Joseph hit the stop button, his mouth as dry as cotton. His fingers were shaking terribly. He pressed the rewind button and listened again. "I didn't have nothing personal against Johnny Quinn either. It's just your turn is all. It comes with the money, pal."

Joseph hit the stop button and put the tape recorder into his inside jacket pocket. He had to pee again. A phantom sensation brought about by nerves. Nothing would come out but the sensation remained. He pulled out his pistol, trembled with the cylinder, made sure it was loaded, put it away, ran his fingers through his hair, inhaled and blew the air out heavily ten times in a row. Be calm, he told himself. Smile. He almost forgot the wallet and then remembered it, quickly jammed it into his back pocket, and exited with a broad smile and a casual strut back to the car.

The kid with the acne slammed the hood as Joseph got in and leaned his head toward Gulatta, who was behind the wheel.

"Your whole gear shaft needs to be replaced," the kid said. "It would take me a day or two to get the parts and do the job. But it's safe enough to drive until you find a mechanic in a town or something. Otherwise you'll be stuck out here on the highway. Just make sure you don't park too close to anyone. Give yourself six feet if you can and ease your foot off the brake and ease your foot onto the gas."

Gulatta handed the kid a twenty-dollar bill for the gas and told him to keep the change. He looked over his shoulder, put the car into reverse, and slammed on the gas. The car leaped five feet forward and then made a terrible noise and caught traction and skidded backward again.

"The fuckin' kid just told you to ease off the brake and ease onto the gas and you floor the fuckin' thing," Rosario shouted. "Take it fuckin' easy or both of us will be stranded up there."

He realized he had made a slip when Gulatta shot him a ferocious look. Rosario turned to Joseph. "Sorry, Joseph, you're so quiet I almost forgot you were there."

"Got another beer up there?" Joseph asked pleasantly.

"Sure," Rosario said. "As long as I'm not driving I might as well have one myself."

Rosario opened two beers, handed one to Joseph. Joseph watched him suck half his bottle down in one gulp, as if it were liquid courage. Joseph took a small sip, and stared straight ahead, his insides fraught with tension.

The sun was much stronger by the time they neared the road leading to the double waterfall. Joseph was amazed at the way in which Gulatta told old stories, joked, sang along with the radio as they drove along. What makes a man tell jokes and sing on the way to murder, he asked himself. How could he keep such a light heart? Sure Gulatta and he were never the very best of friends, but they hung around together and had fought side by side against rivals on the football field, had shared many adolescent things in life together —beer, girls, marijuana.

Joseph knew there would be few campers up here this time of year. Probably none at all, because the waterfall was very secluded and not posted as camp grounds. The waterfalls would be heavy this time of the year after all the rain. The huge pool into which both emptied would be at least thirty or forty feet deep.

Gulatta remembered the route perfectly and he took the left onto the Breakabeen Road, which ran under the shelter of overhanging trees.

Rosario had been silent for a long time now, the only noises coming from him being beer belches. He had consumed five beers inside of an hour.

"Still looks the same, doesn't it, Joseph?" Gulatta asked cheerfully.

"Sure does," Joseph said.

Rosario said nothing as the car slowed along the dirt road. Now the sound of the waterfalls grew very loud, almost deafening, the great awesome roar of nature that no one could stifle. The waterfalls looked beautiful under the high morning sun, with a rainbow bridging the two cliffs. Gulatta nosed the car into the cleared parking space at the top of the cliff that overlooked the first of two falls. There was a silly wooden barrier at the lip of the cliff to prevent cars from rolling off the edge into the two-hundred-and-fifty-foot drop.

Gulatta put the car into park and left the motor running. The three men sat there looking out over the great gorge in the earth, down the massive drop to the wide, deep pool, which opened up into an artery of water that wound through desolate, beautiful forest. The long silver tongues of water fell straight down to the pool of the first falls and then cascaded more powerfully over the second falls, filling the final pool.

"Trout," Gulatta said. "Jammed with trout."

"Yeah," Joseph said as the three sat silently. Joseph could see the massive boulders surrounding the second pool, the giant tree trunks, and the face of the cliff. He had his hand on the handle of the back door. Suddenly Rosario turned to him, his lips quivering, his eyes not quite focusing.

"I'm sorry, Joseph," Rosario said, pointing a pistol at Joseph's head. "This isn't easy, but I'll have to ask you to go for a swim."

"Hey, fellas," Joseph said, his own gun under his jacket in his hand. "This some kind of a joke?"

Gulatta turned to him. "No joke, asshole. Let's see how good a swan diver you are."

Joseph yanked up the handle of the door with his free hand and dived from the car. Just then, from behind them, the roar of a shotgun tore apart the day. Birds took desperate flight. Lou Moran stood on a small hillock up above the car. He pointed his shotgun into the air and pulled off a second round. Rosario was trying to train the pistol on Joseph, but he was not an easy target; he was rolling and flipping all over the ground until he found cover behind the bole of a large tree. Joseph aimed his pistol at Rosario, who was still trying to get a proper aim, and was distracted by Lou Moran.

Gulatta looked in his rearview mirror and saw Lou Moran approaching with the shotgun leveled at them. Joseph had planned on

Lou being there, and now Lou Moran was walking toward the station wagon with his shotgun at the ready.

"Get us the fuck out of here!" Rosario shouted. Gulatta threw the car into reverse, picked his foot off the brake, and slammed it onto the accelerator. The car leaped forward four, then five feet, and Rosario heard the sound of wood splintering. Rosario's eyes grew wide and Gulatta started to scream as the car moved forward another foot and teetered on the lip of the cliff. Both Rosario and Gulatta reached for the handles of the doors, yanking desperately and pushing. But the splintered wood acted as a vise on both sides of the car, jamming the doors closed as the heavy weight of the engine sent it tipping nose first. The back of the car lifted from the ground, slowly, as if being hoisted by a tow truck.

"Joseph, help me, Joseph." Rosario's face was twisted in panic, his eyes so wide Joseph could see the inner red of the lids.

It seemed as if the car was suspended in midair momentarily, with Rosario turned around in his seat, his arm still out, reaching for Joseph, and then all at once the car began its long descent into the foamy tomb below. The nose of the car smashed into a protruding boulder halfway down, making the entire car do a back flip, and then another, until it bounced at the edge of the first pool and almost gracefully sailed outward toward the second pool, twirling as it went, and crashing into a huddle of boulders with a thunderous crunch of metal and glass that was quickly swallowed by the roar of the water. It finally landed upside down in the deep pool, where the long sheets of water fell on top of it.

It spun around in the pool for a few seconds, like a bar of soap under a bath faucet, and then slowly began sinking, sinking, sinking. In a moment it was fully submerged and invisible as the water foamed around it in a huge bubble bath of death.

Lou Moran looked over the edge.

"I never liked them station wagons," he said. "Too big. Bad on gas."

Joseph stared down into the water but there was no trace of death or carnage. It looked majestic and beautiful and sweet.

"They used to be a pretty good backfield," Joseph said as he stared down from the edge.

"They're in the end zone now," Lou Moran said.

Lou Moran had Joseph's car parked up in the trees, out of view from the edge of the cliff. They both got in and started driving back to New York. Joseph was silent for a long time, thinking of boyhood memories of the two men he'd just watched die.

"You gotta let whoever wanted you dead, think you're dead," Lou Moran said. "Get a hotel room in Manhattan. Stay out of sight. Don't come out until the dinner."

Joseph nodded and kept revisiting his boyhood as Lou Moran pushed on for New York.

30

Joseph was getting stir crazy. Four days locked up in a hotel room at the Waldorf-Astoria was not his idea of fun. Lou Moran and Jack Coohill had told him he must stay put. No one else knew whether he was dead or alive. The room was registered under Jack Coohill's name and was being paid for by the funds allotted for the memorial dinner. Coohill told Mayor Bailey that he was using the room as a base headquarters.

Earlier in the day Lou Moran had brought a short simple note that had been mailed by Gloria Weingarten to Joseph's house. Joseph felt like a caged man when he read it. He wanted Gloria Weingarten desperately. He now knew she understood he was involved in something he could not share with her. He was curious about her mention of Daniel Morse. What could she know about Morse? It would have to wait until after tomorrow night. The memorial dinner would take place in the main banquet room of the great hotel the next evening, and Jack Coohill told Joseph it was imperative that he not be seen or heard from until he made his appearance at the dinner.

Joseph promised himself that right after the dinner he would call Gloria Weingarten. The anxiety was disturbing. He was trying to write a speech for the dinner, but every time he sat down to write it he immediately stood up again and paced the room, thinking of Gloria. Every time he lay down on the massive bed, he wished she were there to share it with him. All his meals came from room service. He ordered a bottle of Laforet Blanc 1977, and a shrimp cocktail. When the man taking the order asked how many glasses he should send up Joseph said two. Gloria was so much on his mind that he almost believed for a moment that she was here. He had been ordering food from room service for four days and signing Jack Coohill's name to the tabs.

The Cuban room-service waiter thanked Joseph for the twenty-percent tip he had added to the bill and left. Joseph had not even realized he'd signed his own name to the check. Joseph took a deep slug of the white wine and sunk his teeth into the flesh of a huge shrimp. The horseradish dressing scalded his tongue and the wine was startlingly cold and dry.

He sipped more wine and walked to the large windows of the hotel room, looked out at the city traffic, watched a beautiful woman walk for two blocks, her stride as commanding and confident as a predatory cat. She turned a corner and left his line of sight. I wish to hell you were here, Gloria, he thought. He read her note again and wondered once more about Daniel Morse.

The next afternoon Jack Coohill moved from table to table in the main banquet room of the Waldorf-Astoria and sifted through the envelopes stacked high in his hands. In front of each plate there was a small name tag indicating where each person would sit. In Jack Coohill's hands were envelopes with matching names. He placed the corresponding envelope beneath the dinner plate at each setting. The dinner plates hid the envelopes from view.

The names on the envelopes were those of the people who made up the Brooklyn machine: assemblymen, state senators, district leaders, judges, congressmen, councilmen, school board members, the borough president, high-ranking administrators and commissioners who'd gotten their appointments through the machine. Also campaign contributors, lawyers, accountants, assistant district attorneys, a former mayor, a former governor, several former congressmen who were also former convicts, and, of course, the wives. The list was large and varied, and Jack Coohill had a special surprise in those envelopes for more than half of those who would be eating the veal dinner later this evening. The bandstand was set up for the dinner-hour entertainment, and the stage where the speakers would address their peers was set up too. There was a large poster of Be Be Gonzago looming over the massive room, and there were three different bars set up for the predinner cocktail hour.

Tonight would be one helluva bash, Jack Coohill thought.

Sydney Weingarten applied an astringent to the top of his bald head so that the spotlights would not reflect off it later that night when he was to deliver one of the most important speeches of his life. He laid the tuxedo out on the bed and stood naked in front of the full-length mirror as he toweled himself dry. He turned sideways to regard his paunch. Although it protruded too much, he thought, it would soon be perfectly hidden by the regality of judicial robes.

He began dressing by fitting the special men's corset to his midsection. The paunch might serve him well on the bench, where a portly stature jibed with the business of law, but tonight he did not want to look like a man out of shape, his tuxedo swelling at the sash. He allowed himself a half smile. He was feeling very good. The rejuvenating power of a hot shower was almost amazing, he thought. He felt sparkling clean and fully confident and well prepared for the crucial evening before him. This would be a giant step in his career, one that would bring him closer to the realization of a life-long dream.

He pulled on the pants with the silk stripe up the sides of the legs. The waist was snug but the girdle allowed him to fasten them with little discomfort. He would charm the pants off them all tonight, he thought. He would tell them what a great and sad loss Be Be Gonzago was to the people of Brooklyn. Make that America, hell, why not? He would tell them how difficult it would be to fill Be Be's shoes, and how he would do his humble best to carry on the great work he started for the citizens of this great borough. He would tell them he would do his best to uphold the standards and ethics of this great man. And if he could keep from laughing he would have secured the party chairmanship.

He would, Weingarten thought to himself, help re-elect the governor of New York, which would help Wolfington on the long road to the White House, and later he would get the state Court of Appeals seat, and in a few years, when the opening came up, he would be shocked but honored when President Henry Wolfington appointed him to the Supreme Court of the United States.

Sydney chuckled to himself. He knew the damned Constitution so well he could recite it by heart. He had studied every major decision and amendment and interpretation of this great document. No one would ever be able to doubt his ability.

His one regret, Sydney Weingarten thought, was that Be Be Gonzago would not be there that day to see him sitting above him, peering down at him. Men like Be Be Gonzago would have no place in the America Sydney envisioned. His coarseness and his ego were an insult to public servitude, Sydney thought. Be Be Gonzago, the big hot shot. Weingarten remembered the day Be Be Gonzago publicly humiliated him.

Gonzago had given an exclusive interview to Jason Gotbaum, a young reporter for a Flatbush newspaper. That had been before Gotbaum went to *The Village Voice* and turned on Be Be. Be Be had called Sydney a mediocrity and a man of no ideas who had cashed in on the name of his father. Be Be had been eating peanuts during the interview, and at one point held up one of the peanuts and told Gotbaum that Weingarten's balls were smaller than the peanut. He accused Sydney of racism and bigotry and lack of courage.

The story was picked up by the dailies and the wire services and the television news gossips and had caused Weingarten great embarrassment. Be Be had accused Sydney of collusion with Izzy Siegel, the nursing-home operator, and went so far as to say that Weingarten had sold out his own people, the Jewish people, by running nursing homes that were no better than the barracks at Auschwitz. He accused Sydney of being insensitive to the elderly. What Be Be had conveniently left out was that he had insured all of Izzy Siegel's hovels through his brokerage firm. Well, Weingarten mused, where was Be Be Gonzago now when he would walk to the podium tonight to sing his praises and assume his mantle?

Forget him, he thought as he knotted his tie. This would be Sydney's night, not Be Be's. After tonight he would be able to put his life in proper order. He would arrange with the doctors to place Ruth in one of the very best sanitariums out on Long Island. Then Sylvia Stein would belong to him. He could be rid of Ruth in three days. On his way to a new career. Sam Stone would be safely out of the country by tomorrow night. Caracas. Maybe that's where he belonged. For a while. And Joseph Gonzago was no longer a problem.

Tonight he would take control, Sydney Weingarten assured himself as he pulled on the tuxedo jacket and smiled approvingly at himself in the full-length mirror.

Sydney Weingarten felt like having a martini. There were still three hours to go before he would have to leave for the dinner. He walked down the stairs, and as he passed Ruth's room he felt a mild sadness for her. Once she had been a nice young girl, pleasant and pretty and obedient. Sometimes she could even be fun. Like the time they had gone ice skating and she kept flopping all over the ice. She had a nice laugh then. A pretty smile. She was gentle. But she was in the way.

Suddenly, the telephone rang in the dining room and Sydney Weingarten walked to answer it. He picked it up and said hello.

Ruth Weingarten silently stepped out of her bedroom and walked to the telephone in the upstairs hall. She was curious to see if Sylvia

Stein was on the phone. She had a vague plan about taping some of the conversations between her and Sydney to use as evidence in divorce court. She was going to ask Gloria to get her a tape recorder so she could do this. Earlier in the day Ruth had unscrewed the transmitter cap of the plain black rotary phone and taken out the small transmitting disk from inside. Then she replaced the cap. She knew that when she picked up the extension it would not be audible on the other extension because without the transmitting disk no noise would be generated. However, it was still possible to listen in on the conversation.

She picked up the phone after it stopped ringing and listened to Sydney Weingarten speaking on the phone.

"Hello there, stranger. I'm all ready for the big night."

"Sydney, I don't know what kind of a big night this is going to be," said the voice on the other end.

"What do you mean?" Sydney sounded nervous.

"Joseph Gonzago."

"What about him?" There was a trill of tension in Sydney's voice.

"He's staying at the Waldorf."

"Don't be absurd," Sydney Weingarten said.

"I'm not being absurd. Listen to me. I just got a call from the Waldorf to say that one of their room-service checks was signed by a Joseph Gonzago. In the room that Jack Coohill has rented there for the dinner."

"This is some kind of joke." Sydney's voice was quavering now.

"I'm not laughing and I don't think you should."

"Maybe someone just signed his name."

"No, the Waldorf called to ask if a Joseph Gonzago was authorized to sign for room-service checks in Jack Coohill's room. The room is registered to just one person and they said that if two people are staying there then the rate would have to change. So right away the accounting people asked about it. They called to get clearance. I didn't let on that there was anything wrong with it. But I asked him to have a messenger send a copy of the receipt over to me. It's here in front of me. And I checked his handwriting on the check against an old arrest record from one of those Columbia University riots back in the sixties. I'm no handwriting expert, but it sure as hell looks the same to me."

"This is impossible," Sydney said. "The two oafs haven't reported back to me, but I figured they'd just disappeared for a few days. I told them to take a little vacation. But I just can't believe it."

"Well I don't think we can take any chances."

"Call Stone. Tell him to get ahold of that woman. Have the Stewardess pay him a visit. Make her room service or something. He told me she was in town. I don't care what it costs. I want her to neutralize this son of a bitch once and for all. I knew we should have gone with professionals from the beginning. God Almighty. Do you know what could happen if he showed up at the dinner tonight, acting the moron? Or worse, making accusations? Too much is at stake here. If he is alive, then he must suspect my involvement in the bungled affair with Rosario and Gulatta. We can't have him around. He has to go. He must be dealt with."

"Are you suggesting that we just divert him until after the dinner is over?"

"I am suggesting that we divert him. Period. This should have been done a long time ago. Made to look like he was riddled with grief or something. I don't care what way it's handled."

"Very expensive."

"I don't care what it costs."

"I'll do my best."

"You better, for both our sakes."

Ruth Weingarten heard Sydney Weingarten slam down the phone and she gingerly cradled the phone and walked slowly to her room. She thought she recognized the voice on the other end. It belonged to a face she had seen in this house before. He had spoken of murder. She thought of calling Gloria immediately but Sydney still had locks on all the phones. She could take incoming calls, but she could not make outgoing calls. She went into her room and sat on a chair, trying to decide what to do, her eyes continually moving toward the dresser where the accumulated bottles of whiskey were stashed.

The crane was huge. Francis X. Cunningham stood with a group of other cops as the great hook at the end of the cable lifted the station wagon out of the deep pool of water at the bottom of the two-hundred-and-fifty-foot waterfall. Cunningham lit a cigarette and turned to a state trooper.

"You say there's two of them?"

"That's what our divers said," the trooper answered. "Kids swimming here this morning saw the car. One of them, a young boy, almost drowned because he got such a fright when he saw the two guys inside. They were diving from the rocks there, that's why they got down so far. Our divers got the license number, verified there were two people in the car; we ran a make on the plate and we found out it was registered to this Rosario guy. We sent his name to SBI and they said you might be interested in it."

"Might be."

The winch on the crane strained with a loud metallic whine, and soon the rear end of the station wagon broke the surface of the water. The crane operator sat in his cab, a cigarette dangling from the corner of his mouth, bored. Now the whole car was visible and leaked water as it rose in the early twilight. Soon the crane operator had the car high above the police on the edge of the cliff, and they began backing away as the crane swung the car in toward the road and slowly lowered it to the ground.

Francis X. Cunningham walked to the car and looked inside. Gulatta's face was bloated and fat, with his tongue protruding through his lips. Rosario's face was a study in horror. His eyes were still open and his mouth was wide, with his lips peeled back and his teeth bared. He looked as if he had died screaming and his expression had locked there when rigor mortis set in. Cunningham saw a pistol on the seat beside him.

"Not pretty," said the trooper.

"They won't win any beauty contests," Cunningham said.

"Know them?" the trooper asked.

"Of them."

"Looks like an accident to me," the trooper said. "Of course there has to be a coroner's report. But the back of the car isn't dented, so it doesn't look like they were pushed over."

"Do me a favor, will you," Cunningham said. "After you make a thorough search of the car, will you send me a full report? Everything that's in it? In their wallets, clothes, you know. Everything."

"Sure thing. You know this ain't the first time a car went off here. Had one about six years back. I keep telling the aldermen we need a metal guardrail here. Instead they put up one of these wooden jobs."

"Car sure is damaged," Cunningham said.

"That's what I mean, but just the front end. The back is smooth."

"All right, I have to go. I have to get back to the city."

"Thanks for coming by, Cunningham. I'll let you know as soon as we have the report. Looks like an accident to me."

"That's what bothers me," Cunningham said, and made for his car and the trip back to the city.

Gloria Weingarten arrived at her mother's house at seven o'clock as requested. When she stepped inside, her father was pacing, a nervous wreck. The phone rang. Sydney picked it up and said hello as Gloria removed her small waist jacket.

"You got her? I told you, forget the expense. Yes, within the next few hours." Sydney Weingarten was very nervous, excited, looked at his watch. "Make that two hours. Okay."

Sydney allowed himself a small laugh. "The dinner starts at eight, but I won't be going on until nine. She has to be finished by then. Good then. See you there."

Sydney Weingarten hung up the phone, looking very relieved. Gloria Weingarten did not even look at him. Sydney approached her warmly, his demeanor soft and apologetic.

"Gloria, thank you so much for coming. Listen, flower, I've been meaning to talk to you. I want to apologize for the terrible things I said to you that evening. I'm truly sorry, flower. I've been under a terrible strain these past few weeks, what with the assassination attempt, the party organization, the campaign, Sam Stone, your mother's ill health. I want you to understand that sometimes I say things I do not mean. It's pressure, frustration. Will you forgive me?"

"Let's say I'm willing to forget, Dad."

"Well that's something anyway. I don't blame you for resenting what I've said. But I want you to know that I am willing to eat my crow and admit I was wrong. About a lot of things. Heck, you're a big girl. I have no right to interfere with your life."

"Why the great change of heart?"

"Because I don't want to lose you."

Sydney Weingarten leaned over to kiss his daughter on her lips, but Gloria turned her head and took the kiss on her cheek. He looked peeved for a moment but then brightened.

"We have to get going, flower. Take good care of your mother and let her have her rest."

Sydney Weingarten folded a trench coat over his arm and stepped outside to a waiting limousine with Bernie trailing behind him.

Gloria started climbing the stairs to her mother's room, looking forward to seeing how much further improvement there was in her. She found Sydney's remarks very curious, somehow deceptive. She guessed that perhaps he was riding a wave of euphoria over the dinner he would be attending that night, a dinner that would lay the groundwork for his assuming Be Be Gonzago's place as machine boss.

She opened her mother's door and stepped inside smiling, a smile as fleeting as lightning. There before her, slouched against two overstuffed pillows on the bed, was Ruth Weingarten, an empty pint of Canadian Club beside her and a half-full one in her hand. Her mouth and jaw were slack, and there was a faraway sad look in her eyes. Ruth Weingarten was crying, mascara muddying her face, her hair disheveled. Gloria stood still for a moment. She walked to her mother very deliberately, yanked the bottle from her hand, smashed it onto the floor. Then she went to the drawer where the rest of the whiskey was stored, and she smashed each bottle on the floor as well. Her movements were mechanical, not done in rage, but rather with the dispatch of a solution. Then she walked back to her mother, sat her up straight, helped her to her feet, and walked her to the bathroom. She stuck her fingers down her mother's throat, making Ruth gag and finally vomit a good deal of the booze.

Then Gloria ran cold water over a washcloth, scoured her mother's face, brushed her hair quickly off her face, and walked her back into the bedroom. Ruth went to sit down, but Gloria would not allow her to sit. She made her stand and keep walking in circles, around and around and around the room.

"Mother, you are letting him win. This is what he wants you to do. Now come on, snap out of this. This is stupid and cowardly. This isn't you."

"What would you know?" Ruth Weingarten said. "You didn't hear what he said."

"What did he say to you, Mom?"

"He didn't say anything to me," Ruth's words were slurred and slow. "He never says anything to me. I heard what he said to the other man. I can't remember his name. Just his face."

"What did he say, Mom?" Gloria was still walking her mother in a large circle, trying to get the blood in her body to overpower the whiskey.

"They're going to kill him, Gloria. They're going to murder him."

Gloria thought that her mother was delirious but played along with her, trying to keep her talking and conscious.

"Murder who, Mom?"

"They are going to have a woman do it, darling."

"They are going to have a woman kill who, Mom?"

The weight of Ruth was making Gloria tired, but she kept her walking and talking.

"You took out the banana curls, darling. They looked so pretty. Like when you were just a little girl when everything was so much better."

"They are going to have a woman kill who, Mom?" Gloria was curious now.

"Joseph. They are going to have a woman kill Joseph."

Gloria stopped walking, stared into her mother's blurry eyes.

"Joseph? My Joseph?"

"That's nice. 'My Joseph.' Don't let them take him from you, darling."

"Mother, talk to me, come on." She shook her mother by the shoulders, trying to make her focus. Gloria was standing in a puddle of whiskey and broken glass.

"I heard them talking, darling."

"Mom, when?"

"Tonight. I listened in on the phone." Ruth held up the little transmitter disk and showed it to Gloria. "He didn't know because he couldn't hear me without this, darling. I heard everything they said, darling. The man said Joseph was staying at the Waldorf. What a nice hotel. I haven't been to the Waldorf for twenty years. I went once to a New Year's Eve ball. It was so lovely. I had this silver gown, I'll never forget it. We danced all night . . ."

Gloria was near panic now and she shook her mother again.

"Mother. Now listen to me. Are you saying that Sydney and another man plan to have Joseph killed in the Waldorf-Astoria, tonight?"

"Yes. By the Stewardess."

"What Stewardess?"

"How would I know? That's what Sydney said. They said they'd have her pose as room service."

"What room is he in at the Waldorf, Mom?"

"Jack Coohill's room."

"The number. Do you know the number?"

"No number. No number. How about Seagram's Seven? Would you believe Four Roses?"

"Mom, I want you to go to bed, get some sleep. I'm very sorry, but I have to leave right away."

"Will you come back for me, Gloria? I don't like to be alone."

"Yes, Mother. I'll be back. Just get some sleep."

"Thank you, darling. I'm very tired."

Gloria helped her mother to the bed and pulled some covers over her. Almost immediately Ruth Weingarten was sound asleep.

Gloria raced down the stairs and ran into the kitchen and picked up the telephone. She saw the locks on the rotary dial and slammed it down, furious, nervous. Now she remembered Sydney's phone conversation from when she had entered the house. "Yes, within the next few hours. Make that two hours."

Gloria Weingarten was now convinced that her mother had not been imagining things. Ruth had overheard this conversation. She grabbed her waist jacket, pushed her arms through it, and fled from the house, running toward Nostrand Avenue, looking for and finding a pay phone. She dialed information, got the number for the Waldorf, and with nervous fingers misdialed the number twice. Finally she got the Waldorf on the phone, and before she could speak, the operator asked her please to hold on. Each second of waiting was a jail term. A full minute passed and Gloria started shouting at the mute phone. Finally the operator got on.

"Jack Coohill's room, please."

"I'm sorry, there's a do not disturb on that line, ma'am."

"This is an emergency—"

But before she could finish the sentence the operator asked her to hold on again. Gloria banged down the phone and stood on the sidewalk, pacing. Then she walked to the middle of the street, stood on the yellow traffic line as cars, buses, trucks moved past her both ways. She flailed her arms crazily at several taxis with off-duty lights ablaze. Two, three, five minutes passed. She was shouting at the top of her lungs for taxis now, as cars honked at her and buses roared by.

Finally a checker taxi pulled to a stop. Traffic honked behind the taxi.

"Where to?" the taxi driver asked from his window.

"The Waldorf-Astoria," she said.

Lou Moran unzipped the suit bag and took out Joseph Gonzago's suit and laid it out on the bed for Joseph, who stood in his shorts sipping wine.

"I gotta admit, this is some suit," Lou Moran said. "But that Old Ginzo, I tell ya, if he wasn't so old maybe I would have liked to have dropped his sewing machine on his feet. He told me my suit is garbage, the one I'm wearing when I go in there, tells me it's cheap polyester, that I should wear a garbage bag instead. He fed me some line of shit, I can tell you that. And me, like a mameluke I fall for it. So I buy one of his suits, sets me back three C-notes, and what happens? I go back to the bagel in Barney's who sold me the polyester suit to enlarge his face because he told me it was cotton. Then when I get there he tells me it *is* cotton, that the Ginzo was fulla shit, that he told me my suit was polyester so he could sell me a suit. I don't believe him. He tells me to come with him to another men's shop to ask the people in there what kind of material it is. The guy in the store says cotton. So does the next men's store. That Old Ginzo sold me a line of horseshit you could have fertilized Arizona with. I give him credit for balls."

"The suit he sold you is much better, Lou." Joseph was smiling at Lou Moran, who was admiring himself in the mirror.

Joseph pulled on the suit pants. They fit perfectly, were tapered without being ridiculously tight but not baggy either, the legs just covering the tops of his Gucci loafers. He pulled the vest over the white shirt and regal blue tie and fastened the buttons. His pectorals were emphasized and his trim waist was made to look as flat as glass. The suit jacket fit him perfectly.

"How do I look?" Joseph asked Lou Moran. Lou Moran walked around Joseph Gonzago and nodded with appreciation.

"Like nobility."

Joseph laughed and ran a brush through his hair.

"One thing you gotta hand that old gizip, he could sew," Lou Moran said.

"I can't wait to get out of this room," Joseph said. "I've been cooped up here for five days."

"Another hour and a half," Lou Moran said, looking at his watch. "I'm gonna go downstairs and spread rumors."

"About what?"

"What a good bang I am," Lou Moran said. "When I pay three bills for a suit I expect to have help getting it off."

Joseph shook his head, smiling as Lou Moran walked to the door. "If you need me, I'll be in the bar."

"Okay."

Joseph poured himself a glass of white wine and repeated the lines of his speech over and over in his head.

The Stewardess arrived prepared. She came dressed in a white blouse, a brown skirt, a black string tie, white gloves, and a brown waist jacket—the uniform of the hotel help. She crossed the lobby of the Waldorf-Astoria and picked up a house telephone and requested room service.

"Yes, I'm calling from Mr. Coohill's room, number eighteen-fourteen," she said. "Yes, I'd like a bottle of Laforet Blanc 1977, and a double order of shrimp cocktail sent up, please. Yes. Thank you. How long will that be, please? Fifteen minutes? Thank you very much."

The Stewardess replaced the house phone and walked to the fire stairs, and although heads turned as she walked, she looked like just another hotel worker. She did not want the elevator operator to remember her so she entered the fire stairs and began the long climb to the eighteenth floor. The pocketbook she carried was heavy, and so she took her time because she wanted to maintain all the strength she could.

By the time she reached the eighteenth floor twelve minutes had elapsed. She unbuttoned her white blouse and her breasts swung freely, unhindered by a bra. She looked at the row of elevators down the hall. Three minutes passed. Four. Six minutes. Incompetent clowns, she thought. When they say fifteen minutes they should be here in fifteen minutes. Finally twenty minutes after she had made the call to room service a Latin busboy stepped off an elevator, carrying a bottle of wine, a glass, and a shrimp cocktail on a tray. The Stewardess stepped into the hallway and whistled at him and pulled open her blouse, revealing her lovely breasts.

The busboy almost tripped and fell, looked over his shoulder, appearing nervous as hell. The Stewardess began massaging her breasts now and then motioned with her index finger for him to join her in the stairwell. The Stewardess made vulgar rotations of her tongue and the busboy, swallowing hard and still looking over his shoulder, walked toward her. She held the door to the stairwell open for him, and bug-eyed and flushed, the busboy stepped into the stairwell and bent over to place his tray safely on a step. As he bent over the Stewardess slammed him over the head three times, very hard, with a small sap. The busboy sunk into unconsciousness.

Gloria Weingarten raced into the lobby of the hotel, ran to the front desk, and asked the clerk for Jack Coohill's room number.

"I'm afraid we cannot give out that number, ma'am," he said.

"But this is an emergency," Gloria said, short of breath.

"You'll have to see the night manager, but I'm afraid he's at lunch, ma'am."

Gloria Weingarten, frustrated, walked across the lobby. She spotted Sydney Weingarten chatting with a group of men in tuxedos and fine dress suits. Gloria turned her head away from his direction and walked to the house phone. She asked for Jack Coohill's room. From where she spoke she could see the female switchboard operator talking.

"Can I leave a message then?"

The operator took the message, which said that Gloria was trying to reach him. Then she saw the same female operator hand the message to the clerk who would not divulge Jack Coohill's room number. The clerk turned around and stuffed the message into one of the pigeonhole boxes. Gloria Weingarten kept her eye on that particular slot and walked back to the desk. The clerk looked at her. Gloria looked past him at the box number, which was 1814.

"Is the manager back yet?" she asked.

"I'm afraid not, ma'am."

"Good, maybe he choked."

The clerk recoiled in offense as Gloria Weingarten raced for the elevators and asked the elevator operator for floor eighteen.

The Stewardess knocked on the door and Joseph's voice asked who it was.

"Room service," she said.

"I didn't order any room service," Joseph said.

"This is compliments of the management, Mr. Coohill," the Stewardess said.

Joseph stood inside the door, reluctant to open it at first. But he figured that perhaps management would send up a free bottle because Coohill was in charge of this massive banquet. He unchained the door and pulled it open. Joseph saw the bottle of Laforet and the shrimp cocktail. He knew this must be from room service, or else how else would they know what he always ordered? He noticed the shoulder bag slung over the beautiful smiling woman's shoulder.

"You always take your pocketbook with you on room-service trips?" he asked. She dazzled him with a smile.

"This is my last order of the night," she said. "I'm going straight home from here."

Joseph had not had a woman as a busboy in the five days he was there. What the hell, he thought, she's better-looking than the usual guys.

He accepted the tray of wine and saw that she remained standing there.

"Sorry," he said, searching his pants for a tip. All his money was in his other pants. "Hold on a minute."

Joseph turned his back on the Stewardess and walked across the room. The Stewardess stealthily took the ice pick from her bag, used the bag to jam the door open an inch so she could make a hasty exit, and advanced toward Joseph with the ice pick high above her head.

Joseph was digging some singles from his pants when he heard the scream.

"Joseph!" He spun, caught a flashing glimpse of a horrified Gloria at the door, and then the Stewardess, her face bitten with duty, but half distracted by Gloria's shriek, the ice pick coming down swiftly. Every ounce of agility in Joseph's body reacted at once, as his right hand slammed into the woman's face, sending her reeling across the room, bouncing off the bed, and then landing very hard, facedown on the floor. The woman had tried to break her fall with her blade hand, and now five inches of the long metal spike were visible through the back of her long hair.

Joseph ran to her and realized the ice pick had accidentally gone clear through her neck, and blood was softly beginning to leak from the back of her neck. The Stewardess was lifeless, still lying facedown.

Gloria stood at the inside of the door, her hands covering her mouth, her eyes wide in disbelief.

"Close the door right away," Joseph said with calm authority. "And bring me a towel."

Gloria did what he asked, kicking the woman's pocketbook into the room and bringing him a towel. Joseph lifted the Stewardess's head and saw that the handle of the ice pick was flush against the hollow of her throat, preventing any blood from spilling to the floor. Careful not to touch the handle, Joseph lifted the woman's head and wrapped the towel around and around her neck to keep the blood from leaking to the floor.

A knock came on the door and Joseph looked up at Gloria. The Stewardess was out of view from the door, and Joseph walked over to answer it. He opened the door and standing there was the Latin busboy, rubbing the top of his head, looking very groggy.

"Did a woman come here with your room service, sir?"

"Room service? I didn't order any room service."

"I must be confused," he said. "Somebody hit me on the head. I must have the wrong room. I don't know. I'm sorry."

Joseph closed the door, leaned against it, and Gloria ran into his arms.

"Joseph," she said as she buried her head in his chest. "Sydney did this . . ."

Gloria started crying uncontrollably.

"Calm down, my love. Calm down. Thank God you're here."

"I love you, Joseph."

"I love you too."

He took Gloria by the hand and walked to the telephone, called the lobby bar.

"Lou Moran, please."

Lou Moran came on the line.

"Lou," Joseph said. "Come up here right away."

Joseph hung up the phone and held a sobbing Gloria Weingarten in his arms.

31

The main banquet room of the Waldorf-Astoria was overflowing with people and noise, and the air was filled with the odor of fat cigars. All the tables were full and a dinner of veal scallopini was being served by waiters in tuxedos. The band was playing swing music on the bandstand above the murmuring and chatter and the general din of too many people trying to speak at once. Overlooking it all behind the band, was a massive poster of Be Be Gonzago, his face looming down with his cocksureness and squinted eyes, a face that was memorable and charming, frightening and reassuring, rugged and handsome. It was the face of a man who would have risen above the crowd in any field.

People moved from table to table, carrying drinks and shaking hands and laughing, slapping each other on the back. Some of these people were Gonzago loyalists who had indeed come out of deference to the memory of their slain leader. Others were here because of protocol, because they had no choice, and because they knew the next chairman of the Brooklyn Democratic machine would be informally selected and approved tonight. Besides, it was a chance to get together with friends, exchange gossip and stories and jokes.

Later, when the real ceremonies began, they would all sit quietly at the tables, try not to cough, chink their ice too loudly, drop a knife or a fork, or ask someone to pass the butter. The man who received the loudest applause that night would be the man who would be formally elected to the party chairmanship later in the week.

That would be Sydney Weingarten, and he knew that there would even be a standing ovation. This would mean that in the morning he would be occupying the office on the thirteenth floor of the building on Court Street, which would be a stop on the road to a dream. Sydney Weingarten sat at a table with Dermot Donnelly, Senator Hallahan, and the wives of those two men. Mayor Bailey was at the next table with his top-ranking administrative staff.

The people at the other tables frequently got up and made the obligatory visit to Weingarten's table. They came one at a time, wishing Sydney the best of luck, asking if they could have lunch someday soon, paid respects to the other guests.

Julio Garcia, the councilman from the Bronx, approached, and although Sydney knew he could use Garcia's money and strong-arm men, he wished he did not have to speak with this man. His smile was too wide, his jewelry too expensive, his belly too well fed, his hair greasy and wavy.

"I want you to know, Mr. Weingarten, that I am at your total disposal," Julio Garcia said, smiling broadly, showing his bridge work. "My people will work very hard for you and support you all the way. I'm from the Bronx, but I want you to know how important I think the Brooklyn organization is to us up there. My people look to you for guidance and all the help you can give us."

This man is a run-of-the-mill extortionist and a drug pusher, Weingarten thought to himself. And I have to sit here and listen to him.

"Thank you, Julio," Sydney said, and shook the greasy hand of the corpulent Puerto Rican. "Thanks for your support. We'll need it. Thanks for stopping over."

"My honor," Julio Garcia said, and leaned closer and winked. "And congratulations."

Garcia walked back through the ballroom and took his seat as a congressman from Bay Ridge now came up to Sydney to pay homage to the next boss. After his smile and handshake and kind words, he walked away and was replaced by a state senator, then the borough president of Queens, who was here looking for a handout to come later. To hell with this stooge, Sydney thought as he smiled, shook hands, and listened to a joke. He was always a Gonzago flunky anyway.

The band was doing their last number, and naturally it was "When the Saints Come Marching in," and Sydney Weingarten was happy this part of the evening was coming to a close. Now came the time for the introductory speeches. Someone will come up to tell humorous Be Be anecdotes, someone else will recite some maudlin words of loss, someone else will recall his contributions to the borough.

Sydney Weingarten scanned the seats at adjoining tables. He saw Frank Donato and his stunningly beautiful wife sitting at a table three from his left. There were two empty chairs at Donato's table, the chairs Joseph Gonzago and his guest were supposed to share. Sydney Weingarten smiled. They'd be empty all night, and Sydney Weingarten allowed himself a proud little smile. Then the lights of the massive chandeliers began to dim and conversations turned to whispers and finally silence prevailed.

Spotlights now beamed down on the stage as Jack Coohill, in a tuxedo, stepped up to the podium with a sheaf of papers in his hands. He read a few short announcements, talked about the charity the money would be going to. There was polite applause.

"Okay, we all know why we are gathered here tonight," Jack Coohill said, relaxed and confident from a hundred other similar functions over the years. "We have come to pay our respects to a man who in some way or another touched the lives of each and everyone of us here tonight, in addition to the lives of millions more in the borough of Brooklyn and all of New York."

There was loud applause and Jack Coohill looked over to Sydney Weingarten, who was barely visible in the darkness of the great room. Weingarten was sitting very erect, very pleased with himself.

"I'm talking, of course, of Mr. Walter O'Malley," there was thunderous laughter at Coohill's remark about the man most Brooklynites considered the world's worst quisling for moving the Brooklyn Dodgers to Los Angeles.

"In all seriousness, ladies and gentlemen, I'd like to take this opportunity to ask you all to give a big hand, a hand as big as the one Be Be Gonzago always reached out to those of us who needed his generosity, kindness, and advice over the years. Because wherever he is, in some smoke-filled back room of heaven, I hope, trying to gerrymander God out of his district, he'll be listening, so let's hear it for Be Be Gonzago."

There was a standing ovation, people whistling and hooting, knives and spoons rattling off dinner plates.

"We had originally planned a rather lengthy list of speakers for this evening," Jack Coohill said. "But as master of ceremonies I thought that for once it would be appropriate to conduct this dinner after the fashion of the man we are honoring here tonight. Be Be hated speeches. He epitomized the adage that actions speak louder than words. The words he always spoke came directly to the point. I take great liberty in suggesting what Be Be himself might have said if he were here tonight."

Jack Coohill paused a moment, turned his back, harumphed to clear his throat, then turned to the microphone and twisted his face into a scowl similar to Be Be's and did the best impersonation of the slain Brooklyn leader he could muster. "All right, let's cut the crap and get to the goddamned point here. We're here to pick our new chairman, so let's get it over with, clear away the dishes and open up the friggin' bars."

There was wild applause and much laughter. Now the waiters were moving through the large room removing the dishes from the tables. As they removed the large dinner plates, the sealed envelopes were revealed beneath them. People began to pick up the envelopes, but it was too dark to read, so they just held on to them, looking at the names printed on them in the dim candlelight at each table.

Sydney Weingarten did not have an envelope under his plate and was curious about the one Senator David Hallahan had. Hallahan fingered it, still listening to Jack Coohill speak, sipping a bourbon and ginger ale. Weingarten was not pleased with all this nonsense Coohill was announcing now about the speeches being cut down to just two. Sydney had expected the kind of pomp the evening deserved. This was one of the most important nights of his life, and this washed-up flack Coohill was making a dog-and-pony show of it. But more on his mind was who the second speaker would be.

"Okay," Jack Coohill said. "Before we begin the speeches, we are going to be throwing the lights on for the next ten or fifteen minutes so coffee and dessert and maybe even a brandy can be served. Then we'll get to our speakers and back to the bars."

There was more applause as the lights went on, and the general commotion of a thousand or more voices rose as Coohill left the stage. Coohill stood off to the side of the stage looking out at the crowd. He knew which tables had the envelopes that would cause the recipients the greatest torment.

Now Coohill looked from table to table as these men read the damning documents in their envelopes. A few looked on the verge of tears. They looked around as if for exits but remained glued to their seats, silent for the most part, awaiting some dreadful revelation. Most people read their files quickly, jamming them quickly away into inside pockets, looking nervously at one another. The room became oddly quiet, where only moments before the chatter was reaching a crescendo. Many toyed with their ties and silverware, while wives or companions asked what was the matter.

Coohill looked at David Hallahan reading his file because he knew what Hallahan was reading. He was reading the list of seventeen immigration green cards with the amounts paid to him by immigrants in a corresponding column. That was page one. Page two had a list of the many expensive gifts Mr. Hallahan had received from the heads of several large corporations with international ties —most of them in the Middle East, including one from a firm that did most of its business with Libya. This was most damaging to Hallahan, since he was a very outspoken critic of Libya and a champion of Israel.

Hallahan crumpled the paper into a ball and then thought better of it, smoothed it out and folded it neatly and put it into his inside jacket pocket. He took out a handkerchief and dabbed his brow. Sydney Weingarten looked at Hallahan curiously.

"What the hell is wrong with you, David?"

Hallahan coughed nervously and pretended to have gas.

"The food was awful, Sydney."

"What's in these envelopes everybody is getting?" Dermot Donnelly looked curious too.

"Oh, nothing. Just the usual nonsense. You know, a thank you note from the committee."

"Let me have a look at it," Sydney Weingarten said.

"No!" Hallahan snapped, and then realized he was overreacting. He patted his wife on the arm and excused himself from the table. He walked toward the men's room lighting a cigarette, not speaking with anyone as he walked across the room, looking aimless and very frightened.

Jack Coohill stood in the wings of the stage watching Sydney Weingarten walk over to talk to Mayor Bailey. Coohill knew the cause of Bailey's terrible discomfort. It had to do with the documentation of rigged bidding for city contracts. The same three companies hired to do park renovations had received rotating contracts over the years. The scam was simple. Each year one of the landscaping contractors had his turn to get the job at a bid that was so overpriced as to stagger the mind. The way the lowest bidder would get it that year was by having the other two agree to make bids that were so huge they could not be considered. So the lowest bidder, whose bid was also ridiculously overpriced, would be awarded the contract, and Bailey would get a percentage of this contract back. The next year one of the other two contractors would place the lowest of three exorbitant bids and get the contract. This way one of three very expensive landscaping contractors in the city were guaranteed a gold-lined deal with the city once every three years. The three contractors would split up the money among themselves and a ten-percent fee would go to the mayor.

"I'm not feeling all that well, Sydney," Mayor Bailey said. "I think

I've been overworking myself lately. I think maybe the whole business is catching up on me. I need a rest of sorts. I don't know if I'll be able to stay for the speeches."

Weingarten was surprised. "Aren't you giving the second speech?"

"No," Bailey said. "And I don't know who the hell is."

Weingarten looked around the room. People were putting away the small envelopes with somber alacrity.

The banquet room of the Waldorf-Astoria looked anything but one of majesty and joy; this was not what Sydney Weingarten had in mind for the evening. Slowly he walked back to his table to await his turn to speak. I'll get them going, he thought.

Dumbstruck, he looked over the room. The silence was uncanny. No one was speaking to anyone else. Each eyeing the other as if he were the enemy. Men wiping sweat from their brows and walking back from the bathrooms as if they'd just been sick.

Well, he thought to himself, this is my evening. No one is going to spoil it. In a way it was almost funny. He looked around at the uneasy-looking guests and almost felt like laughing now. Sydney Weingarten waited for the lights to dim and the time to come for him to take center stage. He sipped a martini and started to feel better as he reread his speech.

Jack Coohill stepped to the stage again and now the lights began to dim and a lone spotlight illuminated him in front of the gathered. Coohill smiled as he looked out at the timid wall of darkness before him. He cleared his throat, tapped the live microphone, and held a single sheet of paper in his hands from which he began to read.

"Our first speaker tonight is a man we all know well. He has been around the political circles of Brooklyn for a long, long time."

The crowd was very quiet, except for the occasional cough, sniffle, scrape of a chair leg. Sydney Weingarten sat drumming his fingers on the table, wondering who this first speaker was going to be. He was hoping it was not Mayor Bailey because he was a little tipsy already. Maybe Hallahan. No, he'd already said he wasn't going to speak. He'd been scratched earlier in the evening.

Donnelly? Sydney hoped not because Donnelly was such a fine public speaker and he'd hate to follow him. Of one thing he was sure. The first speaker was not Sydney Weingarten. Acceptance speeches always came last.

"I won't make this introduction long-winded because I know if Be

Be were here, he would be as impatient as the rest of us." Jack Coohill's voice and manner started to irk Sydney Weingarten, who continued to drum his fingers on the table. "And anyway, this man needs no further introduction. Ladies and gentlemen, I give you the speaker of the assembly, Sydney Weingarten."

Sydney Weingarten clapped politely twice before his own name sunk in. Then he realized he had just been introduced. Who the hell did this insolent bastard Coohill think he was? What kind of an introduction was that? No kind words, no buildup, no list of accomplishments? Suddenly Sydney Weingarten realized that only a handful of people were clapping, the sound of a peg on a wheel of fortune. What the hell is going on here, he thought. His eyes began to dart around the room, into the darkness. There was a spotlight and a barren stage awaiting him. Now even the meager round of applause began to die.

Why weren't they applauding? Of course, they are saving the thunder for the end of the speech. That's it. The end of the speech would bring forth the show of hands. A show of confidence. Support. Lasting loyalty. This was, after all, a dress rehearsal for an intraparty election. And this was supposed to be Be Be Gonzago's night, so the true applause would come at the end of the speech, when they would show they wanted Sydney Weingarten as their next chairman. This is what it must mean, Sydney Weingarten thought as he walked uneasily to the steps of the stage. But who is this second speaker? And why will he be the last to speak?

Sydney Weingarten stepped into the beam of the spotlight and instantly felt the heat. He placed the sheets of paper on the small lectern and adjusted the microphone and looked out into the big room. He could make out no faces, just hulks, shapes, white collars and cuffs. He looked down at the speech after an uneasy pause and read the opening words.

"My fellow Democrats, ladies and gentlemen, citizens of Brooklyn, good evening." His voice broke once, but he quickly mended it. "I come here tonight to honor a man we all loved and revered. He was a man who will be impossible to replace. Not just as a leader of men, not just as a friend, not just as a champion of the common man, not just as a seeker of truth and justice. No, more than that, he was a man of ideas who had compassion even for his enemies. He was a fine husband, a loving father, a son of immigrants who came to America to find a new and better life. What they found here was a place where their son would serve bravely in defense of his country in World War Two, haul coffee sacks on the docks of Brooklyn, and work hard in this great system we call democracy, and end up as one of the men who helped shape this city, saw his visions become reality. This was a man who came from the gutters and went on to rebuild the very gutters from which he hailed. Not many men can go to their eternal rest so proudly. He was not a man of privilege, money, status, or even formal education. But he was a man of principles and integrity as tough and unbending as his beloved Brooklyn accent. So, if I may take the liberty to twist a phrase, let me say that we do not come here tonight to bury Be Be Gonzago, but to praise him, because in our hearts, in our minds, on our streets, and in our halls of government, Be Be Gonzago will never die. I suggest to you that Be Be Gonzago is not dead. I say you cannot slay ideas. I say you cannot assassinate history. You cannot bury vision. I say Be Be Gonzago lives on."

There was a pause in Sydney Weingarten's speech where applause was supposed to present a bridge of transition. No more than a hundred hands slapped together in the crowded room.

"We honor Be Be Gonzago tonight because although he lives on in spirit, someone must attempt the monumental task of picking up where he left off."

The words sounded ridiculous without the accompanying thunder of applause.

"So I address you tonight in Be Be's honor because I think I am the man most capable of filling his shoes. I did not come early to this decision to place my name in contention for the party chairmanship. After hard thought, and consultations with friends and family, I was persuaded that I might be able to pick up the ball where Be Be left it and make the hard drive toward the goal line. I pledge to you here tonight that I will do everything in my power, in my own quiet way, to make our organization, the Democratic party of Brooklyn, one of the most vibrant, powerful, important political organizations in this nation.

"So I call on you tonight to assist me in uniting this great organization of ours, to bury old feuds, to seal new alliances, to heal the wounds of yesterday, and to build toward a tomorrow that the great man we honor tonight would approve of. I thank you all, and bid you good night."

He expected the thunder now, the great, long, rolling acknowledgment of a lifelong dream. But all he received was a clickety-clack, like the wheel of fortune, each dull clap like a smack across his face. Sydney Weingarten stood frozen for a moment and then turned to walk toward the steps. He descended the three steps heavily, all grace abandoning him, once almost stumbling. Jack Coohill grabbed him by the arm, steadying him, and their eyes locked.

"Lovely speech, Syd," Jack Coohill said.

"You bastard," Sydney Weingarten said.

Jack Coohill smiled and leaped up the steps again and walked toward the spotlight.

"What the hell happened, Sydney?" Dermot Donnelly said as Sydney took his seat.

"What didn't?" Sydney Weingarten looked at Donnelly, very sad, a man deprived and embarrassed.

He was cut off now by Jack Coohill, who stood on the spotlit stage and began to speak again.

"Thank you, Mr. Speaker, for such an inspiring speech."

Jack Coohill allowed himself a very long pause, to be sure the humiliation of Sydney Weingarten would be complete. "Our next speaker needs very little introduction at all. In fact, I think he would be much better served by introducing himself. So without further ado, I'll pass the mike on."

Now the spotlight went dead and it was like the first thirty seconds in a movie house before the picture starts.

And then, all at once, all the lights in the ballroom went on. It took Sydney Weingarten several moments to adjust his eyes to the light. He heard the speaker introduce himself before he could see him.

"Good evening, ladies and gentlemen, my name is Joseph Gonzago and I would like to succeed my father in his role as chairman of the Democratic party of Brooklyn."

Thunderous applause rocked the room. Now Sydney Weingarten could see Joseph Gonzago on the stage, dressed in a beautiful blue silk suit just like the ones Be Be used to wear. He looked relaxed and he was smiling and the applause built to a deafening crescendo, and then almost everyone in the room stood for a standing ovation. Joseph Gonzago looked at the faces of these people. Few were smiling. Few were pleased. Most were scared, and they were clapping to save their lives, clapping for themselves, each smack of flesh against flesh a groveling plea for mercy. Joseph Gonzago now so clearly controlled their lives that standing there on the stage, looking down at them, as they continued to applaud, he knew the true meaning of boss. He looked up at the massive poster of Be Be Gonzago, and he, too, was smiling down at the gathered in the ballroom. Joseph took a cigar from his breast pocket, one of Be Be Gonzago's cigars, and as the applause continued he lit the cigar and leaned to the microphone.

"Thank you," he said. "Thank you for your support in these trying times." And then he turned and walked toward the steps. Sydney Weingarten was sitting at his table looking weak and sick and half beaten. Only half beaten because there was still something hard and spiteful in his eyes as Joseph approached. Sydney stood. Joseph stood before him as the applause continued.

"What's a matter, Sydney?" Joseph said. "You look like you just saw a ghost."

Joseph blew smoke in Sydney's direction, looked up at the poster of Be Be Gonzago, and winked at the image of his father. As he turned to leave with Jack Coohill, he could have sworn Be Be had winked back.

32

Gloria Weingarten devoured him, held him and clutched him and would not let him go. She wrapped her legs around him, her perspiring body slithering and sliding all over him, feeling his coarse body hair roughen her skin, pulling him this way and that, an animal strength seizing her—and him—taking every inch of him, letting no part of him escape her touch, her caress, her kiss, her smell, her taste. And he held her too, allowing himself to be overpowered by her, permitting her to take of him what she wanted as he took of her. His breathing was deep and frantic, and as he approached climax, in uncontrollable spasms, she whispered almost violently into his ear and pulled at his buttocks for more of him.

"Give it all to me," she said, her voice as much a plea as a command. "All of it."

The fire gutted. The smoke cleared. They lay silent and breathing very heavily for almost a full minute.

"It will be a boy," she said without looking at him.

"You mean . . ."

"I mean."

He laughed aloud. "Sneaky son of bitch," he said. "You never told me."

"You never told me you weren't crazy."

"I wasn't sure."

"Are you sure now?"

"No." He laughed. "Just like you can't be sure you'll even get pregnant. Or, even if you do, if it'll be a boy."

"I'm sure of both."

"How?"

"Because it was you."

They began to untangle themselves slowly.

"Tell me again about what your mother said about Daniel Morse," he said, staring at the ceiling.

Two days later he read the story about Elizabeth Lacey in the *Post.*

> The body of a fully dressed woman whom police have identified as Elizabeth Lacey, 34, who worked as an airline stewardess for Coastline Airways, was found in a laundry bin in the basement of the Waldorf-Astoria Hotel yesterday. The attractive, single blond woman was discovered by a workman in the boiler room of the plush East Side hotel. Police spokesmen said the woman had an ice pick skewered through her throat and that she was dressed in the uniform of a Waldorf-Astoria worker.
>
> Police are puzzled since Miss Lacey had never worked for the hotel, according to the hotel management. The coroner's report confirmed that there was no evidence of sexual molestation. The only fingerprints on the weapon were her own. Police have not ruled out robbery as a motive, but do not think this is the reason for the murder. In fact, police are not certain Lacey was murdered, although the coroner's report did indicate there was swelling under her right eye, which could have been the result of a punch or a fall. No clues were found in the woman's East Side apartment. Neighbors say they never saw her with a man and that she had few friends. It was hinted that a collection of lesbian literature was found in her apartment.
>
> Police are asking anyone with any information at all concerning Elizabeth Lacey to contact them at Manhattan Homicide Headquarters.

Only Joseph knew the rest of the Elizabeth Lacey story. After the speech at the banquet Joseph had asked Lou Moran to take Gloria to his house, where he would join her later. Lou had earlier stashed Elizabeth Lacey's body in the boiler room of the Waldorf. But he had taken twenty-five thousand dollars in cash and some personal belongings from her pocketbook and turned them over to Joseph. There were a few credit cards with addresses, a set of keys, and several photos, all of a young girl whom Joseph did not recognize.

Joseph went up to Elizabeth Lacey's apartment on East Eighty-eighth Street. The place was mostly bare. What little reading material there was consisted of radical left-wing pamphlets and lesbian and feminist literature. There were old SDS and Weathermen posters on the walls, and these almost made Joseph sad but failed to when the rhetoric screamed out at him like lost breath.

Joseph searched the place without finding anything of interest until he looked in the freezer of the refrigerator, the place where he used to stash his grass and political secrets in the crash pads of Berkeley in the sixties.

In the freezer Joseph found the briefcase. In the briefcase he discovered nine stacks of cash, each one totaling twenty-five thousand dollars. Joseph realized that Elizabeth Lacey was a contract killer after leafing through various newspaper clippings he found in the briefcase about nine seemingly unconnected murders all over the United States. All of them were men. All were killed with an ice pick. One of them in a motel in Santa Monica, California, and his name was Jimmy Boyle.

There were other clippings about a young girl named Corrine Mallahey who had been killed in a gang rape four years earlier. There were also love letters from Corrine Mallahey to Elizabeth Lacey. The two had been lovers, and when Corrine Mallahey had been murdered, Elizabeth Lacey had decided to get even. With men in general, or so it seemed. And charged twenty-five thousand dollars a head. Joseph was supposed to have been the tenth head.

Joseph shuffled through some more papers and found the information relating to him. It was scribbled on a single white sheet of paper: "J. GONZAGO. WA. 1814. SHRIMP COCK—LAFORET '77." After this message there was a phone number. The number seemed very familiar to Joseph. He was certain he had recently called that number. He picked up Elizabeth Lacey's phone with a gloved hand and dialed the number. A pleasant female voice answered on the other end.

"Hello, Kelly for Governor Headquarters, may I help you," the woman had said. Joseph stood frozen for a moment and then gently cradled the phone and left with the money in the briefcase and headed back to Brooklyn.

Now, Joseph read the newspaper story without emotion, looked at Elizabeth Lacey's photograph, and thought, too bad, such a pretty girl.

He dropped the paper onto the table and got up from his chair. It was almost eight thirty in the morning. He had an appointment with the Brooklyn Democratic committee at nine A.M. at which the borough's district leaders would vote him into the party chairmanship.

By nine minutes past nine the vote was over. It had taken just nine minutes to elect Joseph Gonzago unanimously to the county leader's seat. The district leaders, men and women, some of whom had voted for him under duress and others of whom were still members of his father's old club and therefore loyal to the Gonzago name, shook his hand as they exited the large conference room on Court Street. When they were gone Joseph stood alone in the office that had been his father's for so many years. He looked up at the portrait of Be Be Gonzago on the wall and nodded, as if to say hello.

Then Joseph Gonzago walked to the window overlooking Court Street, the New York State Supreme Court, the Post Office, Borough Hall, the Municipal Building. He looked off into the distance at the great sprawling metropolis that made up this place called Brooklyn. The spires of steeples, the long running rows of black-topped roofs, the networks of streets running in grids, blotches of green, steam, smoke, traffic, citizens.

Mine, he thought.

Lou Moran and Jack Coohill arrived at ten o'clock. Both men smiled as they walked across the office to where Joseph sat behind the large desk.

"Good morning, Boss," Lou Moran said. Joseph smiled and stood up and shook Lou Moran's hand.

"Congratulations, Joseph," Jack Coohill said. "There's someone here to see you already."

"Oh?" Joseph appeared surprised.

"The mayor."

"Jack, we'll need a secretary," Joseph said. "Middle-aged, very good, and as Tweed might have said, one who understands addition, subtraction, and silence."

"Done."

"Well, let's not keep the mayor waiting. I didn't expect him till about noon," Joseph said. "Let me talk to him alone. I'm sure he's upset enough as it is."

Lou Moran nodded and Jack Coohill led the way into the outer office. Coohill held the door open for Mayor Tom Bailey, who walked through the door with a confident stride, his face austere. Bailey waited until Lou Moran and Jack Coohill left the room before approaching Joseph Gonzago.

"Now just what the hell do you think this is?" Tom Bailey said, his voice strong, like a man who had prepared well for the scene that might fracture his life. "Leaving messages saying that I must come here to see you. Who the hell do you think you are? You think you can waltz here into this city and tell the mayor what to do?"

Joseph sat behind his desk staring at the furious mayor, leaning back in his swivel chair, studying the man. Then Joseph rose from his chair, walked around the desk to the liquor cabinet, and poured Tom Bailey a triple Irish whiskey and walked over and handed it to him.

"No thanks," the mayor said, placing the drink on the desk. "It's too early."

"That's nice, Tom," Joseph said. "I'm pleased you are mending your ways. Because I have a few more changes I expect from you besides what time you take the first drink of the day."

"Oh, you do, do you? Well let me remind you who I am—"

"No," Joseph snapped. "Let me remind you *what* you are. You're a drunk. You're a thief. You're a terrified little man. You're an okay husband and by most reports a fine father. You are the mayor of New York. But you will be a guest of the State of New York in one of their prisons if you don't listen to me, pal."

Joseph picked up Bailey's file folder from his desk. Opened it. Looked at the astonished mayor and quietly spoke as he leafed through the file.

"Mr. Mayor, I have here before me copies of six different conversations you had with my father in which you openly admit to rigging bidding on public contracts in return for campaign contributions, cash gifts, vacations. That sort of thing. Three of these contracts went to the same firm, and the only other bidders in the competition were from your wife's family. You arranged it so that your in-laws would make outrageous bids, thus allowing a certain building contractor to place the lowest bid. Only thing is, the lowest bid was still twice as high as it should have been for this kind of work. You pushed up the price of all bids by having your in-laws bid highest. Then this certain firm that gets the contract gives you a back-hander, which you share with your in-laws, and the contractor makes out too because even with the kickback he's way ahead. Mr. Mayor, I'm appalled. This is all on tape."

"You think you can get away with this, don't you?" Tom Bailey said defiantly. "You really think you can blackmail and manipulate the mayor of New York."

"Yes, Tom," Joseph Gonzago said. "I really think I can. And so do you. Or else you wouldn't be here."

The mayor made a flourish, stood up and stared at Joseph Gonzago, and said, "Go to hell, you bastard."

"I'm already there," Joseph said as the mayor marched to the door. Just as he reached for the knob he stopped, lowered his head, his shoulders finally sagging. Without turning he asked, "What is it you want from me?"

"Your support."

Tom Bailey turned around and walked back to the chair and sat down. He picked up the whiskey and flung it down, coughed, and waited for Joseph to explain. Joseph walked back around the desk and sat down.

"I'm not a spiteful man, Tom," Joseph said softly. "I just want you to tell me the truth about a few things. I want to know anything you know about my father's murder."

Tom Bailey looked up at Joseph Gonzago now, his eyes bewildered, his face damp with sweat.

"I swear to you, Joseph, I know absolutely nothing about it. Be Be had enemies. But I don't believe any of them would want to kill him. Sometimes I differed with Be Be myself, but that's because my loyalty was to Sydney Weingarten, who helped me in my career more than Be Be. Be Be never wanted me to be mayor. But he accepted it. He didn't oppose me full force because Be Be and I were on such a good personal relationship. He liked me. I liked him. He probably could have prevented me from getting the nomination. But he didn't. He told me the reason why. He said because I had a family and I have this problem, as you know, with alcohol. I think he felt sorry for me. It was Sydney who finally persuaded him to let me run. In exchange Sydney agreed not to challenge two of Be Be's congressmen. So if I look like an enemy of Be Be's, it is mostly because I owe Sydney my career."

"I see," Joseph said, steepling his fingers. "But you have more to worry about now than your career, Tom. You have jail to worry about."

"What do you want from me? I'll do what I can."

"First, let me tell you I believe you about not knowing about my father's death," Joseph said. "I don't want much from you. Mainly I want you to act as a liaison between Sydney and myself. I'm a practical man. I understand how much power Sydney Weingarten has in this borough, city, and state. I'm pragmatic enough to know that we might come to terms on some things. When the time is right I'll let you know that I want you to arrange a sit-down with Sydney and Wolfington. There's a good possibility we might work something out."

"But I thought you wanted Kelly," Bailey said, looking at Joseph more calmly now.

"I never said that. The Kelly people have never approached me. I'm not totally sold on him. Or Wolfington. In fact, if I didn't think you might sell the whole state to Jersey, I think you might be a better administrator than either of them."

Bailey brightened and managed a wan smile.

"I also want you to keep me informed on whatever scuttlebutt you pick up around Sydney," Joseph said. "If I make a deal with him, I want to know it won't be signed with my blood. He's a back stabber."

"Is there anything else, Joseph?"

Joseph stood from his desk and held out a hand to the mayor of New York.

"That's all, Tom," Joseph said. "After this election is over I'll give you your file and the original tapes and you can go on with your life."

Bailey shook Joseph's hand, looking immensely relieved.

"Thank you."

"Anytime, Tom. Anytime."

The mayor turned and walked out of the room, and Joseph watched him go, smiling. Jack Coohill and Lou Moran walked back into the room.

"How'd it go," Jack Coohill asked.

"Fine, just fine. I want both of you to listen to me now. No matter what I do, whatever you think of it, whether you think I'm right or wrong, I ask you to stand by me and not ask any questions. There will be some things I'm going to have to ask you to do that you might not agree with, but I want you to promise me that you'll accept them."

"Like what?" Lou Moran asked.

"For starters," Joseph said, "please get me Tim Harris on the phone."

"It's blackmail, Dermot," Sydney Weingarten screamed in his office at the Nathan Hale Club. "There has to be some goddamn thing you can do. You're the district attorney of Brooklyn. Joseph

Gonzago is blackmailing half the political people in this borough. And he's probably guilty of a few murders too."

"Sydney, Sydney," Donnelly answered, trying to calm Weingarten. "There isn't one damn shred of evidence. Nothing. I can't go indicting Be Be Gonzago's son on some trumped-up charge. Are you out of your mind? Calm down. This thing isn't over yet. The primary is three weeks away. We still have time."

Sydney Weingarten finally sat down and drummed his fingers on his desk. He looked at Donnelly.

"You're right. This punk kid thinks he can walk into this borough and just pick it up in the palm of his hand? He's got a lot to learn. I still have clout in this town. In this state. I'll whip his ass. We still have some loyal people, some people smart enough not to have their voices recorded or their transactions written down on paper. Who does he have anyway? Assholes. Anyone dumb enough to get blackmailed can't carry much weight. We're still in this thing. This kid has the fight of his life on his hands right now. I can tell you that."

"The thing to remember is to stay calm," Donnelly said. "He expects you to panic. But we have to outthink him. Muscle just won't work. We have to outpolitick this brat."

"You're right," Sydney said. "We'll have to compile a list of good people who can be trusted. If we need some bodies we can get Garcia to throw in some of his people from the Bronx. They can lick envelopes, make calls, put up posters, watch polls, drive cars. Pull out the plugs on this kid."

"Now you're talking," Donnelly said. "Avakian can get us some money. Sam Stone must still have some of those poverty workers in his pocket too. And Sam must have some money. You don't have friends who carry around kilos of dope without them also having some money. What the hell? And we still have maybe twenty legitimate people with clout Joseph Gonzago doesn't have. Remember some people did clap for you that night."

"All right," Sydney said. "Let's go to work."

Donnelly smiled. At least Sydney wasn't going to take it lying down. The election was still a horse race, and Brendan Kelly was still the dark horse.

Joseph Gonzago had gotten Tim Harris on the phone, and Joseph and he made plans to meet for lunch the next day. An hour after Bailey left Senator Hallahan arrived. Joseph had summoned Hallahan to his office and Hallahan was in no position to defy Joseph Gonzago.

Hallahan's greatest bloc of support came from the Jews in New York. Hallahan was almost fanatical in his support of Israel. He had identified himself with this issue almost exclusively for years—making loud speeches condemning the whole Arab world, not just the PLO.

The Jews were still a very powerful voting bloc in Brooklyn, and Joseph Gonzago could easily have had Hallahan come out for Kelly to try to sway them. But he also wanted to punish this man. Jack Coohill had prepared a major speech for Hallahan to be read from the floor of the Senate. In it Hallahan would condemn Israeli "expansionism," term them unreasonable and warmongering, and say that after long, thoughtful reconsideration of the Mideast crisis he now realized that the Palestinians had been shafted, that the only way to solve the Mideast situation would be to invite the PLO to the peace table, to give back all territories taken by Israel in the Six Day War, to promise that no new settlements be made on the West Bank, and to establish a state of Palestine.

"Why are you doing this to me?" a terrified Hallahan asked Joseph. Joseph looked at Hallahan with a stern, even stare.

"Because you are a greedy, venal man," Joseph said. "And because you betrayed my father when you went with Weingarten."

"Be Be treated me like a little kid," Hallahan explained. "Just listen to the tape about the green cards. My God, you would think I was a child molester."

"Taking money from poor people for green cards is right up there with child buggery, David," Joseph Gonzago said. "And speaking of buggery, remember, it is the number-one pastime in the joint. Do you know what would happen to a senator set loose in the general population of a prison?"

"But, Joseph, all I wanted from Be Be was that he treat me as an adult, as a senator, a United States senator, as an equal."

Joseph smiled and said, "That's where you made your mistake. You were a senator but Be Be was the boss."

Hallahan accepted this and folded the speech and placed it in his inside jacket pocket. "When am I supposed to deliver this speech?"

"One week before the New York primary," Joseph said. "And at the news conference following it you will announce your endorsement of Wolfington because you think his ideas on the Middle East match your new-found ideas. Get it?"

"I get it," Hallahan said. "You know, of course, I will never get re-elected after this. You know you are ruining my life."

"No, not your life, just your career."

Hallahan shook his head and walked slowly out the door. Lou Moran, who had been sitting through all of this in silence, jumped to his feet.

"After he gives that speech and endorses Wolfington every Jewish guy in Brooklyn is gonna rush out for Kelly," Lou Moran said. "They'll empty out the bagel shops, nursing homes, Manhattan Beach, Brighton Beach; they'll swarm to the polls for Kelly. Weingarten will be counting on those people. They're his people. He'll go into coroner's arrest."

Joseph Gonzago laughed at Lou Moran.

"Kelly is still three points behind Wolfington in the polls and I think I know why," Joseph said. "I'll see Tim Harris tomorrow."

He met Harris the next day at a restaurant called Foffe's in downtown Brooklyn. Joseph ate veal piccata and rigatoni and Tim Harris ordered the very same.

After exchanging some stories from the past about demonstrations they had attended together and the old organizations they had belonged to, they laughed about ending up in establishment politics. Actually, Joseph had never been terribly fond of Harris. He felt he had been a sort of sellout. He had chosen the easy way to the top, made his reputation on radical issues, and then when the door opened to make some money and get close to real power, he seized the opportunity without qualification or compunction. But at least he still followed the politics of the left rather than the right. Liberals were the biggest assholes, but he was not really a liberal. Lurking somewhere beneath the exterior of Tim Harris there was still a touch of the radical. A bit softer but still there. Finally Joseph asked Harris about Daniel Morse.

"What can you tell me about Morse," Joseph asked, as he paused to sip some red wine.

"Morse? Oh, I guess he's smart. He's a little lazy. He has always had money problems. His family is huge. Seven kids. He lived beyond his means for a few years. I don't like him personally, but Brendan thinks highly of him."

"Do you know of any reason why he would meet secretly with Sydney Weingarten in Albany?"

Harris stopped chewing, swallowed, wiped his mouth with the

white linen cloth, placed his fork down, and looked at Joseph in alarm.

"What are you saying? Come on, don't beat around the bush with me."

"I'm just asking you a question," Joseph said, watching Tim Harris's reaction, studying the man.

"No, I can think of no reason whatsoever why he should meet secretly with Sydney Weingarten in Albany. Unless it was before this campaign. How recently are we talking about here?"

"A week ago," Joseph Gonzago said.

"Are you suggesting that Morse is some kind of mole for the Wolfington campaign?" Tim Harris did not pick up his fork again. He was sitting in open-mouthed disbelief.

"Why would that be so shocking to you?" Joseph asked. "How many guys did you and I sit around with in the old days, blowing pot, listening to Dylan, and making plans for demonstrations, only to find out that some of our best pals in SDS were FBI agents? I mean how many times did we go through that in the sixties, early seventies?"

"That was a little different, don't you think?"

"I don't know. I'm just surprised you're so surprised. Maybe Morse needed some cash, so he's working both sides of the fence. Maybe it was just harmless. Maybe Wolfington was trying to win him over to work for his side and Morse turned him down."

Joseph thought about the phone number he had found in Elizabeth Lacey's briefcase—the phone number for the Kelly headquarters.

"I better bring this up with Brendan immediately," Tim Harris said. "I mean, this election is so close, three points, and it can still go either way. We can't have people inside working against us."

"Look, we have no idea if it's what it appears to be," Joseph said. "Let it slide awhile. Test him. If he is in Sydney's pocket, you can always feed him bum information, have it backfire on them. That's what I'd suggest if I were supporting Kelly."

"That's a hell of an idea," Harris said. "Like the time we discovered the FBI plant in the Berkeley chapter and gave him the wrong time and site for the demo and the police showed up there while we were across town. Of course. Whose idea was it to do that?"

"Yours," Joseph said, remembering the incident clearly. "Eat. The veal is tremendous."

Harris resumed eating.

"I also think that Kelly had better prepare a pretty good statement on the Middle East."

"Middle East?" Harris said. "This is a gubernatorial election, Joseph."

"This is also a city with over a million Jews," Joseph said. "And a city where certain issues not even remotely related to the election can make the difference. How about mayors and congressmen who have no say in the matter of capital punishment winning on their stance on that sole issue."

"I was hoping that we could avoid the Mideast issue," Harris said. "So damn touchy."

"Well, remember Hallahan is going to endorse Wolfington," Joseph said. "The Jews take a lot of stock in Hallahan. Maybe something to keep in mind. The question of his views on the Middle East will come up when Kelly comes through Brooklyn, I can tell you that. Strictly Camp David would be safe."

They ate in silence for about thirty seconds, and then Harris placed his fork back down and looked up at Joseph.

"Okay, Joseph. We've known each other a long time. We've disagreed on a lot of things. But mostly we are coming from the same place. I won't beat around the bush. Kelly needs you and the machine. What do you want in return?"

Joseph was taken completely by surprise with this question. He had not come here prepared to horse-trade with Tim Harris. He was here to offer advice to Harris on behalf of his dead father. He was here because he knew his father would have been here. He was fulfilling Be Be Gonzago's wishes.

"What do you mean, Tim?"

"What do *you* mean, what do *I* mean?" Harris laughed. "You are now the capo of the Brooklyn machine. We want you. You must want something. If Kelly gets elected because you deliver Brooklyn, we owe you. Tell me what you want and I'll see what I can get done. Jobs, state aid, Medicaid relief, whatever. You know, the stuff we radicals always screamed about. The patronage. Back-room deals. Personally, since I've, shall we say, *matured,* that's the part I like best about legitimate politics. The dirt."

He smiled and sipped some wine. Joseph stared at him without emoting his feelings. So here was the old radical, the campaign manager for the white knight on the ivory steed. Mr. Clean falls in the mud. Beautiful, Joseph thought.

"What makes you think I'm going to endorse Kelly?" Joseph asked.

"You're not thinking of endorsing Wolfington . . ."

Harris looked surprised but not overly concerned.

"My father always kept a little plaque on his desk—it's still there—which reads, 'I said maybe, and that's final.' "

"Well, then why did you invite me here for lunch?"

"Because of the veal."

33

Over the next week Sydney Weingarten assembled his loyal troops —and there still were a good number of them who had to reckon with this man who was, after all, the speaker of the assembly and a man with considerable clout. Other assemblymen in Brooklyn who ever wanted to get their bills through the state legislatures would fear Sydney Weingarten. Most of them, anyway. Joseph Gonzago had the goods on a few of them, and his only demands on them would be to use their influence in their assembly districts to draw out the vote for Kelly. Weingarten would be doing the same thing with those Joseph didn't own.

Weingarten was a clever strategist. Figuring he could deliver the Jewish vote because of his close ties with the United Jewish Appeal and the major shakers in B'nai Brith and similar organizations, and because he was certain Senator David Hallahan would stump for the Jewish vote as well in Brooklyn, Weingarten concentrated on trying to pull votes that many people ignored. The city was not going all black and Hispanic for nothing. Most of those people could vote but rarely did.

If he could get them to come out and vote, it would do his candidate an awful lot of good. So he called in Julio Garcia and his people from the various poverty programs in the Bronx and had them go into the Hispanic neighborhoods and enlist support from those people. False promises of jobs, poverty money, and social-service centers were made to the people who lived in places like Sunset Park, Red Hook, other parts of South Brooklyn, and Coney Island. The canvassers whom Garcia provided spoke Spanish and this mattered greatly. Campaign literature extolling the merits of Governor Wolfington was printed in Spanish.

Weingarten contacted Sam Stone in Caracas and told him that even if he were convicted Weingarten could probably persuade Wolfington to pardon him, and that after the election he could return. In the meantime Stone was to call in all his markers from election-district captains and money people in Brooklyn. Tell them to work for Wolfington through Sydney Weingarten. Stone agreed.

Weingarten knew he could never really ask Wolfington to pardon him. How could an eventual presidential candidate ever pardon a cocaine dealer? But Sam Stone bought the promise.

Sydney did not know of Joseph Gonzago's encounters with both Bailey and Hallahan. Neither man told Weingarten for fear of word leaking back to Joseph, who'd promised to make public their past sins. Weingarten was infuriated that neither man had returned any of his many phone calls. But he knew they would eventually contact him. They had to. Their political careers were at stake.

Sam Stone's help was more than adequate. He still commanded a certain amount of respect in the black community, certainly with the community leaders who had made a handsome poverty dollar from Stone over the years and were indebted to him. So Stone organized a network of black campaign workers that went into the neighborhoods of Bedford Stuyvesant, Bushwick, Crown Heights, East Flatbush, Fort Greene, and all the other areas of Brooklyn with a high-density black population. Stone's people promised to deliver voters to the polls in buses and automobiles, and promises here were made about jobs, money, and other benefits that would, of course, never materialize.

Lou Moran was running the street operation of the Gonzago camp in Brooklyn. Frank Donato had delivered over two hundred bodies from the union to help knock on doors and canvass the vote. A lot more people came from the organizations of the coerced politicians whom Joseph Gonzago had in his files. But Lou Moran was getting frustrated. A lot of people were just too apathetic about politics in general to sit and listen or to make commitments. He also saw that Weingarten was running one hell of a grass-roots campaign. Wolfington was still three points ahead of Kelly in New York and this bothered Lou Moran. He went to see the only man who could advise him, Joseph Gonzago, his boss.

When Joseph Gonzago was presented with this problem, he sat and thought for a moment. He wondered what Be Be would have done in such a situation. It did not take him long to figure out what to do.

"Go collect parking tickets," Joseph Gonzago told Lou Moran.

Lou Moran looked at Joseph Gonzago in utter disbelief.

"Parking tickets? Boss, we're involved in a governor's campaign here and you're talking about parking tickets. You goin' du botz or what?"

"Whenever you knock on doors ask them if they are registered Democrats," Joseph said. "No Republicans. You tell them you are working for the Kelly campaign. And then ask them if they have any unpaid parking tickets. If they do, ask for them and promise they will be taken care of. In return for this favor you only ask that they go to the polls and vote for Kelly on primary day."

Lou Moran was astonished.

"Joseph, with all due respect, I know you're the boss of Brooklyn and you are very smart, but even you can't fix that many tickets. I mean what about that guy in the Lindsay administration, he got caught fixing two parking tickets and Nadjari's guys pulled up with a police van at two in the morning the day the guy's father died. I mean parking tickets ain't so easy to fix no more like they usta be."

"Lou, just collect the parking tickets," Joseph said. "Tell your campaign workers to do the same. There is no need to collect them in the Jewish areas because we're gonna get that vote. But in Bay Ridge, Park Slope, Brooklyn Heights, the black and Puerto Rican areas. And only for Democrats. If the people say they're already for Kelly, don't bother. If they're fence sitters or Wolfington people, get the tickets."

"What do I do with them afterward?" Lou Moran said, exasperated.

"Bring them to me," Joseph Gonzago said.

"This is the most whackadoo idea I ever heard, Boss," Lou Moran said. "You can't fix all these tickets!"

"Just bring them to me," Joseph Gonzago said.

Lou Moran threw his hands into the air and left the room. For the next several days Lou Moran and his campaign workers went all over Brooklyn and started collecting parking tickets. One scofflaw had twelve thousand dollars in tickets and when he tried to give them to Moran, Lou slugged the guy. The man did not come to for an hour. Moran had been insulted by the man's audacity. No one vote was worth twelve grand. The man hit the deck just inside his door as the hundreds of parking tickets fluttered after him through the air. Lou Moran left Wolfington campaign literature on the man's face and closed the door.

Sydney Weingarten got wind of this bizarre operation of Joseph Gonzago's and went to see Dermot Donnelly. Donnelly assured Weingarten that if Joseph Gonzago tried to fix even one of those tickets he would indict him. Joseph Gonzago might be the machine boss, but he was still not above the law. Weingarten and Donnelly were certain the ticket-collecting scam would land Joseph Gonzago in jail. This was the big break they were waiting for.

Weingarten still had not received any return phone calls from Hallahan or Bailey. He had left threatening messages with their secretaries that they would be ruined professionally if they did not get in touch with him immediately. But with twelve days to go until the primary Bailey and Hallahan had a lot more to worry about than their jobs. They had their freedom to worry about, something Weingarten could not grant them. Joseph Gonzago held the power over them.

Ten days before primary day Lou Moran and six campaign workers walked into Joseph Gonzago's office with several boxes of parking tickets.

"Here's your tickets," Lou Moran said. "Now what the hell are we going to do with them?"

"Pay them," Joseph Gonzago said.

Lou Moran's eyes opened so wide that Joseph was afraid they'd fall out of the sockets onto the rug.

"Pay my fuckin' ass, pay!" Lou Moran said. "You got a hundred and ninety-six thousand and fifty-two dollars in tickets here! Pay my ass, pay!"

Joseph Gonzago opened a briefcase on his desk. Inside was the money he had taken from the apartment of Elizabeth Lacey. He counted out two hundred thousand dollars and handed the money to Lou Moran. All the men in the room stood in frozen disbelief.

"Are you out of your fuckin' mind, Boss?" Lou Moran said. "You just can't walk up and pay two hundred thousand dollars in parkin' tickets."

"Why not?" Joseph asked, his voice very calm but secretly amused.

"I don't know why not, but you can't. You just can't."

"Anything illegal in it?"

Lou Moran covered his face with his large hand and mopped the sweat from it. He kept shaking his head and looking at the money. The other men did not say a word; they were completely awestruck.

"I don't know," Lou Moran said. "This is unfuckinbelievable. Jesus Christ on the boards, Boss. Two hundred large in tickets? If it ain't illegal it should be."

"Get fifty men, give each of them a stack so it won't be so conspicuous, and go and pay for the tickets, Lou," Joseph said. "Simple as that. And with the leftover money give everybody an equal share as a bonus and go get loaded. Just don't mention where you got the money."

Lou Moran looked at the other six men in the room. They all shrugged or raised their eyebrows or remained mute.

"You are a lulu," Lou Moran said. "A real fuckin' lulu."

With that he and the other men left Joseph Gonzago's office.

34

Gloria Weingarten was getting used to Joseph Gonzago's irregular hours. Often he slept in the office, working round the clock, meeting with pols, campaign workers, money men. She knew he was always available, but she did not pester him with calls. She knew there would be a time when life would settle down. She had moved much of her clothing into Joseph's house in Flatbush, and had stayed there since they had been reunited. Joseph had asked her to stay there, to move in with him, so that he would know where she was when he needed her. Gloria Weingarten did not hesitate for one moment to accept the invitation.

She sat there on the living room couch, tears streaming down her face, a wineglass in her hand, as midnight approached. She heard the car pull up outside. She wiped her eyes, blew her nose, not wanting Joseph to find her in this state, knowing there were so many other things on his mind already, unwilling to dump her problems on him.

He stepped through the door, and when he did he let out a great sigh of exhaustion and dropped his keys on a small shelf near the door.

"Gloria," he half shouted. "Gloria, you still awake?"

"I'm in here, Joseph," she said, her voice sounding like static.

Joseph sensed there was something wrong before he saw her. He walked into the living room, saw her bloodshot eyes and the forced smile.

"I'm sorry, sweetheart," he said. "I was just snowed under. I'm beginning to understand why Be Be was never around."

She tried to laugh, but broke into a sob instead. He went to her.

"Hey, come on," he said, putting his arm around her, her limp body like dough in his hands. "I'm sorry. Ten more days and it'll be over."

"It's not that." She couldn't hold it back and cried on his shoulder.

"What is it then?"

"Nothing," she said.

"Look, I can't help you if you don't tell me. Your wish is my command."

He was trying to cheer her up. She tried to stop the tears.

"Just tell me," Joseph said.

"It's my mother. Sydney had her placed under a conservatorship and had her committed. Legally he's the only one permitted to see her. Anyone else must get his written permission. He won't even see me, take my calls, anything. He has my mother locked up in some goddamn nut house and he has the key."

She broke down again. "She'll die in there. I know it. She'll kill herself or they'll kill her. One way or the other I'm convinced she'll never come out of there alive."

Joseph held her, tried to soothe her.

"Is that all? That's why you're crying?"

Gloria grew hard and angry.

"Is that all? Is that why I'm crying? This is my mother we're talking about here. Not some district leader or E.D. captain. I'm talking about the woman who brought me into this world. You son of a bitch. My mother!"

"Go ahead, get it all out, cry your eyes out, say what you want, it's good for you," Joseph said, looking into her wet eyes. "But then I want you to stop crying. Because I promise you that your mother will be there at the wedding."

Gloria Weingarten, even in her anguish, gathered enough breath together to say, "Wedding?"

"Yes. Wedding. We'll get married exactly one week after the primary. Seventeen days. I refuse to get married without my mother-in-law there, so she'll just have to be there, won't she?"

"But how . . ."

"My way. Now stop crying and let me make you something stronger than that. Tonight we celebrate."

"Hey, you bastard," Gloria Weingarten said, smiling, sniffling.

"What?" Joseph said innocently.

"What kind of proposal is that?"

Joseph winked at a smiling Gloria Weingarten and said, "Who's the boss here anyway?"

Joseph Gonzago called Mayor Bailey in the morning and told him he wanted to meet with Wolfington and Weingarten that afternoon, that maybe they could work something out. Bailey agreed to try to arrange it.

"I don't want you to try, Tom. I want you to do it. Please, for this afternoon."

Finally Bailey promised.

By the time Joseph Gonzago got to his office his middle-aged secretary, a woman from Greenpoint with six kids and a Brooklyn accent thicker than the girders of the Brooklyn Bridge, told him he had a visitor waiting in his office.

"In the office?" Joseph said. "You shouldn't have let him in the office, Margie."

"I'm sorry, Mr. Gonzago, but the man shows me a badge I figure he's, you know, got a right or somethin'. Where I come from anyways."

Joseph found it totally impossible to get annoyed at Margie. She was the quintessential Brooklyn housewife, he thought. A cop shows her a badge and he's allowed to take the furniture if he wants. Anyone who has ever raised six children understands the law is the enemy.

Joseph told Margie not to worry about it because she kept apologizing to him. He stepped into the office and Francis X. Cunningham stood with his back to him, staring out the window onto Court Street.

"The last time I met you you were an unemployed ex-radical whose father had just been murdered," Cunningham said without turning around. Joseph knew Cunningham could see him in the reflection of the window and was trying to be cool. "Now all of a sudden I am standing in the office of the most powerful man in the largest Democratic county in the state. Was it your resume or your references that got you so far so fast?"

"I took the elevator, actually."

Cunningham spun around and did not smile.

"Remember this, *Boss*, you are not above the law."

"Now I just help make them." Joseph was enjoying the cat and mouse game. "But listen, Cunningham, I'm a busy man these days. Comes with the job. I sure hate standing here wasting time with you while you're on taxpayers' time. The money could be better spent on a stop sign somewhere."

"All right, *Boss*. I didn't see you at the funeral of Rosario and Gulatta. Funny. Such good pals when you were kids. Figured you would have come to pay your respects."

"Yeah, was a sad thing that. Car accident. Didn't the story go that the car had a mechanical fault or something?"

"Yes. That's right. No sign of hanky-panky. Open and shut. Road accident. Both of them were drinking too. Way it goes I guess."

Joseph took his seat behind his desk and buzzed Margie and asked her to order coffee for two.

"None for me," Cunningham said. "I can't stay. I have a meeting with some federal agents in an hour. About this woman named Lacey who was found dead. You read about that one?"

"No, 'fraid not. Anything more complicated than Dick Young and I'm under water."

"Well the federal agents have this hunch, see, that a woman named Elizabeth Lacey, who was found dead in the Waldorf-Astoria two days after you were there at your father's dinner, might be connected to a series of murders around the country."

"No kidding? I didn't read anything about that."

"That part of the story isn't out yet, and I'm hoping you'll keep your mouth shut about it too until the investigation is over. I'll tell you why. One of the people the feds think she might have murdered was a fella named Jimmy Boyle. She was a stewardess on his flight. At least three other guys in cities like Denver, Cleveland, San Francisco, all died the same way and all had Elizabeth Lacey as a stewardess. They're checking on a bunch more, waiting for work records and flight details. Now, Christ Almighty, Gonzago, you were in that hotel the night this broad was murdered. Doesn't it seem weird to you that the broad who might have bumped off your father's killer winds up dead in the same hotel where you appear before two thousand Brooklyn Democrats at a memorial dinner in your father's honor?"

"Listen to me, Cunningham. Up to now I sort of liked you. But you're starting to really bust my stones. Every time I run into you, you make the most ridiculous accusations. What are you trying to say here? Ask me. Get to the goddamn point."

"Did you kill Elizabeth Lacey?"

"No, of course not."

"Did you kill Rosario and Gulatta?"

"No. I didn't like them enough."

"Well, some mother jumper did, man. You know the heat I'm taking on this? From the top."

"Well, then I suggest you go to the top of the agency."

"What?"

"Run it yourself."

"You're crazier than I thought. I can't even talk to you, man."

"Look how far I came in so short a time."

Cunningham was getting frustrated and began walking toward the door. He yanked open the door, annoyed with himself for displaying his anger in front of Joseph Gonzago.

"Hey, Cunningham," Joseph shouted, "you know something? I think someday you'll make it to the top."

"That's what I mean. Nuts."

He slammed the door behind him and Joseph picked up a pencil and wrote his name on a sheet of paper. He also wrote down Tim Harris's name and folded the paper and placed it under a heavy glass paperweight on his desk.

At first Sydney Weingarten had refused to see Mayor Tom Bailey. Bailey had not returned the dozens of phone calls Sydney had left for him. But when the mayor of New York comes to your office, sits and waits for you to grant him an interview, it is impossible to turn him away. It would not look right to any of the other men in the clubhouse. Besides, Sydney was curious to see what Tom Bailey wanted.

When Bailey told Sydney Weingarten of Joseph Gonzago's offer of a powwow, to discuss his possible backing of Wolfington, Weingarten flew into a rage. At one point Bailey thought Sydney Weingarten would physically assault him.

"You son of a bitch," Weingarten had screamed as Bailey sat before him. "I've done everything for you. Helped make you what you are. And then you stroll in here like a delivery boy for Joseph Gonzago."

Dermot Donnelly sat silently, legs crossed, watching the animated scene.

"He expects me to come to see him! This man must be insane. How the hell else would he ever get the gall even to suggest such a thing?"

"But he says he wants to talk to you about supporting Wolfington, Sydney," Bailey said. "Isn't that what we want?"

"Support Wolfington? Sure, in exchange for everything. Every dollar, job, contract. Are you out of your mind? Of course he wants to support Wolfington now, because with nine days left he's still ahead of Kelly. Who wants to go for a loser?"

"Sydney," Bailey said. "Look, the man has incriminating evidence against me. All he's asked in return from me is to come and see you about a sit-down."

"Sit-down. What is this, the Mafia?"

"Please listen to me. Sure, Wolfington is still ahead. But only by three points. You don't know what the guy wants. What can it hurt to see him, for crying out loud? He's the county leader and that has to count for something."

Dermot Donnelly spoke up at that moment.

"Tom, would you mind very much waiting out in the reception area for a minute. Let me talk this over with Sydney. I don't mean to be impolite, Tom. But would you mind?"

"Not at all," Tom Bailey said, and walked out of the office, leaving Sydney Weingarten pacing, his blood pressure rising.

"Sydney, I think we should do it."

"For what? Give me one reason I should sit down with this horse's ass? Just one."

"Okay. The future."

"What are you talking about?"

"Look, the kid is inexperienced. He probably doesn't even understand the power he has. Maybe Tom is right, maybe he doesn't want that much in return. Hell, we have to win this thing. What is there to lose? We thought maybe we could nail him on the parking tickets. What does the idiot do? He pays them! Anyone who spends money that recklessly just doesn't understand what he's doing. We're talking about simple things here. We meet him, have some food, listen to what he has to say. If we don't like them, we reject them. If we can live with them, shit, take them. Think about it for a minute."

Weingarten was beginning to regain his composure.

"You're probably right," Sydney said, exhaling deeply. "I think I flew off the handle because that weakling walks in here like that. A message boy. And who the hell knows where Hallahan is or what this kid has on him? All right. Let's arrange it. Call Brideson. Tell him it's important to get the governor down here today. But we won't have this 'sit-down' in his office where it will be tape recorded. We'll have to pick another spot."

The meeting took place at four thirty that afternoon at an Italian restaurant named Gargiulo's in Coney Island. Weingarten, Donnelly, Brideson, Wolfington, Joseph, Lou Moran, and Jack Coohill shared a discreet table in the rear of the restaurant, which was one of the best Italian places in Brooklyn. Two state troopers sat at a nearby table, watching everyone in the restaurant. They would have no repeat of the assassination attempt here, and kept their firearms in clear view and at the ready.

The meeting had begun cordially, with introductions all around. Lou Moran shook Sydney Weingarten's hand as hard as he could, hoping to break small bones. He didn't, but Sydney Weingarten had yanked his hand away. That was the lone exhibition of bad blood at the table. Everyone else chatted breezily through the salad; Sydney Weingarten avoided Joseph's eyes for fear of growing angry and displaying it publicly in front of the governor. Finally, Joseph focused the conversation.

"We all know why we're here," he said. "I'd like to get to the point. I have not yet made up my mind who the organization will support. The Kelly campaign has not made real advances. So I was wondering what kind of terms we might come to here today."

Lou Moran, already astonished that he was even sharing a table with Weingarten, almost choked on an olive. He could have sworn he'd heard Joseph say he'd like to talk terms with Governor Wolfington. Jack Coohill also was surprised but did not allow his face to show it.

"What kind of terms are you talking about?" Brideson asked.

"Nothing any party leader wouldn't ask," Joseph said. "A few jobs, nothing big, some money to help repair the physical plant of the city. Especially Brooklyn. Access when appropriate."

"The governor has promised most of those things in his campaign already, Mr. Gonzago," Brideson said.

"I want him to make the same promise to me," Joseph said. "Making promises to citizens during campaigns is easy. Who doesn't? If you break the promise to me, I don't have to wait four years to get even like the voter."

The four men in the Wolfington party looked at each other, nodded as if this were acceptable, and waited for Joseph to continue. He didn't. Instead he took a large forkful of linguine and looked at the four men to his right. Then to Lou Moran, who looked as if he'd just been badly injured. Jack Coohill was expressionless, trying to understand Joseph, remembering that Joseph had asked them to accept whatever he did or said no matter what it was.

"And?" Governor Wolfington said, his pasta untouched before him.

"Just two things." Joseph ate some more pasta, swallowed, sipped some white wine, and looked up again.

"When I was a boy my very best friend was a man named Frank

Donato. You know who he is. He is going to go to jail. I don't want him to go to jail."

The four men looked at each other, weighing this request more thoughtfully.

"You're talking about executive pardon?" Brideson asked.

"Yes," Joseph said.

"I'm not even sure if this falls under our jurisdiction," Brideson said. "Dermot, is this a state matter or federal?"

"No, I prosecuted him myself," Donnelly said. "It is state. The last time a waterfront labor leader was jailed it was federal. Donato is state. Grand larceny is what we finally got him on. He beat the federal rap."

"You are talking about after the election," Sydney said.

"No, I'm talking about right away. I can't afford to back the governor and take the chance he'll lose and ever hope for Kelly to do it. I know this is asking a lot. It could embarrass you. But this is a request I must make because this is for a friend. Besides, I think we all know he was framed."

"This needs serious consideration," Brideson said. "But go on. You are talking like a reasonable man. What is your second request?"

"The second one is not even something I ask of the governor," Joseph said. "This is more personal. There happens to be a woman I love very much and intend to marry. This young woman has a mother who recently was placed into conservatorship, with the young woman excluded from visitation rights with her mother. I want this conservatorship dissolved so the woman can come to live with this young woman."

"Who are you talking about?" Governor Wolfington said.

"I know who he is talking about," Sydney Weingarten said as he glanced nervously at Joseph. "I will personally carry out this request myself if the other request is found to be acceptable to the governor."

Wolfington looked at Sydney Weingarten with squinted eyes.

"Do you mean to tell me you are not allowing Gloria to see Ruth?" the governor asked. Sydney Weingarten squirmed in his seat as Joseph watched the two men and ate his linguine.

"It was a technicality," Sydney said. "I just didn't want poor Ruth bothered by every Tom, Dick, and Harry. She's not a well woman. But of course I'll have that amended. Straight away. This is no problem at all."

"Regardless of what I decide on Donato, I think it would be very foolish to keep a mother and daughter separated," Wolfington said. "That's just fodder for the damned gossip columns."

"Nothing else?" Brideson asked.

"No, nothing else. That's all." Joseph kept eating.

The governor rose from the table, shook Joseph's hand, said goodbye to Coohill and Lou Moran. The state troopers flanked him like shells and Brideson, Weingarten, and Donnelly left with him.

Joseph kept eating his linguine, tearing off hunks of Italian bread, dipping it into his white clam sauce, sipping wine. Joseph looked at Lou Moran, who was staring into his plate of food, his head bowed, hung in despair.

"Come on, Lou, eat." Joseph was pleasant and cheerful.

"I'm not hungry," Lou Moran grumbled.

"Lou," Joseph said, "I asked you to trust me. You promised you would. Believe me, I know what I'm doing."

"Yeah, but Joseph, no offense against Frank Donato who's an okay guy, but you know, we sell out the whole thing 'cause one guy is facing time?"

Joseph grew angry now and tossed his bread into his linguine.

"I said I wanted you to trust me, dammit. Now knock it off."

"I'm sorry," Lou Moran said, and said no more. Jack Coohill looked at Joseph Gonzago and smiled. Suddenly his appetite came back and all three were eating again in silence.

35

For the next two days all Joseph Gonzago could do was wait. Then the notification came by telephone. Gloria Weingarten could visit her mother that afternoon at the Jewel by the Sea Nursing Home in Long Island. Joseph agreed to drive Gloria out there, and when they got to the nursing home, Ruth Weingarten was under very heavy sedation.

"I'm taking her home," Gloria Weingarten said. "I'm not leaving her here. I can't wait until the conservatorship is dissolved."

"Fine."

Gloria quickly dressed Ruth Weingarten, placed her in a wheelchair, and began wheeling her out of the hospital. A security guard asked for her authorization card. Gloria explained that she did not have one, but if he checked at the desk he would see her name was on a list. The security guard walked over to the desk, and when he did, Joseph wheeled Ruth Weingarten out the door, lifted her from the chair, and gently placed her in the backseat of the Plymouth. He and Gloria hopped in and Joseph was driving out of the parking lot just as the security guard reappeared at the front door.

"I will never let her go back there," Gloria said as she looked at her sleeping mother on the backseat.

"Of course not."

They drove on the Long Island Expressway in silence for several miles.

"What did you have to give Sydney in return for this, Joseph?" she asked.

"Nothing much. A promise."

"Joseph, I appreciate what you have done, but I think the way you did it is awful."

"Why?"

"Because you have sold a piece of your soul to Sydney. That's all he wants. To be able to own you. Like he owned Mom. And me and Bernie and half the cronies in political office in Brooklyn."

"The only one who will ever own me is you."

He switched on the radio, searching the dial for the all-news station. There was a commercial on for *The Wall Street Journal.* Joseph listened patiently, waiting for the noon update. The lead story crackled over the speaker: "Convicted waterfront labor racketeer Frank Donato was granted an executive pardon today by Governor Henry Wolfington. The startling news came at a ten o'clock press conference this morning in Albany. Citing shaky evidence, new developments, and family hardship Governor Wolfington granted the first pardon of his eight years as governor."

Then Wolfington's voice came on: "As you know, I have never abused this privilege of executive pardon before in my tenure as governor of this state. I have never received either the endorsement or campaign contributions from Mr. Donato or the union he represents. I will not accept any now or in the future. The reasons for my granting this pardon are based purely on the merits of the case in question."

A reporter asked Wolfington if he had spoken to Frank Donato about this case.

"I have never met Mr. Donato. His lawyer, James La Rocca, filed the official papers with my office. I reviewed them and made this decision without speaking to Mr. Donato."

Another reporter asked what effect he thought the pardon would have on the outcome of the primary.

"Hopefully, none," Wolfington said. "I'm still ahead in the polls, and I hope the voters judge me on my record. Not Mr. Donato's."

A gaggle of reporters laughed into their open microphones. Then the newscaster announced that Frank Donato could not yet be reached for a statement.

Gloria Weingarten looked at Joseph Gonzago, shaking her head.

"Why is it I know you knew this was going to happen?"

"You have to look ahead," he said, and kept driving.

Dermot Donnelly sat with Sydney Weingarten in the office at the Nathan Hale Club. Sydney was smiling as he chatted on the phone. Donnelly was smiling too, listening to Weingarten speak.

"I know, I know, Kelly must be going nuts by now," Sydney said. "Sure, because now it makes the governor look like a humanitarian as well as a law-and-order type. Dermot will have no problem with it at all. At first we thought it over and rejected the idea. Take too much flak. Donato is a big fish. But if we present new evidence that Dermot says was withheld from him in the first place, we can pin it on that small-time racketeer. And he's no longer a problem. Just say that Donato was a victim. Of course it doesn't hurt Dermot. He says he went with what he had at the time, which was enough, by the way, to convince a jury. But being a man of justice, this new evidence came up and well, hey, we got the wrong guy."

Donnelly was beaming, pacing the room, finally poured himself and Sydney martinis from a premixed batch in a pitcher. Sydney sipped his.

"That's the hilarious part," Sydney said into the phone. "He didn't want anything else. Just a small personal favor. Of course not. How long can he last there? We'll have him out within the year, but in the meantime the whole organization will be behind us to pull votes for the final week. There's no way we can blow it now. He makes the endorsement official tomorrow on the steps of Brooklyn Borough Hall. We thought about the Abe Stark Skating Rink but figured downtown Brooklyn would be more accessible to the media. Yeah. Isn't it incredible? Yeah, ten sharp. I wish you could be there too, but you're much too valuable where you are right now on the inside. If anyone saw your face there they'd wonder. What did Kelly say?"

Weingarten covered the phone to repeat what the man at the other end of the phone was saying.

"Dermot, Kelly says he hopes Joseph Gonzago roasts forever in the flames of hell. Doesn't that sound just corny enough for him? Okay, I understand, I'll let you go. Keep swinging. See ya soon."

Sydney cradled the phone and rubbed his hands together and toasted martinis with Dermot Donnelly. The phone rang again and this time it was the hospital calling to say that Gloria had taken Ruth out.

"Don't bother me now," Weingarten said. "In fact, don't bother me again, and don't send me any more bills. I don't care where she is."

Joseph Gonzago helped Ruth Weingarten into the house and placed her in the small bed Angela, his mother, had moved into her sewing room when she had first begun to grow despondent over Be Be Gonzago's "infidelity." Ruth was still sleeping, loaded up with sedatives. Gloria sat with her while Joseph called Dr. Licht and asked him to come over to give Ruth Weingarten a complete physical examination.

Joseph was ready to leave when Dr. Licht arrived.

"She's sleeping now, Doc," Joseph said. "But I think they probably loaded her up with Thorazine and crap like that. Gloria said she was fine a week ago, had tried to kick the booze."

"I'll take care of her, don't you worry about anything," Dr. Licht said. Joseph explained that he had to leave immediately, that he had an appointment he was already going to be late for. Joseph then went in and kissed Gloria good-bye.

"Thank you, Joseph," Gloria said.

"I don't know what time I'll be home, or if I even will be tonight."

She nodded and smiled as he left her at her mother's side.

Joseph was ten minutes late for the meeting. Neither man wanted to meet in a public place for fear of recognition. Each asked the other to come alone. Joseph pulled his car to a stop behind a Volkswagen bug parked on Fifth Avenue and Fifty-second Street in Manhattan. Joseph left his car illegally parked and got out and locked it and walked toward the Volkswagen and tapped on the window. The door opened and Joseph Gonzago got into the front seat. He had never met the man before and realized he was taller and broader than he had imagined him to be, although he looked good on television. They shook hands as the car began to move into light traffic.

"Hello, Mr. Gonzago," the man said.

"Hello, Mr. Kelly."

It had been a long night and Joseph was very tired. Tired of talking and tired of listening and eager to get on with the task before him. He had no time to drive back to his house in Flatbush to shower, so he went to the office on Court Street and took a shower, dried his hair, briskly brushed his teeth, and dressed in a fresh shirt, tie, and suit he kept on hand at all times now.

He took two manila envelopes he had picked up earlier at the Water Board and walked out into the hallway and dropped them into the mail chute. One was addressed to Francis X. Cunningham and the other was addressed to Jason Gotbaum at *The Village Voice.* Cunningham's package contained two master tapes concerning the kickback and poverty-program ripoffs in Bedford Stuyvesant and the South Bronx. Each contained a copy of the file kept by Be Be on each man involved in the ripoff schemes.

Julio Garcia would be the man most surprised. Joseph had not placed an envelope for him at the memorial dinner because he had not realized how important his Hispanic connections in the Bronx would be to the Weingarten forces in Brooklyn. Garcia would have an awful lot of explaining to do about narcotics missing from Washington Hospital, of which he was chairman of the board. He would also have to explain the sworn affidavits taken by members of Be Be's Canarsie club from five young men on the methadone programs in treatment centers run by Garcia. They claimed they were forced to work in poverty-money jobs and kick back half their pay to Garcia's machine and purchase their methadone from him with what they had left.

Joseph walked back into his office and made himself a vodka and grapefruit juice because all the coffee he'd had the night before had him wired and edgy. Lou Moran and Jack Coohill showed up while he was mixing his second drink. Lou Moran looked very gloomy but resigned to what was about to happen.

"You sure you're going to go through with this?" Lou Moran said.

Joseph smiled and began to feel good.

"Come on, fellas, have a drink, cheer up," Joseph said. "This is going to be one of the best days of my life. I know you're going to enjoy it too."

Jack Coohill studied Joseph curiously.

"There's something going on you're just not telling us, Joseph," Jack Coohill said. "Come on, now, trust us."

"I don't want to spoil your fun," Joseph said.

"He's nuts, I tell you, Jack. He's waltzin' around like a fairy or something, all happy, drinkin' at nine thirty in the morning on the day they should lower the flag to the height of a rat's ass."

"Bailey is going to do the introductions," Joseph said. "Here's to the mayor."

Joseph smiled and drank up his drink. He even felt like having another one.

There were newsmen from all over the State of New York gathered on the steps of Brooklyn Borough Hall. Joseph could see the television people setting up, and the print people standing idly, their narrow spiral notebooks in their hands, smoking cigarettes, exchanging notes, laughing.

Joseph Gonzago crossed Court Street with Lou Moran and Jack Coohill. He walked confidently, looking young and in control, smiling. Gone was the brooding face of the grieving son. Joseph Gonzago let his jacket and tie flap in the wind as he walked through the reporters who gathered around him. There were over three hundred reporters from all the networks, local TV, and radio stations, from magazines and daily newspapers from Buffalo to Bay Ridge. An awful lot of attention was being paid to Brooklyn in this close race. Kelly had picked up a point in the AP poll overnight, probably due to people's indecision over how to weigh the Frank Donato pardon.

Sydney Weingarten stood up at the top of the steps with Governor Wolfington, Brideson, the borough president, and Mayor Bailey. They were separated from the press by wooden police barriers and members of the Special Events Squad of the NYPD. A group of limousines with darkened windows were parked on the street below. Joseph passed the cars and bounded up the steps.

A wedge of reporters trailed him with pens, microphones, Portopak cameras, asking him questions.

"Let me make my silly speech first, okay, ladies and gents?" Joseph said, still smiling. "I'll talk to you afterward all you want."

Joseph finally outdistanced the reporters, and he and Coohill and Lou Moran ducked under the police rails and climbed the steps of Borough Hall. Joseph checked his watch. It was three minutes to ten. He walked up to Wolfington, winked, shook his hand, and nodded to Sydney.

"Ruth is sure looking swell, Sydney," Joseph said. "The picture of health."

Sydney Weingarten just peered down at him from a higher step. Joseph nodded to a few other pols, then approached Bailey. Joseph moved through these people like butter skiing down a hot pan.

"Tom, it's two minutes to ten," Joseph said. "I told you I want to be up there at exactly ten. Stop fooling around and get it going. I like your suit. You look swell, God bless you, Tom."

Joseph couldn't stop smiling. The sun shone brilliantly off his thick dark hair and his eyes sparkled.

"Ladies and gentlemen of the press," Tom Bailey said as he approached the podium, "I take great pleasure in introducing to you today the new chairman of the Brooklyn Democratic party. He has called this press conference to make a major announcement concerning the present gubernatorial race, in which, quite frankly, I am glad not to be a candidate."

This got a small rise out of the reporters.

"Like his father before him, he likes to get started on time, so may I introduce to you Joseph Gonzago. Thank you."

Joseph stepped to the podium and smiled and looked out at the crowd and then back at Wolfington and Weingarten and Brideson behind him. He winked and then turned back to the press.

"Hiya," Joseph said. "Thanks, Mr. Mayor. And thank you, ladies and gentlemen of the press, for coming here today, in my first public appearance as county leader of Brooklyn. You might wonder why prepared copies of my statement were not passed out to you beforehand, which is usually the way these things go, right?"

There were a few laughs from the reporters.

"Well, the reason is because I didn't write a prepared statement. I studied method acting in school, and they sort of encourage ad-libbing because this way you never know what the hell you are going to do or say. So I figured I'd wing it up here. I'm here to endorse a candidate for governor."

Joseph saw the Volkswagen bug pull up to the curb now, the front door opening.

"This was the candidate my father wanted before he was shot to death. This is the candidate I'd like to see running this state. A man of the people for a change. Ladies and gents, I give you Mr. . . . Brendan Kelly."

Joseph Gonzago pointed to the bottom of the steps of City Hall, where Brendan Kelly stood alone in the morning sun, smiling and looking up at Joseph. Pandemonium broke out in the press corps, and they all did an aboutface and ran for Kelly, swarming him, leaving a shaken and dizzy-looking Wolfington at the top of the steps.

Now a throng of reporters ran toward Wolfington, and the two state troopers each grabbed one of his arms and raced him toward his limo at the bottom of the steps. Sydney Weingarten stared down at Joseph Gonzago in silent bafflement. Lou Moran threw his arms around Joseph Gonzago and kissed him on the mouth.

"You are so fuckin' whackadoo I'd marry you if you had money," Lou Moran said.

Jack Coohill smiled quietly, slapped Joseph on the back. Joseph looked at Jack.

"You knew, didn't you, Jack?"

"I knew something, but not this. You *don't* do this. But you did."

Down at the foot of the steps Kelly was answering dozens of questions. He spotted Wolfington being rushed toward his car.

"Okay, fellas, wait a second, let's ask *him* a question first? Why don't you stand up and debate me on any issue right here and now?

Right here before the media and the citizens of this city and state? I challenge you to debate me here and now, Mr. Wolfington."

Wolfington was halfway into the car, and he could feel the millions of eyes that would see his face on the evening news. He looked at Kelly as if to say the round is yours, then looked more confused as the state trooper pushed him into the car and jumped in beside him as the limousine sped away.

"You saw him. I saw him. I want to give the voters of this state a clear-cut choice in this election. I want to air our views on issues in the open where the citizen lives and works. I think the citizen deserves better than position papers and television ads. I think the public wants a debate. I want one. The only one who doesn't is the man they've elected twice. I say give the voter a chance and a choice. Let us explain ourselves. I want you to decide if I'm worthy of you, not whether you are worthy of me, as our governor's stance toward the voter seems to indicate."

Joseph Gonzago stood up on the steps looking down at Brendan Kelly. They gave each other the thumbs-up salute as reporters swarmed around them.

36

After recovering from the initial shock, Sydney Weingarten settled down and gave long consideration to the campaign, his life, his future.

He had been outsmarted by Joseph Gonzago. Governor Wolfington was furious with him for not forseeing the double cross. Frank Donato was now a free man. Joseph Gonzago was now operating his machine full strength behind Brendan Kelly. The media was still going full blast on the Joseph Gonzago press conference. Even the reform wing of the Democratic party was throwing their support behind the machine. Joseph Gonzago threw his support behind the candidate who was challenging Sydney Weingarten for his assembly seat, a reform candidate named Robert Hershkovitz whom no one had taken seriously until now, one week before the primary.

Suddenly Sydney Weingarten was in danger of losing his own seat in the assembly. Never mind the appointment to the state Court of Appeals. Sydney Weingarten might very soon be citizen Weingarten, a man without title or status in life. A has-been.

Rather than lose control, Sydney Weingarten reviewed his situation carefully. The Kelly-Wolfington race was still close. Kelly was within a single percentage point of Wolfington in all the polls. It was too early yet for a poll on Sydney's assembly race against Hershkovitz because, until now, this race had been ignored by the press. They had assumed that Weingarten would win in a walk.

Two days after the shocking press conference Sydney Weingarten sat in his office at the Nathan Hale Club and watched Dermot Donnelly walk into the room. In his hands Donnelly carried several newspapers. One of them was *The Village Voice.* Sydney had asked that Donnelly bring a copy with him because he had been receiving phone calls all morning from black and Hispanic community leaders. They wanted nothing more to do with the Wolfington campaign. The story penned by Jason Gotbaum in that morning's *Village Voice* was outrageously embarrassing to the minorities. The story bared the information contained in the secret files kept by Be Be Gonzago. Gotbaum went on to say that members of the Garcia and Stone machines were busily working in conjunction with Weingarten to help re-elect Governor Wolfington. These minority leaders no longer wanted their names associated with Weingarten or Wolfington and would likely be shifting their support to Kelly.

Weingarten read the Gotbaum story in silence, shaking his head from side to side, looking very tired. When he finished reading, he looked up at Dermot Donnelly.

"Well?" Sydney said.

"Well," Donnelly said, "first, I checked everything I could on the parking-ticket thing, and I'm sorry to say it is perfectly legal. He beat us there. Second, sure you can pursue the legality of Ruth's conservatorship, but I can't see any probate judge refusing to let Gloria see Ruth. I just can't. Besides, most of the judges are still loyal to the county leader. They have to be. Third, there is a good possibility the Donato thing is beginning to backfire. Mainly because it was a minor problem at first, but compounded with the Stone-Garcia affair, and the debacle at Borough Hall the other day, the voters might put all this together and see the Wolfington campaign as a total can of worms. Fourth, Brendan Kelly fired Morse this morning. Actually Dan resigned, citing differences between them. That might work for us publicly, but it dries up a well inside. Fifth, our great loyal friend David Hallahan is holding a noon press conference after a major speech at a Senate Foreign Relations hearing today. I have absolutely no idea what he's going to say. No one does. Sixth, Kelly is giving a major stump speech on Thirteenth Avenue in Brooklyn this afternoon. He's going after the Jewish vote there. I think we're still okay with that. Okay, to wrap it up, let me say things are not looking good. However, this is not over yet. It is a dead heat and we have to do some damn thing about it."

Sydney Weingarten looked at his watch. It was approaching dead noon.

"Put on channel nine. We'll get the news at noon and see if they have anything on the Hallahan speech."

Dermot Donnelly switched on the small Sony color television. The two men watched the anchorwoman quote from Jason Gotbaum's story in *The Village Voice* as photographs of Stone and Garcia came on the screen. Then the anchorwoman announced that the State Bureau of Investigation had issued warrants for the arrest of Stone and Garcia early in the day. There was a brief interview with Francis X. Cunningham, who said he could not divulge the nature of the information contained in secret documents received by his office, but that arrests were imminent. He also said the documents and tape recordings were received anonymously.

Now there were reaction shots of black and Hispanic civic and political leaders, who were careful to deny association with the two men. Two minority spokesmen were asked if this news story would affect their positions on the gubernatorial campaign. Both said they had no comment yet, which, of course, meant it would.

Then in slick television transition the anchorman came on with an update on the gubernatorial campaign. The resignation of Daniel Morse was announced and an interview with Tim Harris came on. The sight of Tim Harris made Sydney unsteady. Harris was saying that the Morse resignation was of no great significance, that it came about strictly because of personal and family reasons. Harris said he was not at liberty to discuss what these reasons were.

Now the anchorwoman said that they were switching live to Washington, where Senator David Hallahan had just delivered a shocking speech on the Mideast, one in which he made a complete turnaround of his previously consistent views.

Outside the Senate building in Washington, D.C. came the image of Daniel Hallahan answering a swarm of questions from a mob of reporters. In the forefront was a female Washington reporter for channel nine news. Reading from a notebook, she addressed the camera.

"Pandemonium has just erupted on Capitol Hill following New York Senator David Hallahan's startling speech to the Senate Foreign Relations Committee on his views on the Middle East. Hallahan started his speech by saying he now favors inviting the PLO to any peace table; struck out at Israel for warmongering bordering on imperialism; called for the creation of a Palestinian state; and claimed that if Israel's current policies continue, America should not risk the threat of nuclear war to save this single nation.

"The speech echoed through Washington with shock and disbelief because in the past Senator Hallahan had been a staunch supporter of Israel and a critic of the PLO and the idea of a Palestinian state.

"Asked just moments afterward what prompted this stunning reversal in position, Senator Hallahan said that lengthy discussions with Governor Henry Wolfington, whom he expects to be the Democratic candidate for president in two years, helped change his mind on the Mideast question. Governor Wolfington of New York is currently involved in what most observers believe will be a photo-finish primary for the New York gubernatorial primary.

"The revelation by Senator Hallahan that he believes Governor Wolfington will be the Democratic presidential candidate two years from now also sent shock waves through the nation's capital and will almost certainly reverberate through New York and Albany. Questions by New York State's sizable Jewish population concerning Governor Wolfington's stance on the Middle East will almost certainly arise."

The report continued, but Dermot Donnelly leaned over and turned down the sound and looked at a grave Sydney Weingarten.

"Does the governor believe in this hogwash, Sydney?"

"Of course not," Sydney Weingarten said. "Hallahan must have lost his mind to make a speech like this. He'll be lucky if he isn't shot by the JDL, for God's sake. I simply can't believe it."

"You don't think that Joseph—"

"Please, don't even ask. I don't even want to consider it."

"We have to consider it. Hallahan might have been under duress."

"Look, even if he was, it will do us no good now. Our last chance is to take whatever money we have and just wade in at these people. There are a few tactics that we can use against these people that haven't even been tried in this part of the country since Elegant Oakey was still the best-dressed man in town. We need bodies and even if we have to pay for them we had better get them."

"I'll scrape up everything the clubhouse has," Donnelly said. "It'll take until at least tomorrow."

"Fine," Sydney said, standing up and pulling on his jacket.

"Where are you going?" Dermot Donnelly asked.

"This is going to be the most trying week of my life," Sydney Weingarten said. "I need to get some comfort. When anxiety sets in and starts to feel like panic, it is important to pamper yourself, Dermot."

Sydney Weingarten even managed a smile and a wink.

"We're going to win this thing," Sydney Weingarten said. "I can just feel it. I can still feel it. It will take a lot of energy, Dermot. I need my batteries recharged."

Dermot Donnelly smiled as Sydney Weingarten left the office. There was confidence in Sydney's step. This made Donnelly feel just the slightest bit easier. Sydney Weingarten was a man with a track record to match his confidence, he thought.

Sylvia Stein pushed Sydney Weingarten away from her and walked to the mantelpiece and took a cigarette from a pack that lay in front of the framed photograph of her wearing the crown of Miss Manhattan Beach.

"What the hell is wrong, Sylvia?" Sydney Weingarten was more surprised than offended.

"Guarantees, Sydney. I want some guarantees."

"Guarantees? What are you talking about, my love?"

"Cut the crap, Sydney. Join the real world. You're married. I'm single. This ridiculous relationship of ours has been going on for almost nine years. Like a moron I've believed everything you said. But now I want guarantees."

Sydney walked closer to her, concern in his eyes.

"Are you now doubting me too, Sylvia? What more do you need? I give you anything you want. I've given you a fine house. I give you a generous allowance. I have never denied you any kind of clothes, dinners, vacations, jewelry. What do you mean by guarantees, my love?"

Sylvia lit the cigarette and exhaled quickly.

"You think I have nothing better to do than sit around this damned house all day long waiting for Sydney Weingarten to come in and spend a few hours with me and then take off? Come on, Sydney. I'm a *woman,* here. I *feel,* I *hurt* too, ya know. I'm not gonna sit around waiting for menopause while you're home with the wife and kiddies."

"My God," Sydney said, incredulous. "You act as if you're the one who's made the great sacrifice. I've risked my career to be with you. I've risked the contempt of my children. If they ever found out everything about you . . . they'd—"

"Spare me the melodrama, Sydney, please."

"No, I think I have the right to say something here. I have thrown aside a marriage for you—"

"Hold the phone, operator," Sylvia Stein said. "You've been telling me you're going to throw this marriage aside for nine years, and all I ever seem to be, come Valentine's Day, is a kept woman instead of someone's mother, someone's sweetheart, someone's wife. I'm the one who cooks dinners for one, Sydney."

"You are being an ingrate."

"No, Sydney, I'm being Sylvia Stein. The girl you dumped a long time ago for another girl you never loved. You broke her heart and now you want to break mine. Well, I'll tell you something, fella. I've heard a lot of promises all these years I've been with you. You were going to make me the wife of an important man. You would put me in the limelight and show me off a little. You were going to take me to Washington, D.C., for dinners with presidents in the White House. Meanwhile, I've never been farther than Sheepshead Bay for clams on the half shell with you. Now it looks like your whole career is going down the tubes. Well, I'm not going with you. You might not even be an assemblyman come January, never mind sitting on the Supreme Court."

"You damn bitch," Sydney said, growing furious as he turned scarlet.

"I'm the bitch? Hey, I was there at the beginning, you know. We were supposed to get married once, remember? But it didn't work out that way. Maybe if we were man and wife I'd stick around 'for better and for worse,' but see I'm just your mistress, and I don't go the whole 'till death do us part' route. I'll jump ship at 'in sickness and in health,' if you don't mind, thank you very much."

"And just what are these guarantees you're talking about, my mistress? If that's what you prefer to call yourself."

"I want a contract. Something in writing. I want it where I don't have to start looking for some jabone to support me when I'm wearing elastic stockings. I still have a few good years left in me, Sydney. I'm not a bad-looking lady when I give it a good try. I notice the men looking at me, you know. Unless I have some kind of security I'm gonna start looking back."

"You want me to guarantee you money? You do know what you sound like, don't you?"

"Hey, look, I'm no bimbo, you know. I was a *beauty queen.* Remember, I could have had them all, any of them, at one time. But a gal has to live. I have no financial security. I have no real skills. All I have is what I am and what you see. Now I know you're spending a fortune on this campaign. A lot of it is your own money. This Joseph Gonzago kid is whipping your ass—"

Sydney smacked Sylvia Stein across the face. She stood there frozen, staring him in the eye.

"Get the hell out of here," Sylvia Stein said softly. Sydney Weingarten stood shaking, his whole body quaking. He regretted having slapped her the moment he did it.

"Sylvia, I'm sorry, I shouldn't have—"

"Get out, Sydney," she said in the soft voice. "Get out of here and get out of my *life.* I don't need you. You can have your jewelry and your clothes and this house and everything. I don't want anything from you anymore. I'll be gone within the week."

Sydney walked to her on shaking legs.

"Please forgive me, Sylvia," he said as he grasped her shoulders. She pulled herself free of him and turned her back to him and stared at her own photograph on the mantel. She could see a lot more than anyone else could in it. She could see all the years since it was taken.

"Sylvia, please, not now," Sydney pleaded. "I need you. I need your support. I need you there to know someone cares. That you're there. I'll do anything you want. Really, I will . . ."

"Don't grovel, Sydney," Sylvia Stein said. "It isn't you."

"I'll sign anything you want."

"Make it a good-bye note, Sydney."

"No, I refuse to allow it to end like this," he said, standing behind her, trying to get her to turn around. She wouldn't. She kept staring at the photograph. "I'm so close. It will be just a few more weeks. I know you've put up with an awful lot. But I promise you when this is over you won't regret it."

"I already feel free," Sylvia Stein said, smiling thinly. "I've been trying to work up the nerve to say good-bye to you for a long time, Sydney. Maybe you know now how I felt back then when I found out I'd been dumped for another girl. I know it isn't nice. But you'll get over it. There's other women, Sydney. Just like there's plenty of other men. Now please leave."

"No!" Sydney Weingarten shouted. "I won't stand for this. I cannot allow another man to be with you. I cannot. I will not. You are mine and I am yours."

"Was," she said.

"Don't you interrupt me, Sylvia," he snapped, his voice growing menacing. "I have done everything for you. Cheated, lied, maneuvered, killed—"

He caught himself quickly, the words sticking in his throat.

Sylvia Stein slowly turned around, her eyes narrowed, and looked at a desperate Sydney Weingarten. "I beg your pardon?"

"I need you, Sylvia," Sydney said. "Please . . ."

"Please repeat what you just said," she said in an astonished whisper.

"Only a figure of speech, Sylvia," Sydney said, collecting his professional defenses. "I've *ruined* men is what I meant. Ended their careers so that I could secure a place in this world that would be worthy of you. Politics is ruthless. And I've done some things that others have not liked. None of them illegal of course. But I did all of this for you, my love."

"I see," Sylvia Stein said.

"Please don't leave me, Sylvia," he said. "I need you."

Sylvia Stein smiled thinly and touched Sydney Weingarten's cheek.

"I need time to think, Sydney," she said. "Call me tomorrow, okay?"

He nodded and kissed her on the cheek.

"Will you forgive me for hitting you, my love?"

"I'll try," she said, and led Sydney Weingarten to the door and closed it behind him. She stood silently for a moment, aghast.

"Oh, my God," Sylvia Stein said softly to herself, and then looked again at the photo of the smiling young girl in the orange bathing suit.

As far as Sydney Weingarten was concerned, this election wasn't over yet. The two most damaging events in recent weeks had been the Hallahan speech and the Joseph Gonzago press conference. Joseph Gonzago was into dirty tricks. But Sydney Weingarten did not come from Brooklyn for nothing. He knew a few dirty tricks of his own.

Just the night before he had a driver take him out to Crown Heights, through Flatbush, Borough Park, and other Jewish neighborhoods so that he could watch the fun. At three o'clock in the morning a reggae band of Rastafarians, replete with dread locks and stoned on their gunja, drove through these neighborhoods playing their insidious music full blast and imploring in their Jamaican accents to "Come out and vote for Kelly, mon."

Thousands of white people were thrown from their beds as the blacks played their music and chanted Kelly slogans. This had not even cost the Nathan Hale Club very much money. Two thousand dollars. And every one of those people awakened by these malevolent-looking blacks in the still of the night would not fail to remember that they were chanting Kelly slogans and that their truck was plastered with Kelly posters and banners.

That had been the first truly good laugh Sydney Weingarten had enjoyed in some time.

Tonight at the same hour, three in the morning, a sound truck would roll through Bensonhurst, Carroll Gardens, Dyker Heights, bellowing about how Kelly would "Clean up the Italian problem called the Mafia." They were going to use the most defamatory remarks possible about Italians and distribute leaflets with slogans that read: "Not all the Italians are gangsters, but all the gangsters are Italian. Let's let an Irishman clean up the Mafia."

Sydney Weingarten snickered to himself. Some of those little garage mechanics and sanitationmen will not take lightly to that.

In the Irish neighborhoods where the pro-IRA sentiment ran deep, Kelly would be presented as a Lace-curtain Irishman and a quisling to the Irish Republic cause.

Sure the Kelly people could deny this was their doing, but many people would never be convinced by the time they reached the polls.

Then there were the local newspapers in the borough of Brooklyn that, when combined, carried substantial weight. They would all be coming out two days before election day. It wasn't too late to get some paid advertisements into those papers. Sydney Weingarten knew all the publishers. All he had to do was draw up some advertisements and sign Hallahan's name to them. In the ads he could say that Hallahan had been coerced into the speech, that it wasn't true, that the truth would come out after the election, that no matter what he said he was still loyal to Israel.

He could also place other ads knocking Israel and sign them from Kelly. He knew these publishers, such as Arthur Gould from the *Flatbush News.* He could convince him to print the ads, and even though they would later be proved to be phonies, Gould could say he was duped. But by that time it would be too late. The polls would be closed and the votes would be in. These publishers of local papers were greedy. They would run a front-page puff piece on a waiter for a free meal and an ad.

Weingarten would go to see Arthur Gould himself. His paper was the most important of all the locals because it was still read by an awful lot of Jews in Brooklyn. Then he would go to see the other clowns who published these weekly rags. It would be worth something at least. Worrying too much about the Stone and Garcia flap and the minority vote was silly now that the Jews, who voted in greater percentages as an ethnic group, were going over to Kelly, Sydney Weingarten thought.

Arthur Gould was more than cooperative with Sydney Weingarten when he arrived at the offices of his newspaper. Sydney slipped Gould five hundred dollars for himself and then paid the going rate for the ads as well. Gould said if questioned about the origins of the ad copy later, he would simply say that it came over the transom, and it was very unfortunate that they ran without verification, but in the election eve confusion somehow something had gone wrong. They could print an apology in the next issue, after the election.

Sydney Weingarten left the *Flatbush News* feeling a little better. This was going to go to the wire.

After Sydney Weingarten left the office, Arthur Gould picked up the telephone and dialed Lou Moran and explained the situation. Lou Moran told Gould to hold on while he conferred with Joseph Gonzago. Joseph Gonzago then put Jack Coohill on the phone, and Coohill told Gould to read him the ad copy. Coohill instructed Gould how the copy should be revised so that Wolfington came out looking like a rabid anti-Semite and Kelly a champion of the Jews. Gould agreed and hung up. Gonzago then told Coohill and Moran to call all the other local papers they had already visited and extracted promises from, to warn them that Sydney Weingarten was probably on the way. They were to accept the ads from Sydney, for there was no reason they shouldn't make a few bucks from him. But they were to revise them to Coohill's specifications. All the publishers agreed to the letter with the wishes of Lou Moran and Jack Coohill.

While those two men carried out this task in the conference room, the intercom on Joseph Gonzago's desk rang.

Joseph was collecting papers from his desk, preparing to go to lunch with Tim Harris, when he answered the buzzer.

"There's a Miss Stein here to see you, Mr. Gonzago," the secretary said. Joseph thought for a brief moment, curious, then pressed the button again.

"Send her right in."

In a moment Sylvia Stein walked through the door, wearing an orange dress that was much too tight, exaggerating a cleavage that needed no advertising. Joseph motioned for Lou Moran and Jack Coohill to wait in the conference room while he spoke with Sylvia Stein privately; then he motioned for her to have a seat.

He offered her a cigarette and she accepted it and he lit it with a gold lighter. She took a deep drag and stared Joseph in the eyes.

"I didn't want to come here," she said. "At first I was too frightened."

"Of me?"

"You acted like a lunatic at the play."

"That was acting."

She nodded and puffed more nervously on the cigarette.

"Actually I wasn't so frightened of you as I am of what I came to tell you."

"Sylvia, don't be afraid to say what you want to say to me. I promise you, it will never leave this room if you don't want it to. It's about my father. Now tell me because I must know."

"What makes you think it's about your father?"

"Because you're scared. Because the fear I see in you is the fear of a dead man. I know that fear. Tell me."

Smoked leaked from her nostrils as she sat looking at the very composed Joseph Gonzago.

"You know about me and Sydney Weingarten," she said. "I assume you do anyway. It's been going on for years. Anyway, I told him the other day I wanted an end to it. He slapped my face when I mentioned your name, when I said you were beating him in the campaign. Then afterward he came near tears, and he said that everything he's done in the past nine years was for me. I've been hearing this crap for just as long, so it was going in one ear and out the other until . . ."

She stopped and lit a fresh cigarette off the butt of the lit one.

"Until what, Sylvia?"

"Until, he said he had even . . . killed for me. It sent the creeps up my back. He just sort of blurted it out. Then he tried to brush it off. But I know when he's lying. He meant what he said. He never mentioned your father's name, but I knew, I know he was talking about Be Be."

"How do you know?"

"Because he despised him. And the way he smacked me when I mentioned your name. He never smacked me before. And the way he tried to cover it up. Sydney was always ferociously jealous of Be Be, Joseph. He always accused me of flirting with him. Hell, who knows, maybe I did a few times. He was an attractive man. Look, I know a lot of people think I'm some kind of aging whore. I know I'm going. I have mirrors. But I do have some scruples. I guess you just had to be there when Sydney said it. I know he was saying he killed or had Be Be Gonzago killed."

A tear fell down Sylvia Stein's face. "I really fucked up what could have been a pretty good life," she said.

Joseph walked to her and took the cigarette from her fingers and put it in an ashtray. He lifted her face and looked into her eyes.

"You know something, Sylvia," Joseph said tenderly. "You're a beautiful broad."

"Bullshit."

"No, seriously. You're great-looking. You're funny. You have guts. You care about people. You're capable of love and laughter and tears. That still counts, honey. There's thousands of men who'd have you in a minute."

"Doing anything later, gorgeous?" She wiped her eyes, trying to laugh.

"Wish I wasn't. I have a lady."

"I know. She's a real looker too."

"I want to thank you for coming here. It took courage and I admire the hell out of you for it. Now let me get you a ride home."

Sylvia Stein rose, composed herself.

"I'll grab a cab. Spend some of his money."

"No, better still, I'll get someone to take you for a drink. I think you can use one. And I want you to know that whenever you need anything, anything at all, you come to me."

She smiled and shook her head. Joseph called Lou Moran into the room, and when he walked in he looked embarrassed for the first time Joseph could remember. Joseph suddenly realized Lou Moran was shy around women.

"Lou," Joseph said, "do me a favor, will you? Take Sylvia for a drink, maybe a burger, make her laugh, dance with her. She's a little down."

Lou Moran shrugged and looked at Sylvia Stein. "Sylvia, before I do this, I got to tell you something I never told no one before," Lou Moran said. Sylvia smiled.

"Sure, Lou, what?"

"In all my life I only learned to dance two dances. The twist and the Bristol stomp."

"Will you teach me the Bristol stomp?"

"Is a pig's pussy pork? Oh, Christ, sorry, Sylvia, I didn't mean no offense . . ."

The two of them walked out the door with Sylvia Stein trailing a loud wail of laughter.

37

Joseph Gonzago was in his bed, lying next to Gloria Weingarten, whose body was an island of stability in the stormy night. Her flesh was hot and soft and her breathing deep. And yet, while Joseph Gonzago slept, he dreamed he was somewhere over the harbor of the City of New York, staring down at his father, Be Be Gonzago, who was fast drowning in the rain-pocked sea. Clouds rolled by him and Joseph had a special heightened vision and he could see his father's lovely eyes as the waters sucked him under and the expression in the dying eyes was one of acceptance and peace.

A tugboat passed by and Johnny Quinn was dressed in a seaman's cap and warm pea jacket, puffing proudly on a pipe, a man who had learned to master the greedy hunger of the sea. Be Be was shouting Johnny Quinn's name, trying to get his attention, trying to say goodbye. He wanted no salvation. He wanted only to wave a final farewell to a lifelong friend. But each one of his shouts was swallowed by the great roar of the rain and the might of the night wind.

The tug passed and Joseph watched as the image of Johnny Quinn faded into the all-consuming storm. Night became day and the storm passed and the sun shone brightly on the glorious bay. Sydney Weingarten appeared in a sailboat, helming the small craft, smiling and cutting circles around Be Be with a razor-sharp bow, and suddenly the water around Be Be Gonzago was a circle unto itself, with a moat of black void separating it from the rest of the water.

Tim Harris passed by now, pushing the oars of a rowboat, his now Christ-length hair fastened with a red bandanna, love beads about the neck, dressed in hippie clothing, and singing a Bob Dylan song called "The Hour that Your Ship Comes In." He smiled and sang as he watched Be Be Gonzago spin in the autonomous whirlpool of water.

Joseph saw someone else now, probably himself, but faceless, with Gloria at his side, a child, a boy, in her arms, and Joseph was trying to reach his father from the deck of a small schooner. But Gloria told him not to worry, that the baby would replace Be Be. But Joseph did not understand. Gloria told him that he, Joseph, was now Be Be and the baby was now Joseph and that they could start all over again and Be Be had never lived and had never died.

But Joseph rejected this, reaching his hand out, with Lou Moran crying at his side, explaining he did not know how to swim. Joseph could not reach Be Be, who was alone in his private circle of ocean. And now Joseph was indeed Be Be and his father was him. His father was now standing on the deck of a great ocean liner calling to Joseph: "Joseph, Joseph, don't leave me now. I love you, son. I love you. Come to me." "But I am you," came the reply, and Joseph did not understand. And suddenly Gloria Weingarten was no longer Gloria but Angela Gonzago, Joseph's mother. But now she couldn't possibly be his mother because he was Be Be Gonzago and he knew that Angela must surely be his wife and both of them were alive and the baby in Angela's arms was Joseph Gonzago, with the body of a baby and the head and face of the man he was today.

He spun, looked back into the water, and now he was the man-child in his mother's arms and once again he could see Be Be Gonzago in the center of his free-floating pool of water. As he reached out to save him, Joseph realized he was only a baby and could not save his father. He heard himself crying, the voice the shrill siren of an infant: "No, Daddy, no, Daddy, not now, Daddy. I love you, Daddy. I'm sorry . . ."

But it was too late, for as Be Be reached even farther for his infant son, he went over the lip of the water, beyond the edge, and was sucked into the bottomless void that dropped between the two independent bodies of water. Joseph watched from the arms of his mother, who was also his wife, because she was now Gloria Weingarten once more, and the water merged slowly again and all Joseph could hear was the final distant echo of his dying father, the sound coming from the depths of the universe, repeated over and over and over, and Joseph was crying with the infant's wail as his father's final echo came: "I love you, Joseph . . ."

And then suddenly he was awake, in the bed of his murdered father, with the daughter of the man who had probably killed him. He was very wet, and at first he thought it might have been from the sea. But now he knew there had been no sea. Only the dream and he was wet with perspiration.

What day was it? Tuesday. Today is Tuesday, Joseph remembered. But there was something else. His head was thick with cigarettes, coffee, lack of sleep, nightmares.

Election day, he thought. That's it. Today is the primary. Christ! The time?

"Gloria, what the hell time is it?"

Gloria snapped awake. "What time is it?" She only repeated the question.

"I'm asking you," he said.

She picked up her watch from the night table.

"Six fifteen," she said. "Go back to sleep. It's still dark."

"Polls open in a few hours. I have to get up."

Joseph got out of the warm, damp bed, smacked Gloria affectionately on her rump, and walked to the shower.

Tim Harris and Brendan Kelly sat in their suite in the Waldorf-Astoria watching the early morning news. The *Daily News* poll had the contest at a dead heat with Wolfington favored by just two points. The AP poll had it the other way, with Kelly ahead. Everyone admitted it was the closest election since Kean and Florio in New Jersey.

Tim Harris paced the room nervously.

"There must be something more we can do," Harris said. "That *News* poll has me worried because they're usually accurate. Especially in the city."

"We can't do anything more," Kelly said.

"Brendan, I want you to know that if it goes wrong, if we lose it, I want you to know that I'll always appreciate your giving me this chance. And I hope you understand that I'm a pragmatic guy. After this is over I'll be out looking for work. If I take a job with someone that wasn't friendly to us in this campaign, I hope you won't hold that against me."

Brendan Kelly stared at Tim Harris for a long time. Kelly looked relaxed, pleased and happy that the long campaign was finally over. But as he watched Tim Harris pace, snapping his fingers, looking very worried, he thought long and hard about him. And about Joseph Gonzago. Joseph and Kelly had discussed Harris at length the night before the press conference in which Joseph endorsed Kelly.

"Of course I won't hold it against you, Tim," Kelly said. "I understand you have a career ahead of you. And that you'd really like to work in Washington instead of Albany anyway. I have no ambition to go to Washington. If I win this, it will be all I want. I know your future is not with me."

"Thanks, Brendan," Tim Harris said. "I know we've had our differences in this campaign. But all in all it was fun."

"Tell the truth, Tim," Brendan Kelly said. "You will never forgive me for not consulting with you about the Gonzago endorsement before I accepted it. Will you?"

Tim Harris paced the room some more.

"Well, I am the campaign manager, Brendan. Hell, when a major thing like that comes around, I would have liked to have known about it. Personally, I still think it was a circus. Also the stump speech on Thirteenth Avenue in Brooklyn. You didn't even tell me you were going to speak on the Mideast. It was almost as if you knew beforehand that Hallahan was going to deliver his bombshell. I had prepared a speech for you to deliver on the nuclear-energy question. Instead you talk about the Mideast."

"And you never told me Joseph Gonzago had advised you to advise me to prepare a speech on the Mideast. He knows Brooklyn. He was offering free advice on a variety of topics, and you never even mentioned that lunch to me at all. Especially the part about Morse. He told you he thought Morse was a leak and you never mentioned it to me, Tim. I mean, this is all inconsequential now, because the thing is over. But I would have liked to have known about that."

Tim Harris still paced, his steps short and edgy, looking occasionally out the window at the sunny streets.

"How the hell was I supposed to know Gonzago's information was correct? If I came to you and mentioned it, you would have said it was more of the feud between Dan and myself. As for the Mideast thing, hell, I just thought it was too risky an issue to bring into a gubernatorial campaign."

"But I remember asking you to contact Gonzago for weeks, and he claims you never did."

"Well, personally, I never expected Joseph Gonzago to have anything to say in this campaign."

"Well, you were wrong, weren't you, Tim?"

"We'll see," Tim Harris said.

"Yes," said Brendan Kelly. "I guess we will. It's all a matter of time now, isn't it?"

Tim Harris stared at Brendan Kelly, who sat smiling and relaxed on the sofa. Tim Harris broke the stare and changed the television station nervously and continued to pace the room.

Sydney Weingarten picked up the *Flatbush News* at nine A.M. as soon as it hit the newsstand. He went to his polling place in a junior high school in East Flatbush, and as he waited on line he opened the local paper and looked for his ads. When he saw the wording of the copy, he made a high, desperate whine.

"Are you all right?" asked a man standing on line ahead of him.

"Yes, yes, I'm all right," Sydney Weingarten whispered. The man kept staring at Sydney Weingarten and his eyes narrowed.

"Hey, aren't you . . . Weingarten?"

Sydney Weingarten looked at the man, nodding his head, and the man shook his head and turned away, looking disgusted. Sydney saw the man was wearing a yarmulke. He felt as if he were on stage, with people whispering about him. He glanced nervously around the room, but saw that no one was paying much attention to him. Most of the people were reading the *Flatbush News.* Sydney could not believe that somehow Joseph Gonzago had gotten to Arthur Gould. How could he have figured it out? This was madness. Half the people on line had copies of the *News.* They would all see those ads. Then go home and call all their relatives and friends and tell them to read them.

Sydney realized he was next on line. The man who had just a few minutes earlier asked if Sydney was all right stepped out of the voting booth and stared at Sydney. He wore a button that bore the legend: KELLY/HERSHKOVITZ.

"I hope you're proud of yourself for the things you stand for," the man said. "The Jewish people have been good to you, Weingarten, and you stab them in the back."

The man marched away, his anger somewhat softened by his having pulled the lever in the voting booth. Sydney Weingarten watched the man walking away, open-mouthed, shocked. A poll watcher tapped him on the shoulder.

"You're next," the poll watcher said. Sydney Weingarten was momentarily startled and stepped into the voting booth, pulled the handle that closed the curtains, and stood very still for a long time. Wolfington and Kelly each had levers next to their names. Sydney stared at the Wolfington lever. Then at his own name in much smaller print down farther on the panel. Hershkovitz's name was there too. How many people would pull that lever, he wondered. How many people who have seen those newspaper ads? And what about Kelly's lever? Those little black handles in the hands of the voter were so powerful. What would happen if the handle they selected had Kelly's name on it?

Each of those hands would shove him farther and farther away from his seat on the state Court of Appeals. Farther still from the possibility of ever sitting on the Supreme Court of the land. All these hands, he thought, are guided by Joseph Gonzago.

Sydney Weingarten knew at that moment that if he lost this election—if Joseph Gonzago beat him—he would not allow him to have the last laugh. He would deprive him of his spoils. He would not allow Gonzago to sit by as Sydney Weingarten went down the tubes.

And there were ways to prevent him from getting that last laugh. Sydney Weingarten knew that ultimately Joseph Gonzago was not interested in politics or this election. He was thirsty for revenge. What he did want was the names of those responsible for the murder of his father. And he would never get them. But Sydney Weingarten had even better plans. Violence is such a nasty business. But no one will laugh at me.

He pulled the Wolfington lever and then the lever next to his own name and yanked open the curtains and stepped out of the voting booth. A man he had not even noticed before was next on line. He, too, wore a yarmulke and a Kelly button. The man did not recognize Sydney Weingarten and nodded pleasantly as he walked past him. I've done everything I could, Sydney Weingarten thought. Except for one thing.

Joseph Gonzago voted early and drove his Plymouth to the Waldorf-Astoria in Manhattan to see Tim Harris and Brendan Kelly. It annoyed him that he had to drive into Manhattan. Brooklyn did not have one single decent hotel in which to hold a convention or victory party of the size for a gubernatorial election. He made sure to remember that he would have to get some of those tax abatements they were throwing around in Manhattan to hotel developers to bring at least one or two decent hotels to Brooklyn.

After driving through the maddening traffic of Manhattan, Joseph parked the car in a lot near the Waldorf. He took the elevator to the penthouse suite, where two plainclothes security men stopped him. They summoned Tim Harris, who told them to let Joseph by.

Joseph entered the room smiling at Tim Harris, shaking his hand and slapping his shoulder. Brendan Kelly approached him and shook hands warmly.

"Joseph," Kelly said as he patted Joseph's back. "How can I ever thank you for all you've done?"

All three men took seats and Joseph leaned forward.

"I guess that's what I'm here to discuss, Brendan," Joseph said. "I still have an election to run and I can't stay long."

Tim Harris, glancing furtively back and forth, watched the mutual respect between the two men.

"Well, let's get it on then, Joseph," Tim Harris said. "By the way, how does it look in the borough of churches?"

"I think it's a lock. I have no problems."

"Well, I'm certainly glad someone here is confident," Kelly said, looking at Harris. Harris avoided his eyes and looked at Joseph, who smiled at him.

"Well, have you come up with your list?" Harris asked.

"Yeah," Joseph said. "Sort of. Who'd you have in mind to run the State Bureau of Investigation?"

Harris laughed aloud. "SBI? I don't think we've given it much thought, Joseph," Harris said, still laughing.

Kelly did not laugh. He asked, "Who'd you have in mind, Joseph?"

"I'd like to see a guy named Francis Xavier Cunningham made director of SBI," Joseph said.

"Another Irish cop," Harris said. "Can't we think of something a little more original than that?"

"He's the head of the New York office. He's black."

Kelly's ears perked up. "Black man? Hey, I like the idea as long as he's competent."

"That he is," Joseph said.

"Not a bad idea," Harris said, unenthusiastically. "I think we can live with that. What else?"

"Well, the other thing is sort of personal, you know. I have a doctor friend. He's getting a little old for his practice, but he's as sharp as a razor. Is there some kind of place we can find for him? Surgeon general or Health and Hospitals? Coroner maybe? His name is Licht, hell of a doctor, hell of a guy."

Harris was laughing hysterically.

"These requests are absurd, Joseph. No problem taking care of an old geezer. But what do you *want*?"

"That's all, Tim."

Kelly nodded in complete admiration. Harris looked very surprised.

"That's all?" Harris held his palms out.

"Except for what is rightfully ours already. Some jobs for the organization, some money to finance construction, repair work, and a promise to try to help the whole city with things like welfare and Medicaid burdens. But those things we can discuss as we go along in the administration. The only other thing I want is access to the governor and not his flunkies."

Harris did not like the last remark and coughed.

"This all seems more than fair to me," Kelly said. "I want to see this city, this state rebuilt. I think I'm going to need access to you as much as you need it to me, Joseph. My door is always open."

"I'll knock first," Joseph said.

Tim Harris stood, trying to hurry the end of the meeting.

"No gripes from me," he said, and then produced a stack of passes for the party that night and handed them to Joseph.

"The party will be in the main ballroom," Tim Harris said. "There'll be a smaller affair up here in the suite. We have five rooms here, just friends and relatives. No press. Bring whoever you want."

"Okay," Joseph said, and rose. "See you tonight."

He and Kelly shook hands, and Joseph found Kelly's handshake rather limp.

"Good luck," Joseph said.

"Thanks so much, Joseph."

Joseph then shook hands with Tim and looked into his eyes. Tim Harris had trouble holding the stare and half grinned.

"So long, Tim," Joseph said as he looked at him.

"See you later."

"You bet."

38

Sydney Weingarten and Dermot Donnelly sat gloomily in the back office at the Nathan Hale Club. A runner was bringing the results from around the borough of Brooklyn. Brendan Kelly was winning by a huge margin in Brooklyn—almost two to one. The Jewish areas of the borough were going almost unanimously to Kelly. The black areas were going the same way.

Some of the conservative white neighborhoods of Italians and Irish were going a little stronger for Wolfington, but there was not one single assembly district that Sydney Weingarten could call a complete victory. Not even his own. Robert Hershkovitz was leading him by seven percentage points with over fifty percent of the vote counted. Sydney Weingarten had lost. Demolished. He sat staring at Dermot Donnelly, who was watching the television as the returns were being flashed on the screen.

The race was close in most of the state, but with the help of the largest Democratic county in the state, Brooklyn, Kelly was holding on to a five-percentage-point lead statewide.

The runner came back into the room with more figures. Hershkovitz had just gone up another percentage point. This was the ultimate defeat. Sydney Weingarten himself was being disgraced on his home ground by an upstart reformer no one had ever heard of before.

"It has begun," Sydney said aloud, but not directly to Dermot Donnelly. "Now it must end."

Sydney Weingarten slid open his desk drawer and removed a silver .25-caliber pistol. Dermot Donnelly stood up, sweating and very frightened.

"No, Sydney. No more. No more killing. No. We're lucky to come out of this alive and not in jail. Please, Sydney, no more killing."

Sydney Weingarten began to walk around his desk, ignoring Dermot Donnelly as if he were not there, pulling on his suit jacket while still holding the pistol.

"Sydney, stop this. So we lost? Big deal. It happens. Leave it alone now."

Sydney Weingarten spun and looked at Dermot Donnelly with steel eyes.

"You are just as bad as the rest," Sydney snapped. "You could have stopped him. You could have indicted him, fixed something up. But you are a blundering, cowardly idiot. My life is ruined. It's all over. Do you understand that? All my plans, gone, vanished."

Dermot Donnelly detected a gleam of insanity in Sydney Weingarten's eyes. He made a move toward Sydney Weingarten, slow but precise, reaching for the gun hand. Sydney moved before Donnelly could grab the gun and trained it on him.

On the television a reporter was being drowned out by the cheers of the Kelly victory party being filmed live from the Waldorf-Astoria.

"Stay out of my way," Sydney told Donnelly as he held the gun pointed at him. "Just leave me alone or I'll kill you. I promise you, Dermot."

Donnelly backed away from Sydney Weingarten, his palms facing him. Sydney Weingarten backed toward the door of his office and left. He walked down the corridor with the pistol in his pocket. The runner with the tallies was coming his way.

"Go home, son," Sydney Weingarten said. "It's all over."

"That's it?" the kid asked, shocked. "It's . . . you mean, it's done, finished? We lost?"

"Yes," Sydney said. "We certainly did."

They drank champagne.

In his Court Street office Joseph Gonzago smiled and thanked the people who had gathered to celebrate their stunning victory.

The phone rang incessantly, and finally Joseph went and picked it up. Joseph listened for a long time to the person on the other end of the phone, his face became serious and grave.

"I understand," Joseph said. "I don't know if I believe everything you're saying, but I appreciate your call. Perhaps the grand jury will decide if you're telling the truth. Thanks again for calling."

Joseph hung up the phone and looked around the room and spotted the man he wanted to talk to. He led him to the side, away from the others, spoke to him briefly, and the man nodded and walked into the conference room and closed the door.

Joseph rejoined the party, milling with the guests, throwing occasional glances at the front door of the office. A half hour passed and Lou Moran proposed a toast.

"To our boss who knows what he's talking about even though I hardly ever understand him," Lou Moran said. "Congratulations on a great victory. And on your wedding. And the bun in the oven. What the hell, get everyone in."

Everyone cheered and clinked glasses and sipped their champagne. Behind Joseph three televisions were playing, each tuned to a different network. Gloria stood at Joseph's side, looking tall and elegant and smiling broadly. Ruth Weingarten was sipping a club soda and standing close to Dr. Licht. Jack Coohill was still manning the phones. Frank Donato stood with his wife, looking calm and confident, very much like a free man. Sylvia Stein sidled up to Lou Moran and looked bashful. She was also thinking about the confrontation she had had earlier with Ruth Weingarten. Ruth had told her that in a way, Sylvia was responsible for freeing her from a terrible marriage and life. Sylvia Stein had been unable to find any words except to say that she was sorry. Ruth had told her that being involved with Sydney at all was penance enough.

"I want to thank you all," Joseph said, "for helping me carry out the wishes of my father."

The victors clapped and cheered wildly.

"It was a tough fight, but you came through," Joseph said. "I will always be indebted to you. I want my friends to know that if there is ever anything I can do for you, come to me and ask."

"All right," said Lou Moran. "You could start by tellin' us where you come up with that there idea about the parking tickets."

"My father's idea, Lou," Joseph said.

Everyone was laughing when the voice came from the back of the room.

"Be Be Gonzago was a low life," came the bellow from Sydney Weingarten, who stood just inside the front door with his pistol drawn and trained on the room.

"Father, put that gun away," Gloria Weingarten shouted.

"Don't call me *your* father, you little tramp," he said softly, his eyes wide and wild. "Anyone who would share the same bed with that scum is no child of mine."

Ruth glared at him.

Sydney grinned viciously at Ruth. "Oh, darling Ruth, I see they've let you out of your cage. So how many quarts have you had today?"

"Leave her alone," Joseph said as he placed his champagne on his desk. "And get the hell out of here."

Joseph made a move for Sydney Weingarten, but Weingarten raised his pistol and aimed it at Joseph's face as he sidestepped toward the door to the conference room.

"Go ahead, Sydney," Joseph said. "You going to kill me like you killed my father? Go ahead, Sydney. Only this time there will be witnesses and you'll be the speaker of cell block ten. Go ahead. Let's see if you have the guts to pull the trigger yourself."

Sydney saw Lou Moran make a move for the desk, which was situated several feet from the conference room.

"Get away from there, monkey," Sydney said to Lou Moran. Sydney walked to the desk, his back now to the conference room door. He opened the right-hand drawer and took out the gun Lou Moran was going for. Sydney saw Sylvia Stein now, clutching Lou Moran's arm.

"Even monkeys now, Sylvia?" Sydney Weingarten said, sneering.

"At least monkeys can get it up, pal," Lou Moran said.

Sylvia Stein said nothing as Sydney smiled at her.

"So, you have been discussing me, have you?" Sydney said as he tossed the pistol from the drawer out the window and down thirteen stories. Several seconds later he heard it clatter to the street. "Good old Sylvia Stein, Miss Manhattan Beach, talking about *me.*"

"You disgusting son of a bitch," Gloria Weingarten said.

"You dare call me disgusting while you're carrying around the child of a grease ball? You think I don't know?"

Sydney started laughing as Sylvia Stein held her head high. Sydney stopped laughing, and turned to Joseph.

"You'll never know who really killed Be Be Gonzago," Sydney said. "Never in a million years. I was in on it, sure. But I didn't arrange it. I didn't conceive it. It doesn't matter now because I don't intend to live to see tomorrow. There's nothing to see there anyway. But I want to watch you all squirm a little before that happens. And poor Sylvia, I did it all for you. Then you had to betray me. So sad. We could have been happy. Instead I'll have to kill you because I cannot leave you for someone else to have. So I'll have to take you with me. First I will kill Sylvia so you can all watch. Then you can watch as I take myself. Because I won't leave myself around to be ridiculed by the likes of you, Joseph Gonzago. I'll be gone, and with me goes the name of the man responsible for killing your father. For the rest of your life you will be haunted by it."

The room was eerily silent. He looked at Sylvia Stein again.

"Come here, Sylvia, and kiss me good-bye," Sydney said to her.

"You better shoot me first, rat shit," Lou Moran said.

"No, I know there are plenty of people in this room who would like—enjoy—taking my life. But I won't give any of you the pleasure. Frank Donato would enjoy it. You, monkey man, you would enjoy it. Joseph Gonzago would enjoy it. None of you will have that pleasure. Just me. I'm the only man in this room worthy of killing Sydney Weingarten."

"And I thought I was crazy," Ruth said.

"Sylvia, come here, darling," Sydney said, the dementia dilating his eyes.

"Kill me from there, Sydney, but I won't beg," Sylvia Stein said.

Sydney grew enraged for the first time now, raised the pistol, and aimed it at Sylvia Stein's head. She closed her eyes, awaiting the impact of the bullet, her body quivering, but refusing to give Sydney Weingarten this last pleasure.

"Cunningham!" Joseph shouted.

Sydney was momentarily distracted, shifted the pistol in Joseph's direction. The door of the conference room smashed open and Francis X. Cunningham charged through, his pistol drawn. Sydney Weingarten turned the pistol on himself and was about to fire a round into his own forehead when Cunningham slapped his hand away and grabbed the wrist, twisting it, forcing Sydney to drop the gun. Sydney broke loose from his grip, turned toward the open window, and made his move for it. Joseph caught him by the back of his collar and his right arm, which he twisted behind his back. Then Joseph spun him around and slammed him onto his desktop.

"No, please let me do it . . ."

Sydney Weingarten pleaded with Joseph Gonzago, who held Sydney by the ears, banging his head against the hard wood several times.

"No way, Sydney Weingarten," Joseph said slowly and hard into Sydney's face from just inches away. "No way am I going to let you take the coward's way out of this. No, I want you to *live.* That's the greatest punishment for you. To have to live. What you did to my father, you son of bitch, was the biggest mistake of your life. Because now you are a nobody. Zip. Nothing. A two-bit hood. You've lost your wife. You've lost your mistress. You've lost your daughter. You've lost your job. You lost your last friend when Donnelly called to let me know you were coming. You've lost what little respect you've ever had. You've lost your freedom, pal. But most of all you've lost tomorrow, lost your future. I own that, old man. I took it all away from you. Are you listening to me?"

Joseph pointed with his right hand to the large portrait of Be Be Gonzago beaming down from the wall behind the desk.

"Me and my father, we took it from you, Sydney. He beat you from his grave. You couldn't keep him buried, Sydney. He's back, do you understand that? As long as I'm alive he'll be haunting you. And I'll outlive you, Sydney. See, I thought about killing you. I thought of doing it in every way a human being could think of. I dreamed about it. But I found out that when I beat you, when I had your life ruined, I wasn't going to let you die. That would be almost humane. No, I decided I wanted you to lose everything but your crummy little life. This way, you could live every rotten little day knowing you lost it to me. All of it! To Be Be Gonzago's son. Every day you are going to wake up in a cell, a little more dead than the day before. With nothing. Just absolutely nothing, because I have everything you ever had. So all I have to say, Sydney, is here's to your health and I hope you live a long, long, long life."

Joseph pulled away from him and Francis Cunningham snapped a pair of handcuffs on him. Sydney Weingarten stared at the floor, unable to look at anyone. Gloria Weingarten stared silently at him, tears in her eyes. Ruth Weingarten looked at him with pity.

Two members of the SBI showed up and Cunningham turned Sydney Weingarten over to them and began leading him out the door. Before he left Sydney Weingarten turned desperately back to the people in the room.

"Ruth!"

But she turned away.

And finally, Sydney Weingarten was gone, his voice trailing off as he was led down the corridor.

Ruth Weingarten was standing in front of one of the three television sets now, shaking her head from side to side. Gloria was standing with her, along with Dr. Licht.

"Once, he was a nice man," Ruth said. "But so long, long ago."

Ruth stared at the television screen which showed Brendan Kelly walking onto the speaker's platform at the Waldorf-Astoria ballroom for his victory speech. The crowds were surging before him, and he was smiling and shaking his fists in the air. Ruth was watching with such intensity that Joseph found it incongruous. Her husband had just been led away for murder.

"Lou," Joseph said. "Turn off the damn TVs, will ya."

Lou Moran left Sylvia Stein to turn off the televisions, but Ruth Weingarten lightly touched his hand.

"No," Ruth said, very softly, almost a whisper. "No. Don't turn it off. That's him. Right there. See. That's him."

Curious, Joseph walked over to Ruth.

"That's who, Ruth?"

"The man I told you about," she said, talking so softly Joseph had to bend to hear her. "Right there behind Kelly on the stage."

"What man you told me about, Ruth?"

"The one from the house. The one I overheard talking about Be Be with Sydney. They thought I was asleep. Or drunk. I don't know. I was lying down on the couch. I saw them. I saw him. And I heard them talking about killing Be Be. I'm certain that's him."

Now Francis X. Cunningham was listening to her as she pointed to the man on the stage. Joseph leaned close to the television set to get a closer look at the man who was standing, unsmiling, unmoved, behind Brendan Kelly.

"Mrs. Weingarten, are you sure of this?" Cunningham asked.

"Oh, I'm quite sure. Faces I rarely forget. Names I forget. But never faces."

"Ruth, once more, you're positive? Try to remember what they said exactly," said Joseph.

"Oh, I don't recall exactly what they said. But something about paying a woman to eliminate the middle man. This way they would never be able to trace it because the woman wouldn't know the man she was to kill was the man who killed Be Be. I never told anyone because no one ever listened to me. And I didn't know his name. And I wasn't even sure for a while if I had dreamed it or imagined it or if it was real. Now I know it was real because there's his face. That's him. Who is he anyway, Joseph?"

Joseph looked once more at the man on stage, half obscured now by Brendan Kelly. "His name," Joseph said, "is Tim Harris."

39

The lobby was jammed with Kelly supporters and campaign workers and reporters with camera crews. There were a lot of college kids who'd had a lot to drink and were celebrating the victory of their candidate. Some of them stood in the lobby making out with each other or just hooting it up. One chubby young girl was sitting on the floor crying tears of joy.

Kelly buttons, Kelly hats, Kelly posters, Kelly literature, Kelly photographs, Kelly pens, Kelly shopping bags, littered the floors. Plainclothes security men with dark glasses and earplugs stood around as conspicuous as summer snow.

Joseph strode across the thick carpet of the crowded lobby and located a security head at the entrance to the ballroom. Joseph wrote a short note on a small piece of paper: "TIM HARRIS. Must see you immediately. Complications. Come alone. I'll be in the suite upstairs. Joseph Gonzago."

The security man assured Joseph that he would get the note to Tim Harris immediately. Harris was still in the ballroom, partaking of the obligatory protocol of greeting and thanking workers, talking to newsmen, supporters, contributors.

Joseph rode the elevator to the penthouse and walked to the suite he had been in that morning. The doors were open and there was a bar set up awaiting the guests. Joseph walked to the bar and fixed himself a straight Irish whiskey. He belted it down, letting the hot amber liquor scald his chest cavity. He repeated the process and waited for Tim Harris.

He arrived ten minutes later. When he walked into the room he was smiling and walking as if on springs.

"Joseph, you did it," Tim Harris said. Joseph smiled and obliged Harris's outstretched hand. "We couldn't have done it without your help."

"I know."

"Well, modesty was never one of your great virtues," Tim Harris said as he walked to the bar.

"Murder was never one of yours, Tim." Joseph spoke softly and did not even turn to face Tim Harris. Harris was stunned, stopped in his tracks, and walked in front of Joseph to look at him.

"What the hell did you say?"

"I said murder was never one of your great virtues. But then, that was in the sixties, Tim. Back when we believed in what we did for all the wrong reasons like morality, justice, that kind of shit. Today it's for power. For a place in the world. For history. Right, Tim?"

"What have you been drinking?"

"My father's blood," Joseph said.

"You are flaking out on me, Joseph. I don't know what you're talking about."

"Come on, Tim," Joseph said. "Sydney Weingarten was arrested tonight for the murder of my father. He spilled everything. He said you masterminded it. I just wanted to see you first to ask why? Why, Tim?"

Joseph's manner was totally calm, reserved, and this made Tim Harris panicky.

"You're bluffing," Tim Harris said. "You're so blind with revenge that you are looking under every bed. Why the hell would I want to kill your father?"

"Stop it, Tim," Joseph said, standing and walking to the bar. "You had Weingarten have the wise guys on the waterfront get a hood, a hit man to kill my father. Then you got a woman named Elizabeth Lacey to kill him. She tried to kill me too, but well, that didn't work out so well. I first suspected it when I found out she was an old radical, Tim. Weathermen. I know you were in that organization too, at the same time she was. The FBI records say so. You knew she dropped out, and started to kill for a living. But only men. So you used her, Tim.

"I also knew when I told you about Morse. He was a stooge, Tim. You had to have a stooge on Wolfington's payroll to justify the leaks. You needed a guy to use as a fall guy in case Kelly realized Weingarten and Wolfington had bought somebody inside. So you used poor Dan Morse, family man, cash poor, in hock. That took you off the hook."

Joseph made himself an Irish whiskey, and when he turned around Tim Harris held a .38-caliber pistol on him.

"Why'd you have to come back, Joseph? Why couldn't you just have stayed in the academy? Let it pass. You hated the old bastard anyway. You told me that hundreds of times. You said it publicly. Why'd you have to come back?"

Joseph looked at the gun and laughed.

"Get off it, Tim," Joseph said. "You might hurt yourself with that thing. Put it away."

"I've used one before, Joseph," Tim Harris said. "Believe me. You always had that attitude. That gays and women were somehow weak."

"I've met some strong ones, but not you, Tim."

"No," Tim Harris said. "I'm going to have to kill you. You spoiled it, man. I had a shot. Wolfington was going to Washington in two years. Don't you understand that? The presidency of the United States! I could have been on the inside! Sydney was going to see to that. Can you imagine what someone like me could do inside the White House? I'm smart, Joseph. We always talked about overthrowing the government. That was kid shit. This would have been for real. If Wolfington had won tonight, he would have been the president in two damn years, and I would have been there with him. On the inside, working against the system just as I did with Kelly."

"You didn't do such a good job with Kelly," Joseph said, nonchalantly. "You wanted to make sure he'd lose and he won anyway."

"That's because you came in and fucked everything up," Harris said. "What is Kelly? He has no intentions of ever going to Washington. He actually wants to stay in Albany. Do you believe that? So I used him. I used him to help me get in with Wolfington, who could have gone all the way. Could have gone to the White House. But you fucked it all up. You and your harebrain ideas and your silly vengeance for a machine hack."

"Who approached you?" Joseph asked.

"Initially Brideson did, but he's a moron too. Wolfington himself and Brideson still don't know that Be Be was meant to be killed. I was simply asked to make the Kelly campaign implode from the inside. None of us thought he had a chance, but he's not a bad piece of political property when you put him in front of people.

"But we found out Be Be was going to support Kelly. I approached Weingarten with the idea of getting rid of him. It took time, but eventually he agreed for a variety of reasons. He didn't like Be Be very much, did he?"

"The feeling was mutual, Tim."

"We tried to persuade Be Be to go with Wolfington. At least Sydney did. And Wolfington. And finally we resorted to the final plan and had him killed."

"That's it?"

"In a nutshell, yes."

"All right, kill me now."

"You crazy bastard."

"You better kill me because my drink is almost gone, and when it's gone I'm going to get up and beat you to death, Tim."

"I'll do it, Joseph, I really will."

"Then go ahead, Tim. I only have a sip left."

Tim Harris began backing out of the room with his gun still aimed at Joseph. Joseph rose from his seat and followed him to the door. He quickened his pace, and anger was mounting in him. Tim Harris was growing panicky now, holding the pistol straight out at Joseph.

"I mean it, Joseph, stop."

"I mean it too, you murdering bastard."

Joseph threw the right hand so fast and so hard that he did not even see the punch land, felt only the impact. Tim Harris sailed through the open doors into the waiting arms of Francis X. Cunningham.

"That man might have killed you," Cunningham said, as the groggy Harris lay in his arms.

"Nah," Joseph said. "I knew him in the old days. He was a coward then. He still is. Besides, you wouldn't have let that happen to me, would you?"

"What, and miss my chance of running the agency? No way, bossman." Cunningham giggled.

"You get it all on tape?"

"All of it."

"I'm gonna go, Cunningham. You know where to find me."

Cunningham handcuffed Tim Harris, whose distorted nose and mouth were leaking blood.

"See you around," Joseph said to Cunningham. He was about to leave but paused to take one last look at Tim Harris, who was standing on shaky legs. Joseph shrugged and hit him with the left hand now, sending the manacled slight man into a heap on the floor.

"Shucks," Cunningham said. "Don't go hitting my prisoner."

He watched Joseph Gonzago walk slowly down the corridor then around a corner and out of sight.

Joseph took the car out of the lot and started driving slowly home toward Brooklyn. For a few moments he wished that he had killed Tim Harris. But the desire passed. He could smell something that had to go now. It was the ashes and butts of Be Be's old cigars in the ashtray. Joseph stopped for a light at Twenty-third Street and took the ashtray out of the slot and was going to empty it into the street. He thought a moment and decided against it. He placed the ashtray on his lap and kept driving.

He thought about what had happened to him over the past weeks. He was now the boss of the Brooklyn Democratic machine. He had access to the governor. He had a good woman he loved, a child on the way, and some pretty damned good friends. He figured he'd make Jack Coohill head of the Longshoremen's Union. Frank Donato got in too much trouble down there. He could always give Frank the head job at the Water Board instead, which would pay him decent money and give him all the time in the world to be with his family.

Lou Moran had his bar, but Joseph would have to keep Lou around. Bodyguard, driver, laughs, something.

If Bernie Weingarten behaved himself maybe he'd let him eat. Now wasn't the time to be vindictive. Besides, he was Gloria's brother. But Joseph had other things to think about. There was a councilman's seat left vacant by Sam Stone, who wouldn't be coming back anytime soon. Hallahan's Senate seat was up next year. Bailey wouldn't be running again for mayor. Brooklyn was going to need a new district attorney. There were a lot of people who had worked hard on the campaign who deserved jobs. Then there was that other two and a half million people called Brooklyn to think about.

Joseph took the Brooklyn Bridge, felt the familiar wonderful tingle of the tires whining over the gratings. There before him, spread out like a lovely old dream, was Brooklyn, sprawling and wicked and wonderful and sad. And his.

Joseph was smiling broadly as he exited the bridge and headed up toward Atlantic Avenue. He was home now and he took the ashtray from his lap and let the old dead butts and smelly ashes scatter into the breezy night. He was home and the rest of the world could go to hell. His father's murder was now avenged, his wishes fulfilled. It was time now for Joseph Gonzago to get on with the rest of his life. To sleep and play and laugh and cry. To make love and new friends and new enemies. To raise a family and love his wife and go to work.

It was time for Joseph Gonzago to be the boss.

Epilogue

Lou Moran picked up the telephone as Joseph Gonzago sat behind his desk reading Dick Young in the *New York Post.* Joseph had his feet propped up on the desk and was sipping coffee as Lou Moran fielded the call.

"She says it's the governor wants to speak to you," Lou Moran said.

Joseph did not look up from the paper, instead just kept reading, sipping his coffee.

"Tell her to have him hold on, I'm on a long-distance call to Washington," Joseph lied.

Lou Moran nodded.

"Tell the governor Joseph is on a call to the president. He'll be with him in a few minutes."

Lou Moran hung up the phone and watched the hold light blink incessantly.

"You want to go to the fights tonight, Lou?"

"Sure, Boss, where at? Garden?"

"Yeah. There's this young kid from Brooklyn, a real banger with the hook, named Santiago. I'd like to see him. If he's any good get him a job somewhere so he doesn't wind up shooting junk into the left arm."

"Yeah, all right. What weight?"

"Forty-seven. I hear good things. Eighteen KOs in twenty fights."

"Maybe the Parks Department."

"Yeah, outdoors, so he can do roadwork or something."

"Done."

"Give me the phone, Lou."

Lou Moran handed the phone to Joseph Gonzago. Joseph held it with three fingers, still scanning the *Post* sports pages and sipping coffee.

"Yeah," Joseph said. "Hiya, Brendan. What's up?"

He read while he listened and put his hand over the transmitter and spoke to Lou Moran. "Call the Garden, reserve two seats."

"Okay, Boss."

Joseph listened some more. "Okay, Brendan, look, let's stop the nonsense. In the four years you've been governor you've done very little for my people. A few jobs here and there. But nothing else. You pave seventy miles of the Hamptons when you can't even drive a bike down to Coney Island. You build schools in Buffalo when they're shutting them down here. The subways are so bad hobos wouldn't hitch a ride on them. Now you're up for re-election and I hear from you. You don't mind spending some state money on a phone call to Brooklyn when you're up for re-election, but in four years how many times did you call me? Ten? Maybe twelve? Did you ever offer me anything, Brendan? I mean really offer me anything? No. I never asked for much, from the beginning. Now you're asking me when you never gave what little I asked. I'm telling you, Brendan, because I like you personally, but this other guy who's making noise from Brooklyn, Hunt, is starting to look pretty good to me. Sure you can come down and see me. Sure, arrange it with my secretary. That's if you still know how to get here from there. No, I'm not trying to be a hard guy. I'm trying to be a sensible guy. Brooklyn needs help, but I'm not a panhandler. I expect a fair return. We'll talk next week sometime. Talk to my secretary. Okay, Brendan. See you."

Joseph's eyes never left the paper as Lou Moran hung up the phone.

"Get those tickets, Lou?"

"Yeah, they'll be at the box office."

The intercom rang and Joseph pressed down the button with the heel of his shoe.

"Your wife and son are here, Mr. Gonzago," the secretary said.

"Send them in." Lou Moran took the cue and stepped out of the room. Gloria walked into the office looking stunning. Her four-year-old son Anthony held her hand. The boy had large dark eyes and silky black hair and looked astonishingly like his dad. The boy broke away from his mother and ran across the room and hopped onto Joseph Gonzago's lap. Joseph started tickling him and the boy writhed with laughter.

When the boy was able to catch his breath, he leaned up and hugged his father and kissed him.

"I love you, Dad," Anthony said.

"I love you too, kiddo," Joseph said. Joseph hugged his little boy close to him and then kissed Gloria, who leaned over, smiling.

"Mom and Doc Licht are coming over for dinner tomorrow night. I hope to hell you're free. It's their third anniversary, so please don't make any plans."

"Tomorrow is fine, sweetheart. But I'm busy tonight. I have an important meeting about a job for a guy. I can't miss it, so I won't be home for dinner, okay?"

"Sure, no problem, what time does the fight start?"

"How the hell did you know I was going to the fights?"

"I started reading Dick Young, that's how I know. The only way to know what's going on up there. This morning's column he mentioned this kid Santiago, hits pretty good with the hook."

Joseph laughed and kissed Anthony again. Anthony was staring up at the portrait of Be Be Gonzago on the wall.

"He was your daddy, right, Dad?" Anthony asked.

"That's right, kiddo. Your grandpa."

"But he's not around anymore, right, Dad?"

"Oh, I don't know," Joseph Gonzago said. "I'd say he was still around somewhere."

Then the little boy kissed Joseph Gonzago good-bye and Joseph hugged him tightly. Joseph rose and kissed Gloria. The mother and child left the office and Joseph spun around and looked up at the portrait of Be Be Gonzago smiling down at him. Joseph smiled right back, looking Be Be in the eyes.

"Right, Dad?"